Praise for …

Solitary

"A YA novel for the hip, the savvy, the thinker-outside-the-box—and anybody else who wants a great read. And don't even try to predict this one. Just hang on and let it take you straight into the real world of the newest generation."

Nancy Rue, best-selling author of tween and young adult fiction

"*Solitary* is a cautionary tale, startling and suspenseful. The characters are unforgettable, the prose stark, and the dialogue masterful. Travis Thrasher is a versatile storyteller who walks his readers through life's uncertainties while leading them toward glimmers of hope."

Eric Wilson, *New York Times* best-selling author of *Valley of Bones*

Praise for …

Travis Thrasher

"Thrasher just keeps getting better."

Publishers Weekly

"Each time I read a novel by Travis Thrasher, I close the cover and tell myself that was his best. But I find it hard to imagine that Thrasher is going to be able to surpass *Broken* easily.... The story literally drove me to tears. The action is intense, the pace breakneck, the aura of mystery palpable, the sense of the supernatural mysterious. In the vein of *Isolation* and *Ghostwriter*, Thrasher gives us *Broken*, one of his best stories to date."

Josh Olds, author and book
reviewer at LifeIsStory.com

"How does Christian horror actually work? I'm not really sure, but fiction writer Travis Thrasher has successfully figured out the formula. He's combined Christian faith with a Stephen King–esque setting to explore what happens to your psyche when you are in the midst of a spiritual attack."

Rachel Laudiero, author and book reviewer
at OldMustyBooks.com

"Not only will *Isolation* scare you, it will also challenge your faith and remind you of the all-encompassing power of the love of our Savior. [Travis] only gets better with each new offering, and this latest tale might just be his best yet."

Jake Chism, author and book
reviewer at FictionAddict.com

TEMPTATION

Also by Travis Thrasher

The Promise Remains
The Watermark
The Second Thief
Three Roads Home
Gun Lake
Admission
Blinded
Sky Blue
Out of the Devil's Mouth
Isolation
Ghostwriter
Every Breath You Take
Broken
40
Letters from War
Paper Angels
101 Writing Tips

The Solitary Tales
Solitary
Gravestone
Temptation

THE THIRD BOOK OF

THE SOLITARY TALES

TEMPTATION

A NOVEL

TRAVIS THRASHER

TEMPTATION
Published by David C Cook
4050 Lee Vance View
Colorado Springs, CO 80918 U.S.A.

David C Cook Distribution Canada
55 Woodslee Avenue, Paris, Ontario, Canada N3L 3E5

David C Cook U.K., Kingsway Communications
Eastbourne, East Sussex BN23 6NT, England

LCCN 2012930869
ISBN 978-1-4347-6417-1
eISBN 978-1-4347-0503-7

The Team: Don Pape, LoraBeth Norton, Nick Lee, Caitlyn York, Karen Athen
Cover Design: Amy Konyndyk
Cover Photo: iStockPhoto

Printed in the United States of America
First Edition 2012

1 2 3 4 5 6 7 8 9 10

012912

For Madison

Tonight I think I'll walk alone
I'll find my soul as I go home.

—"Temptation" by New Order

PREFACE

The night changes everything.

So she told me.

Final words to her little boy.

In the passenger seat of the SUV, I look out and see the city. It glows and breathes and welcomes me. I hear the words and believe them.

I never knew Chicago could look so beautiful.

It's late, and I feel like we've been driving forever. My ears are sore from the earbuds attached to my iPod. My butt is sore from sitting in place for so long. The last time we stopped was around Lexington. I'm ready to get out and stretch my legs and step back onto flat Illinois land.

Solitary is over a dozen hours away.

Not far enough, if you ask me, but it'll have to do.

It's quiet in the car. I look out the front window at the skyline in the distance. That's where we're headed, toward the city and not the suburbs.

The city means more people. More people means more help in case—well, in case of anything.

"You awake?"

I glance over at my father. "Never fell asleep."

"You closed your eyes."

Sometimes it's better that way.

I yawn and wipe my eyes.

"You're going to enjoy it here," Dad tells me.

"Yeah."

I don't really believe this. I want to. I really want to. But I just need to be away from that cursed town for a while. Maybe I can slowly begin to forget. Maybe I can slowly start to live again.

But that's what you tried doing in the summertime, and look where it got you.

I don't want to think about the last few months. The only thing that will bring is hurt, and I've got enough of that as it is.

"I think you'll like the apartment," Dad says.

"I think I'll like anything that doesn't have winding dirt roads around it."

Or secret hidden tunnels below it.

Dad doesn't know quite what to say. I don't blame him. He probably still aches for Mom. Maybe he's angry with himself for not being able to do anything more.

That's how I feel. Angry with myself, with nothing left to say.

When someone dies, all you can do sometimes is stay quiet and keep moving.

I thought that losing Jocelyn hurt. But this … this is different. This is worse.

The first time you did too little. But this time you did too much.

"Hungry?" Dad asks.

I was until I turned off the music and started hearing the voices. "No."

The city with its lights and life invites us in. I'm glad to see civilization again. I no longer feel so remote and so alone.

Yet there's a part of me that says I should have stayed.

There was no reason to stay.

There's so much to think about that my head hurts. I can't sort out the details. I think of the motorcycle, of the cards, of Marsh and Staunch, of Oli, of *him*. I can feel the Zippo lighter in my pocket.

Then I picture her face and feel the hurt again.

"I know Mom is proud of you."

I let out a chuckle and then keep my voice down. "Proud of me for what?"

"Proud of you for being strong for her."

It's been quite some time since I've felt proud or strong. The irony is that it's my father telling me this.

Seven months ago, there'd have been no chance ever that I'd be riding here with *him*.

But life sure has a way of crashing and burning around you.

The interstate eventually merges into Lake Shore Drive. Even though I can't see it, I know Lake Michigan is out there in the darkness. I can feel it watching and waiting in silence. Eventually we take an exit and drive for a few minutes down block after block.

"This place will be busy tomorrow night around this time," Dad says.

Everybody will be celebrating and toasting and laughing and living.

Wanna know what I was doing last year on New Year's Eve, Dad? I was discovering that this girl I'd fallen crazy in love with had her throat slashed by a bunch of freaks in robes.

Even though Dad knows a few things, he doesn't know that much. He can't know much. I still don't know everything, but I know enough now. I know a lot of answers to questions that circled inside my head a year ago.

Answers might fit the puzzle pieces together, but they still don't block out the gaping hole in the picture. The hole that's my heart.

1. Elegia

It's June, and there's a guy—a kid—a boy stuck in a ditch that's called his life.

Sixteen.

Sad.

Stuck in summer school.

Stuck without a license. Without a job. Without friends.

Stuck in a town he hates and fears. Stuck in a family that's leftover parts, with a mother who only has leftover love to give.

Surrounded on all sides by those who claim they know him, who claim there's something about him, who claim this and that. Threatened and watched by unseen strangers.

A boy still haunted by memories of a girl he once knew.

A boy still haunted by memories of all the things he could have done.

There's a teen who's supposed to be playing the next track on the next album but instead is stuck repeating the same sad, endless song that keeps going around and around the turntable.

Yeah, there's *that* guy. That poor, miserable guy.

But that guy's not me.

2. Made for You

The front door used to frighten me. Now it frees me.

I swing it open, daring them to seize me. I walk downstairs, daring them to trip me. I know someone watches me, but only God knows why. But we know where things stand between me and God, don't we, so let's not go there.

I'm done going there.

I should be tired of not having a license and not having a car, but I'm not. Instead, I'm breaking the law on a Triumph motorcycle as I start it up and get on out.

I'm not afraid.

Yes you are.

I'm not plagued by the last eight months.

Says who?

The faster I rev this machine and turn the corners, the more unbound I feel. I can almost, almost, really almost escape.

Nope.

But I can and do, and soon even those nagging stupid swirling thoughts inside my head go away.

Just like that.

I don't hear them anymore.

But I do see the road ahead, and for once I'm happy. I'm a happy boy. I'm not running for my life and I'm not covered in blood and I'm not seeing ghosts and I'm not crying.

Nope. I'm happy.

I'm happy because the sun is shining. School is over, and I don't have to feel like a sore thumb sticking out. I can't sleep in like Mom does because I've got summer school, but that's fine. It just means I can avoid finding a job since my last one burned down. I can avoid thinking about all that, and you know what? The wind and the whipping streets all make it go far away.

It's been a few weeks since graduation, and it's gone away.

This is the fifth day back at the dump I'd gotten away from, but I'm a different person.

I'm changed.

I am different from the guy who climbed the steps of the school last October and proceeded to slowly waste away with worry.

I pull my bike up in the parking lot and get off.

I'm riding a bike. I mean—come on.

It's a new day.

The first day of the rest of your life.

So I've been telling myself over and over and over.

It's a Friday, and the weekend is almost here. A weekend that no longer frightens me.

I'd take off my helmet, but I didn't wear a helmet because that's how I roll.

You don't roll anyplace.

"Shut up," I say.

Then I look around to make sure nobody saw me talking to …

Yeah, myself.

Guess some things never change.

3. The Breakfast Club

The beautiful thing about being here at Harrington High is that nobody else is there to taunt or watch or mock or spy. This is the first of my two three-week summer school sessions. Nothing like spending most of the summer at the school I desperately wanted to get away from. But after a week of this, everything has changed. The dark, creepy cobwebs have been cleaned up. Now everything is actually …

Normal.

The weeks since graduation—since everything happened with Pastor Marsh—have been awesome because I've gotten used to not doing anything. Not hearing anything going BOO in the middle of the night. Not having to deal with any craziness. Just living day after day as a normal teen. Learning how to start and ride the motorcycle that an elderly woman named Iris left me, the one that belonged to Uncle Robert when he used to work for her at the Crag's Inn. No Iris or missing uncle has been spotted, which is okay.

It's all okay.

I've come to realize that whatever the reason my teachers decided to fail me (well, not my French teacher, because I deserved that F, but my English and algebra teachers), it doesn't really matter anymore because this is a glorified recess. Summer school is like a study hall minus the studying and the students.

So far, I'm not really sure *what* I'm supposed to be doing and how I'm supposed to be graded, but then again, it's a new day, and it's a new Chris.

There are reasons for that.

One in particular.

I'm among the first to get to the class today. I take my regular seat, a second chair from the back row. Since the first day, we've all sat in the same seats, all seven of us. Thankfully there's no Gus. That was my big fear. But I remembered who his father was and bet that he probably wouldn't have to spend his summer mornings at school regardless of his grades.

There weren't any formal introductions to the kids in the class. There were only two I actually recognized. One who terrified me a bit until he started amusing me.

And then …

Well, I'll get to that in a minute.

Gin is in the back row, her monstrous black glasses and straight falling black hair hiding her face. I honestly don't know yet if Gin can speak English. Or if her name is Gin or Jen or Ginny. Her last name is Chang or Wang or something like that. The teacher said it quickly the first day, and that's been that. I'm not sure if she's Chinese or Japanese and whether this is all one big blur to her. Someone said they thought she was a freshman.

So yeah, all I know is that she wears big glasses.

The pudgy short kid with the red curly 'fro is Shawn. He's a junior, and he's just—Shawn. He's *that* kid. The one everybody knows, nobody really loves, but everybody loves to not love. He makes you laugh, but he says the most outrageous stuff. You wonder what he'll be doing when he grows up. Here in school, he can be dumb and say crazy things, but there's no telling what the guy will do when he gets out of here.

"Christopher," he says to me in a Russian-sounding accent.

No connection to anything. Probably some random thing going off in his head.

Shawn sits in front of me, which is fine because that way I can avoid Mr. Taggart. Mr. Taggart is the last one to show up every day. Usually he stumbles in looking like he went to the same party my mother went to the night before. He's mostly bald, with a nice thick mustache that looks two decades out of place and a nice thick belly that looks two belt sizes out of shape. They say he used to be the coach of the football team.

These are things I hear mentioned casually. Like Gin being a freshman.

The next to come in is the movie-star wannabe. Roger struts into the classroom as if it's a red carpet and the paparazzi are out in full force. He smiles a crystal smile that shows through the airbrushed beard he's got going on. I still haven't quite figured out how he can cut it *that* short, so short it looks like shoe polish. His hair slants forward and upward in a faux-hawk style.

Guy has to use a lot of gel to get his hair to do that.

He fist-bumps Shawn, who idolizes the guy for some reason.

Roger is a senior who needs this summer class to graduate. He says he's going to the University of Southern California. I don't know whether to believe him or not.

But at least he's not telling you he's your cousin. That didn't turn out so well, did it?

"How're we gonna kill three hours today?" Roger says to me.

Roger's one of those kids who doesn't really talk with you. He talks at you. I shrug, because he's not really looking for an answer.

He looks at the quiet figure in the back. "Hey, Gin."

Roger's not a bad guy. He's just a politician. A politician or a

Don't say it

pastor.

Something about both of those professions makes me skeptical.

I'm waiting in my chair, waiting for the moment that made me get out of bed and get on that motorcycle and rush here.

Soon it arrives.

Harris comes in first, the bright-eyed smiling guy who looks like Will Smith's clone from his television days. As usual, Harris is dressed like a preppy. He's laughing at something. He looks behind him, and yes, there she comes.

Lily walks into the room, and suddenly it shifts like one of those houses at an amusement park. Everybody watches her. I can't see Gin, but I'm sure she's looking at the golden-haired beauty too.

Good morning, Lily.

This is what I say in my mind. I don't say it out loud because—well, Lily and I have had two conversations. Just two. And they've been the throwaway kind, not the get-to-know-you-better kind. The kind where she says something, I say something stupid in response, and then she just looks at me with pity.

As usual, just as she did on her first day, Lily takes the seat over to the right of the room, right across from Harris. They're best buddies, of course.

Today she's wearing an Atlanta Falcons jersey and small shorts that almost don't show, since the jersey's so long. Lily is tall and athletic, and her legs show it.

A part of me sighs, and another part tries to look cool.

It's easier to look cool riding a bike than sitting in this rigid seat.

I glance over and see those perfect lips widen into a smile as she says something to Harris. Oh, I'd like to hate him, but I can't. Harris is possibly one of the nicest guys I've ever met. And he's just like the rest of us—pretty much smitten with the new girl.

That's all I know about Lily. She's the new girl. She looks twenty-five but will be a senior next year. Her hair is curly and wild, as if she just skydived before coming to class.

There's something about being in this room with her that makes me feel alive.

Yes, maybe I should've learned some things from my track record with girls. But—it's not like there's anything happening here. It's just a beautiful girl who doesn't really know me who happens to go to Harrington High....

Stop me if you think you've heard this one before.

That's a song I just heard the other day. Kinda fits.

I stop thinking of this when Brick walks into the room. He looks like he's trying to mimic Clint Eastwood's character in those spaghetti Westerns, except Brick isn't wearing a gun (that I can see anyway). He's in a leather vest and a white T-shirt, and his hair is about the same length as Roger's beard.

He first looks at Lily, then grins and winks at her. "My little flower."

She laughs. "Good morning, Brick."

He eyes the rest of us in a sinister way.

He did this the first day, and I thought, *Oh great, here we go again. A skinhead Gus.* But after a couple of days I realized that Brick just looks mean. Yes, he's a skinhead, and yes, he doesn't like authority. But I'm not an authority on anything, so he's grown to like me.

So much so that he now sits across from me and usually will talk to me throughout the class. Mr. Taggart stopped telling Brick to quit talking, since it never has any effect.

Brick messes up my already messy hair and nods at me. "Miss me?"

"Like the plague."

He laughs. This is probably why he likes me. He thinks I've got a funny, quirky sense of humor. He told me so. The third day, after hearing some of my comments, he just examined me with squinting eyes. Then he said, "You're kinda funny, Buckley."

Shawn told me the story of how Brick got his name. Turns out he literally threw a brick through the glass doors lining the front of Harrington High when he was only a sophomore. It was after hours, and he was coming to get something that Principal Harking had taken from him and left in her office.

Obviously that got him a nice suspension, along with a visit from the cops and a fine.

Not that the cops do anything around here. Just saying.

Brick proceeds to tell me again why I need to sell him my motorcycle. Something about it being worth a ton and about an actor named Steve McQueen. I nod as if I'm paying attention, but really I'm just wanting to look over at the blonde who's not paying either of us attention.

Soon Mr. Taggart stumbles in, looking lost and disinterested. He's got a bit of stuff to hand out—some reading material and a quiz related to it. Stuff that would take a monkey about half an hour to do. We have three hours.

"And if you finish it, just start—I don't know, do something."

That's our summer school teacher. Dazed and confused and saying things like *do something.*

I'm wondering if we'll see Mr. Taggart nod off today. We like taking bets to see if and when he will.

My guess is that his weekend has already started, and that mentally he's a long, long way from this classroom.

Surrounded by these strangers who are quickly becoming not strangers anymore, I strangely find myself at home.

For the first time since coming to good ole Solitary.

4. Memories

Middle of the morning, we have a fifteen-minute break where kids can go check all their social sites on their phones (as if they weren't already doing that for the last hour and a half), or go to the restroom, or go smoke if you're Brick. He offers me a cigarette every time he's ready to go. I always politely decline.

There's this crazy hope that I'm going to somehow find myself talking to the golden-haired goddess. Then again, I know I'd sorta stammer and say something stupid like the last couple of times we've talked.

After coming out of the restroom, I see her leaning against the wall while Harris, Roger, and Shawn circle her.

There's really no room for someone else. What's that called? *Fifth wheel?*

I walk slowly and hear Roger talking about some party. Suddenly it's my junior year again.

Seven people, and I'm still on the outs.

"You should come. Meet some more of the wonderful people who go to this school."

Shawn laughs, says something. I'm almost past them when I hear Roger say, "You can come too, Harris. Hey—Chris—you, too."

I stop and give my best *Oh you guys are talking about something 'cause you know I'm so cool I didn't notice.*

Lily glances at me, and the glance stays for a moment. She smiles.

No, I take it back. She's amused. She finds this—probably all of this—comical.

"Go where?" I ask.

"Big party Saturday night," Roger says. "Del's having it. His parents are gone, and they don't care anyway."

"I'll only go if Harris goes," Lily says. "Wanna be my date?"

I think all of us want to be your date.

Harris, of course, looks blown away. If he was as pale as me, perhaps he'd be blushing, but he just beams and acts like his day has been made.

It's funny, because Roger runs in different circles from the other popular senior I got to know. Ray didn't talk much about him. But I know Roger normally wouldn't invite people like Harris and me to his party. It's because Lily is standing there. He's finally figured out a way to get her to come.

We talk and laugh and then see Mr. Taggart walking past us in the hallway. He stops and looks over at us, his droopy eyes looking tired and sad.

"Don't ever have kids, I'm tellin' you straight," he says, then keeps walking.

We wait until he's in the room before bursting out laughing. It's funny.

I follow the gang into the room before remembering I left my notebook in the bathroom.

I jog back down the hallway.

The lights are on in the school, and it strangely feels like it's just the start of a regular day.

I slow down before getting to the restroom.

I slow down, and I remember.

"Good. We'll take you. You fit with us. Plus … you're cute."

That meeting in the hallway with the three girls. Jocelyn, Rachel, and Poe.

All gone in one way or the other.

I shut my eyes as if that can shut out thoughts. But memories are hard to keep contained.

"Don't say anything. Okay? Not now. Just wait for later."

Jocelyn's words after she found the note that I wrote but probably never intended to give her. Her words in these very same hallways.

I think of Joss, and Poe, and Newt, and Kelsey.

You can't just shut the book on them. They're still out there, even if they exist only as ghosts or memories.

I open the door to the bathroom and try to escape from all those names and faces and voices.

The school year is over.

The stuff that happened—it happened yesterday.

I find the notebook and grab it.

You can't just bury it.

I laugh and look at the guy in the mirror.

"Let's see if I can't."

5. Keys

"When are you going to find another job?"

I've managed to make it home minutes before Mom is ready to head out the door.

That is not so coincidental.

"My last one burned to the ground."

Mom is all made up and is running around like she always does before she goes to work at Brennan's Grill and Tavern.

"What'd they ever find out about that?"

"It probably went in the same file as everything else does."

Some big fat file in a dark abandoned room.

"Poor Iris. I hope she had insurance." Mom stops and thinks about things for a minute. "Have you ever heard from her?"

I shake my head.

Iris.

I don't tell my mom that every day since summer school has started, I've gone hunting for the scorched remains of the Crag's Inn.

And every day, I've come home without even finding the road that leads to it.

A road can't just disappear.

But the road leading to the inn, along with the inn itself and its keeper, have just suddenly and mysteriously *vanished.*

Hey, if a mysterious island can do that, maybe so can an inn …

"Well, when you see her, tell her if there's anything I can do …" Mom says.

I'm wondering what she has in mind. Replenishing the bar?

"Did you ask the teacher about getting your license?" she continues.

I laugh. "Mom—you don't ask Mr. Taggart anything to do with … well, anything."

"What do you mean?"

"If you saw him, you'd understand. He just walked off the set of a zombie movie."

"You have to get your license, Chris."

"I know."

She gives me a look. With the sun spilling into our small cabin, I can see her up close. Her eyes are red and watery. No amount of makeup can hide that.

"I've got some leftovers in the fridge. Half a chicken sandwich and some spinach dip."

"Together?" I make a face.

She shakes her head and starts for the door, then realizes she doesn't have her car keys. I find them on the counter and hand them to her.

"Get that smirk off your face," Mom says in a feisty tone.

"What?"

"You know *what.*"

I shrug.

"Just because you're able to ride around on that motorcycle doesn't mean you're grown up. I'm not going to keep paying for gas, you know."

Uh-huh. She's one to talk about being a grown-up. And part of me really thinks she likes paying for the gas. It keeps my smirk and her guilt far away.

Mom looks at her watch. "I'm gonna be late."

Exactly.

I see the door shut. And suddenly, there it comes again.

That lightweight feeling.

The quiet. The

dare I say it for fear of rats morphing into bats crawling out of the closets

peace.

It's close to one o'clock on a Friday afternoon on a summer day. I make sure Midnight has a bowl of food, then give her a good-bye pat on her head. The little black Shih Tzu seems content to sleep the day away on the couch.

I find the other set of keys and pick them up.

It's time to find the woman who gave them to me. Or at least find the place where she's buried.

6. Trying to Outrun Reason

"Hi, Chris."

I see Mr. Page's face as I'm just finishing gassing up the motorcycle, and a feeling of guilt tears through me. I can see his truck behind him at another pump, and I just know that Kelsey's sitting in the passenger seat. Sitting and watching. Wondering whatever happened after I last saw her at prom, after our dance to the last song of the night.

"New bike?" he asks me as he admires it.

"Uh, it was a gift," I say.

"Wow. Some gift. How's your summer going?"

"Good." I can't exactly see into the truck, but I just know—I have a feeling—

"Kelsey just left for Florida to visit her cousin. She'll be there a couple of weeks."

I hear the *phew* go off inside my head.

"Sounds like fun," I say.

"Yeah. She begged me, and her cousin came up here last summer, so we decided she could do it."

I think of the couple of times she's called and left messages. Of that last message still on our answering machine at home. Asking me to call, telling me to call soon if I can.

"Everything all right?" Mr. Page asks me.

Both of Kelsey's parents are just plain nice. No wonder she's such a sweet girl.

And no wonder she needs to stay far away from your life.

"Yeah. Everything's great."

"Maybe we'll see you sometime this summer. We'd love to have you over for dinner again."

"Yeah, sure," I say with a forced smile and interest.

If it's up to me, I won't go.

Nothing against Kelsey, or Mr. Page, or their nice little family. It's just—that's not for me. I don't belong in that picture.

I belong in another picture. Rated R for violence and horror. The kind where kids get killed off one by one.

I mount my bike and try to start it up. For some reason, it won't go.

I try again. And again.

I glance over at Mr. Page, who's smiling at me.

I feel like such a tool.

Finally, after a few more tries, I start it up. I wave to him and take off down the road, not really sure where I'm headed but just getting away from the niceness of that man and his family and especially his daughter, who I've been avoiding thinking about because it's easier that way.

I ride for a while, getting out of the town limits of Solitary. Sometimes it seems the farther I drive the easier it is not to think about everything. But today, it all comes back. Maybe it's because I saw Mr. Page and was reminded that just because I'm not answering doesn't mean they're not out there.

If I close my eyes and think about it, I can still picture Kelsey's glance while we danced at prom. I can still remember feeling lost and free. Of course, I can't shut my eyes at this very moment, or I'd probably end up wrapped around a tree in the woods I'm passing. Maybe that's another reason I like this bike. No time to daydream.

Then I think of Poe, of her telling me not to bother stopping by to say good-bye. Of her telling me that she'll contact me at some point down the road. But every day I don't hear anything, and I wonder when exactly "down the road" is going to be. Will I end up at a nursing home one day and see her sitting across from me in a wheelchair?

Think you'll live long enough to see a retirement home?

The whole Poe-Kelsey thing that happened last semester—I still don't know how to make sense of any of it. There was never supposed to be a Poe-Kelsey thing to start with. It kinda creeped up on me, and then when I realized it, the mouth of the beast swallowed me in. Things got too dark too fast for there to ever be Team Poe shirts and Team Kelsey pages.

This reminds me of my current predicament. No, not predicament. Situation.

The latest pretty girl I can't stop thinking about.

The road winds around, and I keep going faster, trying to outrun reason. I'm getting the hang of riding this motorcycle even if I don't have a license and don't know exactly why I was given the bike in the first place.

I'm trying not to think so much these days. But I'm not doing that great a job.

7. Back Roads Party

The following evening, I show up to Del's home, using the directions that Roger scribbled down for me. His house is really just a one-bedroom shack, to be honest, but it's got a huge yard that everybody seems to be parked on and hanging out in. There are probably a hundred people that I can see when I pull up and get off the bike.

As usual, I get people admiring the bike and commenting on it. I can't lie. It feels good to be noticed in a positive way.

I go in search of any of the summer school students, hoping to find someone I know to stand near instead of looking like a kid lost at a busy mall. It doesn't take me long to see Shawn, but he just nods and keeps going in search of something. Maybe more beer.

The backyard has more people just standing and listening to music and drinking beer. Someone hands me a cup and I thank him, and then he tells me it's ten bucks. Instead of telling the guy I'm not going to drink, I just give him a twenty, and he says thanks and disappears.

I stand there with an empty cup, waiting for my change. Then wondering if the guy knows I needed change. Then just giving up.

I see Roger talking with a group, and he says hi to me. I walk up, and he asks if I rode my bike, then asks about riding it later. I tell him sure but plan on forgetting about it the same way the guy forgot about my change.

"Dude, you need a refill," he says.

He grabs my cup and then tells someone to get me a beer.

Suddenly I see Shawn, and he's saying hi to me and bringing me a full beer.

Gotta love high school and cliques and popularity.

Some of the people standing around here look like they're in their thirties. Others, like me, look well under the legal age limit. But getting caught for underage drinking seems so yesterday, so Illinois-suburbs-where-people-aren't-sacrificed.

I take a sip but don't like the taste of the beer. I don't even like the idea that I'm drinking.

Mom's been doing enough of that for the both of us.

But I sip to fit in.

And that's exactly what I do. I fit in. I suddenly morph into the crowd, listening to awful hard rock and even more awful country. I wonder what they'd do if I suddenly threw in some Arcade Fire. Torch it? I listen to Roger talking and talking more, and I feign laughter and find myself doing nothing better than I would have been doing back at the cabin. I still feel isolated and out of place even though I'm surrounded by all these kids.

What am I doing here?

But eventually, as the sun disappears and the tiki torches surrounding the backyard glow and that first beer I was going to sip has turned into my third cup, I see a streak of golden sunlight split the sea of students and strangers. Lily.

I realize why I'm here.

She doesn't have to see me. I don't mind.

She's a sight to behold in this mass of ordinary people.

"Girl, you look *fine,*" Roger says in a way that makes me hate him.

I only wish I could say something with such ease.

Lily and her golden dress give Roger a hug. Thankfully I'm not the only guy standing here looking like a dog with its mouth open, staring at a bone.

"When you said back roads, you really meant *back roads*," Lily says.

"It's better that way," Roger says. Then he whispers something in her ear, and she laughs.

I hope I'm not going to have to watch them all night.

"Hey, Chris," a voice calls from behind me.

It's Harris. He's getting just as many looks as Lily did, but for a whole different reason.

"How's it going?" I say with a nod.

Harris stays and talks to me. Either he's oblivious to the stares, or he just doesn't care. Nobody offers him a cup, but he doesn't mind.

"Did you come with Lily?" I ask.

"Yes, definitely."

"Like a date?"

Harris just laughs at me. "That was funny."

I nod and smile but wonder why he thinks I was making a joke.

A popular country music song begins to play, and some of the crowd start dancing. I look for Lily or Roger, but they're nowhere to be found.

"You look almost as out-of-place as I do," Harris says.

"Really?"

He nods. "Come on—let's go to the front of the house. Where it's not as loud."

Back on the front lawn, there are several groups of kids hanging around the backs of their trucks, drinking beer and dancing and listening to bad music. Harris and I watch them for a while, amused by their antics.

"So you're the guy who set the record in hurdles, right?" Harris asks.

I nod.

"They keep asking me to go out for track. I try not to make it a racial thing, you know, but it's hard to understand why year after year they keep asking."

"You like any sports?"

"If I tell you I don't, will that break all stereotypes for you?"

There's a redneck song blasting that says something about the singer getting "whiskey bent and hellbound."

"No. But if you tell me you like this song, I'll be worried."

Harris laughs so hard that he almost chokes. I guess that's a good thing.

After a while he asks another question, this one not so funny.

"You were the guy hanging around Jocelyn Evans, right?"

I nod but don't say anything else.

"The thing about this place—the most interesting people always end up leaving. It's a known fact. That's what I told Lily. That's what I told her she should know. She'll be here for a while, and then she'll be gone. Just like that. It always happens."

He says this in a matter-of-fact way, not in any spooky bedtime-story way.

"I liked Jocelyn," Harris continues. "She was wild, you know, but still—there was something about her. Something authentic."

Suddenly I want to finish this beer and have another. So I do.

I don't want to talk about Jocelyn. Or hear how wild she might have been. Or how authentic she might have appeared to be.

I don't even want to hear that name.

So I grab another beer.

And I stand in the glow of the warm flickering lights. And I hear the strumming of warm flowing music. And I suddenly see a warm smile facing my way.

Not long after that, I'm gone.

8. A Night Like This

The sound of the motorcycle wakes me up. I feel the breeze against my head and face and know I'm riding back home.

The problem is that the world keeps spinning sideways and doing a tilt-a-whirl around my head.

"Don't let go of me, or you'll seriously die!"

I tuck my arms and hands back into something both soft and hard. I'm dizzy and wondering if I'm standing with my arms wrapped around someone. But then I realize that no—I'm on my bike—I assume it's my bike—it better be my bike—with my arms around someone.

"I swear if you're faking this just to be able to grab me all over, you're seriously going to get your butt kicked on Monday."

"Joss—" I say, but the wind swallows the word before it makes a sound.

Strands of thick curly hair whip against my face and forehead.

It's not Joss. It's Lily.

But of course, it's another dream. Like those I used to have of Jocelyn.

"We're almost home, kid," she tells me like a parent. "Come on—hang on tight."

Even though this is a dream, she feels real. She even smells real. She smells like—flowers.

Of course she does. And when you get to her house she'll have a bed of roses waiting for you.

I see streetlamps and lights and realize that we're downtown in Solitary.

"Why are we here?"

"You told me to get you downtown. That you forgot how to get home."

"I don't want to go home."

The voice in front of me laughs. "Yeah, well, you're not coming home with me. That's for sure."

"I know of a barn somewhere."

Another thought suddenly pops into my delirious head.

How'd I get this way?

I didn't have *that* much to drink. I know it. I know it for a fact.

"What happened?" I say with a major slur.

A silver sports car comes out of nowhere. It looks expensive and snazzy, and I see Harris behind the wheel. He asks Lily something, and she answers, but my head can't keep up.

"Okay, think you can tell me how to get home from here?"

She says this with her head half turned. I see the profile of her face, the full pouty lips and the narrow cheekbones.

"You're beautiful," I say.

She laugh. "You sure don't get out much, do you, Chris Buckley?"

My head hurts. "I would if I could."

"That so?"

"Yes. Drive anywhere you want."

She nods. "That's nice, but you, my boy, need to get some rest. Maybe another time. So tell me. Where do I go from here?"

I look around and then mumble directions to my house. I hear the sports car following us.

This was definitely *not* how this night was supposed to go.

9. Like Mother, Like Son

I wake up around ten Sunday morning and drag myself downstairs. My head throbs, and my mouth is dry. For a few moments my brain can't even manage a straight thought. I go to the fridge and open it to find very little inside. I get a glass and fill it with water from the sink, then sit on the couch.

My mom strolls out of her bedroom, looking hungover and groggy. She sits on the other couch and for a while says nothing.

Her hair is messy and her eyes are bloodshot and she looks like New Year's Day.

Just like you probably do.

I wonder if this is what they call irony. I don't know. I can't stretch that word out long enough to grasp its meaning.

When Mom finally notices me, she looks puzzled. Her lips almost go to say something. Almost.

Then they close again, and she squints her eyes the way she does when she has a migraine.

Here we are, just the two of us.

"Hungry?" she eventually asks.

I nod.

Mom slowly gets up and heads into the kitchen.

Eventually I follow.

10. You Owe Me

Six other students, and I'm ashamed to show my face in our class.

It's the Monday after the party, and I'm still just as hazy about what happened as I was twenty-four hours earlier. At least I finally feel more like myself, but I don't understand what happened. I can't even remember being dropped off. My last memory is being downtown in Solitary and seeing Harris pull up beside us in his fancy car.

There's no way I can get out of this class or that I can undo what happened at the party. Or afterward.

When I get to class, everybody is already there. As if they planned on coming early in order to mock me.

"There he is," Roger says with the same dynamic smile as always. "The wild child of the party."

I laugh nervously. I look at Lily and Harris next to her.

"How you feeling, buddy?" Harris asks.

"Fine. A lot better." I notice that Mr. Taggart hasn't slid into class yet. "Parts of the night are a bit foggy."

Lily laughs. "No, really?"

"How'd I get in my bed?"

"Oh, it was right after we had to undress you and give you a sponge bath."

Lily says this loud enough that everybody can hear. They all laugh at her joke. Of course, it really *better* be a joke.

"I helped you in," Harris said. "You were gone."

I sigh. "I swear—I didn't have that much to drink."

"Man, it happens to the best of us," Roger says to me like an older brother.

Brick asks Roger if he had a party and why he didn't invite him—that gets them talking about the party and the focus off of me.

"I swear—really—I had a few beers," I tell them. "That was it."

I'm convinced of it. But Harris and Lily just look at me like I'm in junior high.

"I had fun," Lily says to Harris, then looks at me. "I got to drive your motorcycle. It was awesome."

"Thanks."

Her green eyes don't look away. "You owe me," she says in a playful way. "Especially after what you said."

"What I said when?"

Steps shuffle behind me, and I hear a voice bark out, "All right, hush up everybody; Chris, sit down."

I start to head over to my regular seat, but Lily taps the seat in front of her.

"Sit," she says. "I won't bite. At least not today."

I nod and take a seat in front of her. I wonder if there are any pimples on the back of my neck and whether she's examining them. Mr. Taggart is talking about the handout he's giving us when I feel her hair brush up against my right shoulder.

"This guy is even more bored than we are," she says.

I turn and nod and then keep looking ahead. I hear whispers between Harris and her but can't make out what they're talking about.

It's week two of summer school, and I've managed to make a connection.

Whether it's based on friendship or pity—I guess we'll have to see.

11. Just a Shadow

I'm walking out of the school into the bright sunlight, following Harris and Lily. I can't help but notice Lily and those jeans. The jeans and the top that looks like half a top with tiny little straps. I can't help watching her even as she occasionally says something and glances back at me. I try to keep my eyes at head level and am reminded again that I need some sunglasses.

I don't see the cop car until we're standing on the blacktop of the parking lot.

"Uh-oh," Harris says. "Someone's in trouble."

Sheriff Wells is leaning against the car, looking at us. "How're you guys doing today?"

We nod and say fine and keep walking.

"Chris—do you have a minute?"

Harris and Lily look at me.

"Sure."

I can't help but think this has something to do with Saturday night.

"See you later," I tell them.

I won't confess. Not that I really have anything to confess to anyway.

It's been a while since I've seen the sheriff. He's on my To Avoid list. It's a pretty long list.

He scratches his gray goatee and then clears his throat. "Summer school, huh?"

I nod.

"Your grades that bad?"

"Guess so."

He nods, not really sharing what he's thinking. Then he glances around, even though the parking lot is basically empty.

"That your bike?" he asks.

"Yeah."

"That used to belong to your uncle."

"Did I do something wrong?"

Calculating eyes cut into me. "Oliver Mateja was found dead this morning."

For a minute this doesn't mean anything to me. *Ma-tay-hah?* Not just the name, but the fact that the sheriff is telling me that someone was found dead.

Jaded to the core. Most kids might freak, but you stand there still thinking about Lily's jeans.

"Oli," the sheriff says to clarify.

I want to shake my head as if I have water in my ears and didn't quite hear that right.

No.

Gus's ugly, fat face comes to mind, and I know that in some way he was involved. He, or his father, or all of them together.

There's no way.

I suddenly feel guilty, though I haven't had any sort of interaction with Oli since the incident in the art room.

When he stuck up for you.

"How'd he die?" I ask.

Trying to stay cool and trying to keep from screaming.

"Drowned."

That makes as much sense as Oli being dead. I try and think of the places around Solitary he could have drowned.

"Lake Toxaway. I don't know all the details yet—they're just coming in."

Didn't even know his last name.

"When was the last time you saw him?"

"School. That was it."

I'm feeling a bit woozy, like the sky above me is going back and forth the way it does when you're on a swing.

"He was part of the crowd giving you a hard time, right?"

I've had several conversations with the man in front of me. I'm used to seeing him and his badge and his edge.

They don't scare me anymore.

I've learned there are bigger things to be frightened of.

"Am I a suspect?"

The sheriff shakes his head. "No. It's being categorized as a drowning, Chris. Not a murder. Do you know anybody who would want to hurt Oliver?"

The guy who moved here with his mother after the divorce happened—that guy would have told the sheriff everything he knew.

The guy who rushed for justice and answers after Jocelyn's death—yeah, that guy would have told the sheriff everything too.

"No," is all I can say.

I don't trust this guy any more than I'd trust Santa Claus if he showed up to teach me summer school.

"Anything you know can help."

"I don't know anything about drownings or lakes."

The sheriff lets out an annoyed curse. "What's with the attitude?"

"There's no attitude."

His face grows grim. "Chris—listen to me. I'm on your side."

"There are sides?"

He shakes his head, looks around again. "You seen much of Gus this summer?"

"Nope."

"Any of his friends?"

"Somehow they all managed to escape summer school."

"Yeah, I see."

I stand there and wait. Not offering anything. Not sharing the story of how Oli stuck up for Kelsey and me in the art room. How he threatened Gus.

If the sheriff asked me point blank, I'd probably tell him that yeah, sure, I think Gus might've killed him.

But that's not my problem. Oli. Gus. The sheriff. Kelsey.

All on the To Avoid list.

"You staying out of trouble?"

I look at him.

There's a part of me that has started to hold him responsible for what happened to Jocelyn.

"Have you seen me any this summer?" I ask.

"I'm just trying to help out."

I nod. "Kinda late to be a hero, isn't it?"

Sheriff Wells glares at me but doesn't say anything. I walk away from him.

I feel goose bumps and chills and adrenaline coursing through me as I get on the bike.

You just told off a sheriff.

But I know the guy's a scared little mouse. He's not going to do anything to anybody.

I start up the bike and see him still standing by the car.

Just a shadow of a man.

A shadow you can walk straight through.

12. Pity Party

Give me a freakin' break.

I sit there on the edge of an unnamed road in the middle of an unknown forest. I shut off my bike, and then I wipe the tears away from my face. They make me angry. The feel of them. Streaming down my cheeks as I'm riding on my motorcycle. That's so *not* cool. That's so *not* how to ride a bike.

I climb off and head to the edge of the trees towering over me.

I don't want the sky to see me.

Just in case.

Just in case they're looking down. They—whoever they may be.

I let it out for just a few minutes.

I let it out, realizing the truth.

Oli was protecting me and Kelsey, and that was it. And now he's dead.

I don't care what anybody else says—he didn't just drown.

Get control, Chris. Get control, and get over it.

When I leave this cursed place, I'm going to be a master of my mind and soul. A master at being able to let things go or at least bury them deep inside.

My eyes burn, and I wipe the silly, stupid tears away.

I think of Oli.

Oliver Mateja.

A part of me wants to know his story—his real story, the story behind why he chose to help me out when it meant abandoning his friends.

Why would he do that?

And this is what it got him. This is what happens when you stick your neck out for others. You find yourself at the bottom of a lake.

But not you, Chris. You're special. You're different.

Then the words spoken by Jeremiah Marsh seem to whisper in my ears.

"We can live and die afraid, or we can live to defy, Chris. It is up to you."

I don't get it. I don't understand.

All we have is ourselves. That's all. Nobody else is looking out for you. Nothing is there to come and save you and defeat the evil monster.

I hear a rustling in the woods. For a second I think—no, I *hope*—that it's the bluebird I used to see at Iris's place and shortly after the fire. But I haven't seen the bluebird in a long time.

Something's in the woods—I know it. I can feel it.

But it's bigger than a bluebird. Bigger, and probably meaner.

Every man for himself.

And this man decides enough's enough. The pity is over.

The party, however, is just about to start.

It's called letting go.

13. Warning Sign

That afternoon, as I'm watching television because I don't have much else to do, I hear a knock on my door. It startles me. I can't help it.

I see someone peering through the window. Newt's big glasses are easy to recognize.

Newt's an odd kid, but he's one of the few people at Harrington High who seems to get how awful things are in Solitary. He's also one of the few people I trust.

It can't be good that he's standing at your doorstep, since he's never come by before.

I open the door. "What is it?"

He glances down the stairs behind him before he quickly moves by me to get inside. Once inside, he locks the front door.

I used to think his silly fears were a bit extreme, but I don't anymore.

"How'd you get here?" I ask.

"Rode my bike. Did you hear?"

"About Oli?"

"Who told you?" His eyes seem to keep getting bigger, like someone blowing up a balloon.

"The sheriff."

Newt's bangs are sweaty, and his face is flushed. I ask him if he's okay, if he wants to sit and have something to drink.

"Oli was the most athletic guy in our school," he says, ignoring my questions. "He didn't drown. There is no way he drowned."

He doesn't have to tell me this.

"How did you hear?" I ask.

"Word's getting around school. I saw it on Facebook."

I nod. I haven't been online for a while, much less on Facebook.

"I heard about what happened with Oli and Gus and you in the art room," Newt says.

"I'm sure a lot of people have."

"Don't you think it has something to do with that?"

I shrug. "I've stopped thinking."

The beady eyes look at me as if they're trying to comprehend what I just said.

"I'm tired of playing detective," I tell Newt.

He shakes his head.

"What?"

"You can't just—"

"I can't just what?" I ask. "Stop? Stop asking questions? You're the one who always said I should be careful."

"But that was before—"

"Before what? Before Oli died? Before they got to Jocelyn? Before they made Poe leave?"

"No. It was before—before I saw what they did to you."

I don't get what he's talking about. "What do you mean, what they did to me? Who are you talking about? And what'd they do?"

"Nothing," he says. "They didn't do anything."

I'm still not following.

Newt sighs and looks back at the door.

"Nobody's coming, man," I say. "There's no boogeyman listening to us."

He looks at me, his eyes flitting around.

"What?"

"See this?" Newt points to the red streak on his face.

I nod.

"You want to know how I got this? And the one on my arm?"

"Yeah."

"Stuart Algiers. The kid who disappeared before you moved here. That's how."

"He did that to you?"

"No," he says in frustration. "It was after he went missing. After the rumors really started getting crazy. I started looking into it."

"You did?"

He nods. "Stuart was always nice to me. He stuck up for me when others didn't. He was—he was kinda like you. And after he disappeared during Christmas break, I knew something bad must have happened to him. So I started looking around. Asking questions. Playing detective. And that's when this happened."

"*What* happened?"

"I was walking home from the park when a couple guys wearing ski masks jumped out of a van and grabbed me, then knocked me out. I woke up somewhere dark with a whole group of them standing around me, threatening me. They took something hot and sharp—like a knife left in a fire—and they did this."

I can't help but wince, looking at the scar.

Now you know, Chris.

"They said the only reason they didn't kill me was that I was going to be a lesson. They wanted me to walk around with this, to warn other students not to mess around. Not to ask questions. To go about their lives being quiet and not curious."

"I'm sorry."

"So then you come in and start hanging around with Jocelyn and asking questions and snooping around. That's why I've been careful. Why I act this way."

"I've been warned too," I tell him.

"Yes, but—Chris, for some reason you're different. I don't know. You just—you are."

"Why?"

"Because people are looking out for you. And because—because they haven't gotten to you."

"Says who?"

He just looks at me, the eyes behind the spectacles, the scar on his cheek, the flustered face.

He is the picture of a warning sign.

"They got to Oli just like they got to Stuart. Or to Jocelyn. Or to others. But not you, Chris. You're different."

I shake my head. I don't believe it. "So—what's that have to do with anything?"

"So you can't stop," Newt says with as much strength as his little form and feeble voice can muster. "Not after everything. That's what they want you to do. You have to keep going."

"Keep going? Keep going where?"

I think of the pictures I found of Jocelyn dead and bloody. I think of Pastor Marsh, of the blade I thrust into his chest, of the realization that I'd killed a man in cold blood.

But you didn't. He's still around, still preaching some kind of message on Sunday mornings, still smiling his creepy smile.

As if everything that happened to us in the woods was just a dream. Or a nightmare.

Is there a difference?

I think of the following days and nights where I walked around as if a ghost or a goblin might grab me at any moment. Where I tried to make sense of it all.

I still can't. It doesn't make any.

"There's nowhere left to go," I say.

"Chris—"

"Newt, no. Enough."

"You just can't—stop."

I laugh. It's probably a little bit too loud and too crazy, because Newt suddenly looks scared.

"This is not my problem. I'm—I'm sorry to hear about Oli.

Really. But I didn't have anything to do with it. And this—all of this—I didn't sign up for this. I'm done. With all of it."

14. Similarities

I get to Harrington High a bit late and see Brick standing by the entrance, smoking. He watches me get off the bike and then offers me a cigarette when I get near him.

"No, thanks."

"You do drugs, Buckwheat?"

I never know what exactly I'm gonna get from Brick.

"Just got out of rehab, so I gotta cut down, you know," I say.

For a brief second he thinks about what I'm saying, then he laughs. "Funny."

"I try."

"You know, they don't like drugs around here."

"I hear they sure like them in Nebraska, though."

This time he really doesn't get my joke. Or he doesn't think it's funny.

"I'm serious. Like—it's kinda weird."

"People not liking drugs?"

He flicks his cigarette away and then shakes his head. "Nah, man. It's how they leave you alone. If you're part of that crowd."

"Who's 'they'?"

He opens the door to the school. "Look, you're still new. I'll show you sometime. Okay?"

I'm not so sure I want Brick showing me anything. "Yeah, sure."

"That guy Staunch. I know all about him. I could write some books."

He says this with a laugh.

The very mention of the name makes my skin crawl. I want to ask what he knows, but I don't. Part of me wonders if he's trying to get me to ask him, then he'll fill me with lies.

"They don't mess with me," Brick continues. "Think I'm just a useless druggie, you know. But those are the ones you gotta watch. 'Cause those are the ones watching you."

Mr. Taggart is standing by the chalkboard with his wrinkled long-sleeved dress shirt sticking half out of his pants. He's writing something in really messy cursive. Brick glances back at me and gives me a *What now?* expression. I take my new seat close to Lily and Harris but don't get much of a greeting. Especially from Lily.

The teacher turns and looks at us. "I don't know what I'm doing up here." Then he curses.

I look at Harris, who is looking at Lily.

We're all thinking the same thing.

What are we *doing here?*

"Any of you any good at algebra?" Mr. Taggart's groggy voice asks.

He's asking *us,* the ones sitting in class during the summer.

Brick raises his hand, which only gets a dismissive nod from the teacher.

"Do they use algebra in *Call of Duty*?" Brick asks.

Several people laugh as Mr. Taggart gives him a dead person's look.

"Very funny, Franklin. You're gonna need that humor in prison."

"Trying my best, *sir,*" Brick replies.

This is gonna be a long class.

After class, Harris seems to remember the visit from Sheriff Wells and asks me about it as we're walking out.

"It was nothing."

"Have anything to do with Oli?"

So he's heard. Of course he's heard.

"Where'd you hear about that?"

"Everybody's talking about it on Facebook and Twitter."

"Talking about what?" a voice out of nowhere asks.

Little Miss Sunshine strolls up to us, still playing with her iPhone. Lily hasn't said much to me today. I felt like a doorknob sitting in front of her. A doorknob that nobody's bothering to turn and open. And I specifically tried looking a little nicer today, whatever that means since doorknobs never look particularly interesting.

"This kid at our school drowned in a lake," Harris says.

Lily stops texting or doing whatever she's doing and stares at him. "Seriously?"

"Yeah."

"That's awful. Did you guys know him?"

Harris and I shake our heads. She brushes back the curly golden locks and looks genuinely upset.

"How old was he?"

"Seventeen," Harris says.

"Just a kid," she says, staring down the hallway and lost for a moment. "Wow."

We're heading out of the school on another gloriously sunny day. I'm getting ready for the regular routine of telling them I'll see them later when Lily says, "Now I'm seriously bummed out."

She stops Harris as if she's had a bright idea. She looks like a model today in her bright pink top and dark pink shorts.

"You want to go to lunch today? Do you have time?"

"I don't work until three," Harris says. He works at a golf resort not far from Asheville.

"What about you, biker boy?"

"I don't have a job," I say.

"Great. Let's go somewhere, then. My treat. I don't exactly have a job either. But I have money."

I nod and realize I have no idea where Lily lives or what her story is.

"Want to follow us, then?" she asks. "Harris and I will figure out a place to go."

I nod. As Harris and Lily walk over to his car, I see Brick coming up behind me.

"Puppy dogs."

I smile and nod, not knowing what he meant by it.

"You keep sniffing and you'll get your nose cut off," Brick says to me in his good-old-boy accent. He makes himself laugh as he keeps walking away from the parking lot and down the hill.

I guess he doesn't drive to summer school.

As I follow the shiny sports car that looks like it just got washed and waxed, I'm wondering why Brick thinks we're puppy dogs.

And why he thinks we might get our noses cut off.

I think of Jared, my so-called cousin. All he ever wanted was to keep tabs on me and fill me with wrong information.

Don't worry, Brick. I'm not trusting anybody again. No way.

We drive fifteen minutes away from the school, so far that I seriously start wondering if they're playing a joke on me. We get off the main highway and head into a small town called Flat Rock. They eventually stop at a smokehouse that looks pretty busy for a Tuesday. It takes us a few minutes to order and then take our food outside to sit at a table.

Lily wears large shades that seem to lose themselves in her windblown hair. She's ordered fries and a barbecue beef sandwich as large as her head. Something tells me she doesn't eat like this every day.

"So what's your story, Chris?" she asks me after we've started eating.

Harris sits next to her in a pair of mirrored sunglasses. I can't tell if either of them is even looking at me while they eat.

"I moved here last October."

Last October feels like two years ago.

Make that two lifetimes ago.

"From where?"

"Libertyville. A suburb of Chicago."

She finishes a fry and then sips her soda. "I absolutely love Chicago."

So here's my chance. To ask her what her story is.

Yet I just can't.

"Why'd you move?" Lily asks.

"My parents divorced."

"You kidding?"

I shake my head.

"Same here."

"Really?" I ask, genuinely surprised.

"Who'd you move with?"

"My mom."

"Same here! What—was your old man cheating?"

"Uh, no."

"Mine was. What a nightmare. It just proves that it doesn't matter who it is. If it's a guy, then it can happen. Right, Harris?"

"We're all pigs," Harris jokes.

"You are." She picks up one of the ten napkins around his plate and flings it in his direction.

I don't want to tell her that my parents' divorce was due to God and not because of breaking one of His commandments.

"Where'd you move from?" I ask.

"Just like you—a suburb. Dunwoody. North of Atlanta."

The obvious question on the tip of my tongue is—

"So you're wondering why in the world Solitary. Right?"

"Nobody moves to Solitary," Harris says. "Then Chris comes along. And now you."

"Why'd you move here?" Lily asks.

"My mom grew up around here. And my uncle—he used to live here."

"Ah, family then," Lily says. "We're sorta the same. Well, kinda. My mother's mother had a place here. She recently passed and left it to us. After everything happened back home—my mom just wanted to split."

"Sounds familiar," I say.

"You guys should start some kind of recovery group," Harris says.

"Hey—shut up," Lily jokes. "Divorce isn't funny."

Harris nods. "Especially when you have to move to this place."

"How was your first year at the school?" Lily asks.

I seriously almost choke on a bite of my burger. I finally swallow and am not sure how to answer her.

I mean, could things have possibly gone any worse?

"That bad?" she asks with a laugh.

"Wasn't that good."

"Great," she says. "You guys sure know how to make a girl feel welcome. Especially after she buys you lunch."

"What do you want us to say?" Harris asks. "We're just being honest."

"Gee—I can't wait for school to start!" Lily exaggerates.

I wish I could see her eyes. They really do tell a lot about somebody. And I just want to see them in order to get some idea, some hint of who she might really be. Right now she's like the sun above us. Bright and cheery and carefree.

I want to tell her things about this town.

"Maybe my mom will decide that she can't take any more and move us back to Atlanta."

Maybe it's from her good looks or maybe it's from where she grew up, but Lily carries a confidence that's surprising even for someone like her. It's not like she's talking down to Harris and me. But she definitely controls the conversation and the tone and, well, basically everything about us sitting here.

And you like that, don't you?

Coming from a house where my mom controls nothing—absolutely nothing—the feeling of having someone in control is kinda welcome.

Especially if that someone is someone like Lily.

"I gather that the two of you aren't exactly typical Harrington High boys, are you?"

"Oh, no, it's almost seventy-five percent black," Harris jokes. "Right, Chris?"

"Yeah, sure. And everybody *loves* alternative music."

My joke is definitely the weaker of the two. But Lily smiles at both of us, the two boys sitting at her table.

"I'm expecting both of you to show me around when school begins. Deal?"

Harris and I both nod. I'm pretty confident both of us are more than happy to show Lily around. At least I am.

15. Bad Romance

That night, I find myself in a circle of girls. At first I think it's just some kind of school function, but then one of them tells me this is an intervention.

I wonder if my mom's there, but no. She hasn't managed to be responsible enough to make it into my dream.

"I just wish Chris had the guts to actually stay in touch with someone," Poe says to me.

I notice that since she's moved, she's become even darker, like *The Girl with the Dragon Tattoo* dark.

"I just wish Chris knew what he wanted when it came to girls," Kelsey says.

She's got gigantic glasses on and one of those contraptions for braces that I've only seen in movies, the kind where it looks like you're in a neck brace and have wires all around your head.

"I just wish Chris had gotten to me in time," Jocelyn says. "We all know that record he set in hurdles wasn't really a record at all."

Jocelyn doesn't look like herself at all.

That's 'cause you're forgetting what she looked like. Isn't that right, Chris?

"Why are you all talking about him in the third person?" Lily says, standing up and taking my hand. "Come on, Chris. Let me take you out of here."

"All Chris ever does is ignore me," a permanently smiling mannequin says to me as I stand up.

Suddenly I hear a Lady Gaga tune blaring.

What was in that burger I had at lunch?

Then I see my mom's aunt Alice next to the mannequin. She looks puzzled as she says, "Rah-rah-ah-ah-ah-ah!"

As I take Lily's hand, I wake up and find myself no longer stuck in a bad romance.

It's just me and my crazy mind and my narrow bed and the window I'm so used to seeing right next to it.

16. End of the Discussion

The next day Lily shows up late—like half an hour late—and she looks like she had a long night. Not the way my mom might. No, Lily still is a morning shot to the system, but she's wearing a designer white cap and shades as she strolls in front of the class.

Where's she going?

I'm sitting where I've been sitting, in front of her regular seat across from Harris. But she strolls by us and heads for the other side of the room.

"Well, good morning, Miss Lily," Mr. Taggart says as he stops whatever rambling nobody was listening to. "Did we interrupt your beauty sleep?"

"We're all terribly amused," she says as she sits in a desk near nobody.

All of us look at each other. Harris shrugs and then keeps thumbing his phone.

I look over at her and wait for some kind of glance or nod or anything. I see her head look my way, but I can't tell if she's looking at me from behind her sunglasses.

Does it really matter anyway, Chris?

But it does. Because deep down—well, yeah, deep down there's this crazy little hope.

Mr. Taggart sometimes reads from his notes. We're covering several subjects, and sometimes he drones on without ever seeing if we're paying attention, like a machine on an assembly line automatically squirting jelly into jars. But they haven't been able to make machines that pump information into kids, not yet, so Mr. Taggart is trying his best to correct that reality.

Harris is still texting, and I see Lily working her phone as well. They might be talking. Then again, so is Roger. Shawn is sleeping, his round chubby cheek so soft he's probably using it as a pillow. I look at Gin/Jen/Linn. She's listening to Mr. Taggart, making me wonder what she really and truly is doing here. Then there's Brick, leaning back in his seat and just staring ahead with his mouth open and his eyes fixed on the nothingness of life.

Harris laughs. Then I see him glance over at Lily, who nods.

I gotta get a phone. And service. And connected.

But that would mean I'd need a job. And yeah, I don't want to go down that road again. Especially now that I can't even find the blasted road.

During break, Lily doesn't move from her seat. She's still got the sunglasses on and still looks like she doesn't want to be bothered. I head out to use the restroom and then get some air outside.

These hallways have a weird white glow about them, like they could double as the halls for a mental institution. I've always assumed it was the strangers inside these halls that caused my mind to grow slowly numb, but now I realize the funky lighting contributed.

As I'm walking out of the restroom, my hands still wet because there were no paper towels to dry them on, I'm heading toward the main doors where the empty cafeteria sits and waits for all the heapings of bad food to be dished out next year.

I'm almost to the door when I see him.

A tall guy in sweatpants and a sweatshirt. Walking down the other hallway, away from the front doors and from where our classroom is.

He turns and glances my way, then keeps walking.

I blink because I swear …

No you didn't just see that.

But half of his face kinda appeared—dark and grisly and gone, like the blond-haired guy at the end of *The Dark Knight.*

Imagination and boredom, Chris.

The hallway lights on that side of the school are turned off, but he's still walking over there.

I feel cold. Like an air conditioner suddenly got plugged in and a gust of cold air is blasting over me. I shiver and can't help it.

A part of me wonders if it has anything to do with the guy I just saw, but …

Knock it off, Chris.

I refuse to spook myself out anymore.

This life isn't some script from a horror movie. I'm tired of being in that story.

Brick is standing outside with a cigarette and nods to me as I come out.

"Where's my smoke?" I ask.

"You finally want one?"

I shake my head. "Just kidding. Hey—did you see a tall kid walking by?"

Brick shakes his head.

It's easy to forget about that kid I saw. I'm sure he was just another Harrington student who needed to come in for some awful reason.

We finish early, since Mr. Taggart is anxious to get home and do nothing, and I wait for Lily to walk out the door. As the others head out of the room, she moves slowly. So do I. Then she moves even slower.

It's obvious that I'm waiting for her.

"Yes?" she eventually says.

"Everything okay?" I force myself to ask.

"Now why would you think something's wrong?"

It's the same tone she used with Mr. Taggart.

That's not a good thing.

"I just—I don't know. You're kinda quiet."

"Not sitting next to you guys is different from being quiet."

"Okay. Yeah, I guess so."

"After you," she says. "I insist."

I walk out the door and head down the hallway. She follows from a distance.

I pause and turn around. "Anything I can, uh, do?"

What a stupid question, Chris.

She shakes her head and gives me one of the smiles that an adult gives a child.

You're not going to find another Jocelyn, so just move on out.

I keep walking and don't say another word to her. And I think that I'm probably right. Jocelyn was this beautiful girl who I discovered wasn't just some silent, stuck-up beauty, but much more. There was so much more going on with her.

With her and surrounding her.

But some girls who happen to be hot act like they know it and that's it. End of the discussion.

As I get on my bike, I see Lily getting in the car with Harris. I wonder how she got here this morning, then realize it's stupid thinking about someone who's not thinking about you.

17. A Slap and a Punch

When I get home, I find Mom already wasted.

It's not even lunchtime.

I open the door and see her in the kitchen and know something's up, since she always works lunch and dinner during the week.

"Chris, you're home," she says.

And right there I know.

On the way up, my mom sounds like this. Happy and light if not a bit slippery and slurring. On the way down, before she blacks out, she's either half unconscious or she's half possessed.

She's good to go.

The question is where she needs to go *to*. I think AA would be fitting.

"I'm so glad, because you and I are going to have a magnisifent lunch."

Oh dear.

I don't tell her that she needs a spell-checker.

"What are you doing home?" I ask.

The sky outside is overcast. I just had a feeling this was going to be one of *those* days.

"We need to celebrate."

"Celebrate what?"

"How about a birthday celebration?"

"Your birthday is July 15."

I'm hoping she hasn't actually forgotten her birthday.

"I know. But you only turn forty once, right? And I need to start really trying to feel good about it." She comes over and puts her arms around me. "Where's my little baby?"

I sigh and gently move out of her embrace.

"Come on," she says. "What are you hungry for?"

How about sobriety? How about an embrace that doesn't smell like the backside of a brewery?

"I'm not really hungry."

"Oh, come on. I just went shopping."

I can see the bags of stuff on the counter. And it really is a bunch of "stuff." She must have gone a little crazy in the store and bought one of everything.

"How much did you get?" I ask.

"Don't worry about it—I had a good night last night."

"Are you serving tables now?"

"No—just—don't worry about it." She goes back into the kitchen and starts unpacking bags.

"What about work today?"

"They gave me the day off. 'Celebrate good times, come on!'"

When Mom starts singing, it's time to get out of here, and fast.

"And why did they give you the day off?"

She shrugs and keeps her back to me, still humming as she unpacks the bags.

I see a half-empty bottle of wine in the corner. In the garbage can, another completely empty bottle that wasn't there this morning.

I'm beginning to notice a lot more things, living with Mom.

"Did they send you home?" I ask.

She looks at me with an *Are you kidding me* look that confirms it.

"Mom, come on."

"What?"

I curse.

"Don't use that language."

"What? What'd you just say?'

"I said not to use that kind of language." She talks in a way someone talks as if trying desperately not to slur their words.

"Oh, I'm sorry. Did that offend you?"

"Chris—"

"No. I mean—come on. It's barely noon."

"So."

"So? Oh, okay. What are the rest of your plans today?"

"I don't know. I thought we could go sightseeing."

I look at her and just laugh. The look on my face has to be

similar to someone just discovering that there are martians living in the bottom of his shoe.

"And where would we go?" I ask.

"I've always wanted to check out the Biltmore Estate. I think that would be fun."

Yeah. And I'd have to get a stretcher to carry you back home.

"Or maybe Grandfather Mountain?"

So you can fall off?

I just stare at her. "Why did you—what's the deal?"

"Nothing is the *deal,* Chris. I'm just living life a little."

"Good to see."

She brushes her hair back and shakes her head. "Do you know something?"

"I know a lot of things, actually."

"You're the most dramatic sixteen-year-old I've ever seen. And you're a *boy.*"

This would have hurt less if she'd slapped me in the face and then punched me in the gut.

The slap's for the dramatic comment. The punch is for the boy comment.

I stare at her. This woman across from me still doesn't have a clue. She has no idea the nightmare she's brought me into by moving here.

I want to say it, to say what I'm thinking and say it while she's still halfway coherent.

Oh, yeah, well, you're the worst example of a mother I've ever seen.

Or *Oh, yeah, well, suddenly Dad's place is looking a lot more appealing.*

Or something else like the hundred other nasty and mean feelings swirling around in my head.

But I just shake my head and force myself to keep quiet.

I leave this cabin that doesn't feel like home and never will.

18. The World Will Be Yours

Do you ever wish you were someone else?

I hear people say this, but I've never once wished I was someone else.

I just wish I were me living in someone else's life.

Because it's not me that I hate so much, it's the stuff surrounding me. Like all those bags of groceries full of crap. Just so much stuff that came out of nowhere. That's what my life is right now.

I don't want to be Ray Spencer, the homecoming king who graduated and I'll probably never see again. I don't want to *be* him, but I sometimes wouldn't mind his life.

Parents and friends and yes, *Mother,* a drama-free life.

Maybe I would have less drama if I hadn't moved to this dramatic little town.

Ever think about that, Mom?

The overly dramatic sixteen-year-old is on his motorcycle and driving to get away.

To maybe come along a side road that takes him to another life, another place, a place called hope and happiness. To a place called home.

But I keep driving, and that road never shows up.

Mom had the right idea about going sightseeing. That's exactly what I'm doing in Asheville now. I'm browsing in a Best Buy store when I think of something else I miss about living in Illinois.

Apple stores.

It's not that I ever did a lot of shopping at them, but I used to go there with my father. Back in the days when he actually spent most of his time working at the law firm. Maybe he thought of it as a father-son outing, but it was really just an excuse for him to go check out the latest Apple gizmos. The store itself looked a lot like an Apple computer: white and futuristic with that logo front and center. It certainly didn't look like any of the other stores surrounding it. But I guess that was the point.

Thinking about those half-hour trips to the Apple store makes me think of my father.

And of his apology after he found God.

I'm sorry for neglecting my duties as a father, Chris.

I was fifteen and had already spent most of my days as a son living under his roof. Even if he and Mom didn't divorce, I'd only have a few more years to see him suddenly try to step up to the plate and assume his duties.

I didn't say anything at the time, good or bad. I just nodded and felt a bit embarrassed for both of us. The man was on his knees as if he'd done something criminal or something. The man—this guy who'd always been so controlled and so tough and so unemotional—was on his knees, in tears, asking for my forgiveness.

Looking at the latest iPhones at the Best Buy store, I'm thinking of my father's tear-filled apology.

I try and shake the thought as I play with the phone. I think of Lily and Harris texting each other. I think of all the other thousands of times in the past year when it would have been nice to own a cell phone.

At least it would provide a little temporary escape.

"Picking up a new phone?"

The voice chills like a screech on a chalkboard. I look up and see Jeremiah Marsh standing at the counter next to me.

For a moment I'm stuck back at the falls, facing him down in some kind of possessed rage, forgetting who I was and what I was doing as I took the knife and stabbed him.

But of course you didn't really do that, Chris, because if you had, how could he be standing here?

"I love my iPhone, I have to tell you," Marsh says, showing me his in a black case. "Though it is a bit addictive."

I look around us to make sure that I'm still here in this Best Buy, surrounded by others.

I haven't seen him since the moment I walked into graduation and saw him speaking on the platform.

A voice from the grave.

"You look like you've seen a ghost, Chris," he says. His pearly white smile strangely seems to match his bleached-out hair.

I can't think of anything to say. A part of me wants to bolt, but another part can't move. And that includes my lungs and my heart.

"How's your summer going?"

"What do you want?"

He looks perplexed, as if he just can't quite understand my attitude at the moment.

"Well, to be perfectly honest, I came here for a CD. But that's the thing about technology—it just keeps changing. I remember when Best Buy had thousands of CDs. But not anymore. Everything is a download these days. Everything is electronic. And it's a bit sad, because I believe there's a really impersonal nature about that. People don't ever have to leave their rooms to buy or sell or communicate. So what does that ultimately mean?"

I can't tell if there's a point to what he's saying or if he's just talking to sound deep.

He glances at me with those eyes that feel about as warm as the flatline on a heartbeat monitor.

"I keep thinking we've gotten off on the wrong foot, Chris."

He says this as if—as if there's actually a chance that there could be any kind of *normal* relationship between us.

"I can understand your feelings," Marsh says. "I've been there."

I don't think he understands anything about me.

"I was sixteen once. But then again, you've got a birthday coming up, don't you? This summer, right?"

I nod. I can't help it. This is surreal.

I saw you drop over the falls. I saw you fall to your death.

"What if I made a peace offering?" He points at the iPhone. "How about I give you one of these as a token of our starting over? A clean slate. Let the past stay in the past."

An iPhone? He seriously wants to buy me an iPhone?

That wouldn't cover one strand on Jocelyn's head.

Perhaps he can see my reaction from the flushed feeling my face suddenly gets. He smiles, so calm, so smug, so pastorlike.

But I no longer think of him as a pastor. Not anymore.

"Chris—let me ask you something."

"No."

"Just wait. Please. Then I'll let you go. You've been here—how long?"

"Since October."

He chuckles, shaking his head. "Of course. Don't you understand—I know the exact date you and your mother came to Solitary. I know pretty much everything about you, Chris."

"Okay."

"But you still don't know the reasons *why* I know about you. Aren't you mildly curious?"

Anger is bubbling inside of me.

I spent six months being curious until that curiosity killed the cat. Until my nine lives were shot and I was sent into sweet denial.

"You continue to fascinate me, Chris. You really do. I've been wrong about certain things. That's been my fault. But I just want to say this. What if you didn't have to just look at that phone? What if you didn't have to wait and wonder if you could ever own something like that?"

He's talking in his pastor voice, so soft and sweet, like some kind of poisoned candy.

"What if you could have anything—and I mean *anything*—your heart desires?"

The way he says *anything* makes a wave of bumps cover my skin.

I feel locked in this store. Locked in place. Locked in fear and frustration. I want to lash out at the man across from me, but I already tried that. And look where it got me.

I think of the "anything" he could give me. I picture Jocelyn. I picture the way she looked when I found her last New Year's Eve all bloodied and gone.

"Clean slate," he says again, as if reading my mind. "Chris—she was not part of the plan."

"Who?"

"You know who. The reason you're still so angry. The reason you still can't let go."

I shake my head. How can he read my mind? *Is* he reading my mind?

"A mistake, for sure. But I never thought—I didn't foresee that happening. But that was yesterday, and this is today."

He's still talking like a man speaking in another language, making no sense whatsoever to me. Slowly he reaches out his hand and holds out his palm. As if he's holding something in it.

"If you let it go, Chris—if you let *her* go—and if you just let things happen, you will see."

"See what?" I ask.

"See what you can become. See the person you can be."

"I don't—I can't—I don't want to be you."

He smiles and puts one hand in the other. "That's the thing, Chris. The thing you don't understand. I know you don't want to be me. But I've always wanted to be you. To be the *you* you're meant to be. And I mean it when I say that if you just … let … it … go, then the world will be yours."

"The what?" I laugh. This is crazy. "If I do what? What do I have to do?"

"Just ask, Chris. Just ask."

19. The Fantasy

As if seeing Pastor Jeremiah Marsh put a hex onto my summer, everything suddenly seems to turn gray and stale.

The weather shifts from blue skies to dark overcast and thunderstorms.

Mr. Taggart seems to shift too. He seems to realize suddenly that his life hasn't worked out the way it should, and he decides to take it out on us. Not with homework or anything like that, but by being irritable and coming down on everybody for random things like taking too long of a break or not paying attention or wearing something "inappropriate." Brick gets the worst of it, but then again it seems like Brick doesn't really care.

I find myself alone on one side of the room. Harris moved over to where Lily is sitting. Now the closest person to me is Gin, and she's several rows back and probably doesn't know that regular school is over and this is summer school.

Things get even better when I overhear that Roger is going out with Lily on Friday night. And I hear about a July Fourth party tomorrow. Neither of which I'm invited to. It's not like I should be surprised or jealous or anything. My one big chance consisted of her driving me home on my bike.

Yeah, nothing says love like drunken stupor. Right, Mom?

Mom misses a couple of days of work, but I'm just ignoring her like the tunnels I found underneath the cabin. I know they're down there, but I'm ignoring them.

Everything suddenly seems darker and meaner, and it all starts to come back.

The bitter taste.

The bitter feelings.

My anger and hurt and frustration.

Midway through Friday's class, I'm sitting in my old seat behind Roger and Shawn. I see Roger texting Lily and the rest of the students looking bored and oblivious. Meanwhile the creepy pastor's voice continues to go off in my head.

See what you can become. See the person you can be.

All my heart desires.

Yeah, right.

Sounds like an invitation to join the army. To be in Marsh's legion of doom.

In the shadows of this room, while Mr. Taggart does a horrific job of trying to explain algebra to us, I look over at Lily.

She's in this sleeveless light blue dress that has a slight band at the waist and stops a few inches above her knees. It's the perfect dress for a girl like her to wear while frolicking in a field. I'm not sure exactly what *frolic* means, but I think it has Lily's face and body beside the definition. Maybe this is the dress Lily will wear while she frolics around with Roger.

Then again, my mind imagines that she'll dress up for tonight. The frolicking girl will become the wild girl, the sexy girl.

She's really truly oblivious to the guy sitting a few chairs back and a few rows over.

Yeah, that would be me.

And as I think of Lily, I can hear what Marsh said to me. About having anything my heart desires.

Yeah, sure. That's what I want.

But it's not just Lily.

It's the idea of Lily and me.

It's the notion that I am the kind of guy who lives in Lily's world. That I can be someone who just goes up to her and talks and we hit it off.

Lily is in a different world and a different league. And yeah, maybe it's that world and league I want to be a part of.

Maybe I know that a girl like her is never going to be into a guy like me.

Kinda like Jocelyn?

But I shove the thought away. Jocelyn was different.

What about Poe? What about Kelsey?

These thoughts only make me angrier. Poe moved away, and Kelsey is out of town. And in either case, it wouldn't have worked out anyway.

And it would with Lily?

I shake my head.

I don't want something serious, something real.

What I want is the fantasy—something that won't end in heartbreak and tragedy.

I just want something that will feel good.

And that will make me forget about all the other things that are so stinking bad.

20. Poe

Friday night, and I'm thinking of a girl I want to be with but can't.

I guess this is just what I do.

I don't want to say that you can insert whatever name you want into that "girl" I'm thinking about, but then again, I'm not so sure.

I do something I don't usually do when I'm bored. I go online. And that's when I see it.

An email from Poe.

She told me she'd be in touch, but she also told me not to hold my breath.

She said that right after giving you a kiss on your cheek.

She said that after seeing the tears in my eyes.

Then she said something that I've tried to avoid thinking about but can't.

"Don't let this place change you, Chris. You're too good for that."

I sigh. *Too good for that.* I'm not too good for anything. I shouldn't have let her go. I should've fought. I should've been in touch. I should've figured out some way to make her stay. Or to at least not end the way it did.

Part of me still finds it ludicrous that the school actually believed that the drugs they found in her locker belonged to her.

I see the email and seriously wonder about opening it.

I wonder if somebody is still reading the emails I get.

Everybody is watching. Everybody.

For a long time I just stare at the unopened message, wondering what it says and how she's doing. She hasn't called in the army or the marines or even the National Reserve. No FBI agents have shown up around town. No detectives or SWAT teams or Navy Seals have come to my rescue.

What would they be rescuing me from? Huh? A weirdo pastor?

I delete the email without reading it.

If I can't read it, that means no one else can either.

"Sorry, Poe."

I am sorry.

Sorry that I never knew she liked me in the first place. Sorry for what might have been.

Story of your silly, sad life, Chris.

21. Answers?

When are you going to get started?

I'm sleeping and don't want to be bothered.

People are getting impatient it's time Chris it's time.

It's time for me to sleep.

No. It's time for answers.

I open my eyes.

I swear ... it's like this voice in my head ... it's like it was right there next to me, whispering in my ear.

"I'm waiting," I say in a hoarse morning voice.

Waiting on some answers.

But I refuse to go looking for them anymore.

22. A Little Care

There are reminders everywhere, things I just can't seem to let go of. It's one thing to try and bury memories or simply walk around ignoring them. It's another to actually throw away something associated with a memory.

There's the laptop that Iris gave me. I haven't used it for fear that she might suddenly pop up on Skype or something. I know that sounds crazy, but I've seen a lot of crazy around here, so nothing would surprise me.

That picture that I found in my locker—the one of me smiling. It's completely blurry and useless, like a snapshot someone took of the sun while riding a bike. Yet still I haven't been able to throw it away.

A painting that I did in art class last semester.

The picture of the woods and the poem underneath it.

All the stuff that belongs to Mom's brother, Uncle Robert. Other than the records and the T-shirts, everything is going untouched.

Even Midnight reminds me.

The Saturday sun is bright, and I just want to feel as good as I did a couple of weeks ago. I'm not going to let the darkness slip in again.

I'm a senior. Sure, my school and town are from hell, but besides that, I'm staring at my future. Soon I'll be able to leave this place. This town and this cabin and all the secrets that surround it. I'll let my mom figure them out. Or not. It's up to her.

I tried.

I tried and failed.

What more can I do?

It's eleven in the morning, and Mom is still sleeping when I answer the phone.

"This Chris?"

"Yeah."

"Hey, man, it's Harris."

I hadn't spoken with him much at the end of the week, so getting a call from the guy I barely know is a surprise.

"What's up?"

"Look—I was going to tell you about the party we were talking about in class, but you took off Friday."

"Uh—I left after you did," I correct him. "You were waiting for Lily."

"Oh, right," he says in a way that doesn't sound like he's lying, but rather in a way that says he hadn't noticed I was still there. "Well, then, that's a bit strange."

"What?"

"Well—Lily was the one who told me to give you a call. That girl … man."

"What about her?"

"She's like kinda crazy. In a good way. Mostly good, I guess."

"She wanted you to call me?"

"Yeah. She was texting me last night. You know she went out with Roger?"

"And she was texting you?"

"Yeah. *While* she was on the date."

I can't help but laugh. "So it was that good, huh?"

"Oh, man. That Roger—he's something else. He shows up high as a kite thinking Lily was into that. He takes her to some party in the middle of nowhere with a bunch of potheads. Brick even showed up. She was texting me the craziest stuff. It was better than paying to see a comedy."

I'm glad to hear about the date gone bad. But I'm still not sure what it has to do with me.

"Listen—she was asking about the party tonight. Then she asked if I'd invited you, and I told her no, I forgot. She was like totally moody last week. Stuff going on in her personal life."

"Like what?" I can't help asking.

"I don't know. I didn't ask. Probably the parents drama, you know."

"Yeah."

"Anyway, it's going to be a pre-July Fourth party at Ray Spencer's house. Probably the last he'll have for a while."

"Ray's place?"

Suddenly the invite doesn't sound so inviting.

"You know him, right? I remember seeing you guys together."

"He ran track," I say.

"That's right. Yeah, cool. Well, it's going to be huge. I'm not always invited to Ray's parties, but with Lily—well, word's gotten around. Ray wants to meet her. As you can guess."

"Sure."

"So anyway, just wanted to let you know. Starts in the evening sometime."

"Cool."

"Sweet," Harris says. "See you there."

I get off the phone and look outside. I think of the last few weeks of school, where Ray basically ignored me both on the track field and in the school hallways. Not on purpose, at least not that I could tell. It just seemed like he was busy thinking about college and the end of the school year and graduation and all that. I was busy chasing ghosts and nightmares.

I think of Ray meeting Lily. He'll surely throw himself at her with his charm and good looks.

The party I went to with Jocelyn seems like a long time ago.

You had a chance to be buddies with Ray, but you never really let him in.

Who could blame me? I let my so-called "cousin" in, and that got me nowhere. Now Jared's a distant memory like so many others that I got to know during the school year.

Mom comes walking out of her bedroom.

"Just in time for lunch," I tell her.

She looks at me with a wrinkled smile. "You know—I get enough lip at work."

"Hey—I'm going to a party tonight at Ray Spencer's house."

"Okay."

"I'll probably be late," I tell her.

"Okay."

She's telling her sixteen-year-old, who's riding around winding mountain roads on a motorcycle without a license and going to a party, "Okay."

I'd appreciate even a mild "Be careful" or "Be safe" or "Don't drive yourself off a mountain ledge and impale yourself on a sharp branch."

These are the small things I wish for. Not much. Just a little care.

23. What I'm Doing

I get to the party deliberately late. I don't want to go in and not see Harris and then feel like a knob for coming uninvited. Not that I picture Ray caring much, but Ray is Ray. He'll be Mr. Friendly, but his use for me, whatever that was, is clearly gone.

There are cars parked alongside the road winding around to the stone and log monstrosity that is the Spencer house. I've been here several times, a few during the end of the track season. But I'll always remember the first time.

Coming here with Jocelyn.

I park the bike close to the house so some drunk moron doesn't decide to do something stupid to it. I hear pounding bass coming from inside the mansion. The door is half open. A burst of firecrackers goes off, followed by some pounding booms of M-80s or something like that. I see a few people I don't know coming out of the house.

You really want to go in there?

Maybe if I could do everything over again, I'd choose to enter Ray Spencer's world—this world—and never look back.

That's a lie.

Maybe I'd decide to ignore all the weird stuff, just like I'm doing now.

You'd do everything the same except you'd find a way to save her.

I go inside where I see a party raging and where the music will drown out my thoughts.

Soon enough, Ray finds me.

Somehow he looks more mature. As if getting his high school diploma has suddenly made him older and wiser. I probably still look like the scrawny teen he tried to take under his wing.

"Chris! What. Is. Up?" He puts an arm around me like we've been friends forever. "Can't believe you came out."

"Yeah, me neither."

"Hey—let me grab you a beer."

"That's okay."

"No, it's cool. My parents are here. 'Chaperoning.' Whatever that means." Ray laughs. "I heard about the wild party last weekend. You animal."

Ah, word gets around.

"Yeah, partied a little too hard last week."

And somehow I don't even remember it.

"Well—it's cool. It's all good. You here solo?"

"Meeting some friends."

"Okay, cool."

Then for a second, just a mild second, he seems to look at me in a weird way. Almost with …

Suspicion?

But that doesn't make sense. I'm not sure why he'd be suspicious of anything with me. Then I see that smile, and he takes off to keep entertaining.

Near the open area next to the large kitchen, I find them. Harris and Roger and—

Whoa.

"He made it," Harris says. "We thought you were going to ditch us."

"Uh-oh. Keep the beer away from this one." Roger laughs at his own joke.

I'm surprised to see Roger standing next to Lily after what Harris had said about the failed date.

I try to act cool, but I don't know exactly how that works. I don't say anything to Lily and don't look at her, but then I hear her say, "And how's Chris doing tonight?"

As I smile and nod at her, my words suddenly get stuck. It's pretty easy to see why.

She's wearing a black skirt—no, I think black shorts, though I'm not really inspecting them so I can't be sure—but they're black and they're short. And black boots that go almost up to her knees.

This is Solitary not Hollywood, come on.

Her black-and-red striped top is quite revealing except for the light sweater she's wearing over it.

"Hot," I say out of the blue.

What?

Lily waits for me to follow that up.

I am such a boy.

"I'm kinda hot," I say.

And yes, I am starting to sweat from being outside and from wearing a long-sleeved shirt for some stupid reason. But that was a slip. The guys don't react at all, but Lily knows.

She knows she's hot, and she also thinks it's kinda cute that I slipped up.

"There are ways to correct that," she says. "Let me get you something to drink."

I shake my head. "No, it's fine. I think—last weekend was enough for a while."

"Well, there are other things you can drink besides beer."

"Yeah, sure."

She keeps looking at me and then nods in the direction of the kitchen. "Come with me. We'll find something."

She glances at Roger, but he's oblivious, talking to Harris about something.

She wants to escape. She wants to use me as an escape.

"Sure."

So I follow her.

Just like the gaze of pretty much every guy in the room.

They're surely wondering the same thing I'm wondering.

Who is this girl, and what am I doing with her?

24. The Card Game

Lily pours herself a diet soda, and I haven't yet managed to say anything to her when the host of the party comes up.

"Having fun yet?" Ray asks me.

There it is again. That look.

Ah, now I get it.

This is a really weird déjà vu. At the last big party here, I was with Jocelyn. The girl he used to date. I never learned their history, but it was definitely a history.

Now Lily.

Not that I'm here with Lily, but I'm one of the few guys here she knows.

Lily turns around to look at Ray. Somehow she seems to move her lips to make them more pouty, more sexy.

"So who's your friend?" Ray asks me, but as he speaks he looks at Lily.

Lily just laughs. "Harris pointed you out. This is your house, right?"

"Yes. I'm Ray."

"Of course you are. Nice party."

A stream of fireworks goes off in the back. The music changes to another loud, bass-heavy song.

"So you're going to be a senior at Harrington this fall?" Ray asks.

"Looks like it."

She's not smiling anymore. Her eyes are cold and sharp. Something tells me this sort of scene has happened many, many times before.

"So I missed you by a year."

"Ah, yes. The tragedy of it all. Otherwise, who knows what could have happened?"

Ray doesn't seem to be getting her sarcasm. Or maybe he's just undaunted by it. After all, he's the prom king and homecoming king and blond king and all that stuff.

"College is a long way off," Ray says.

"I'm even farther," Lily says, then grabs my untucked shirt. "Come on, biker boy."

I feel like she's babysitting me. Yet as I follow her, I can't help but feel a mild bit of satisfaction. Not that I hate Ray. He's just—he's just a guy I'll never be. A guy I'll never be best buddies with.

Lily is actually a little taller than me in her boots. More heads turn.

We get out of the main room where there're the most people and the loudest sounds. In the next room a bunch of kids are sitting around a glass table, playing some kind of card game while another group stands around them, watching.

I know this.

They're playing with cards that I recognize. The same kind I found at the mysterious cabin that belonged to Jeremiah Marsh.

At the other party, Jocelyn got angry when I asked about the cards.

Dial down the curiosity factor, she told me. *Don't go there. Those weren't tarot cards, okay?*

But this time I'm not the only one curious.

Lily moves past a couple of guys and looks over.

"What are you guys playing?" she asks.

The faces look at her but don't speak.

"What kind of cards are those?"

Nobody says anything.

"Uh, hello? Anybody? Is this some kind of Solitary special club or something?"

I see the cards and their different designs, a stack of cards with black back sides on either side of the table. And there it is again. The ashtray with something glowing in the middle.

"You really want to play?"

The voice seems to surprise everybody. It's Ray, who has followed us in here.

Lily looks at him, then nods. "What is this?"

"This—why, Chris didn't tell you about this?"

I can feel my face start to turn red, but Lily either doesn't see it or doesn't care.

"No, Chris has more grown-up things to do with his time," Lily says.

There are a couple of muffled chuckles. Ray smiles even wider, as if he's holding some big secret.

"You *really* want to play this game, huh?"

"Yes, I *really* do," Lily says in an exaggerated, mocking way.

Everybody else is watching us.

"Fine. Go ahead. Dave, get off the couch. You guys move too. Lily wants to play."

"So does Chris," she says.

I really would rather haul tobacco leaves than play this game, but there's no way I'm telling Lily no. Or backing down from Ray. He only nods and then tells Lily and me to sit. He takes a seat right next to me.

He can't keep his grin down.

"This game—it doesn't really have a name. We just call it the cards. It's only brought out at special occasions. Since these cards—well, they're quite special."

All the cards I'm looking at have different pictures on them. I see a small dog. A car. A candle. Other things I don't immediately recognize.

"So how do we play?" Lily asks as she glances over at Ray and me on the couch facing her.

"You just pick a card and then hold—"

"Uh-uh-uh." Ray interrupts a little dark-haired guy I've never seen before. "Let me explain, Doug."

Ray looks at the cards, then back at Lily. It's as if nobody else is in the room.

"Every now and then, I have the great privilege to play with these cards. They are—well, on loan, I guess. They're what I call magical cards."

"Magical cards, huh?" Lily asks.

"Don't you believe in magic?"

"I believe there are men in this world who like to play games and cover up secrets," she says. "Sometimes they call their little tricks magic. But that's all they are. Little tricks."

"You don't believe in the supernatural?"

"Like ghosts and goblins?"

Ray just chuckles, shaking his head. She's mocking him in front of everybody.

That's fine, he seems to say. *That's quite all right.*

I look behind us and see that more kids have gathered around to watch.

"A lot of people don't believe the magic of the cards at first. That's the fun. That's their power."

"Do they tell your future?"

Ray shakes his head. "They're not those kinds of cards."

"Then what do they do?"

Ray looks at the others sitting around us. "What do they do? The big question." He reaches over and takes a card from one of the decks. He turns it over and shows Lily.

The card is blank. Just white and empty.

"Looks like you got a dud," Lily says.

"Where are you from again?"

"I never said."

Ray nods. "This is what you do. You take a card. Pretty hard, huh? They'll always be blank at first. *Hopefully* just at first. You take your card and hold it a few inches above the ashtray."

"And what's in there?"

"Just part of the game."

Lily glances at me and continues looking skeptical and amused.

Ray holds his card over whatever is glowing or burning in the ashtray. After a few seconds, a picture begins to form.

The image forming on Ray's card first looks like a sun—it's yellow—but then a smiley face appears on it. He puts the card down just like the others on the table.

"That's it?" Lily asks.

Ray nods.

"Wow—that is absolutely captivating. A sunny face. What an amazing trick."

"Are you always this, um, friendly?"

"I can be *very* friendly," Lily says in a very adult manner that shuts Ray and the rest of the room up.

She goes to pick a card, but before she does, Ray holds out his hand.

"Let me just—jokes aside, okay—let me warn you."

"Warn me about what?"

"This is serious. Even if you don't believe the game, it's serious."

"What? Little pictures pop up on the cards. So?"

"They're very real. And they're always very different."

"What are they supposed to mean?"

"The pictures say something about the person holding the card. About who they are."

"That's it?" Lily asks, sounding amused and annoyed in the same breath.

"The rules of the game go like this," Ray says. "You only pick one card. The card represents you—here, tonight. If someone happens to pick up a card that has the exact same image as yours, you leave the party with them."

"For what?"

Ray stares at Lily and just smiles. "I think you know for what."

"Says who?"

"Says the cards."

"Oh, now I get it. This is some silly way for kids to hook up."

"It doesn't happen often."

"Why don't you just get a bottle and spin it?"

Nobody laughs. Which is eerie because normally people—people my age—would laugh at this. Or at least at something a girl like Lily says.

"If your card has a number, that means there will be a task you are to perform the next week."

Lily shakes her head. "Ludicrous."

Ray isn't finished. In fact, I've never seen him look this serious. "If your card has nothing on it—if it's just blank—"

"What's that mean?" I can't help asking.

"It's not good. That's all I'll say."

Lily rolls her eyes and picks up a card. It's blank just like Ray's card initially was. She places it over the ashtray. As she waits, she makes an "ooooooh" sound like a silly ghost in a movie. Nobody is smiling, however. Everybody is watching and waiting.

An image appears. First I see what appears to be a leaf. Then I see something spiky. Then an image of a flower forms at the top.

All the amusement and the color and everything drain out of Lily's face.

What is it?

She looks at the card with surprise and almost horror. Then she looks back at Ray.

"How'd you do this?"

"Means something to you, right?" he says.

She curses at him and stands up. "Seriously—I want to know."

"All I see is a picture of a rose. What do you see?"

Again, she swears at him as though he's done something. She

whips the card on the table and then moves through the crowd to get out of the room.

I look at Ray.

"She wanted to know," he says.

"I'd better go get her," I say.

"Wait. Pick a card, Chris."

I don't want to, but the others are looking like I'm about ready to do something dangerous for the first time.

Just do it man.

Peer pressure.

What's the harm?

I pick up a card and hold it over the glowing rock in the ashtray. I wait. And wait. But nothing happens.

This isn't good.

I keep waiting, and finally an image starts to form.

I see the same lines being drawn, the same leaves and thorns and then the same rose.

I've never seen Ray look more surprised. Not just surprised, but a bit pale.

"What's it mean?" I ask him.

The others in the room all know. I heard what he said too, but I don't quite get it.

So now I go home with Lily?

I don't think it's going to be that easy.

This time it's Ray who curses in disbelief.

"What?"

"You lucky dog, you," he says.

"What do I do now?"

"You follow her. And you show her the card. Take hers, too, or she'll think you're using hers."

"But what's this rose supposed to mean?"

He shakes his head, brushing back his blond locks. "I don't know. But it sure means something to her."

"What's yours mean to you?"

"Uh-uh. You don't tell. You *never* tell."

I take the cards and then stand up to go find Lily.

Now that I know what the game is all about, I still feel like I know nothing about it.

Just like the town of Solitary.

25. Following the Rules

I don't find her with Harris or Roger. I go through the house and out on the back deck and through the mob that's laughing and dancing and drinking and setting off fireworks. Soon I head back out to the front of the house.

Lily is sitting on a lawn chair outside the three-car garage that's open and full of people.

"You okay?" I ask when I reach her.

She shoots me a cold look. "Do I look okay?"

"Uh, yeah." I think she does.

Not sure how I'm supposed to answer that question.

"I'd be a lot more 'okay' if I could be left alone."

I nod, think about going back inside the house, then pull out the cards from my pocket.

"Here."

I give them to her and she takes them, examining both.

The thorny rose on each one.

Again a look of surprise comes over her face. Not just surprise, but total speechless surprise.

"I'm sure it doesn't mean anything," I say.

Yeah, sure, then why are you showing it to her?

Lily looks at me and shakes her head. For a minute, she just looks at me. Studying me.

"What?" I ask.

"Is this some trick, Chris?"

"No." Then I add, "I mean, yeah, I'm sure it's a trick. But I don't know how it works. I wasn't part of it."

"But you still had to show me the cards, right?"

She's not stupid.

Those eyes look me up and down. Then she flings the cards onto the ground and holds out her hand.

"We have to follow the rules, don't we?" she says. "Help me up."

I take her hand and pull her out of the lawn chair. She looks at my face that surely shows that I'm nervous and don't know what to say.

"So I'm supposed to leave the party with you. Let's leave."

"And go where?"

She smiles. "This time *you* drive. Just—wherever you go—I want it to be far away from this place."

"Ray's house?"

"This town."

26. Banana Split

I feel her arms and legs wrapped around me, holding on tight.

I can understand why guys like riding around on motorcycles with girls. Maybe that should've been obvious to me a long time ago, but a lot hasn't been obvious to me. Ever.

Lily seems to fit very nicely around me. Her long legs seem even longer. I'm picturing a thousand different things besides the beam of the light of my motorcycle. Those legs of hers and that look and smile are among them.

She doesn't say anything or get my attention in any way. I head toward Asheville, the biggest city close to us, the only place I can really think to go.

What is it about the girls who keep showing up in my life?

A pretty face that suddenly makes me get all teenage-boy all over the place. I mean, yeah, I know, I *am* a teenager, but why do I have to act like one?

I wonder if she's going to be gone soon, another character lost in a sad little tale. Gone with no answers. Gone with this empty hole left in my heart.

I get this weird déjà-vu feeling.

Trying to retrace your steps, Chris?

Heading to Asheville. Why does this seem familiar?

Trying to relive your time with someone else? Another unattainable girl who ultimately gave you her heart?

I think of Jocelyn and of visiting the Grove Park Inn on the hill late at night.

Is that where you're headed?

I couldn't find that place even if I tried. But I'm not going to try.

We get off the highway and head toward the downtown area of Asheville. At a light, I ask Lily where she'd like to go.

"Anywhere. Seriously. You choose."

My mind races and wonders, but I keep driving.

I can think of a lot of places.

Then again, I'm not a Ray or a Roger or a Harris.

So instead of some place to park and make out, or some seedy motel room (not that Lily would agree to that, but as I said, I can think of a lot of places), or some club that you have to be over twenty-one to get into, we end up somewhere in the past.

Maybe somehow the motorcycle—this special, magical motorcycle that belonged to my missing uncle—transported us back in time.

To a soda fountain, the kind you might see in a movie set in the fifties.

We're sitting at a round table on hard chairs in a brightly lit place called Woolworth Walk—a strange combination of an art gallery with a genuine soda fountain from yesteryear.

This seems to brighten Lily's mood, and we order a banana split with everything on it. Actually Lily orders it, and she pays for it even though I try several times. When we sit down, she dives into the dessert like she hasn't eaten all day.

"You better take some bites, or this will be gone," she says with a laugh.

"Is this your dinner?"

"You kidding? I had a burger and fries from Hardee's earlier. This is just dessert. I do this all the time."

I must look very surprised, because she taps my arm and laughs. "You're funny, Chris."

"What?"

"The way you look."

"Oh, okay. Well, that's very nice."

"You really think I eat Hardee's and banana splits on a regular basis?"

I shrug.

"Uh-uh," Lily answers. "Not to keep looking like this."

This might be one of the most arrogant things I've ever heard someone say, but strangely, it doesn't seem arrogant coming from her. It's just the truth. I mean—the way she looks is the way she looks. I can already see half a dozen guys looking at her. I'm looking at her in a way that seems like I'm scoping her out. And I'm at the same table she's sitting at.

"That party was a bore anyway," she says.

"Yeah."

"You know Roger pretty well?"

"No," I say. "Not at all."

"Did you hear about last night?"

I nod. "Harris told me some."

She shakes her head, then moves her wild and curly hair to one side of her head over her shoulder. "I've never gotten the appeal of pot. It just makes people stupid. Stupid and hungry for some Krystal burgers."

"Krystal burgers?" I ask.

"That's right. You're from up north. They're like White Castle."

"Technically the Midwest."

"Technically the Midwest," she mimics.

"Having fun?"

"I'm not *not* having fun."

I try to think what that even means as she takes a bite and glances around the room like she's very pleased.

"Tell me, Chris. Have you ever had your heart broken?"

Where did that come from? One minute we're talking about the South's version of sliders, and the next she asks me about love.

"Sure."

She laughs. "Sure." She's mocking me again, repeating the way I said it so casually.

"What?"

"You say it like I asked if you've ever stopped in at a Waffle House. 'Sure.' Ah, yes, just another day, another broken heart."

"That's not very nice."

"Oh, come on. Seriously. I'm being serious."

"So am I," I tell her.

It's just you make me a bit nervous, don't you get that?

She takes another bite of the banana split. "What do you know about love?"

"You talk to me like I'm some little boy," I tell her.

Lily raises her eyebrows in an *Oh yeah?* sort of way. She looks born to be feisty, born to fight, born to flaunt those lips and long eyelashes.

"All men are little boys at heart. Post puberty, of course. But that's where they stay."

"And you know?"

Of course, even as my mouth utters this, I don't need an answer.

Her eyebrows rise as if to say, *Are you daring me?*

I know she knows.

Something just screams that she knows all too well.

"The last time I shared a banana split was—well, it was in a different life," Lily says. "That's why I brought it up. I just thought of it."

"A good memory?"

She shakes her head. "No, actually, it wasn't a good memory. Not at all. Once all the smoke and fire die down from the passion, once you can finally see straight in a relationship like that, you realize that there weren't too many good memories. Simple memories. Happy ones."

Lily waits for a while to see if I'm going to say anything. Then I see her staring at the dessert. One last bite.

"Go ahead."

She smiles and takes it. "Do you not like desserts?"

"Sure I like them."

"Banana splits?"

"No," I say. "I actually like them a lot."

She smiles even bigger.

"What?"

"See—that's what I'm talking about."

"What?"

"Little gestures like that. Letting me take the last bite."

"That's just common courtesy."

"Exactly. But sometimes little common courtesies get overlooked. Sometimes love overshadows them. Until you're no longer in love and you're just left with a lot of bad memories. Memories of not being able to take the last bite. Time and time and time again."

I think that I kinda understand what she's talking about.

No you don't you don't have a clue.

"Are you still hungry?"

Lily looks at me as if I've totally *not* understood what she was talking about. It amuses her.

"They were right about you," she says.

"Who?"

"Just—people at your school."

"And what did 'they' say?"

"They said you were a nice guy."

"I'm not always nice."

"A bit naive, but nice."

"Naive?" I ask. "About what?"

"Come on. Let's go."

"Go home?"

She stands and shakes her head. I sit there for a while and look at her.

Then I repeat the motion she did in her lawn chair, holding out a hand for her to take and pull me up.

For some reason, Lily really seems to like this. She takes my hand with both of hers.

"Come on, Mr. Buckley," she says. "Show me the town. We only live once, right?"

27. Rolling in the Deep

We walk down the main streets in Asheville and blend in with the other couples who are coming from dinner or going out. I like imagining for the moment that I'm on a date with Lily. That I'm not sixteen (almost seventeen) and that I'm not stuck in some YA novel.

Eventually we see a bench opening up, so Lily takes it. I move slowly toward her. I guess too slowly, since she moves over and pats the seat.

"It's okay," she says. "You can sit next to me."

As I do, we see an older couple, probably in their twenties, walking hand in hand and talking and laughing.

"So why doesn't a guy like you have a girlfriend?"

I shrug. "I don't know."

And I'd rather not tell you my little horror story.

"I mean—it's not like you're a dud or something."

"Thank you," I say. "Such a compliment."

"See?" she laughs. "You're kinda funny in your own nervous way."

"Am I supposed to feel good about these comments?"

"You're cute, too. The messy hair and that little wise-guy grin."

I'm trying *not* to grin, but I can't.

"At a place like Harrington, you can't find a girl?"

I think for a minute. "Let's say this—it's hard to keep a girl."

"And why's that?"

I don't want to tell her about this high school or the town or anything like that. I don't want all that invading this date-that's-not-really-a-date but that I really want to try and believe is one.

"It's just a strange place," I say, leaving it at that.

"Trying to forget about someone?"

This time I don't say anything. I just nod.

She takes my hand, and once again I'm feeling like a little boy out with his babysitter.

His extremely hot babysitter.

"Then let's forget together."

"Okay," I say, not exactly sure what that means but certainly wanting to forget.

"One more week of summer school."

"Not for me. I've got a whole other session."

"Brutal. You being punished for something?"

"Yeah. Don't laugh—it's true. I think the principal hates me."

"But why?" Lily asks, looking over at me and still holding onto my hand. "Why would anybody have anything against you?"

"They don't like newcomers."

"Great. They'll just *love* me."

"The guys will."

Some girls might say *Really?* but not Lily. She knows they will.

She knows they'll take one look and fall instantly in love without needing or even wanting to get to know her.

I don't know her, not really. But I want to.

"You have some deep, dark secret you're not telling everybody?" Lily asks.

"No. Not that I know of anyway."

"Everybody has secrets. I think the important thing is to allow people to have them. To just let them be. It's easier that way."

So what are your secrets?

That's what I want to ask. But she stands back up and in some kind of restless way tells me to come on.

We walk down another street. As we pass a store, we hear a song blasting.

"Ooh—Chris—I love this song!"

And she starts dancing. On the sidewalk, in a world of her own, her legs in those long boots moving to the pounding beat. She claps her hands and sings along, then looks over at me.

"Come on," she says, taking my hand again.

We're not alone, but you certainly wouldn't know it. Or maybe she likes people watching. They're certainly watching us. Or watching *her.*

"I love Adele," she says of the soulful singer that I've never heard before.

She sings the words to me. Something about scars of love and having it all and being breathless.

We haven't even started to have it all.

She mouths the words and spins around me, and I really, really try not to dance like a donkey. But I'm not doing a great job.

It only amuses her.

She lifts a hand, and her lips curl up as she closes her eyes. She needs a mike and a stage, not a stagehand stumbling around her like I am.

The music stops except for singing and clapping, and she urges me on—clapping. "Come on, white boy, show a little soul."

Then she keeps dancing, a girl in her own world, not caring a bit about the onlookers, the guys checking her out and the girls wondering who in the world she thinks she is and the older people amused at her passion.

The song ends, and she just laughs, locking an arm in mine. "So you wish you were still at that party, shooting off fireworks?"

"I went there hoping you'd be there," I blurt out in an honest way, just like her dancing seconds ago.

"Guess it was all in the cards. Pun intended."

We are back in the dark, sleeping town of Solitary in front of the place Lily guided me to. It's a large Victorian house not far from the main strip of downtown.

"This is your house?" I ask, glancing at the two-story home partially hidden in the woods.

"Ha. Hardly. This is a bed-and-breakfast. My mom and I are staying here while we go through my grandmother's place. It's pretty messy. Not really in any condition to stay there."

"This looks nice."

"It's very—well, quaint. Kinda like you."

"Quaint?"

"Totally quaint," she says with a smile.

We're standing at the sidewalk leading up to the inn.

"I don't think many guys would like being called quaint."

She walks up to me, and since she's tall enough in her heels to look directly at me, that's what she does. She moves her head inches away from mine.

"I wouldn't call many guys quaint. But you are, Chris. You're sweet."

"Oh, come on, if I—"

She interrupts me with a kiss. A soft and mesmerizing and confident kiss. And Lily knows just how long to kiss me, because she gently moves away and smiles at my surely dumbfounded face.

"This was really nice, Chris."

The kiss? The evening?

"All of it," Lily continues, as if reading my mind. "Hanging out. Getting away and just forgetting."

"Yeah, I know."

"Thanks."

"No, thank you," I say. "I want to forget. I need to forget."

She studies me and waits for more.

Maybe more will come eventually. But not tonight. The only more I want tonight is to continue where that kiss left off.

"Have a good night. And a good weekend."

"I don't—" I start to say, thinking about the long weekend and about whether or not I'll hear or see or—

"You'll hear from me. 'Kay? Soon."

I think I've started to breathe again. "Okay."

She smiles and then walks off into the shadows and up the steps of the inn. Then she's gone.

And yes, just like that—just that easily—so am I.

Lost again in the lair of some beautiful girl I want to know and love.

28. Rolling in Something Else

I come back down to earth when I enter the cabin and smell the unmistakable smell of a party gone bad.

For a moment I check to see if Midnight is somewhere down here, laid out on the floor after getting into something she shouldn't have eaten. But no—it's as I thought. As I feared.

The stench comes from my mom's bedroom.

I walk in and see the bathroom light on. For a second my heart and stomach drop, and I rush over to look at the sink. I open the cabinet doors and look at the piece of plywood at the back that I recently nailed shut.

It's still there. Hasn't been touched.

My heart is beating fast, and I go back into the bedroom. Mom is lying on her back. The sheets and comforter are all on one side of the bed, like she was wrestling with them. I pull them down and then see it.

See and smell.

Mom got sick and threw up on her bed. On herself.

I swallow and then shudder.

I think of a kid who did this back at our high school in Libertyville. The kid died on his own puke. A senior who had too much too soon and then choked in his sleep.

My hand reaches out toward Mom. I'm scared. I don't want to touch her, not because it's gross but because I fear the worst.

But she's warm. Too warm, in fact. I see her mouth move up and down. It sounds raw and dry.

Now that I know she's alive, I'm furious with her.

For a while I just stand there, thinking of what to do.

Leave her there to wake up in her own mess.

But I can't. I can't and I won't.

I know I have to clean her up.

Even if she's unconscious.

I see a bottle of vodka on the dresser. It's empty.

I stand there and look at it. I look a long time.

Trying to understand.

Trying to fathom what exactly was in that bottle—in every bottle—that Mom is looking for so desperately.

I don't have a future in the field of nursing.

Nope. Definitely not.

It takes me a very long and very hard hour to clean up my mom. She's not dead, and I'm thankful for that—yes, I am—but she might as well be dead since she's limp and totally gone. I call out to her and nudge her and then use a damp rag to clean her, but she doesn't wake up.

I don't change her—nope, can't do that.

But I manage to wipe up the mess mostly. I pull the sheets and blankets off of her. Leaving her on a bare mattress that's still a bit stained. I wipe off the mess as best I can, knowing she's going to wake up with crusty clothes that she passed out in along with a crusty mouth.

She does manage to sip a little bottled water, but that's it.

I find another blanket in the closet and put it over her, propping her up on the pillow she didn't throw up on.

Then I toss the empty bottle of vodka into the garbage can and turn off the lights in her room.

In some weird way, this is normal. It's not shocking, not like the quasi-date with Lily. It's just the sad reality of my life.

I think of Dad and wonder whether it's time to call him.

No.

But somehow, this life is not working out. Not for Mom.

Whatever she's trying to do to herself—whatever she's feeling—whatever she's trying to run away from—*this* isn't working.

And as hard as I can try to ignore it, just like I'm ignoring everything and everyone else, I can't overlook this nightmare at home.

In my bedroom, holding Midnight by my side, I think of Lily. The memory of tonight makes up for the mess I came home to.

Even in my thoughts and dreams to come, I'm able to escape for a while.

Escape the darkness and downward spiral that wants to suck me under.

29. A Slice of Normal

I don't know why I go.

Partly because I don't want to see Mom when she wakes up.

Partly because deep down, I know I want answers. Answers to everything. Not just why my mom drinks, but why everything is so messed up. Why I have no idea what is going on.

I go because he has the answers.

I go to the church with the families and their children and all the people who seem real and happy. They seem normal. They're not wearing hoods or upside-down crosses. They don't have horns or 666 tattoos. They're just normal people who probably didn't puke all over themselves last night. Normal people going to church.

Pastor Marsh is there, and he looks normal and says normal things. He's not normal—I know that. But to everybody else, he's the pastor saying nice things like believe in yourself and fight the good fight and know there's a reason for everything. He says these clichés, and they all seem very normal to me.

But I didn't come here because I wanted a slice of normal.

I came here because I want the truth.

After the sermon, I wait for him. It doesn't take long.

In some weird way, it's like the pastor knows I'm here.

"Hello, Chris."

Deep inside I'm shivering. At least it feels like that. But I stand firm and shake his hand and look him in the eye. "Good morning."

"It's a nice surprise to see you here."

"I want to know."

Jeremiah Marsh doesn't look surprised or shocked. He nods, and then his eyes focus behind the narrow glasses. "I can understand one's need to know. May I ask why now? On this particular beautiful summer morning?"

"I'm tired of just—of not knowing. Of living somewhere that just seems—really messy."

Saying that makes me think of his house. The one I broke into while Poe waited. There was nothing messy about it, except his raving lunatic of a wife screaming at me.

"I can't tell you everything at one time," he says. "Even if I wanted to, I couldn't. It's too much, too soon."

"You said if I let things go—if I just asked. Well—the letting go part is already done. And I'm pretty good at that."

"I know," Marsh says.

"But I'm here—right now—I'm here to ask."

His serious gaze focuses on me. "To ask for what?"

"I don't even *know* what I'm supposed to ask for."

He nods. "What is it you really, truly want?"

I think of everything in one brief heavy downloadable second.

Leaving Illinois and meeting the girls and the mysteries and the love of Jocelyn and the nightmare to follow and Jared and Poe and Kelsey and Mom and Dad and Lily.

"Relief," I blurt out.

Because that's true.

I just want to feel lighter. The way I've almost started feeling this summer.

The pastor smiles, and my skin grows cold and I shiver as he places both his hands on my shoulders.

"You're going to get that and more. And then you're going to thank me. For everything."

30. Sun in Your Eyes

July 4 arrives with a clear sky and a refreshing morning sun. The rest of my Sunday was uneventful, including not seeing Mom at all. Part of me wonders if she even knows what I did on Saturday night. Part of me wonders if she remotely cares. But it's 8:00 a.m., and she's still asleep and thankfully isn't messy.

Awaiting me on the table, lit by sun leaking through the blinds, is a box.

I get closer and see it's an iPhone.

Just like the latest model I was looking at in Best Buy.

For a second I look around the room, then I glance at the door. It's locked. But that doesn't matter. Locked doors don't matter in a place like Solitary.

I open the box, and instead of the phone being wrapped up in packaging, it's ready to go with only a small sticky note on its black surface.

For a moment I think it's from Mom. An apology of sorts, a bribe maybe. Something to make up for yesterday and the days and nights before.

But no.

I read the short note.

One less thing you have to worry about—being out of touch.

Your friend, J. M.

I pick up the phone and see that it's charged. I slide it on and see that it's loaded and ready.

Then I notice my hand shaking.

Throw it away toss it in the creek down below.

But I just keep holding it.

Sun streaks through the room, bright slivers making me squint my eyes.

I look and see that there's a text from somebody.

I open it up.

RELIEF CAN ONLY COME WHEN YOU FULLY LET GO.

It's from him, of course. From J. M.

What have I done?

I shut the phone off and slip it into my pocket.

The Chris from last month would have found the pastor and tried to make him eat this phone. But not today's Chris.

It's a phone. It's a gift. And it's mine.

I get my motorcycle keys.

It's time to get out of here and see what kind of fireworks I can find.

Then I think of something else. I run upstairs and grab the phone number that Lily gave me.

The blurry, mostly blank snapshot still sits on my desk. It's almost a reminder of a guy I used to be. Someone who slowly disappeared.

I'll take a new snapshot today. One of Lily and me. And I'll take it with this phone.

I head out.

31. Anticipation

So you finally got a phone?

The phone chimes when the text from Lily comes. I'm out of Solitary, feeling like I can breathe a little better, eating a sausage-and-egg biscuit at Bojangles. When I first came here not long ago, I made a joke about the name, but the food is no joke. It's greasy goodness.

Buying breakfast and driving out here with little left in my gas tank reminds me that I need to get a job. Or rob a bank.

Maybe you can just get a wad of cash from your new benefactor.

I think for a moment about what to respond to Lily.

Now I need a job.

I wait for her response. It comes quickly.

What are your plans for today?

I pop the last bite of biscuit into my mouth, then smile and wipe my hands. I drain my iced tea, which I've decided might be the best morning drink ever.

Nothing much.

Which is my way of saying I'm doing jack squat and I'm texting you because I desperately want to hang out.

Want to go sightseeing?

For a second, I wonder if this is a joke. Her sarcasm. *Yeah, sure, let's go look at some trees and rocks.*

I want to text something like *every day in summer school there is a sight to see, and it arrives when you walk in the room.*

But that is about the corniest line ever.

Sure, I text.

Don't sound so excited. I was going to get Harris to go with me.

I type back, my thumbs not used to texting or this phone.

I'm sure Harris would enjoy seeing the sights with you.

I wait.

I'm sure you would enjoy it even more.

I smile.

I'm sure I would too.

That's a good boy.

I just laugh. Breathe in. Feel alive. My mind taking it all in.

I'm her little pet.

What time? I text.

Noon.

Okay.

Can you wait that long?

Again I smile and shake my head.

I'll try, I say.

ANTICIPATION IS A MARVELOUS FEELING. ENJOY IT. SEE YOU AT NOON.

SEE YOU.

I stare at the iPhone. It's only around nine, and I've got three hours to kill. Three hours to anticipate seeing her. Three hours before we go sightseeing.

Three hours before who knows what.

And yeah. It feels pretty marvelous.

32. A Great Day

I sit next to this girl who's no longer a stranger as fireworks go off above us. She's not draped in my lap in some romantic way that I would have liked. No, she's just sitting next to me after a fun day full of laughter. At some point in the middle of the colorful display over Lake Julian, Lily pokes me.

"Relax, Chris."

"What?"

She laughs and looks at me, and I smile.

Yeah okay fine.

Easier said than done. Especially now that night has come and ... well, I don't know.

A day of riding around and seeing some sights like a famous mountain and a cool bridge.

Everything's happening so fast.

How'd I get here from

No stop not here and now.

So yeah, I stop. And listen to Lily. I let out a silent sigh and keep looking up, but I'm not paying the fireworks any attention. I'm keeping her in my peripheral vision. She watches and comments on the colors and claps and acts like a little girl.

It's nice to see her relaxed. No—she's always relaxed, but in a standoffish sort of way. Now she's just free and easygoing.

Especially when she moves closer to me on the blanket.

We stay on that blanket after the show is over and let the crowd disappear and leave us alone.

Or at least that's what I'm thinking and hoping.

"Summer of sixth grade. Running around with all my crazy cousins in Georgia. In the *country.* Shooting off bottle rockets and Roman candles and almost putting someone in a hospital."

This is Lily's fondest Fourth of July memory. She laughs at her own comment, not believing how crazy her family used to be.

"Do you ever see them?" I ask.

She shakes her head and doesn't say more. She's resting on her elbows while lying on her stomach, staring out at the dark lake in front of us. I'm doing the same, but I'm watching her more than anything else. Even in the dim light of night, I can see her clearly.

"You miss Illinois?" she asks.

"Every day."

"I can understand. Maybe I need to come live in Asheville."

"Too bad your grandmother didn't live around here," I say.

For a moment Lily looks at me, then she nods and smiles. "Yeah, too bad."

I want to ask about us, what we're doing and what this means and if there's some kind of chance—

"Chris?"

"Yeah?"

"I see smoke coming from your ears."

I laugh. "That bad, huh?"

"I see that mind spinning."

"Sorry, it's just—"

"*It* is fine," Lily interrupts. "Relax. I mean it. Relax. I'm not going to bite. We're not going to do anything tonight, and we don't have to worry about anything. You don't have to tell me how much I mean to you, and I don't have to ask how you're feeling and any of that nonsense."

I kinda like that nonsense.

"I'm just a girl. Okay?"

"Yeah, okay."

Once again, I crack her up. "What?"

"That was *so* unconvincing."

"Sorry."

She moves over and then moves her lips toward my ear. Then she bites me. Hard.

"Ow!"

I move and sit up on my knees, rubbing my ear. "Wha—"

Lily sits up as well, laughing with a playful look on her shadowed face. "I'm going to keep doing that until you just ease up."

"I'm eased up—I'm relaxed."

"Yeah, right."

"That killed."

"Good," she says, then adds, "Oh, come on, be a man."

I raise my eyebrows as if to say something, but she just looks at me, waiting.

"Yeah?"

"I don't get you."

"Join the club, pal." She then slides up beside me as if we're on a bus and have to cram next to each other. "You okay?"

"That really hurt."

"Do I need to make it better?"

I look at her and so badly want to say that yes, she needs to make it better. I want to have the James Bond reply that has a double meaning, but I just can't. I'm just way too nervous to say anything.

"You really are cute, Chris," she says. "I'm not just saying that."

"So are you."

Her face grows serious, and she shakes her head. "No, Chris, I'm not. There are some things I am. *Many* things I am. But cute is not one of them. I was cute a long time ago. Not anymore."

I don't know what to say. As usual.

We sit there for a while and continue to look out at the lake. We don't make out in outrageous passion, nor do we continue this playful back-and-forth. I picture it in my mind, but here and now we're just sitting in the quiet.

"See, it worked," Lily says eventually.

"What?"

"The bite."

"What about it?"

"You look relaxed now."

"Either that, or you gave me rabies and I'm slowly going unconscious."

She just laughs. "This has been a great day, Chris."

"I'm not going anywhere."

She studies me for a moment. I wish I could read thoughts. Especially girls' thoughts. Because I've never been able to figure out what they're thinking.

She's thinking something big, but I can't tell what.

"Me neither," Lily finally says.

Later, after dropping her off and receiving a sweet hug that was just that—a sweet hug—I'm back at home in my bedroom, and I can't stop thinking of her.

Then it dawns on me. The text from Marsh. About relief and letting go.

He's right.

This thought—these two words—terrify me.

33. A Voice from the Past

It's a funny thing about girls.

Sometimes they seem to forget.

Other times they seem to remember.

The final week of summer school is fine, but fine isn't on the same level as wonderful. Fine is riding in the backseat with your friends going somewhere fun. Wonderful is riding on your motorcycle with your girlfriend's body draped around you.

Somehow it seems like my some kind of wonderful has turned into some kind of okay. Not because of anything Lily does, but what she doesn't do. The whole day we spent together never gets acknowledged. Not that I want a personal write-up of her thoughts and feelings about July 4—although actually, come to think of it, *that* would be some kind of wonderful.

Instead I get the ordinary passing of time.

Occasionally she texts me, but even this isn't particularly memorable.

The call I receive on Thursday, however, is quite memorable. And surprising.

I pick up the home phone, thinking it's Lily, but a part of me should have known. Wouldn't she be calling my cell phone now that she has that number?

The voice on the other end surprises me. It's too high to be Lily's, too soft and too unsure of itself.

"It's Kelsey," she says, helping to remind me.

"Hey, yeah, how are you?"

"Good."

"Great."

Awkward.

"My father said he saw you last week."

"Yeah," I say. "Are you back from your trip?"

"Yes."

"Cool."

Uncomfortable.

"I just wanted to see if you got my messages," she says.

"Yeah, I did. I'm sorry I haven't called."

"It's okay. I just was checking. I would've emailed, but I just thought—"

"No, it's—I should've called back. I'm sorry, really. I've been busy with summer school and, you know—"

Summer school and girls named Lily …

"Sure, no problem," Kelsey says.

There's a pause that seems thirty minutes long. Then we both start to say something, then both pause, and do the go-ahead thing.

Why'd I pick up why?

"So are you like, uh, working this summer?" I finally get out.

"I'm working out at the Asheville Racquet Club."

"Oh. I didn't know you played."

"Harrington doesn't have much of a team, but I play in different leagues. I help run programs with kids for the summer."

"That's cool."

"You like tennis?"

I can't remember the last time I held a racquet in my hand.

"Sure."

"Maybe we can play sometime," Kelsey says.

"Sure."

"When you're not stuck in a classroom. Or on your motorcycle."

I laugh, but overall this is a fail of a phone call.

And once again …

Silence.

"Well, you know, I just—" Kelsey starts to say, then pauses. "Just wanted to say hi, since I didn't get a chance to see you much at the end of the year."

After prom, she's surely thinking.

After that dance, she's probably wanting to say.

"Yeah, sorry, it's just, yeah."

Those aren't exactly the words I'm wanting to say.

Kelsey says a quick good-bye, and I hang up. For a moment I look at the phone.

It's just, yeah.

What kind of moronic statement was that?

I sigh and feel bad. I feel bad for never even bothering to say anything after prom. Granted, I had some other issues going on with my life.

Issues someone like sweet Kelsey doesn't need to know about.

Her voice is a reminder of last year. Of everything that happened.

Of all the things I'm desperately trying to forget.

I stand there feeling like a moron for a few moments until a text comes on my cell.

ONE MORE DAY OF SUMMER SCHOOL. WHATEVER WILL I DO WITH THE REST OF MY SUMMER?

It's from Lily, who's obviously being sarcastic. It's good to hear from her. It's good to hear from my summer life so I can forget about my spring self. Perhaps my summer life will result in a fall guy that I like a lot more than that kid talking on the phone with Kelsey, fumbling over his words and feeling like an idiot.

I spend the next hour texting Lily. We could be talking or

hanging out, but at the moment this is still better than anything else I can think of.

34. Mess with the Bull You'll Get the Horns

We're all very upset that Mr. Taggart isn't here on our final day of class.

And by upset I mean absolutely elated.

But that's short-lived when some wise guy comes into class, stands before us all, just looking and staring, then says, "Well, well. Here we are."

No one is impressed. Brick makes a fart noise.

"I want to congratulate you for being on time," our new teacher says, then stops and shakes his head like he's got some thought dying to come out. "Anybody? Anyone?"

All we can do is look at one another.

His name is Mr. Charleton, and he says he's taking over for Mr. Taggart, who can't be here. No other reason, no credentials listed, nothing like that. This guy could have killed Mr. Taggart and put him in his trunk and decided to fake us out—we don't know. But everybody seems bored and ready for class to be over.

Mr. Charleton looks like he's energetic and eager to do something. He seems like a nice enough guy—at least for a teacher. He looks like he's my mom's age.

"How many of you have heard of John Hughes?" an excited Mr. Charleton asks a totally dead class.

Nobody reacts. Then Brick asks if he's an adult film actor, which makes us laugh.

"Seriously. No one has heard of the director John Hughes?"

"We have cable," Lily says in a classic snotty-girl attitude.

"So that's a yes?"

He's not getting any favors from us today. Nope.

Mr. Charleton leans against his desk as he looks at all of us. He's dressed casual—a polo shirt and jeans—and he acts casual. He just doesn't realize how done we are with this class.

"I just quoted from one of his movies when I first came in. I was hoping … Well, honestly, I'm feeling a bit nostalgic today. Anybody heard of The Psychedelic Furs?"

Brick starts to say something, but Mr. Charleton gives him the cut-it signal. "Anybody?"

I raise my hand.

"Good man. Doesn't make me feel *that* old. This band was one of my favorites in the eighties. Wrote the title song for *Pretty in Pink,* a Hughes classic."

"That movie was lame," Brick says.

"Anyway, they're coming in concert tonight in Asheville, yet I'm going to be attending a swim meet for our eldest daughter, which is quite a shame …"

"Excuse me, sir?" Shawn says.

"Yes."

"Are you going to be teaching anything today, because if not …"

Everyone laughs.

"Very funny. Listen, I'm going to show you a clip from the *The Breakfast Club.*"

I've seen the movie before. Twice, actually. He shows us a clip on his wide-screen laptop that seems about as big as the television at our cabin. The scene is when the teacher welcomes the five students making up the Breakfast Club to class, then gives them an assignment. Bender, the rebel, speaks out, and the teacher gives him the "Don't mess with the bull, young man, you'll get the horns" quote.

The clip runs for a couple of minutes, then Mr. Charleton shuts his screen.

"How many of you have seen that movie?"

We all raise our hands.

"There's hope for your generation yet. So this is what we're going to do today. Taggart—excuse me, Mr. Taggart—described you guys to me, and I thought—this will be perfect. I'm going to give you a task to do this morning."

Brick raises his hand. "Are we going to have to write a thousand-word essay on who we are?"

"No, but close. I'm only going to make you come up with a hundred words."

"Good," Brick says. "I haven't written a thousand words in my entire life."

"One hundred words. That's all. Describing who you think you are. It's that simple."

Lily, who already seems in a bit of a foul mood today, doesn't raise her hand, but just blurts out a question. "And we just hand it in to you?"

"You share it at the end of class."

There is a collective groan.

"Come on, indulge me. I'm sure you'd rather do that than spend time going over English and algebra, correct?"

"I think Mr. Taggart covered those topics pretty well for all of us," Brick says.

Mr. Charleton chuckles and hands out a sheet a paper and a pen for everybody, just like in the movie.

"This will be fun. I'm curious as to what your answers will be."

"Will you be counting our words?" Shawn asks.

"I'm sure you can manage to come up with one hundred. I have confidence in you."

"Then you don't know Shawn," Roger says.

I stare at Lily, who rolls her eyes and taps the pen on the piece of paper in front of her. Then I glance back at my own page.

I don't need a hundred words to define who I am. This piece of blank paper pretty much sums it up.

35. The Cold Hard Facts of Life

Roger volunteers to go first. He's wearing a vest with a short-sleeved button-down shirt with a fancy design on it. His hair looks extra faux-hawked out, and his beard looks extra thinly cut. He smiles, and I wonder if he still thinks there's a chance with him and Lily.

I know the answer to that one. No vest is going to help him with that.

"This is me," Roger says, and glances up from his paper to see if we're listening.

"Wow, that's truly moving," Brick says.

The teacher tells him to be quiet and let Roger continue.

"This is me. Six foot one. One hundred seventy-five pounds. Loving and giving. Crazy and fearless. Hopeless romantic. A dog person, not a cat person, but could live with a cat person if she allowed a dog person into her life. Panthers fan. Tarheels fan. Sugarland fan."

Roger keeps going like this. It begins to sound like an ad for a dating service. He apparently didn't get the memo about one hundred words. He doesn't mind sharing all these wonderful, random tidbits about himself with us.

When he finishes, Mr. Charleton nods and thanks him, then asks who's next.

"I'll go," Shawn says, sliding out of his seat and heading up front. He adjusts his pants as he turns to face us.

"People don't know this about me, but deep down I'm really shy," Shawn starts. "Deep down I love grandmothers and help them across the street. I love puppies and mice. I like to babysit. I love vegetables, especially the green kind. I love doing homework and can't get enough of school (that's why I took summer school, you know). I love romantic comedies, especially when one of the characters dies in the end. I love dances and slow music. Oh, and I love Katy Perry and her music and videos. I love singing in the shower and working out. If you believe me you can call 1-800-it's-a-lie."

He looks around to see if anybody is laughing, but nobody thinks it's funny. Especially not the teacher. Once he said, "deep down, I'm really shy," I think we all got the joke.

Ha. Ha.

I'm wondering if Mr. Charleton is regretting assigning us this task. Especially now that Brick has come up to share his thoughts.

He clears his throat to be dramatic.

"They call me Brick and think I'm a hick
They see my hair and think I don't care
They hear my tone and then leave me alone
They see my friends and think they offend
They grade my tests and never let it rest
They think I'm poor but never wanna know more
They see me smoke and think I'm a joke
They close the books without a second look
'Cause they always look but they never really see
They seem to hear but they never really truly listen
They think they know but they will never—ever—fully know."

Brick folds up the piece of paper and takes a bow as we all clap. I gotta admit—his little poem was actually quite good.

"Thank you," Mr. Charleton says. "Great job. Who's next?"

Harris goes up and reads his piece on why he loves flowers. He goes through every known flower he can think of until he gets to—surprise—his favorite flower, the lily. He pauses for dramatic effect and glances at Lily to see her shaking her head and saying "corny" out loud.

Gin is next, and everybody seems to know that this is going to be interesting. I'm thinking that none of us will even understand what she even says, but then again, I'm wondering if she understood the assignment.

"My name is Yin, yet I live in a Lin/Jen/Gin world that I've grown accustomed to," she says in the most ordinary, American, non-accented voice I've ever heard.

Roger and Shawn look at each other, and even Brick laughs out loud.

"It's easy to hide behind big glasses and long hair. Sometimes it's easier that way. While they think I'm doing math equations and eating Peking duck, I'm beating them online at a video game or eating fried chicken while watching *Battlestar Galactica.*"

"Awesome," Brick says.

I can't help but laugh.

You're a nice surprise, Yin.

"They have a phrase called fanboys, and they lump them with nerds and geeks who love sci-fi and *Lost* and comic-book movies. But what if—what if among these you included a girl with a Taiwanese background who blends in and never gets noticed?"

She looks up at us and smiles. "We live in a different time and age right now when a book shouldn't be judged by its cover. Because frankly, nobody is buying books anymore. They download them. They pop up instantly."

Suddenly I feel a bit ashamed. I definitely judged this book by its cover.

"My name is Yin, and I have always been part of the background as far as everybody knows. But little do they know that when I go home and turn on my computer, I'm part of their world and their conversations and their lives. Just under another name and another persona."

She walks back to the back of the room, and we all look at her, stunned and wondering who in the world this Yin girl is. Where'd she come from?

No way I can top that.

"All right, great job, *Yin,*" Mr. Charleton says. "Final two?"

I glance at Lily, who says, "All yours."

I open my sheet of paper.

"For a long time I considered myself a Foo Fighters or a Snow Patrol song. Cool and upbeat, but nothing *that* terribly different. Yet ever since coming to Solitary, I've realized that I'm really not that at all. I'm a Cure song off *Disintegration.* I'm a Smiths song off *Meat Is Murder.* I'm a Tears for Fears song from *The Hurting.*"

They're looking at me, not really getting it. Or at least that's what I think.

Except for Lily. She's looking and smiling and getting it. Getting me.

"I never knew who I was deep down until I moved here and realized that in many ways, I was living in the wrong decade. I should've been living in my mother's and uncle's decade, where songs reflected—well, me."

I look back at the teacher. "That was one hundred, exactly."

"The Cure, huh?" he asks with a big grin. "How'd you discover them?"

"My uncle."

Or more like my uncle's closet.

"He's got good taste. Thank you, Chris. Okay, Lily?"

We all watch her like we usually do—all the guys anyway—as she walks to the front. She's wearing a black tank top with really tight white pants. Her shoes aren't very high heels, but high enough for a summer school course.

"For the record, I think this assignment was rather lame," Lily says.

"Thank you," Mr. Charleton says.

For a second, standing there, Lily glances at me. Then she gives me a nice little smile.

What's that mean?

I'm not sure. Like many things with girls and especially *this* girl, I don't know. I can't know. I'm only beginning to try and know.

"I grew up a happy girl, loving life and loving those around me. The future was always like a colorful movie poster with beautiful smiling stars on it. I found love and my leading actor and lost myself in them."

Something strange is happening. Right at the time Lily said *I found love*, her voice starting shaking a bit. Now her eyes are tearing up a bit as she pauses.

Now this is really something.

"Being lost in love is dangerous. Because once you lose that someone, you can lose yourself. You can suddenly look out and wonder what happened to the story. You question whether the whole thing was made up to begin with. Your hero is just another hired gun. That movie poster suddenly turns from color to black and blue."

Lily pauses and wipes her eyes and doesn't look at any of us. I'd like to rush to her side and give her a hug, but then again, so would most of the others around me.

"I've realized that you don't start over again. There are no do-overs. There are no second chances. Some lives are like epic movies. Some are just sad reruns."

Lily turns and faces the teacher, who seems as surprised as all of us. "You happy with that? Those hundred words good enough for you?"

She flings her piece of paper his way and walks out of the room.

36. Don't You Forget about Me

Mr. Charleton thanks us all for doing the assignment. He doesn't take our papers. Instead, he tells us to keep them and to continue updating them.

"I gotta tell you," he says with a surprised look on his face. "This—was amazing. It gives me hope that youth is not necessarily wasted on the young."

He lets us go half an hour early, and we all tell him good-bye as we leave. Before I take off, I ask him if I can give Lily her sheet back. He nods.

"Tell her I said thanks for being open and sharing. That took a lot of guts."

"Sure," I say taking the paper Lily wrote out. "Yeah, she seems to have a lot of those."

When I walk out of the room, I remember that this is the final day of our summer class. At least for this particular group of people.

I suddenly have this awful thought.

Lily is gone, and I never even had a chance to tell her good-bye.

I won't see her the rest of the summer and she'll have her own life and she'll go and forget about me.

I hear the song that Mr. Charleton was playing as we left the room, the main song from *The Breakfast Club*.

This is what's going to happen. Lily is going to forget me, and then we'll start school in the fall and she'll be dating some football stud and will forget about me and my stupid, silly notions of living out a life in the eighties with my uncle's records and my mother's nightmares and—

"You lost?"

Lily is standing there by the doors of the school.

"Hey."

"You look sad," she says as she walks up to me.

"I thought you'd be gone."

"Who's gonna take me home?"

"I think you could get anybody you want to take you home," I say.

"I want *you* to take me home."

I nod and smile.

"But only for a short while, okay?" Lily adds, taking my hand. "'Cause it's Friday, and I know what I want to do."

"What?"

"I want to go back in time with you, Mr. Wrong-Decade-Boy."

"You have a time travel machine?"

She stops and forces me to look at her up close. "I could take you to places that would blow your little mind, Mr. Buckley."

I want to melt.

I mean, really, truly, that's what I feel like doing, standing there like Play-Doh in front of her.

"Okay," I say so weakly.

She just laughs, then puts a hand gently to my cheek. "You're adorable, you know that?"

"Are you all right?" I ask.

"Yes. I am now. Come on."

We walk down the steps of the high school and get on my bike, and I know that Lily isn't going away anytime soon.

37. How Old I Am

Before the concert begins, the one that Lily was somehow able to get us into even though we're both under eighteen and neither has a parent anywhere around, I look at her standing in the middle of the floor and come right out with it.

"Is this all some big act or something?"

We're at the Orange Peel in Asheville, and the average age of the people surrounding us has got to be fifty. It makes me wonder when exactly these Psychedelic Furs were popular anyway.

Lily, with her normally curly hair straightened out, definitely looks older than her age tonight, in tight, dark jeans and a pink and somewhat sheer tank top and a big pink necklace coming down almost to her belt.

I feel like a total moron next to this girl.

She's the adult I'm with. The babysitter. And that's what's led to this question. All of a sudden out of the blue.

"Is what an act?" Lily asks.

It's not air-conditioned, and I'm already sweating even though a huge fan swirls around above us. Lily doesn't seem to sweat. Of course she doesn't. Girls that pretty never sweat.

"This—being here—you hanging out with me."

"You have a problem with it?"

"No, it's just … I don't know."

"*What* don't you know?"

I've been around her long enough to know that she doesn't like me taking a long time to get out something I'm thinking.

"Did someone put you up to this?"

"To *what*?" She still doesn't know what I'm talking about.

"Going out with me. Hanging out."

"Why would someone 'put me up' to it? Like a dare?"

I'm suddenly thinking of Jared.

I don't know who put him up to that, but in the end I realized I'd been had.

"I don't know."

"I think you know what you're saying," Lily says.

"It's just—"

Then the band begins to play.

For a moment, I see Lily staring at me with cold, distant eyes. But just for a moment.

Soon we're lost in the crowd while this band from yesteryear plays songs I don't know. Until, of course, "Pretty in Pink" comes on and everybody recognizes it, including Lily and me.

Suddenly I get why she's wearing that shirt and oversized necklace.

She dances next to me during the song and takes my hand and forces me to do the same. It's strange because I don't feel as stupid making a fool of myself around all these old people. Some of them are dancing too.

Some of them *shouldn't* be dancing.

Near the end of the song Lily comes up beside me and whispers something in my ear. Actually, she's probably half screaming in order for me to hear.

"I think you're endearing, Chris. And if you don't already know that by now, there—I've said it. Believe it. I'm not lying."

She moves away and I see that beautiful face and those lips and I know she's going to kiss mine so I close my eyes …

But only for a second.

Because when I open them she's already in front of me again dancing.

I glance around to see if anybody saw that utter display of stupidity.

An overweight slightly balding man holding half a cup of beer looks at me and nods. He's not mocking me.

Nope. He's giving me a glance that seems to say, *I used to be young and in love back when I had more hair and less of a gut.*

I smile and suddenly forget how old I am.

Lily has that effect on me.

38. Dreams

Lily's watching me drink the coffee drink that she ordered for both of us.

"You don't like it?" she asks.

"No, it's fine."

"Do you even like coffee?"

It's actually worse than coffee because it's cold and sugary and gross.

"I can stand coffee."

"But that?"

I move the drink back to her. "You can have the rest."

She shakes her head. We're on the second level of a double-decker bus that kinda reminds me of Harry Potter. It's in the middle of the city. It's a coffee shop, except the shop is a bus. Kinda cool, gotta admit. That's why it's crowded. We're sitting next to each other in the cozy space, and I'm willing to down the whole cold coffee thing in order to stay here.

"Why don't you ever speak your mind?" Lily asks me.

I shrug. "I'm not sure."

"Is it because you're nervous?"

I swallow and nod.

"Why?"

I scratch my cheek, look down.

"Chris—" She gently puts a finger on my chin to raise my head. "Look at me. Talk to me."

"Okay."

"Why are you nervous?" she asks.

"Because of you."

"But I already told you—I want to be here."

"I know."

"Why are you nervous then?"

"I don't know."

Those green eyes don't let me move. "Do you always get like this around girls?"

"No. Unless—"

"Unless they're what?"

"Unless they're gorgeous."

She lets out a laugh, causing people around us to glance our way.

"Oh, Chris. You are something."

"See—I say what I'm thinking, and I get mockery."

She shakes her head. "I'm not laughing at you. I'm laughing at—I don't know—just how earnest you are."

"I'm serious about what I said," I tell her.

"I'm sure you are."

She takes a sip and looks down at the drink. Then she glances back at me.

"You know—I always dreamt of being some gorgeous movie star when I was younger. I wanted to move to Hollywood. Become glamorous. Go to the Academy Awards. Have magazine spreads written about me. All of that."

"Who says you can't?"

She looks at me but suddenly seems far away.

I decide to do what she's asking and keep talking. "Just because you moved to this place—to Solitary—doesn't mean you can't get out. *I'm* getting out."

"Good for you."

"I'm serious. We're both seniors—almost seniors—so what—what's another year?"

"Yeah."

But something about that "yeah" doesn't seem so convincing.

"Maybe you can at least go back to Atlanta."

I see something in Lily's body seem to stiffen when I say that. Her expression turns dark and serious. "I'm never going back there. There's nothing left for me there."

I nod, then shake my head. "Can I tell you what I'm thinking now?" I ask.

"Sure."

"I'm thinking that whoever broke your heart back in Georgia really did a good job of it."

She curses and shakes her head. "He didn't break my heart."

"Then what is it?"

For a moment she seems about to respond. For a moment.

"Come on—let's get out of here," she says. "I'm feeling cramped and uncomfortable."

Sad, 'cause I was just beginning to feel totally opposite.

Maybe it's those lights that seem to hover and glow and spin around me.

Or maybe it's the coffee thing that Lily ordered hovering and spinning around in my stomach.

Maybe it's the fact that I'm following this girl around like a puppy and I don't care.

She smiles at me and acts like she knows some big secret. But something tells me it's just her, that a girl like her will always have secrets.

I don't care.

She takes my hand. "It's okay, you know."

She can be answering a hundred questions and I know that yes, it is okay. It's okay and it's fine and it's almost midnight and I'm out late even if it's a summer Friday night.

"Come on," she says, and she doesn't have to ask anymore.

At the center of the city is a fountain that we walk around a few times. I don't know how many for sure, because I'm following her and not paying attention to anything else.

"You don't have a curfew, do you?"

"I'd break it if I had one," I say.

Lily smiles.

And I wonder. What am I doing here? The middle of summer and there was a war going on and then suddenly she showed up and all the battles stopped.

I stopped.

"What are you thinking?" she asks me.

"I'm trying not to," I say.

"Good boy."

She talks to me like some little boy and all I can say is I like it. I like her and the way everything about her makes me feel.

She takes my hand and leads me down the sidewalk toward the somewhere I know I want to be.

I'm walking with her down a city street, dreaming of tomorrow and the next month and the next year.

But when Lily takes my hand, I'm suddenly dreaming of our future.

I know that this is all too fast and sudden and crazy, but don't blame me. Blame the humid night and the still air and the passing strangers. Blame Lily and every round and wonderful thing about her. Blame her take-control attitude. Blame my let-go attitude.

The minutes evaporate, and soon I find myself back in Solitary, thinking foolish thoughts.

I don't want this night—or early morning—to end.

Somehow she's made this tiny town in the middle of nowhere suddenly come alive. I park the bike near the main strip, and we walk the rest of the way to her bed-and-breakfast. She holds my hand, and I'm not going to let go until she does.

We're walking under an ancient oak tree and I'm laughing at something she says and then all of the sudden I hear her scream.

She's screaming because I can't scream. Because some dark, hideous figure has jumped out of the shadows on me. I'm sprawled out on the sidewalk while someone is kneeling into me.

I hear curse words.

Then I see him. A face I recognize.

Wade.

Jocelyn's Wade. The guy living with Jocelyn's aunt, the sleazy redneck guy I threatened and shot in a moment of outrageous courage.

A gaunt and grizzled face looks over me and spits. He laughs, breathing heavily like he just ran ten miles, then jams something stiff and blunt in my stomach.

"If you're gonna shoot someone, you better kill him, because if you don't, this is what happens."

And before I can think of where he came from or what he's doing here or what's going to happen to Lily or my mom or anybody else in this town—

39. Bloodline

When I wake up, I'm tied up at the bottom of the hole in that dirty old cabin not far above Uncle Robert's place.

Wrong story Chris.

I'm in the woods, feeling dizzy and delirious after stabbing Pastor Marsh.

Uh-uh pick again.

I try to open my eyes but feel a burning, sickening feeling against my side. Then I realize that I didn't dream Wade coming out of nowhere and shooting me.

"Hello, son."

It's Dad. He finally made it down here, finally came to help out the family he abandoned, to get Mom straight and fend off the evil wackos around here with his super spiritual Christian powers.

"Just lie back down," the voice says.

Since when does Dad have a Southern accent?

I blink a hundred times it seems and then stare upward. I'm in a bedroom. I see a man standing next to me. He's tall. He's got on dark dress pants and a blue shirt with sleeves rolled up. Bloody sleeves. His hands are bloody too.

Is that my blood?

I feel light-headed.

"Go on, close your eyes. It's gonna be a long night."

It's Mr. Staunch.

I'm in Mr. Staunch's house.

So Wade works for Staunch? No surprise there.

"You're okay, Chris. You're going to be just fine."

"Erd ee sept eere?"

I'd tried to say *How'd I get here?* but that's what came out.

"You're okay. The girl is okay too. And the man who did this—"

I blink again and see the smile on Mr. Staunch's face.

"He won't be bothering you again. Or anybody else, for that matter."

I try to understand what this means, but I can't because I slip back down into the shadowlands.

Wake up Chris wake up.

But my eyes are closed and my side is still sizzling and my throat is dry and my mouth is numb.

Wake your life up Chris wake your soul up.

It's the same voice, but not. Maybe not. I don't know. It sounds like there are others that are standing around me.

You are special and it's time to take your place.

But I don't feel so special. I feel unconscious, and my place should be at a hospital, not Staunch's house.

You are part of a bloodline Chris and nobody can take that away from you.

And here I go, knowing this is jibber-jabber stupid talk. One minute it's Jocelyn and the next it's some creepy old man in the tunnel and the next—

You're the last one remaining. Your uncle and you, and your uncle said no.

But the voices—and there are two voices now, I know that—don't know what they're saying because my mom is still there so ha, take that, voices in my …

Then I open my eyes.

"That's right, Chris, we're right here."

Jeremiah Marsh is sitting in a chair next to my bed.

Voice #1.

"You hear what we been sayin'?" Voice #2 says.

It belongs to Mr. Staunch—Ichor Staunch, which I still can't believe is a real name, I mean, come on—who is standing at the foot of the bed.

In a hooded robe with some kind of long blade in his hands …

But no, he's just there in the same outfit, except he changed his shirt, and his hands are clean.

My side still throbs.

"It's going to be tender for some time," Marsh says as I wince.

"What happened?"

Marsh glances at Staunch to see if he's going to tell me.

"Good ole boy Wade decided to bring a little payback to you," Staunch says. "Seems he's been waiting for some time to come back around. Looks like he had no choice after his money dried up. And he just couldn't resist paying you a visit."

"How do you know all this?"

"Because Mr. Staunch is the man who gets things done, that's why," Marsh says. "Listen, Chris, you almost died tonight."

"Lily?"

"The girl you were with?" Marsh asks.

I nod, looking around the room. It's some kind of guest room—average and homey feeling.

"She's fine," Staunch says. Or actually repeats, since he told me before. "She's back at the place she's staying."

"And what about—"

"Everything is under control. We spoke to Wells and his men. Nobody else was around when it happened. Wade knew it would be deserted around there."

"Where is he?"

Staunch's eyes dart to Marsh, then back to me. "When you're better, I'll show you. Okay?"

"Show me what?"

"I'll show you what control looks like," he says.

Then he leaves me alone with the pastor. Which I normally would have been freaked out about, but strangely I feel relieved that Staunch is gone.

"Is this his house?"

Marsh nods, then rubs his eyes underneath the glasses.

"What—what time is it?"

"About three in the morning."

"My mom—"

"Is fine, Chris. Listen to Staunch. When things are handled, they're *handled.*"

"Meaning?"

I expect the same routine, just like every other time. Some mysterious, cryptic answer. But instead I hear an explanation.

"Staunch runs everything around here, and when I say runs, I mean he runs. I still don't always know how. But I know why."

"But I—what does—I still don't get—"

Marsh holds a hand up. "Chris—listen to me. Staunch and I—but mostly Staunch—work for a man you don't know, but you need to know. He is the reason you're here. Not just here in this room—the reason we were keeping tabs on you and were able to get you help tonight—but the reason you were born."

"My father?"

"No. Your great-grandfather. Your mother's grandfather."

This makes about as much sense as seeing Wade coming out of nowhere right when I was beginning to think Lily and I were going to be walking into happily-ever-after land.

"You remember when you took that little visit to the grave site in the middle of what used to be old Solitary?"

"You saw that?"

Marsh shakes his head. "No. But you were seen. You've been watched ever since you got here. But you already knew that, right?"

"The gravesite? You mean the church?"

My head is hurting, but I want to hear this.

"That is the gravesite—the newly built gravesite—for the original founder of this town. And Chris—that man was your relative. The reason you're alive too."

"But what—he's alive?"

Marsh shakes his head in amusement. "No, not Louis

Solitaire—he died in 1842. But Walter Kinner is alive, and he's the reason *you're* alive too. He saved you tonight."

"Who did?"

"Your great-grandfather."

"How? Why?"

If this is all made-up talk, like the lies that Jared fed me about being his cousin, I gotta admit—they're pretty wild.

"The how—well, that's beyond even my belief system. But the why. The why, Chris. The *why* is the thing I've been saying to you ever since you stepped foot in this town, but you have never once heard me. The why is the most important thing of all."

I look at him.

Waiting for an answer.

Please, don't leave me in suspense anymore. Please don't leave me hanging—

"You said it yourself, Chris. You wanted relief. And soon—very soon—you will have it. Complete and total relief from all that wonderful stuff you're carrying around with you."

I try to sit up a bit more, but I can't. Another bolt of pain goes through my body.

"By morning the pain will go away," Marsh says. "I promise. It's just—it's a good thing we were there. Any longer and—you would be gone."

So Staunch and Marsh … Staunch and Marsh *saved* me?

"That's why—even though it might be a bit premature—it's time, Chris. You need to know the big picture. Once you see it, I think you'll finally understand."

"Understand what?"

I know I keep asking questions, but I can't help it. I'm in pain and I feel groggy and tired and I just want Marsh to keep going even if the answers coming from him don't make perfect sense.

"You'll understand why I'm not the bad guy you've made me out to be. Someone like that Wade guy—that's a bad guy."

I want to remind him that there was this girl named Jocelyn who got abused by Wade but ultimately got *killed* by Marsh and whoever else he was involved with.

I want to say that, but I'm too weak and tired. And this all seems a bit—insane, to be honest.

Maybe I'm dreaming.

"There will be more answers, and more proof, and more of everything, Chris. I promise. Just—just be patient and … and be careful."

This man is telling me to be careful. Like he's on my side.

"You don't want to mess with him."

"Staunch?"

"No. The—other guy I was talking about. The one you're related to."

40. Handling Things

There's a scab on my stomach where there should be a … a hole or a gaping, bloody wound. But I'm touching my stomach, and I can feel the crusted-over skin that feels like I got scraped by a branch.

Like that time my skin got punctured by a tree limb when I was running for my life away from those crazies in the hoods.

I healed quickly then, and it looks like I've healed now.

But last night I got shot. Someone rammed a gun into my gut and pulled the trigger.

I don't get it. I really don't get it.

First Marsh, now this.

This is all I can think as I follow Staunch down a wide, dimly lit hallway into a large room. I try to take in my surroundings. The main thing I notice are the animal heads. Bears and deer and that sort of thing, like he's some kind of hunter. There's a massive brick fireplace with a large oak mantle above it. Then I stop.

"What is it?" Staunch asks as he stops and looks at me.

I'm staring at the black wolf that's hovering above the mantle. Of course, it's just his head, but it looks alive and real.

"I shot that on our road, the very road you live on," Staunch tells me with an amused look on his face. "Nobody believes me when I tell them that, but that's fine. It was standing in the middle of the road."

I think of the other wolves I've seen since being here, and I believe him. Then I think of the mountain man with his large dog. I haven't seen him in a while.

Then, of course, I think of the demon dog that turned into black smoke.

There it is, right there on the mantle, Chris. It was just taking a nice evening stroll on his property.

"Come on."

I'm waiting to see something else, something creepy, something scary that might be dead but suddenly moves. I pass a table and see a picture of Gus. In a tie. Trying to smile but not really succeeding.

Well, that's creepy enough, thanks.

Staunch leads me out a sliding glass door onto a deck. The same deck that overlooks his property, the same one I saw the old man looking off from the second time I wandered onto Staunch's land.

"Come on, I want to show you something before you go."

Staunch leads me down the grassy hill to the edge of the forest. He opens a black iron gate and then descends a stairway, urging me to keep up with him. There's a creek below us, and the sound of the small waterfall I discovered when I was trespassing is quite different from the pounding waters of Marsh Falls. I see the clearing in the woods with the early morning sun streaming down.

I want to ask him so many questions, but I haven't been able to ask even one.

Before Staunch stops, I see him.

A figure at the base of the waterfall, right where the water is dropping into the small pond. One hand chained to what appears to be a rock. Black tape X-ing out his mouth.

It's Wade, looking tired and angry and confused.

For a moment, as we stand above him, looking down at him, he doesn't see us. The splashing water echoes all around us.

"There you go," Staunch says. "*That* is how you take care of problems."

Wade seems to hear him, although there's no way he could from that distance. He jerks his arm, trying to breaking it free, screaming underneath the tape over his mouth. Staunch just looks down at him the way he might look at some wounded, dying animal.

"So what do you want to do with him?"

I see bright blue eyes glancing down at me, unmoving and unfeeling. "What do you mean?"

"You control this situation now. You can do whatever you'd like to this thing below."

I swallow, shake my head, my mouth opening but unable to speak.

"It's simple. You decide. If you decide nothing—say nothing and never bring it up again—well, that is a decision in itself."

"What's going to happen to him?"

"Well, if you don't do anything, he'll stay down there and die."

"No."

Staunch nods, then reaches into his pocket.

"Here's a key. It's to the lock on his wrist."

"No."

"Take it."

I try to back up, but he forces the key into my hand.

"Listen, Chris—you have to start handling things yourself. This is a good test for you. To see how you'll deal with things."

"I'm not going to let him die."

"Fine," Staunch says, looking back down at the skinny, soaking figure of Wade. "But let me remind you of something. He just put a bullet in your side. A .45. You should be dead. I'm not going to tell you how it is you're alive, and I'm not looking for thanks or anything like that. I'm just looking for you to grow up and be a man. I get teens. I got a seventeen-year-old oversized brat for a son who's probably that way because I didn't hold him enough when he was younger. That's fine. That's another world, Chris. That's not your world. You're different. And I think you know it."

"No," I say in a very weak voice.

"You say that, but deep down I think you know. And don't forget why Wade shot you. Or why you shot him."

"How do you know about that?"

Staunch leans over and looks me directly in the face. "I know about everything that takes place around here. Not that you even tried to keep that one a secret. But the guy's a piece of trash, Chris. I'd be wasting a bullet if I stuck it between his ugly little eyes."

This is too much too soon too fast. I feel like I'm about ready to fall off this minor ledge here. But I'll be falling and won't hit the ground.

"You want to blame others for Jocelyn's death. You blame Marsh—you surely blame me, too. You want to know who was under those hoods. Right? Everybody seems to know *about* it, but nobody is confessing to actually having been there. But what if—what if that very man down there was the one who orchestrated it all?"

"No—he's too—"

"What? Dumb?"

I nod, swallow. I feel like running.

"You calling men and women who dress up in robes and carry torches in the middle of the night smart?"

He's got a point.

"I have things to do, and you best be going back home. Take the key. You decide. You let me know if I need to do anything."

"Like what?"

He just looks at me with heartless eyes. "Anything you need."

Staunch begins to walk back up the hill. I hear a high-pitched, muffled wailing coming from below.

"How did I—how come I didn't die?" I ask before he's gone.

"What if you did die, Chris? What if you're a ghost and don't even know it?"

Before I can react, Staunch just laughs out loud, then continues to walk back up the hill.

I follow, trying to get away from the stifled cries below.

I don't know what to do with Wade, but I'm beyond trying to figure it out at the moment.

I need to go back home and …

And what, Chris?

I picture her face and know that I need to call Lily. I'm not sure what happened to her last night, but I'm sure she's probably wondering what's going on with me.

I'm walking down the long, circular driveway leading to the dirt road our cabin is on when it dawns on me that I have a cell phone in my pocket.

I keep forgetting that, and keep forgetting that it belongs to me.

41. Prisoners

I only get Lily's voice mail. It worries me, not being able to talk to her in person. I just leave a message saying I'm fine and I hope she's fine and to call me soon.

It takes a few moments to get to the bottom of the drive.

So now I know what's behind the gate. Sorta.

A normal mansion that's decorated in Ernest Hemingway macho-hunter style.

And the suggestion that my great-grandfather is alive and keeping tabs on me.

I hear the crunching of dirt and rock underneath my tennis shoes.

I want to know how everything could have suddenly gotten all—all dark and dreary again. It's this road. This road and these woods and everything stuck inside them.

I want to find Lily and take her away the same way I should have taken Jocelyn.

This time I'm going to learn.

The more I understand, the more confused I am.

I remember that gravestone I found with the French writing and the name Solitaire.

I don't know. I don't know anything anymore.

I'm walking and breathing heavily, and I realize that I'm shaking all over. I stop for a minute and try to control the shaking, but I can't. I can't. I realize that I've been holding back on the terrified shakes, but now they've got me like some heroin addict who's been clean for twenty-four hours.

I need someone to come and grab me and tell me I'm not losing my mind.

To tell me I haven't lost my soul.

Maybe Staunch was right. Maybe I was shot dead and I'm a ghost wandering around these woods like the ghost dogs and wolves I've seen.

I lean over and put my hands on my knees like I'm some marathon runner who's just finished a long race. For a moment I'm dizzy. The morning sun beats down on me.

Then I stand back up and keep walking.

I don't feel special or different. Being watched and haunted doesn't mean you're special. It just means you're a prisoner.

No different from the guy shackled to a rock below the waterfall.

Maybe we're all prisoners in one way or another and don't know it.

I just want to be released from all of this. Every little bit of it.

I want to go about my life just like I was doing before Wade showed up last night.

42. Some Weird Voodoo Stuff

"Hey, Chris."

My mom smiles as I walk through the door. I was already surprised to see my bike in the driveway. Somehow Staunch got it there without a problem. Now Mom is smiling at me as if it's just any ordinary morning.

"Did you have breakfast?"

Yep, just finished some French toast with Wade. Oh, and your grandfather.

At first I shake my head, then I nod. My head doesn't seem to know what to do with itself.

"Was that a yes or a no?"

"No—I'm fine—thanks."

"Okay. Hey—I wanted to tell you the good news. I got a promotion yesterday. Actually just a pay increase, but still. It's something."

I nod, feign a smile, look around to see if anything else seems strange or if it's just me.

Hey—wanted to tell you my good news too! I got shot, but somehow I survived. Thanks to good old great-grandpa, who I'm dying to meet. Get it, Mom? DYING??

"I'm busy—gotta run to Asheville before work. Want to come?"

I shake my head.

"How is Oli doing? You guys have fun?"

I feel something scraping against the scab on my stomach. Then I hear a laugh. And even though these things are only in my mind, it certainly feels and sounds like they're happening.

"What do you mean?"

"Oli—the guy you spent the night with? Hello?"

I tighten my lips and nod. I raise my eyebrows and force a smile. "Good."

"Bring him by sometime."

I don't think you want me to do that, Mom.

She continues to get ready as I try to unpack my brains on the sofa.

It just never stops.

That was a warning, Chris. Just like everything else. A warning. A little hocus-pocus shazam to show you.

I sit on the couch and close my eyes.

Sleep comes, but like everything else, it's short-lived and not satisfying in the least.

Lily is hysterical when she calls.

All I get is "phone died" and "charged" and "thought you were going to die" and then some curses and a very loud and very distinct "What happened?"

She sounds like she's outside walking, because she sounds out of breath and her connection is cutting in and out. I just keep asking where she is, so I can get on my bike and go see her, but then the call drops completely.

Yet when I hear the knock on the front door, along with the handle turning and the door swinging open, I see I don't have to call Lily back.

She's managed to get to me very quickly.

"I left the moment I got your message," she says, rushing up beside me and then wrapping me up in her wonderful arms.

I'm buried in her soft and sweet-smelling hair and skin for some time. She just holds me, shaking, maybe crying, though I can't see it and I don't know. For the longest time she doesn't say anything.

When she finally lets me go, I stand there feeling a bit light-headed from being so close to her.

"You okay?" she asks me, touching my stomach gently to see if there's a hole or anything in it.

"I'd get shot again if I'll get one of those every time."

"Chris—seriously. What—you don't even have bandages or anything?"

I shake my head.

"What happened—who were those men that took you?"

"Listen," I say, "I don't really know what happened."

She lifts up my shirt and sees the scab. "That's impossible."

"I know."

"Chris, I saw you get shot. I was there."

"I don't know what happened."

She shouts my name and curses, as if I just vanished into thin air or something.

"What if it was all an illusion?" I ask, trying to come up with some explanation.

"I heard the gun go off."

"What if it was a fake? A prop or something?"

"I saw blood. I saw you."

Yeah, and I *felt* blood.

"What if—I don't know—what if somehow he just shocked me to think I got shot—then everything else was acting? Like made up."

"Chris!"

"What?"

"How can you—oh, I don't—I just can't—"

"I know," I say again.

"You know what?"

"It's this place. And the people here."

"That's some weird voodoo stuff going on here. First that card game, and now this."

"What about the cards?"

"I didn't tell you—Chris, nobody, and I mean nobody except *one* person in this whole world knows about that rose tattoo. Nobody has ever seen it except him. It's not exactly in a place where people can see it."

"A tattoo?"

"One that looks exactly like the card. That's why—I just couldn't believe it. I still don't. But this—you're walking around like it was a toy gun that went off."

"Maybe it was."

Lily curses in disbelief. "No. It's something—something evil. Something wicked."

"You don't have to tell me."

She looks at my cabin, and I realize she's never been here before. Not that I need to give her the grand tour or anything. I wonder how she got my address and then remember that she took me home from the party that night.

"Chris—"

"What?"

"What is going on here?"

"I don't know."

"But you're not freaking out like you should be. I mean—feel this."

She takes my hand and puts it against her soft blouse and even softer skin. I guess I'm supposed to feel her beating heart, but I'm a bit taken aback by having my hand thrust *there.*

"Come on—stop being a boy and start talking."

"I can't—Lily, no."

"What?"

"I can't just start talking. I don't even know where I'd start."

Then I think about this cabin and the tunnels underneath.

I think about the cell phone that doesn't belong to me. That maybe lets someone else know just where I am.

"Come on, let's leave and go somewhere," I say.

"I'm driving."

"You have a car?"

"Of course I have a car," she says.

As I follow her outside, I leave the iPhone behind. Just in case.

43. Partial Answers

"You're not telling me everything."

We've been sitting in the parking lot of the grocery store for some time, the car off and the convertible top down. It's starting to get really hot in this two-seater. Lily said that her old Mazda Miata doesn't have air, that it's broken but she never bothered to get it fixed. She doesn't seem fazed by the morning heat coming on like an electric blanket.

"I've told you enough."

"Enough? Chris—what's happening here? I want to know everything."

In the half hour it took us to get out of Solitary and then find a spot to park and talk, I decided that I couldn't tell her everything. Everybody who ends up knowing something leaves. Rachel and Poe, two prime examples.

For a while this summer, it was nice to have Lily be a part of another life and another world, one that didn't involve darkness and evil and weird happenings. But now she's right in the middle of it.

"Are those men bad?" she asks me.

"The one who attacked me was."

"Why'd he attack you?"

"Because—because I threatened him once with a gun. Actually, I shot him."

Lily can't believe it. I nod.

"But why? And what were you doing with a gun?"

"It wasn't mine. I was helping out a girl I knew."

"Who?"

"You don't know her," I say, and leave it at that.

We continue to play the back-and-forth game.

"Chris—you need to tell me. Did you get shot?"

Of course I got shot, but how am I supposed to explain something I don't understand?

"No."

"Chris—"

"I think the whole thing was a warning."

Lily shakes her head, her hair more curly since last night, her face pale because she's wearing almost no makeup. "A warning for you to do what?"

"Stay out of people's business. Which is what I'm going to do."

"We need to get help."

"No." I find my hand grabbing her wrist.

She looks down at it, and I let her go.

"Lily—please. Don't do anything. Don't—not now at least."

"Why?"

"Because—listen, they're starting to tell me what's going on. Why people are so interested in me around here."

"And why is that?"

I shrug, wiping my damp forehead. My back is getting nice and wet. "I think—they say it's because someone who founded the town of Solitary is a relative."

"So?"

"Yeah, I know. I don't know why that's noteworthy."

Of course, I'm not really being honest, because I have ideas. They don't all make sense, but I've seen enough movies to know that being related to someone can be a big deal.

"Is there some evil cult thing going on in this town?"

"Yeah, something like that."

"The pastor you mentioned—is he involved?"

I nod. "In some way."

"This car isn't bugged, you know."

But I don't know anything. Whether I can trust her completely, whether I can believe what Marsh and Staunch were saying, whether I am going to make it to my senior year of high school.

"Lily—I just want to get the school year over and then leave. That's all."

For a moment I see her staring at me. She looks so determined and fierce.

"Let's leave. Right now. Right this very instant."

I laugh. "Yeah, right."

"I'm serious."

"And go where?"

"I don't know."

"And do what?"

She shakes her head, but doesn't reply.

"Lily—I—my mom is not doing so great."

"Is she sick?"

"Yeah, I guess you could say that. I'm afraid—I've thought of it before. Of leaving. But I can't leave her. And I know she won't come with me."

"Does she know about this?"

Oh yeah, sure, give her some more reason to drink.

"No."

"Does anybody?"

"Everybody who does—the people I tell—all end up leaving."

She moves in her seat so she's facing me square on. Then she grabs both of my hands in hers. "I'm not going anywhere—you hear me? Nowhere."

"They have a way of changing that."

"They?" she shouts. "I want to know who *they* are!"

I nod.

"Chris—this is what you need to do. Find everything you can about these people—whoever they are and what exactly they want."

"Why?"

"So they can be exposed."

I think of all my attempts to do just that. Everywhere I tried to get help turned into a dead end.

I think of Sheriff Wells. A picture of someone weak, regardless of whose side he's on.

"I've tried, Lily. Believe me. And I don't want to risk anything else happening."

"You'll be fine," Lily says.

"No—I'm talking about something happening to you."

"I'm not afraid."

"You haven't been here long enough," I say. "Give it time."

44. Now We're Even

Lily might be right. I don't know.

I guess you need proof in order to go to the authorities. Or to go to *somebody.*

I'm not sure what the next step is. It's probably not up to me. But I do know one thing, and I'm taking care of that right now.

I'm not a monster and never will be.

It doesn't take me long to walk down my road and stop at the gate that warns intruders away. The one with the *No Trespassing* sign and the camera on the ground. This time I know I'm being watched. I know they're expecting me.

The wrought-iron gates aren't locked.

The choice is up to me, he said, and this is my choice.

I slip through the gate and keep walking.

Daylight is almost gone, and when I head into the woods at the base of the Staunch mansion, I have to watch my footing in the shadows.

Wade is still down below, still chained to a rock at the base of the small waterfall, still being doused. He's slumped over, not really able to sit but resting sideways on the rock.

I nudge him to see if he's still conscious. He jerks and moves and then flails his arms.

I put my enclosed fist out toward him, then open my hand.

"It's yours. You can go."

He just looks at me with confused, frightened eyes.

"Take it."

For a moment I wonder if he's so tired and hungry and out of his mind that he thinks he's dreaming. A shaking, bony hand finally takes the key.

He knows just like I do that he shot me, that I should be dead.

Maybe he believes I'm a ghost. I don't know.

I'm not sure what he's going to do once he frees himself.

This is the man that hurt Jocelyn and tried to kill you.

I'm not trying to be noble here. I shot him. He shot me.

Somehow we're both alive to talk about it.

I walk away from Wade, hoping that we're now even.

When I get to the top of the hill and leave the forest behind, I see a figure sitting on the deck. It's dark—too dark now—to really make out who it is. But it's not Staunch—this person is smaller. It looks as if he's sitting in a wheelchair. Like an old person might.

Like someone who could be your great-grandfather might.

I stare and wonder if I'm going to hear voices whispering to me. Or if the wind is going to suddenly start blowing and getting creepy. But nothing like that happens.

The figure on the deck doesn't move, but just faces out, looking down at me.

I'm tempted to wave, but I don't. I leave the Staunch property behind.

45. Another Story

The letter is just one more thing for my mental To Do list:

– Get a job.

– Be on the lookout for anybody who was shackled to a rock, who I let go a couple of days ago.

– Check the piece of plywood underneath Mom's sink to make sure it's still got all the nails holding it down.

– Remember to feed Midnight. And take her on a walk.

– Find out how to go about getting my license.

– Find the road that leads to—that used to lead to—the Crag's Inn.

– Start working out.

I put that on there because I saw a few minutes of one of those weight-loss reality shows, and I vowed never to be on one.

– Get something for Mom's b-day (nonalcoholic).

– Learn to fire a sidearm (figure that could come in handy).

– Buy a gun (see above).

– Be prepared in case things with Lily suddenly go to the next level (this being even more unlikely than me buying a handgun).

– Did I mention find a job?

– Open the letter that just came in the mail from Kelsey.

I look at her handwriting. The envelope feels light, not too light but light enough. No ten-page letter inside. It's not a card. It's a good old-fashioned letter.

She tried to call and that went nowhere.

I really don't want to open this letter. Like the email I got from Poe that I deleted, I don't want to read this.

Maybe it's just something friendly, like her way of saying hello.

But with everything going on in my mind—all the stuff that I can't keep track of—I don't want … no, I don't *need* something else to think about.

I put the letter on my desk upstairs, unopened. It's still only July. Eventually Kelsey will move on and find someone like her. Cute and unwatched and unchosen and all that. Someone who isn't thinking about a new student named Lily, along with wondering what the guys up the street are going to do next.

Kelsey is for another story and not this one.

46. One Big, Gigantic Pool

I'm thinking of the remaining few days I have before the next session of summer school starts. This has been a nice break, despite, you know, getting *shot* and all.

I'm downtown Solitary at Brennan's Grill and Tavern, eating a bacon barbecue burger, and I'm almost done when someone slides into the booth across from me. For a second I think it's Marsh, but this guy is too big to be the pastor.

"Chris," Sheriff Wells says.

"Hi," I say with my mouth full.

"So how you doing?"

I nod and tell him fine. He looks at me with grim, suspicious eyes.

This was the guy who told me to lie low and keep to myself. Now he keeps popping up for some reason.

"Nothing abnormal going on in your life?"

"Nope."

Abnormal around here would mean nothing was happening. So I'm not really lying.

"How about your mother? Is she doing well?"

"Yeah, last time I noticed, which was like five minutes ago," I say. "She's over there behind the bar."

And speaking of bar, she's well on her way to rehab, if that's the "well" he's referring to.

For a few minutes he asks me questions and I keep answering them in short, mouth-full-of-food answers.

"Well, it's good to hear that everything is under control. I just had some information that I thought you might like to know. Considering everything."

I nod, staring at the deep wrinkles on his face and the heavy bags under his eyes.

"They found Wade Sims dead this morning after he drove his car off the side of a mountain. All reports show he was drunk. Probably didn't feel a thing."

I suddenly have an eerie image of Staunch looking in the window and waving at me, an evil grin on his face.

Act normal just act like this doesn't shock you.

"Wow, that's crazy," I say.

I guess the sheriff's new role is to come and see me anytime something bad happens to someone I know.

I *really* don't want to see this guy anymore.

"You didn't happen to see Wade recently, did you?"

I shake my head, but it seems as if both the sheriff and I know I'm lying.

"Well, the funny thing is—not really funny, more interesting, I guess—is that Wade came back around here. There are no reports of Helen Evans being spotted anywhere in Solitary. The old house is still abandoned. Just took a drive there before coming here."

The sheriff continues to look for a reaction from me, but I'm not giving him anything. The time came and went for that.

"Chris—I'm on your side here," he whispers.

"Sometimes it seems as if there are no sides," I can't help saying. "That everybody is swimming in a nice round pool around here."

"I can't help it that we lost that young girl, Chris."

"*I* lost her. I don't recall you losing anything."

Except maybe your guts and courage to stand up and do what's right.

"Do you understand that within a very short time, two people who have recently had altercations with you have tragically died?"

"You think I had something to do with it?"

He shakes his head and then rubs his goatee. "I don't know. I know it wasn't you—but I think they're tied together."

"But didn't you say Wade had been drinking?"

"It looks that way. But there are a lot of things around here that look a certain way."

"So what are you going to do?"

He doesn't seem to like my tone. He leans over and talks between clenched teeth.

"You listen to me—I'm just trying to help."

"It's a little late for that, isn't it?"

I can hear the snotty, flippant attitude reeking off my words. But I don't care. This man is as much to blame for Jocelyn's death as Pastor Marsh.

One big, gigantic pool. Jump in, Chris, the water's still warm!

"I'm still keeping an eye on you, just so you know," the sheriff says as he slides out of the booth.

"Good. So's the rest of the town."

47. Drama

The drama seems to die down for a while.

I guess I should rephrase that, since I don't want to use the word *die* anymore.

The drama goes away.

But Lily doesn't. She remains nearby.

And my feelings toward her—these wild and uncontrollable urges inside of me—only continue to grow.

There are reasons for that.

And they're not all because she's the most beautiful thing I've seen around here since …

Don't.

No.

Lily is more than a pretty face.

She also seems to be the only one around here interested in taking care of me. Not interested in what I'm doing and why or where I'm doing it. But just interested in how I'm doing.

Period.

There are others but you just don't want to think about them.

I silence this voice by putting black duct tape on its mouth. I don't want to think about anybody else. I just want to focus on Lily.

I lose track of how often we text each other. We'll talk on the phone and I'll drive out to see her, but the rest of the time I'm constantly sharing random thoughts with her.

I still don't know what "we" are or if we're anything at all. I know she's expressed feelings—well, some feelings at least. She's even kissed me. But there hasn't been that thing that I keep wondering (hoping) will come. The moment when I stop being the little boy hanging around with her.

You never had a chance with Jocelyn because she was gone in a blink.

I don't want to think that, but it's true.

I don't want to waste time with Lily. So I'm not.

Yet—I still don't know how she feels toward me. Besides liking me and my company. Which is all fine.

But.

I'm just not sure.

But wait. Didn't you say the drama was gone?

Maybe I'm doomed to be surrounded by drama. Even if it's of my own making.

48. Alone

It's strange to be stood up for a date by your mother. But that's my world.

It's July 15, and Mom said yesterday that we'd go out for dinner to celebrate her birthday. She said that she would try to get off early, that it shouldn't be a problem.

It's already eight at night, and it looks like something indeed was a problem.

Maybe you're the problem, Chris.

I shove the Debbie Downer voice away even though I've tended to think that way recently when it comes to Mom. I've always wondered why she and Dad didn't have more children. Did they even try? Or did they have me and then wipe their foreheads and shake their heads and go, "Phew! No more of those!"

I don't know.

I just know that the present I bought her (and had nicely wrapped, thank you not so very much) is sitting on the breakfast table all by its lonesome little self. I don't want to call—nope, I'm not doing that. I've checked our landline, and it works. I don't bother checking my cell since I haven't told Mom about it (since it's from Pastor Marsh and all).

It's eight fifteen when I decide to head out.

I used most of my remaining money from working at the Crag's Inn on the present. Fifty dollars. Not much, but it got me a nice gift card from Ann Taylor, a store Mom used to shop at a lot back home. I've heard her complain many times about her clothes—a complaint she never used to have back home when Dad worked and Mom spent.

A small Happy Birthday note is in the card. I hate regular Hallmark cards with phony phrases. I don't have a lot to say to my mom. Everything I *want* to tell her isn't particularly good, so the note simply says, HAPPY BIRTHDAY, MOM. I HOPE THIS NEXT YEAR IS A BETTER ONE FOR BOTH OF US!

It's true. Maybe it's a selfish note. Maybe I should tell her she's special and beautiful and that I haven't given up on her. She *is* special, and she certainly *is* beautiful, but I think I have given up on her. Sorta like I've given up on this town.

The less I have to think about Mom or Solitary, the better off I am.

I get the key for the motorcycle and leave the gift on the table.

Hopefully Mom will come home before I do, open the gift, and feel sorry for forgetting about her son.

I know that's kinda mean. But maybe it'll get her attention.

Something has to.

I drive up to the bed-and-breakfast. It's barely noticeable behind the trees and fading light. I'm hoping that I can surprise Lily. I told her that I was going to be spending the evening with my mom, and I even half considered inviting her. But I sorta want to keep Lily all to myself. I don't want my mother and all *that* suddenly intersecting with her.

I shut off my motorcycle at a spot across the street. For a second I think of texting her to let her know I'm here.

But only for a second, because just then I actually see her.

Walking down the sidewalk arm in arm with some guy.

Some older guy. Like in his late twenties or early thirties.

I'm a bit breathless as I try and make out what I'm seeing.

Lily's smile—flirtatious and dreamy—and her hand that gently strokes back her hair. She touches her grinning lips, then laughs at something the man said, then nudges him with a hip.

She's wearing a short skirt and a low-cut top, like some kind of skimpy outfit for a night out on the town. But Solitary isn't a town, and Lily isn't …

The dude next to her sure isn't her big brother.

He's got a big, fat grin on his face, the kind that professional athletes have that says, *I have it all.*

A big, fat grin.

I still want to believe or hope or try to imagine that it's nothing, but then she kisses him.

On the lips.

For a long time.

I'm watching the whole thing, and they're oblivious, this couple across the street, walking away from the B and B.

Oh man.

My mind is doing cartwheels as I just sit there on my bike, trying not to flip out. I see the guy get into some fancy, expensive silver car. Then, as he pulls out, the empty space allows Lily to see me.

She doesn't say anything. She doesn't even react. She just looks at me and stares. Since I'm not that close, I can't see the true expression on her face.

I shake my head and try to start the bike back up.

I don't need her. I don't need her, just like I don't need my mom or anybody else.

"Chris!"

I keep trying to start the motorcycle, cursing, and then suddenly Lily is standing next to me, touching my arm.

I yank it back and look at her. "Don't touch me."

I have a weird déjà vu but don't recall what it is.

"Chris, please."

My heart is pounding, and I really have no idea what to say.

"What was—who was that?"

"Calm down."

She's so calm and unfazed, but I continue to shake my head and laugh. "Oh, okay, sure."

"Chris, please, just—get off the bike, okay?"

"Who was that?"

"Just an old friend."

I laugh. "Yeah, I'd say he's an old *friend.* Looks like you guys were really good friends."

"Don't."

"Don't?" I ask. "Don't what?"

"Don't be a jerk."

"Don't—oh, sure—fine. Yeah, I'm the jerk."

"I thought you were with your mother tonight."

"She had other ideas."

And I guess you did too.

"There's nothing going on with him."

Sure doesn't look that way.

I can't say anything.

"Chris, listen—he's an old friend of the family. We go way back. That's all. He stopped by to check on my mom and me."

"Where's your mother?"

"She's inside."

I look at her, and suddenly I see Jared all over again. Another person coming into my life to lie and cheat and steal from me.

And I don't have that much to take. That's the craziness of this.

"You want to go inside and see her? Let her tell you who Kurt is?"

"Kurt?"

The name sounds obnoxious and fake.

I look ahead down the street and remain lost for words. I hear the katydids droning on in the trees around us.

"Chris—"

"What?"

She grips my shirt in her hand, and she yanks at it. Hard. She pulls my whole body down, and I suddenly can't believe how strong she is. She forces me to look her in the eyes, and then she curses at me and tells me to cut it out.

"Don't be some stupid guy getting jealous over nothing."

"Over nothing?"

"Yes, Chris, over nothing. I'm not going to play games here—not here, not with you, not this way. You got it?"

She releases my shirt, and I bring my aching shoulder back up.

"You want to come in for a few minutes or what?"

Not now, not like this.

I shake my head.

"Well—I can't hop on your motorcycle if that's what you're wanting," she says. "My mom is pretty upset, okay?"

Yeah, well so am I.

I don't know what to say.

"Call me tomorrow," Lily says.

I nod.

"And stop, Chris. Don't do that."

"Do what?"

"The sad puppy dog eyes. The little lost boy routine. Just stop. Grow up, okay?"

Ouch.

"That—that's the last thing I need, okay?" Lily says.

"What?"

"Guilt. Suspicions. Jealousy. I swear—men are all the same. Doesn't matter how old or young."

She curses again and starts to walk across the street.

For a moment I want to follow her, but I don't.

I watch her disappear under the trees, and I wait for a few minutes, then try to start the motorcycle again. This time it works.

I hope I'm never going to be running for my life and needing to start this old bike. Because the horror movie cliché is *totally* going to be there when I can't start the stinking thing and the zombies come to bite into my flesh and carry my heart away in their mouths.

That's the image I'm thinking of as I drive away from Lily.

A blood-sucking zombie with my heart in its mouth.

I drive into the night, feeling tired and very much alone.

49. Broken

That night I have a nice little pity party.

Lily texts me with an apology and a long explanation, but I don't really care.

I get home, and Mom offers me an apology and a longer explanation, but I don't really care.

I don't text Lily back and don't respond to my mom.

Instead I go up to my room and let my anger boil over. I turn up my stereo, daring my mom to come upstairs to tell me to turn it down, but nope, she doesn't.

I've been searching so long, trying to work things out.

But not anymore.

I just—I just really—

I don't care anymore.

Nothing's going to be all right anymore.

Nothing.

And I tell myself this the next day when morning comes.

And the following day.

I even tell myself this when the second session of summer school starts, and the group of five kids isn't as interesting and colorful as the first batch.

It doesn't matter.

I'm going to come in and endure the few hours of class and then leave. Without saying a word. Without getting to know anybody.

Because it doesn't matter.

It's the same thing over and over again.

Walking uphill and being turned around and around.

I feel like a broken man but am constantly and continually reminded that I'm just a boy just a little boy just a boy Chris boy oh BOY.

And in the midst of running and walking and feeling the anger inside day and night, it's funny how time flies.

50. Summertime Rolls

My birthday in August comes and goes without much of anything.

So uneventful.

I was hoping that someone besides Mom would know and celebrate. But then again, there aren't too many people out there to celebrate with. I've ignored calls and texts from Lily, and maybe I shouldn't but I'm just tired of the confusion and the lies and the mysteries. So very tired. Mom tries by giving me a few gifts (including a gas card, which I've desperately needed), but it doesn't help me escape the monotony of everything else.

Not even a call from Dad. Not that I wanted one, but still.

Poe—well, she's long gone and has no idea it was my birthday. The kids in my second summer school session—I haven't gotten to know any of them, and they seem content not getting to know or even interact with me.

Ho hum.

On a whim, I decide to open the letter that Kelsey sent me. I feel like hearing from someone, anyone, now that I'm officially seventeen.

I open the letter and see a simple note. Short and sweet.

> *Hi Chris.*
>
> *All flowers in time bend toward the sun.*
>
> *Kelsey*

I read and reread the note and try to make sense of what she's saying.

Okay??

Then I shake my head.

This was why I didn't open this letter. Some other mystery. Some other random mysterious message that I don't get. I'm tired of not getting. Tired of not understanding.

I fold up the letter and put it back in the envelope.

Not much later, I slam the phone down and curse at my weakness.

I'm not a chosen anything.

I'm not a special anybody.

I actually seriously almost dialed all the numbers belonging to my dad's new place. I got the number from my mom's purse after searching long and hard the other day. I scribbled them down with the full intent to call him with an SOS, whatever that might look like. I figure that just my calling and saying that we needed help would be enough, but then again who knows. Maybe he's got a twenty-four-year-old girlfriend who believes in God too, and they're going to get busy populating the world with godly children.

I go upstairs and search through records and find the one with a cover that Mom surely wouldn't like. I've heard of Jane's Addiction before but never really listened to them. I put on the record and listen. Mom is gone—when is she not gone? She could be here inside this house and she'd be gone—she could have headphones on and waving hello at me and she'd still be gone. It doesn't matter.

I crank up the stereo. The loudest I've ever had it. The room and the bed and the floor vibrate.

The album is called *Nothing's Shocking.* Is that not just so utterly and wonderfully fitting?

The songs are loud and wild, and I like the fact that they're kinda crazy, but I don't like any of them, not really, not until the laid-back song called "Summertime Rolls."

It starts off moody and drifting and sorta sums up how I feel. Spiraling and circling this house like a vulture in need of something but unable to find what it needs. The cloud of smoke drifting upward higher and higher.

It's stoner music, and I maybe should give Roger or Brick a call. But that's not my thing. I could invade Mom's liquor stash—oh, I know, Mom, you think I don't know about it—but I don't because that's not my thing either.

Instead, I dream of dancing with Lily to this song, her arms wrapped around mine, her eyes on me, her smile welcoming me.

"Me and my girlfriend," the singer sings, and that's what I want.

"She loves me, I mean it's serious," he sings, and that's what I need.

Right now.

I don't need to figure out the rest of the world and whether we go somewhere else after we die. I don't need to know about the spirits circling above and the tunnels dug underneath. I don't give a rip about any of that. I just care that it's summertime and that it's rolling and that the days just pass without all those dark omens beating me over the head and heart.

I want summertime to keep rolling.

To keep rolling.

And for me not to feel bad. Or fear the bad. Or think bad thoughts.

I need Lily.

Whatever this singer is talking about—that's what I want. Crazy passion.

So so serious.

"As serious can be."

I finally give in and text.

Lily help me. Come back to me. I need you. I need someone.

But she ignores me like I've ignored her.

51. Who Knows

So the remaining August days come and go.

And summertime does indeed roll.

And in some crazy, impossible way, I find myself actually looking forward to school. To seeing other students and maybe starting over.

And then an invitation arrives in the mail. Addressed to me.

The Annual Staunch Labor Day Bash

Labor Day

Starting at 4 p.m. and going until ????

I hold the heavy card with the fancy design and shake my head.

Why not?

I have nothing more to lose. I've seen the house, and it's not that frightening.

I'm bored. And lonely. So fine.

Maybe I'll get some more answers and will learn that I can fly.

That would be great.

I turn the invitation over and see handwriting.

> Hi, Chris. Please feel free to bring a guest. We hope you can come. It will certainly be in your best interest if you can make it.
>
> IS

I stare at the initials. *IS.* Just call me Is.

I decide that I'll go and that I'm going to get the rest of the story on who I am and why I'm important and then …

Well, then, who knows.

52. The Spoon

I decide to head down the street to the Staunch house around six. I take my bike just in case I want to leave quickly (or have to escape for some reason). I like the security of the motorcycle even if the drive is only a few minutes.

Maybe that's why Iris gave it to you.

I hate thinking of Iris because I have no idea what happened to her. I hate not knowing.

I find the gate opened and see a hundred people roaming around outside the Staunch residence. Nobody's wearing a robe or carrying a machete.

Turns out, half of Solitary seems to be at the Labor Day gathering. All standing on the lawn, holding plates of food or drinks like some kind of church picnic.

I see Sheriff Wells. And his deputy who hates me, Kevin Ross. Principal Harking is there talking to some people (probably parents). My track coach, Mr. Brinks, sees me and shouts out a big "Chicago!" He comes over and feels my arms and stomach to make sure I'm not getting flabby.

Ah, feels just like home.

Then I see a couple walking down the slight hill hand in hand. A strangely attractive couple, smiling and looking polished like a pair of fancy shoes.

Jeremiah Marsh spots me and starts to guide his wife, Heidi, toward me.

This is the first time I've ever really seen her in public. She's a stunning figure, but not because she's good-looking. She's older and looks almost—regal or something. She's white as a ghost, but I think that's on purpose. Like some of those movie stars or models who look pale.

Maybe it's because she's kept inside her house locked up.

I wonder if she's going to act like she recognizes me, but when Marsh comes up and shakes my hand, Heidi only smiles at me.

"Chris, I don't know if you've had the pleasure," Marsh says in a more distinct Southern drawl, as if he's trying to show off. "This is my beloved wife, Heidi."

She has blonde, almost white, hair that seems to hover around her head and glide onto her shoulders. A sleek hand brushes it away from her face right before she reaches out to shake my hand.

Her hand feels like cold silk.

"Hello, Chris."

Up close, I no longer think of her as some movie star. She resembles one of the elves in Lord of the Rings, striking but also a bit—otherworldly.

This is the same lady who screamed at you in her house and looked like a maniac.

"Do you live near here?" she asks me.

I'm not sure if she's acting and already knows or if she doesn't remember me. I tell her where I live.

Her blue-green eyes seem to change shape like some kind of expensive crystal in the sunlight.

This is the same woman who sent you to try and save Jocelyn.

Maybe she really *is* an actress, because she's certainly fooling me by acting like she doesn't know me.

"I've always loved this property," she says in a high-class sort of Southern drawl as well. "The creek and the sprawling lawn and the beautiful house. I told Ike that we'd buy his property if we had the money."

Ike?

Is that short for Ichor?

As we talk—or mainly as I listen while Jeremiah and Heidi talk to me—I notice that the pastor never stops holding her hand. At one point he laughs at something she says and then puts his other hand on her bare arm to stroke it. But it's kinda weird how he does it.

Like the way someone strokes a cat or something.

"Well, Chris, you certainly must have some of that delicious brisket they're serving," Heidi tells me.

"Sure."

"Not that she would know," Marsh says. "It takes a lot of willpower to look this beautiful."

"I had my three bites, thank you very much."

Marsh looks at her and seems to momentarily forget about me. He smiles and makes some weird face at her, then pecks her on the cheek.

"Oh, Chris, be sure and see the host before you leave."

Those beady eyes stare at me from behind those sleek glasses. I nod and watch them walk away. Still hand in hand, as if she might try to escape if he let go.

It's really weird. Not seeing them—well, it's *always* weird seeing Marsh—and not just seeing Heidi act like she doesn't recognize me.

It's weird seeing Marsh around his wife.

He really acts like he loves her.

But in a weird, sick kind of way.

I have my full plate of food—beef brisket, corn on the cob, baked beans, corn bread, coleslaw—when I hear a curse and then feel something ram into my back. My entire plate of food gets smashed into my chest before spilling all over the rest of my clothes. I turn around, but I've already recognized the voice.

There he is. The big, fat face I've missed so much this summer.

"What do you think you're doin' here?" Gus demands as if stunned that I'm walking on his lawn.

I'm wiping my clothes off. "I got a personal invitation."

"You get out of here or your face is gonna look like that shirt of yours."

I'm glad I wore a white T-shirt. Makes the stains stand out all the more.

I see the crowd around us watching and I decide I don't need this.

"You know, school hasn't even—"

I stop as I see something rushing toward us from the corner of my eye. Then I see Ichor Staunch come up beside Gus with one of the large metal serving spoons that I'd just used for my plate and whack him over the head several times. I'm startled and move back as Gus crumbles to the grass with his hands over his head, as he screams for his father to stop.

Then Mr. Staunch takes his free hand and grabs Gus's neck.

"I have warned you, boy, and you do not listen to me."

He swats the metal spoon against Gus's thick jaw, laying him out over the lawn. The sound makes me sick.

Then I hear another sound.

Gus is crying, his hands covering his face as he lies curled up like some baby on the grass.

I suddenly feel sorry for the big guy.

Everybody is now watching in silence, but nobody is doing a thing. Teachers and cops and mothers and fathers.

Nobody does a thing.

It's almost as if they've seen stuff like this before.

Or they're too afraid to do something against a man who will be this crazy.

Staunch looks around and raises a hand. "Sorry about that, folks. Don't let Gus here ruin our party."

And that's that.

It's like someone just had a heart attack and everybody around him is going on talking and eating and minding their own business.

One man can't have this kind of control.

Staunch comes over to me and shakes his head as he looks at my messy shirt and pants.

"I'm truly sorry about that, Chris."

And you thought your *father sucked.*

I just nod. Others around us have seemed to get a clue and are now talking again.

"Come on up to the house," he tells me. "I wanted to talk with you in private anyway. I guess that moron of a son of mine actually made that happen."

Gus is now sitting up, but he still has his face in his hands and is whimpering.

"You coming?" Staunch asks me. He's still holding the spoon.

I'd hate to see this man with an actual weapon in his hand.

I nod and follow him.

I'm sad, but not just for poor Gus.

I mean, it was his fault.

But no. I'm sad because I really wanted to have some of that brisket.

53. PETRIFIED

After changing into a set of clothes that belonged to Gus a few years ago—clothes that are still way too big on me—I walk out into the main room with the immense fireplace and the hanging animal heads. Staunch is on the sofa smoking a cigar, looking comfortable.

"Sit down, boy."

The way he says *boy* makes me nervous.

"Sorry I don't have anything else, but Gus is a porker. Has been since he was little and his mother gave him too many treats to eat. Stopped his crying, but didn't stop his belly from growing."

I want to ask about Mrs. Staunch but don't dare.

"Please, Chris, sit. Go on."

I sit on the leather couch across from him. There is a huge coffee table between us with a variety of things on it, including a big leather book of some sort.

"Yeah, that's what I want to show you," he says, putting his cigar in an ashtray and picking up the book. "It's a scrapbook of sorts. I want you to look through it."

It's a heavy book, so I leave it on the table and open the thick leather cover to see a page with handwriting that says *Kinner*.

My mom's maiden name.

The scrapbook turns out to be a photo album. The first page has a small black-and-white picture of a couple. Good-looking couple, dressed up. Maybe on their wedding day or honeymoon.

Samuel Tapson Kinner and Nellie Henrietta Solitaire, 1856.

There's that last name again.

Solitaire.

The same name that was on the gravestone in the church in the middle of nowhere.

So this is a picture of my great-great-great-however-great-grandparents?

"That is the first Kinner," Staunch says, biting on his cigar. It doesn't appear lit. "That's the first picture I've been able to locate. And I've tried hard."

"Kinner."

"Yep. Same spelling and everything."

For the next few minutes, I'm looking through the years at pictures of men and women. None of the names or faces mean anything to me, but I keep looking, acting like this interests me.

The only think I really want to do is get out of Gus's clothes.

I turn a page and see a kid with light-colored hair sitting on a beach.

"Hold it," Staunch says, then he turns the photo album, looking at me and then at the pic. "Yeah, sure, I can see it."

"See what?"

"The resemblance. A bit."

The boy in the picture doesn't look anything like me, but whatever.

"That, Chris, is your great-grandfather."

I see the words written in black ink.

Walter Robert Kinner, b. 1921.

"Chris—Walter is still alive."

"What?"

"Yes."

He takes the photo album from me before I can see any more. Then he stands.

"Listen—I have to mingle and do my thing. You be a good boy and stick around. Hear me?"

I nod.

"I want to introduce you to your great-grandpoppy."

"He's here?"

"No, not in this house. But yes, Chris. He's around. Just wait until the party is over. Stick around."

A short while later I'm finally managing to eat the brisket, but suddenly I'm not hungry anymore. All I can think about is having to stick around here until later, whenever that might be. I think about this supposed relative I'm going to meet.

Last time I met a cousin, that didn't work out too great for me.

But another part of me wonders why Staunch would lie to me.

If I'm "important" for whatever reason, maybe it's because I really do have a great-grandfather who is somehow connected to the history of the town.

But so what?

Maybe I'm going to get a huge inheritance of money and shrunken goat heads.

The corn bread tastes thick and the beans taste goopy.

I so don't have an appetite.

I make small talk with some people, including a few kids from school, but I wish that I had decided to bring someone. Mainly Lily.

I text her to see what she's doing.

It takes a while to get a reply.

SO YOU'RE NOT GOING TO LEAVE ME ALONE, HUH?

WHAT ARE YOU DOING? I ask her again.

SPENT THE DAY SHOPPING IN DOWNTOWN SOLITARY.

REALLY?

No she sends back. Then quickly adds WHAT ARE YOU DOING TONIGHT? CAN YOU SEE ME?

I'M AT A PARTY.

I WANT TO SEE YOU she types back. DOESN'T MATTER WHAT TIME.

It's good that she wants to see me. And everything in me wants to see her. It's just—I'm still annoyed at her. Still unsure about her history and her secrets and not sure I want to go there.

Who cares about her secrets? Don't ask, don't tell.

CHRIS?

YEAH.

I WANT YOU.

I look at the text and wonder if she left off "to see" in it.

I feel something stirring inside of me as I read those three words.

I REALIZE THAT NOW another text from Lily reads.

I'm not sure what to say.

I just know I'm definitely not hungry anymore for beef brisket.

YOU THERE?

YEAH I type with a nervous hand.

I'LL BE HERE she says. WHATEVER TIME WORKS. IF IT WORKS.

OKAY.

BUT CHRIS—I WANT TO SEE YOU BEFORE SCHOOL STARTS. TO GET THINGS STRAIGHTENED OUT.

How? I ask.

YOU'LL SEE.

I was already nervous about later tonight.

Now I'm petrified.

54. Cold and Soft and Dead

I follow his footsteps through the towering trees along a narrow path that I can't even see but trust is there below me. The flashlight Staunch carries doesn't even stay on the path, but rather bounces around the trees. The woods around here always feel dense, but tonight they feel suffocating.

"Come on," he says in a low voice. "Keep up with me."

We've been walking for ten or fifteen minutes. I keep thinking that he's taking me out to kill me and be done with me for good.

But he could have done that easily some time ago.

I wonder if something's going to jump out at me. Some figure in a dark robe, some figure holding a knife or a gun. Or maybe an animal will attack.

The night air is cooler and I feel it against my sweaty neck. I've got Gus's pants gripped by one hand to hold them up. It's seriously so dark.

They're all going to be there—everyone from the party, but now they'll be wearing sacrifice garb.

"Here—right up there," Staunch tells me.

This path leads upward from the Staunch mansion. For a moment I expect another little log cabin like the one behind my house, but I see something in the clearing that says this is different.

I can only make out an outline in the darkness, but it looks like a massive stone … castle?

But no, it's not a castle. And whatever it is, it's not all there.

It's half caved in, whatever this is.

The structure in front of me makes that run-down shack that I discovered, the one containing Marsh's belongings, look to be in great shape. There's not really even a structure to look at. It's more just some stone arches that were once part of a larger house long ago.

"This is the original house that Solitaire built after settling down here," Staunch says as he stops and shines his light over the walls.

It looks like something out of ancient Greece or Rome, something from the *Gladiator* movie.

"This house was supposed to be fireproof, though only the rock turned out to be so."

We walk through one of the arches, with Staunch now shining the light on the ground.

"Be careful—follow me closely," he says.

I do as I'm told and follow him to the center of the area around the stone arches. I can see a little better with the help of the moonlight above. The half-crumbled stone walls look like crouching beasts around us.

Staunch shines a light on my face, blinding me. I close my eyes.

"Stay here. He'll show up in a minute," Staunch says.

I open my mouth to protest.

You're right—you are *going to be sacrificed, but this time your great-granddaddy is going to do it.*

"Wait—what do you mean he'll show up in a minute? My great-grandfather?"

"Nothing's going to happen to you," Staunch says. "Here, take this."

He hands me the flashlight.

"But I—what if I—I'm not sure how—"

"Shut up and stay here," he says.

I watch him walk away, back underneath those tall arches and into the woods.

I'm left in the dark. In the middle of these hollowed-out ruins of some house that burned down.

Now it's where they burn stupid, silly seventeen-year-old boys who want answers to questions they should never have asked.

I feel the cool breeze and fold up my arms and wait. Clouds block the moon for a brief moment. The sounds of night circle around me. Somewhere nearby, an owl hoots.

It's a terrifying sound, to be honest.

Then I hear something directly in front of me.

As if it's been there since we walked in.

Something cold touches my arm. Something cold and soft and dead feeling.

Then the voice comes and I know.

I know exactly what it's going to sound like.

"Chrisssssss."

I jerk back and then lose my footing and nearly fall backward. I stand up and look around but can only see darkness.

Of course that's the voice of my wonderful long-lost great-grandfather.

"I'm right here," the old voice says to me.

Make that ancient voice.

I shiver and squint my eyes and I can make him out. A figure standing there hunched over.

"The time has come, my son."

I need to start breathing again so I can feel my body and so that body can start to make a sprint toward anywhere but here.

"You have a mission now," the grainy, creepy voice says to me.

I want to ask what, but I can't speak.

I want to turn on the flashlight, but I can't move my fingers.

I want to do anything, but I really can't.

I'm too scared.

"There is nothing to be afraid of in the dark. They will come to fear you like they fear me. You will go out and you will do big things. And these people and this town will be like this house we're standing in."

I exhale with a tremble and lean in to look at his face. I want to see this man or creature or whatever it is.

But he's gone.

It's gone.

I wave my hand out and then I turn on the flashlight, but I don't see anybody. No trace or sign.

Nothing.

Nothing but bubbling, raging fear deep inside of me.

55. Breathturn

I'm sitting on the steps leading up to our house, not wanting to go inside, not wanting to stay out here. I'm shivering, but I'm not cold. I'm breathing fast, but I'm standing still.

I'm not sure how long I've been outside.

I'm not sure of anything.

Then again, when have I been sure of *anything* since arriving here?

I don't hear the car engine, but I do hear the door shutting somewhere below in the dark. I just sit and wait. If they've come to get me—the bad guys or the shrinks or the priests—then so be it. Let them.

But instead I see an angel walking up my driveway.

She wears shorts and a tank top and she holds her arms as if she's cold. When she reaches the edge of where I'm sitting, she just stares at me.

If I could have any superpower, it would be to read the minds of girls. Then and only then I'd be indestructible.

She walks closer to me and reaches out to take my hands.

Suddenly I'm not thinking of the house up the road. Or the mother up the stairs. Or great freaking gramps hovering around somewhere. Or anything else except these soft hands touching mine, then touching my cheeks, then holding my head gently and moving it toward hers.

Lily doesn't say anything as she leans over and kisses me.

I kiss her back and try to make up for the lost kisses I've wanted and dreamed about. To make up for the lost time I've spent avoiding her for some reason I couldn't honestly tell her.

As I reach out in hungry teenage desperation, Lily moves away for a moment and then whispers to me.

"Chris—let's take it slow."

I nod, but I don't want to wait on anything anymore, including this.

"Just—give it time," she says. "Not now, not tonight."

But then she kisses me as if to make a promise.

I wish I could make the kiss last the night.

"I don't want to leave you tonight," Lily tells me, looking down at me in a way that I haven't seen before.

Not trying to look glamorous or sexy or seductive. But looking just like—like a girl who's a bit lost and even more confused.

"I thought—"

"Just because I said I want to take it slow doesn't mean I don't want to stay with you."

I'm not sure how to answer this because—well, this hasn't really happened before.

"Can I sit next to you?" she asks.

And I feel like a moron, apologizing and then moving over so she can fit next to me on the step. I see her shiver, and I put my arm around her. Lily leans into me and gets comfortable.

"Yeah, just like that," she says. "Is this okay?"

I nod, suddenly feeling like—like somebody. Like a man. Like a protector.

"I want to just stay like this for a long time," Lily says softly.

"Me too."

So we do.

56. A Different Story Again

It's not something we plan, but then again, it's the only way I've wanted Lily to walk into Harrington High on her first official day.

I remember just how lonely I felt walking through those doors and into those hallways. Granted, Lily's the sort of girl who should never, ever feel lonely, simply because so many guys are going to want to talk to her. But after picking her up on my bike and driving her to school, we enter the building holding hands like those lovesick couples who seem attached at the hip. It's actually Lily's idea, taking my hand and laughing and then proceeding to walk in with me.

It's a great feeling. Knowing that there's someone there beside me to take the blow of having to come back here for a whole other year.

The guys are all looking at us. So are the girls. Basically, everybody is interested in the new girl.

Before reaching my locker, a locker that's in a new place this year, I spot someone that I've somehow managed to forget about.

Kelsey smiles at first, but then sees Lily by my side.

Then Lily says she has to go. And she gives me a nice little peck on my cheek.

Someone bumps into Kelsey, but she doesn't look around. She just keeps staring at me.

I want to say hello and say something—ask how her summer's gone—but she's a bit too far away. And by the time I reach into my locker and put my bag and books away, she's gone.

That dance at prom with her seems like years ago.

That guy dancing with her seems long gone.

I discover that Harris is in three of my classes, which is great. I've seen Brick several times—the first time getting a nice bear hug from him. I've even seen Roger and Shawn and said hello.

Tiny steps. Or baby steps, they say.

This year will be endurable.

Right?

But then midway through the day, I find something that seems like—well, that seems like a typical Harrington High experience.

I roll my eyes and sigh.

It's an envelope

of course

that opens up to a letter

naturally

that's handwritten and mysterious

would it be anything else

and that's signed at the bottom by Poe.

I stop and look at the name. Yes, it's from Poe. I recognize her handwriting.

You can delete emails but you're going to have to physically throw this sucker away.

My heart is beating faster and I look around to see if Poe is anywhere near. Not because of Lily—no, it's because—there's a hope that she's around because—I don't know. I'd just like to know she's around.

I read the letter immediately. No more of this secret, spy-like behavior. I'm done with that.

CHRIS!!??

WHERE ARE YOU AND WHAT ARE YOU DOING?

I SENT THIS TO THE ONLY PERSON I COULD THINK OF WHO I KNOW HAS YOUR BACK AND USED TO HAVE MINE. HINT, IT'S NOT A SHE. AND BOY DOES HE LOVE HIS M&MS.

I'VE TRIED SEVERAL TIMES TO EMAIL YOU THIS SUMMER. I TRIED CALLING A COUPLE OF TIMES BUT THEN GAVE UP.

WHAT IS HAPPENING WITH YOU? ARE YOU OKAY?

I DID SOMETHING STUPID THIS SUMMER. I ACTUALLY SPOKE TO SOMEONE WHO IS AFFILIATED WITH THE FBI. I DIDN'T TELL HER EVERYTHING. OR ANYTHING, ACTUALLY. I JUST SORTA TESTED THE WATERS. BUT IN THE FOLLOWING WEEK, I SWEAR SOMEONE STARTED TO FOLLOW ME. I'M PARANOID. DAD HAD SOMETHING BAD HAPPEN AT WORK, BUT MAYBE IT WAS JUST COINCIDENCE—I DON'T KNOW.

I HAVEN'T GIVEN UP,. BUT I JUST—I HAVE NO IDEA WHAT'S HAPPENING WITH YOU. ARE YOU IN TROUBLE? PLEASE—JUST CONTACT ME SOMEHOW. JUST TO LET ME KNOW YOU'RE OKAY.

POE

The letter makes me angry. Not because of what Poe said, but because I've ignored her for so long.

Some friend you've been, huh?

I feel guilty.

You can try to bury the past but it will never go away.

I'm heading to class when I see Kelsey again. She looks more tanned than I remember her being. And where are her glasses?

She spots me and looks away, brushing her hair and quickly moving with the group she's with. I'm not about to chase her down. I don't have art this year, and so far she's not been in any of my classes.

You're already feeling bad about Poe, don't go feeling bad for Kelsey too.

I really don't want to feel bad. I want to be a new person and let things go. I'm older—I'm *seventeen.* A lot has happened that neither of the girls knows about.

Lily spots me and comes by and gives me a hug.

Things are different now. The story has changed.

I really want to believe that.

But somehow, I don't think I can.

57. Stuck and Hidden Somewhere

"When'd you get in last night?"

I'm trying to come down on Mom. Her coming and going—or more like going and staying gone—is fine by me. She stays out of my business, and I don't have to be reminded of hers. But I'm just curious on the first Saturday after an uneventful first week at school.

"Why so curious?"

She's sipping a cup of coffee and isn't looking hungover, so I figure it's safe to ask.

"Just wondering."

"Late."

I see her give me a courtesy smile that makes me know that something is up. The way she's been gone more often, and getting dressed up more than usual, and trying to look young and pretty—

Bet there's some guy.

I'm not about to ask, however. I'll save that question for when I want her to stop asking me questions.

Such a nice young son, Chris.

I check my phone for texts or emails but don't have anything. As my thumb's getting a workout, I spot my mom watching me.

"Where'd you get the phone?"

Oops.

"I've had it for a while," I say without having to lie.

"But where'd you get it? How'd you have money to buy that?"

"I had some money leftover from my job at the Crag's Inn. And they were having a great deal through school."

Yeah, that one was a lie.

"I haven't seen any bills coming in for you."

I shrug. "I get a trial run. There are a lot of restrictions on it."

"I'm not paying a hundred bucks every month for you to have an iPhone."

You don't have to, Mommy Dearest.

"Don't worry."

She brings up the subject of work, and I try and get out of that one. I do want a job, but so far I've managed to get by without one. Lily pays for a lot, which I don't mind. She keeps reminding me that they just got a huge inheritance after her grandmother passed away, and she *wants* to spend money. How can I say no?

I'm going to take a shower, but before I head upstairs Mom asks a question that surprises me.

"By the way, Chris—you didn't happen to talk to your father anytime recently, did you?"

Where's that coming from?

"Yeah—we had dinner last night. He took me to a ball game afterward. Oh, and later we're going to throw a football outside."

"Stop it," she says.

"I haven't talked to him in ages."

"You're sure?"

"Why? Have you?" I ask her.

"No. It's just—I want to make sure you'd tell me if he called."

"Why wouldn't I?"

She has a look of heavy, deep thought, and I don't want to get into it, especially if it has something to do with Dad.

"Just make sure you let me know if he ever calls you."

"Yeah, sure," I say.

There are many mysteries even in this tiny, cramped cabin of ours. It's no wonder that I want to get out of it every chance I get.

I'm resting on my bike and cursing, looking at a dead end.

There are many things I've given up on, or more like tried to forget about. But this is not one of them. I can tell Mom or the rest of the world including Lily that I'm just riding around, but I've actually been looking for the way to the small inn on the top of the mountain. The place where I met Iris and the place where I learned about the history of Crag's Inn.

I've seen a lot of weird things happen around here. I've been a part of some of them, stuff I can't even explain. Like getting shot and then suddenly feeling fine. Or stabbing Marsh and then seeing him walking around fine and dandy. But a missing *road*? That's even harder to accept. It has to be that I've just gotten turned around.

This place is a light in the darkness, Chris.

Iris's words seem to drift through the air out of the woods and the cut-off road I'm on.

A space in between. That's what the Crag's Inn is, Chris. It's always been in one of the spaces in between.

I think of those words and believe them more than ever. Whatever she meant, the inn certainly seems stuck and hidden somewhere. It's definitely a space in between.

No—it's in *a space in between.*

Ever since stabbing Marsh and then deciding that I can't go on searching and wondering and trying to figure things out, everything has been different.

There have been no strange animal sightings.

I haven't been able to locate the Crag's Inn.

And there haven't been any conversations with Jocelyn in an airport or a plane.

Are these things related?

I recall Iris saying something else, something about a passage in the Bible. Daniel something.

The tenth chapter of Daniel.

I never did take her advice. Why should I?

But Iris told me once to read it and think about her place and the spaces in between.

I decide to check it out. But first I have to find a Bible. I know we don't have one in our house.

Last one we had got chucked over the falls.

58. The Boy Who Cried Wells

I'm in the library and have read Daniel chapter 10 several times through (after taking just as long to look it up) and I still don't understand anything. Something about Daniel having visions and a man looking like dazzling light with eyes like torches. Daniel's terrified, seeing the guy, and I guess I would be too. For some weird reason I picture one of those guys from Blue Man Group, which I saw once with Mom and Dad. Instead of blue, he's gold, but still looking weird like that.

Probably not a good sign, when reading the Bible makes me think of Blue Man Group.

I put the book back in the reference section where I found it and leave the library. For a moment I think of stopping in and seeing

Mom, and maybe getting a free lunch, but I decide against it. I think of dropping in on Lily as well, but remember how great that went last time I tried it. I'm supposed to pick her up later for a party (which she was, no surprise, invited to).

I'm about to get on my bike when I hear it. A muffled sound, like a strange groaning. Like someone in pain.

I look toward the street but don't see anybody.

Hey, look, it's the mountain man with his big dog!

But nope, thankfully I don't see him.

The groaning is coming from the alley between the library and the building beside it. It's narrow, and light shows that you can get through the buildings to the other side by walking through.

In the middle of the pavement is a figure writhing in pain.

I rush to the person, a dark-haired guy clutching his hands to his face and making a loud, droning "ohhhhhhh" sound.

I stop a few feet away from him. Just to be safe. Just to be careful.

"Hey—are you okay? Hello?"

I see stubble on the man's face as he peels his hands away.

I suddenly back up and almost trip over my own feet.

The man in the alley is missing his nose and a nice portion of his upper face. I let out a gasp and swallow and look to make sure I'm seeing the right thing.

The nose—where the nose used to be—is a bloody mess, and the upper part of his face—his cheek and his ear—looks like a bomb ripped it off. It's dark red and bloody and pulsating.

Run get out of here get away.

The man opens his mouth wider, and I see blood dripping down its side.

Yeah, I run.

I bolt out of that alley and run down the sidewalk toward the police station.

This time they're gonna do their job.

This time they're gonna get off their butts and do something to help someone out.

I open the door and *so* hope that Sheriff Wells is there and yes.

Thankfully he's there, standing by a desk and holding some kind of file.

I blurt out something that probably doesn't make much sense, and he slows me down. I see Kevin Ross sitting at a desk, but I ignore him.

"Chris, what's wrong—calm down."

"You have to come—now—right now—someone's dying in the middle of the alley."

I go back outside and the sheriff follows me, along with Ross.

It's only been a couple minutes. That's all. That's not long enough for someone to come and help the bleeding, dying man out of the alleyway.

And yet …

The alley is empty.

I go toward where I had seen him

and I did see him

to try and see if there are blood spots or anything.

But no.

"Chris?"

I shake my head, looking at the walls on either side, walking to the end of the alley and then back.

"What did you see?"

I close my eyes.

Here we go again.

I open them again and try to say something, but I can't. I don't know what to say.

"If this kid thinks he can keep wastin' our time with these—"

"Ross, shut it," Wells says. "Go on back to the station."

Ross says a few nice curse words in my direction, and Wells tells him again to go. This time he obeys.

"What did you see?"

I shake my head. "I don't know."

"Yeah, you do."

"I thought—I thought I saw a man—older—your age—lying in the alley bleeding to death."

"Bleeding how?"

"His—he was moaning, and I heard him." I shake my head again and look at the sheriff. "I know—I don't blame you for not believing me."

"I'm not sayin' I don't believe you."

"Yeah, well there's nothing here."

"I've made that mistake before," he says. "I don't like repeating it."

For a few minutes he checks out the alley and the surrounding buildings. Then he walks me back to my motorcycle. I already know the question is going to come before he utters it.

"Is everything okay, Chris?"

"Yeah—yes."

"Are you sure?"

I wonder if this man ever sits around a table laughing and playing board games and telling jokes with his family or friends. Maybe he does, but I've only ever seen him looking stern and grim. His hair and goatee look more thick and gray than usual.

"I saw something."

"Tell me, Chris—did this man look like he got beaten up?"

"No."

"No?"

"He looked—it was worse than that. A lot worse."

Sheriff Wells nods. "Listen—I'll check around the town for anything strange. You go on home."

"Okay."

"And Chris—don't tell anybody else what you saw. Just—keep it between us."

I nod.

Not that anybody would believe me anyway.

59. Madly Crazy

I think Lily is just trying to look hot to get looks from everybody at the party and laugh about it. Which is fine by me because she's by my side the entire time and doesn't seem to mind being there. I've become one of those guys I can't stand, the one always hovering next to his "lady," the one looking at others looking at his girl. The "stupid guy with the hot girl."

Part of me doesn't even know yet if we're together. I mean, we are—she likes me, and I want to run off to Mexico with her. So yeah, that's together, right?

I guess I don't need a ring or anything.

The party is at a house in Hendersonville. I guess this guy used to go to Harrington and then got kicked out. Makes me wonder what he did. His parents moved to Hendersonville, and the big question is whether or not he ever finished high school.

Doesn't matter, because half the students at this party are from Harrington. The drinking isn't as obvious as the last party I went to, but I can still tell that kids are drinking or doing other stuff. I'm fine just being here with Lily. That's enough for me.

I'm having a great time laughing and not thinking about anything. No distant ancient relative with a lisp is anywhere in sight. Nor is a pastor or a near-dead person on the street.

Just some teenagers and some college-aged kids. That's all.

Just people like the tall, leggy blonde walking around in a short skirt.

Wait a minute.

That's not Lily I'm talking about.

No—Lily's wearing jeans with a pretty revealing top.

No—this is—

Leaving me speechless.

"Hello, Chris," Kelsey says.

Or the woman who possessed that cute girl I got to know in art class.

"How's it going?" she asks.

Wonderful, come to think of it.

"Good," I manage to get out.

"Good," she says.

Her hair seems a little more—messy perhaps? No glasses, the outfit, the attitude, that smile, and something else.

"You—you don't have your braces?"

She keeps smiling, proud of her teeth that have finally been set free. "I know. About time."

"You're *so* not going to believe this," Lily says, interrupting us and grabbing my arm before she sees Kelsey. "Oh, hi, sorry."

"No, it's fine."

The formerly confident face suddenly breaks out in a full-on blush.

Just like something I'd do.

And Kelsey seems to know it, too, because she puts a hand up by her cheek to shield it. But her whole face is red.

"Well, aren't you a cutie," Lily says, making me smile. "What's your name?"

"Kelsey. I go to Harrington. We're in English."

"Yeah! That's right. I thought I'd seen you. I love the dress. Where'd you get it?"

It's great to watch this, because Lily isn't being nice just to be nice. They start talking like girls, and I zone out.

Everybody is watching us.

That's right, keep looking. I'd be looking too, but nope, I'm right here, that's right. These are my ladies and

"Hello, space boy, come back home," Lily says.

"What?"

"Kelsey said you guys went to prom last year."

I nod, wondering where I'd gone and how they had this conversation while I was in my happy place. "Yeah."

I'm surprised Kelsey said this since we didn't technically go with each other.

Are you?

"You two make a cute couple," Lily says.

We do?

As if to make sure that Lily's point isn't thought about anymore, Kelsey looks across the room and waves. "Excuse me—I gotta go."

"Who's that?" Lily says.

"Todd," Kelsey says. "He goes to UNC-Asheville."

"Older boy. Good for you."

Kelsey leaves, and Lily stands there watching her. "You didn't tell me about her."

"What's there to tell?"

Lily rolls her eyes.

"What?"

"I've seen her this week."

"Yeah?" I ask.

"She didn't look like that."

"Well, she's got a hot date."

Lily looks over at Kelsey and Todd and then nods as if unconvinced.

"What?" I say.

"I don't think she wore that for Todd. Who, by the way, doesn't even look like he's into chicks."

"So then who'd she wear it for?"

Lily smiles, then gently touches my cheek. "See—that is why I'm falling madly crazy in love with you."

She laughs and then makes me come with her to talk to some other kids.

I don't believe that she's "falling madly crazy in love" with me, but still.

I mean—she could, right?

It's not the craziest thought, is it?

This whole place is full of crazy, so why can't I be a part of that craziness?

60. Losing My Mind

The bathroom downstairs has a long line, and Lily suggests I go upstairs, saying she asked the kid who's hosting and he said why not. I tell her that he might say something different if I asked him, and Lily tells me he can get over it.

I love her fire. I guess looks can do that, give you an inner strength.

Yeah, but she was born strong, and looks didn't have anything to do with it.

I head up the stairs and get to the top and suddenly feel something.

A cold. A cold like I just stepped into a walk-in cooler.

This isn't good.

Any time the temperature just changes—that's not good. That's like the couple in the woods, about ready to go skinny-dipping, hearing something. That can't ever be good. That's the sign—you *know* it's a sign—to bail.

But I have to go to the bathroom, so I try and not think about how cold it became. Maybe the air is on up here.

I open the first door I come to, thinking it's the bathroom.

But it's a bedroom. A kid's bedroom, with a lot of pink all around. I'm guessing a girl's bedroom.

I hear someone crying.

Leave now Chris just leave.

It's a soft whimpering sound.

The air is still cold. I can tell my arms have bumps all over them from the temperature change. A small lamp on a dresser is lit, but I can't see anybody.

"Hello?"

The crying continues.

The sound is coming from a closet behind two folding doors.

I open them up and see a little girl hiding there, her arms clutching a big bear, her face buried in its soft white fur.

"Hey—what's wrong—are you okay?"

Then the girl looks up at me and I don't actually believe what I'm seeing.

Her face is all bruised and swollen. Not bloody, but rather literally black and blue.

I back up in fright.

One of her eyes is so swollen it can barely see me. Her lips are cracked and cut up. Her jaw seems swollen as well.

She has to be—I don't know—five or six years old.

I reach out to touch her

'cause maybe deep down I don't believe what I'm seeing it's just like that guy in the alleyway

but as I do she jerks back in terror and howls in pain, as if I'm doing something to her.

"No, no—it's okay. Really. I'm not going to hurt you."

But she buries her smashed-up little face back in her teddy bear and continues to cry.

I feel sick to my stomach, wondering who could have done something like this to her. I leave her in the closet and hurry away to find someone, anyone, to help this poor girl out.

I'm downstairs and then I spot Lily.

I think of what happened at the police station.

"What's wrong?" she says.

I'm not sure what to tell her.

Don't Chris don't tell her.

"What's going on?" she asks.

"Can you do me a favor?"

"Yeah, what?"

I ask her to go to the first bedroom at the top of the stairs and tell me what she sees. Surely she will find the little girl and freak out and find the owners of the house.

Lily appears curious, but she does what I ask. Minutes later she comes back down.

Her expression tells me that she didn't find any little girl crying.

"So?" Lily asks.

"What was in there?"

"Just a bunch of boxes. A desk that's not being used. Why—what'd you see in there?"

My head is hurting, and I have no desire to stick around.

"Chris?" Lily asks.

"Would you mind if we took off?"

"Why? What's going on?"

"You can stay if you want."

She just gives me a look that makes me feel stupid.

"What?"

"Yeah, I want to stay here because this party is so rocking," she says.

"I'm just saying."

"What's wrong with you?"

"Nothing."

"What did you see upstairs?"

"Nothing."

She's not buying it, but she doesn't press me.

"Okay, fine. Come on."

I follow her out. But before I leave, I spot Kelsey one final time. She looks over at me and gives me a friendly smile. I haven't seen it in a long time. No matter how adult and different she might look, she still has that sweet and friendly face.

It's quite the opposite of the sweet but beat-up face I saw upstairs in the closet.

And even though I'm not going to tell Lily this, I *know* I saw it. I'm not losing my mind.

If I lost my mind I did so months ago.

61. The Sex Chapter

I don't want to just drop her off and go back home.

No way.

I feel Lily holding on to me as I ride my bike, believing that this machine is maybe the best thing to have ever happened to me. I refuse to let her just go away into the night. I want to stay with her. I want to do things other kids our age are doing. I want to—finally—just give in and get it over with so I don't have to be thinking about it all the time.

But when I get to the familiar bed-and-breakfast where Lily stays, I see a man waiting by a car. She curses. It seems like he's waiting for her.

"What?"

"Nothing—I need to go."

"No."

She gets off the bike and stands, brushing back her hair. "Yes, Chris."

"I don't want to leave you."

"Well, you're going to have to."

"Who is that guy?"

"Nobody."

But he definitely looks like somebody. Everything about her has changed.

"I'll go ask him myself," I say.

"Chris—that's my father."

I can barely make out the guy—he's about my height, pretty solid build, still has his hair, which looks dark. The guy doesn't seem *that* old.

"Please, Chris."

I'm so tired of dropping her off and letting her go. So tired of seeing Lily and smelling Lily and then sending Lily home.

Half of me wants to go up to the man and introduce myself.

Hi, my name is Chris, and I want to marry your daughter.

But I realize that marriage isn't the thing weighing on my mind right now.

I'm sorry, but my name is Chris and I just want your daughter.

Lily leans over and kisses me on the cheek. "Thank you, Chris."

"Are you going to be okay?"

She glances at her father, who's still just resting against the car. "No. But that's okay."

"I can wait."

"No. I'll—I'll contact you later."

Soon I'm back on the road, driving in darkness, the beam of light looking as lonely as I feel.

No, it's not lonely. It's hungry.

When I get home—

Do I even need to say it?

Repeat track "Home Alone" over and over again. It's a long track on the album *Cabin Fever.*

I check the fridge but don't see anything worth eating. I turn on the TV but don't see anything worth watching. I keep checking my phone, even though it's only been fifteen minutes—now twenty—now thirty—since I saw Lily.

I go upstairs feeling restless, just like always.

I really had some strange feeling that it might happen tonight.

And that's weird because it's not like I've ever done it. Not officially, technically, all that. Trish and I were a thing back in Illinois, going out then not going out, changing status on Facebook (well, she changed hers—I think it's stupid even having a status to change). And the subject came up, but Trish was scared. She said she felt like it wasn't right to do before marriage, and I remember laughing, wondering who even said stuff like that. Then she said most of all she was scared.

We got close. But that was it.

Then I moved.

Then came this dark-haired beauty named Jocelyn, and there was that one time—but that was different. Everything was different with Jocelyn.

Everything's been different since coming to this hole in the world called Solitary.

I sigh, because I don't want to think of Jocelyn. I don't want to wonder if she's up there in the clouds watching me wanting to have sex with Lily. I'm seventeen, eighteen soon enough, and I can't really say I'm saving myself for marriage. Mom sure would like me to and Dad has told me that's the right thing to do.

But they're not here.

Then again, nobody else is here either.

I wait to hear from Lily.

And I keep waiting.

And I keep waiting.

62. The Dream Is Never the Same

I can see her in the distance.

She's not coming to me like she used to before I told her once and for all to leave me and my dreams alone.

Yet I can still see Jocelyn sitting on the deck behind her house. Lounging in the sun. She's wearing sunglasses, so I don't know if she sees me, but I can see her.

I look up and see dark skies above and wonder how she's getting sun, but then I realize that she's miles away. I look down and see the ground drop, as if I'm standing at the edge of the Grand Canyon. But this is deeper and wider.

I call out to her, but she doesn't hear me. I keep trying, but she doesn't even know I'm here.

"Chris?" a voice calls from behind.

I look behind me and see an old cabin. It looks like a haunted house, worse than the abandoned place Marsh used as his secret hiding place. At one of the windows is a face that I first recognize as Lily. But I look again and see that it's not Lily but some monster with snakes on her head and holes for her eyes.

"Time for din-din, my love," she says, opening her mouth and letting out a snake that was lodged back down there.

I'm feeling a bit woozy now.

"This is what you always wanted, what you always dreamed about. Come back in so we can make some babies."

Then she starts to scream, and that's when I wake up.

I might have spent the next few moments thinking about how big of a loser I am to be dreaming weird and wacky dreams like that one, but I hear a sound that makes me get out of bed.

It's the sound of an engine running.

I go downstairs and see that it's around two in the morning. No Mom is to be found.

Well, not until I look outside and see her car running, lights still on.

I go outside and feel the cool breeze against my bare legs and arms. When I get to the driveway, I don't see anybody in the car.

Then I open the door, and Mom spills out of it. I mean literally spills out onto the driveway.

I wonder what's happening until I see a big wad of something white sticking out of the tailpipe.

"Mom!"

As I reach down to lift her up, I really honestly believe that my mom is dead.

63. Coming Back Again

Cold harsh light.

Men and women, doctors and nurses, strangers busy at the hospital, asking for answers that I don't know about insurance and coverage and physicians, asking what happened.

Empty hall.

A buzzing coming from somewhere.

Someone giving me a cup of coffee. Drinking it and forcing myself to finish it.

Waiting.

More questions.

Waiting longer.

Drifting off.

Wondering. About calling someone. Dad, of course. Dad certainly. Dad finally.

Denying.

Rejecting.

Fighting.

Refusing.

Closing my eyes. Drifting further.

"Oh, Chris."

Mom utters this the moment I walk into the small room and come alongside the bed. Her face crinkles up, and she begins to cry. But it's not just that. It's the look on her face. It's so sad. So sad, and probably ashamed.

I want to ask her things, but instead I just hug her.

She's so skinny. I didn't realize how bare-bones she really is.

There's a lot you haven't noticed.

She's apologizing to me, and I feel tears in my eyes and I let the hug linger so I can get back control.

But everything in me knows that some of this—not all, and maybe not even half, but at least some of it—is my fault.

I've been the only one around and have been too blind to notice what's happening.

I move away from her and stand looking down. I wipe the tears out of my eyes.

"I don't know what happened, Chris, I really don't."

I nod.

"I didn't—I was just out of my mind last night. Please—just sit for a minute."

I take a seat in the armchair next to the bed. She's hooked up to an IV and has a few other things connected to her. The people talking to me earlier said she's going to be fine. But they said that in a cautionary way, as if she'll be fine *this time.*

"I haven't told you everything," Mom says.

Really? Well, join the crowd.

"There was someone I met at work. I—I mentioned him once to you."

"Mike?"

She looks surprised that I remember.

"You were aiming a shotgun at me the day you mentioned him," I say. "So yeah, the name stuck."

"He broke things off—whatever they were."

I might be young and stupid at times, but if a relationship causes me to get out the shotgun, something tells me that it's probably not going to work out.

"Did you call Dad?"

"No."

"I'm sorry—I was just wondering."

"No. I haven't spoken to him and don't plan to."

She looks away for a moment. "Turning forty was hard, Chris. Harder than I thought it would be. And Mike—he was a diversion. He allowed me to not think about everything I wanted that suddenly seemed gone. He made me feel …"

Those tears are in her eyes again. Then a weak voice says very softly, ". . . young again."

That's all she says about Mike.

I've got another name to add to the Push Off a Cliff list.

I sit there for a while, not saying anything. It's ironic how she so desperately wants to feel young again, while I can't wait to be old.

"Chris—things are going to get better."

She's said this before.

"No—I know—I know what you're thinking. This time I'm going to get help. I have to. I just—there are some places I can check in to."

I just nod.

"I mean it, Chris. This—*this*—is not me. This is not your mother."

I nod again.

She reaches over and grabs my wrist. "Stop just nodding. Chris—I'm sorry. And I mean it. I haven't been around for quite some time. I just need help coming back again."

64. A Little More Trouble

I see the two of them walking down a dirt road, holding hands. Looking at each other and laughing. They're younger and happier. They're my parents. And they still love each other.

They look back at me and then wait.

"Come on."

They wave me on, and I start running up the hill.

There is a spot in between them where I belong.

I keep running, and running, and running.

But I can't get to them.

And soon they just turn their backs and keep walking.

Except they start walking in opposite directions, making me scream out to them to turn back around and wait a minute and just hold on …

I'm nudged in the seat and look up to see Lily standing there. I'm in the hospital room in Asheville where I rode in the ambulance with my mom. She's still in bed sleeping, though it looks like there's sunlight behind the closed blinds.

"Are you okay?" Lily whispers.

"Yeah." I stand up and motion to the door.

We walk down the hall and out to the main waiting area. Lots of doctors and nurses are walking around this morning. I had texted Lily last night and told her what happened in a nutshell. I tell her everything again but don't have much more to add.

"She's fine?"

"I guess," I say. Which is true because I'm not sure how to define "fine."

I don't think Mom is fine or will be for some time.

"Can we just go?"

"Go where?" Lily asks.

"I don't know. Anywhere. I just want you to take me somewhere."

We're standing on the front lawn of the massive Biltmore Mansion, and I seriously am feeling like I've entered another universe.

Maybe that's Lily's whole point in bringing me here.

"Are we going inside?"

She shakes her head. "Only if you want to."

We actually waited until nine o'clock to pay and drive onto the massive estate. We're walking over toward the place called the Italian Gardens, where pools and lawns are connected and hidden by walls of stone and shrubs. As we walk, Lily takes my hand.

"Imagine that this place is ours."

All I can do is laugh.

"No, seriously. Come on."

"Okay," I say.

"We've been married a year. This is our estate."

"Really?"

I look at her, her long hair pulled back in a ponytail this

morning, her workout pants and shirt still making her look incredible.

"What?" Lily asks.

"Well, if we were married—"

"Stop. Do guys all have a one-track mind?"

"Well, I'm just being honest."

She stops for a minute. "And that's all I am to you, huh? Some pretty face with long legs?"

"I never said that."

"What do you like about me—about *me*—the me part that's below the surface?"

"I like how you take control."

She seems to like my quick answer. "Okay."

"And I like how you're confident in, well, pretty much everything."

"Not always."

"A lot more than I am."

"You should be confident, Chris. Really. You have everything going for you."

"Oh, yeah, of course. I mean, my family life is crazy and just getting crazier. But sure—I have everything going for me."

"I mean you. Nobody else but you."

We find a bench to sit on in front of a pond. Lily sits toward me with one leg folded into the other.

"I really mean that, Chris. You know—I've met some real losers in my life. I've dated some too. You're different. You really are."

"Why? Different can be bad."

"You're just—you're a gentle soul."

This sounds ridiculous. “Oh, okay.”

“I’m serious.”

“Look—I’m not always gentle. I can be rough.”

Lily looks at me and shakes her head. “Oh, *okay*,” she repeats.

“I’m serious, too.”

“Maybe I need something gentle in my life. Hmm? What do you think about that?”

She places a finger over my hand and rubs the tiny hairs on it. Then she turns my hand over and does the same on my lines.

“Going to read my future?” I ask.

“Yes.”

“Okay—go ahead. What do you see?”

“Hmm—I see you happy. Yes, I see Chris Buckley finally happy. Smiling in the sun—laughing even.”

I think of that snapshot that I found—that I was given—the one that faded.

It’s just a coincidence that’s all.

“What’d I say?”

“Nothing. Keep going.”

“I see love in your future. A love that surprises you.”

“Really?” I smile. “So do you see yourself there?”

“No.”

I fold up my hand. “Ouch.”

“Those two things don’t go together.”

“What don’t?”

“Happiness and me.”

“I’m happy right now.”

“I only bring temporary happiness, Chris. That’s all. And for now, for you—that's okay. But you need more. You *definitely* need more than I can bring."

"Stop—what—why are you saying that?"

"I'm just being honest."

I shake my head and take her hand. "Lily, you make me very happy."

"You need someone—you need someone like that cute blonde at the party. What's her name?"

"Kelsey."

"Yes, Kelsey. I can see her in your future."

"I'm not interested in Kelsey," I say. "I'm interested in you."

"I know. And sometimes—that's just not the best thing, Chris."

I look at her and have no idea what she's talking about. "I can't think of anything better."

She smiles and then looks away. I want to ask what she's thinking, but I don't. I don't because it looks serious and sad and I don't want any of that, not this morning.

"Come on—let's check out the grounds," Lily says, standing and pulling me up too.

"I liked sitting there with you."

"I know," she says with a nod. "I was liking it too. And that—that could be trouble."

"So what? A little more trouble in my world won't matter. I'd like *that* kind of trouble."

She looks at me for a moment as if she's considering something, as if she's actually contemplating my words. But then she just starts walking.

Naturally, I follow.

65. Lies

I'm walking into the main entrance of the hospital in Asheville to take Mom back home. I drove her car, figuring she wouldn't mind. She just tried killing herself during a drunken blackout, so I don't think she's gonna come down on me and my lack of a license.

Before I can head down the hallway, I feel a hand clamp against my arm. I jerk around to see Pastor Marsh.

"Wait just a minute, Chris."

Normally I might ask him what he's doing here, but I don't. I'm sure he knows, just like all the others who are supposed to know.

And strangely, I'm used to this now.

"Can we talk?"

I nod, and he leads me over to a sitting area.

"I spoke with your mother today."

Again, this should surprise me but doesn't.

I mean—hey—he *is* a pastor, right?

"She has agreed to enter a rehabilitation program that I told her about."

That can't be good.

"It's a place here in Asheville. I told her that the church can pay for it, too. I know there's the issue of not having health insurance."

"Yeah, well—"

"It's taken care of."

I don't know how or why, but I just shake my head.

"Now, Chris—listen to me." The pastor looks around, and then moves in his seat to get closer to me so he can whisper. "Do not tell your father about what happened. Understand?"

"Yes."

"Your mother is going to think that she needs to tell your father. Because—since she has to go away for a while—who are you going to stay with? But listen to me—I know—I can see it on your face. You don't need your father. So convince your mother you've talked to him and set up all the details. Make sure that your mother doesn't talk to him in person."

"But how—"

"She is very ashamed of what has happened," Marsh says. "She doesn't want to talk to your father if she doesn't have to. But convince her. Understand?"

I nod. He looks around again, which is strange because he's usually not like this.

We're not in Solitary. That's why.

Marsh adjusts his glasses and returns his gaze toward me. "How are you doing?"

"Fine."

"Have you been experiencing anything strange lately?"

I think of the body in the alley and the little girl in the closet at the party. I just shake my head, only to get a chuckle from Marsh.

"Chris—you really are a bad liar."

"Shouldn't that be a good thing, at least in your world?"

"The things you're starting to see—don't let them frighten you."

"What are you talking about?"

"You know what you're seeing. The thing is—why are you seeing them? Right?"

"Seeing what?" I ask him.

I want to know how he knows. Or if he knows what I'm seeing.

"Horrific visions. Stuff from nightmares. Nightmares blending into reality. Am I right?"

I'm too tired to even try and lie. "Yes."

"It's all part of the process. Just—try not to freak out."

"Oh, okay, sure," I say.

"In time you will understand, Chris. I grew to understand myself. But I'm not like you. Not even a bit."

There he goes again. I want to say something like *I left my Superman cape at home* or *The Batmobile is underground,* but Marsh still freaks me out a bit. I don't like the guy. But the fact that he knows what I want to know—that makes me bite my tongue and not say anything.

"There are big plans in the works—huge plans. The countdown is already underway. And in time, before next summer, you will know everything. But for now—convince your mother. Try your very best to make up a story. Okay?"

We've been home for an hour when I take Marsh's advice.

"I called Dad and told him."

It's not just a little lie. It's a doozy. But considering everything—I don't feel bad. I'm doing it as much for Mom as for myself. I'm saving her embarrassment (is that why they call it saving face?) and I'm saving me the misery of having to deal with my father. I don't know what is going on with him, but I do know that he'd come down to pray over Mom's wretched soul and then go about trying to save mine.

"You told him what?"

"Everything."

Mom moves on the couch she's been resting on. It's the most movement and expression I've seen from her since this all happened.

"Did you tell him about Mike?"

"No."

Go ahead and tell him I tried to kill myself, but don't dare tell him I'm into another man!

"You said you weren't going to call him."

"I know."

"Chris …"

"Mom," I say, trying to shut this conversation down so she believes it and moves on.

"What did he say?"

"That's he's coming immediately."

"But how—how is he able to do that?"

Watch yourself here. She knows more than you do.

"He just said he could. Not *right* away, but as soon as possible. I called him from my cell."

"Chris—"

"What did you expect? Would you rather have called him yourself?"

"I need to talk to him."

"And you will. He just—he's in shock."

She looks eager to know how Dad is feeling about everything. I understand that expression because I'd love to know too.

"Did he say anything—about—about the last time we spoke?" Mom asks.

"What do you mean?"

"I was—I wasn't very nice."

"Yeah, he said something like that."

Liar.

"I told him that if he came down here to see you it would be over my dead body."

He wanted to see me?

"Well, it almost was," I say.

Mom looks at me and tears up again.

"Mom—I'm not trying to make you sad again."

"I know."

"Dad said it would be better that you get help and worry about that," I say. "Don't worry about anything else. Including him."

Liar, liar, pants on fire.

"I don't know how long I'll be gone."

"You just call home and let us know."

Us? Yeah right.

Mom sighs and drinks her water. She's staring out the window into the sky in the distance.

I wait for her to say something, anything. I still half expect her to want me to prove I spoke with Dad.

"But you didn't say anything about Mike?"

"No. But he wanted to know details. He really kept asking. I told him I didn't know. But if he talks to you …"

She shakes her head and sighs again.

Ooh, that was a good one, Chris.

I don't like lying to her, I really don't. But I have to.

Not because Marsh told me so. No.

I'm not about to do what Marsh tells me to do.

I want a breather from Mom and from everybody else. Dad coming down would just make everything worse. If Mom gets help, then maybe things will be okay.

You know why you don't want Dad coming down here.

I check my phone and see the text. From Lily.

IS EVERYTHING OKAY? HOW'S YOUR MOTHER?

And that's why.

EVERYTHING IS FINE.

I think about the situation and look around the little cabin.

Suddenly, it doesn't seem so cramped in anymore. It actually feels kinda cozy.

I send Lily another text.

ACTUALLY EVERYTHING IS PERFECT.

I look at the phone on the counter and wonder how I can make sure that Mom doesn't get any random calls from Dad.

But she's not about to. Their last conversation was awful.

I get another text.

WHY IS EVERYTHING PERFECT?

I think of Lily coming in and staying here in this cabin. For however long she wants. Doing whatever she'd like to do. Just locking the doors and trying to leave the rest of the world behind.

My whole body tingles with excitement.

I'LL TELL YOU SOON ENOUGH I text back.

Soon enough.

66. When the Creepies Come Calling

That night I hear scratching coming from somewhere.

Normally I might get up or get freaked out. But then again, normally I'd be asleep.

I can't go to sleep because I keep thinking of my current situation with Mom leaving in another week or two and being gone for who knows how long. I keep imagining inviting Lily over here and then … Well, I'm imagining stuff any teen might imagine. Or any guy who is into a girl like Lily. Or really any guy into any girl. Period.

With thoughts like this, my mind wanders and floats and goes back and forth. I think of crazy things like when Mom and Dad were young, did they feel the way I'm feeling? I guess they must have, but that seems like the Dark Ages or something because I never knew them to be anything close.

I'm thinking of what Lily might say after I tell her the news when the scratching sound starts.

It first sounds like it's downstairs. But then I realize that it almost sounds like it's coming from …

From under my bed?

No. That's crazy.

But I feel Midnight shift on the bed and then hear her slowly growling. A muffled, weak little growl that wouldn't scare an insect. It's more cute than courageous.

"Come on, Midnight," I say as I reach over and scoop her up.

The scraping sound seems louder. As if someone is under my mattress trying to get out. I peer over and look down but know that there's no way to look *under* my mattress. The mattress and box springs are in a rectangular wooden frame that suddenly makes me think of a coffin.

That's great.

Nothing big could get in. Not even an animal like a squirrel or a chipmunk.

I'm trying to not get spooked out. I'd rather keep thinking of Lily. But the scratching continues.

It keeps going until I finally feel something sharp and rough rubbing against my back, like Freddy Krueger giving me a backrub.

I jump out of bed, flailing like a crazy person and reaching for the lights. I half expect a snake or something on my bed.

But all I see is my tangled sheet and light blanket. Midnight is just sitting there giving me a look that says *Can we sleep now?*

I look around the three sides of my bed, trying to see if anything is off. But nothing looks abnormal. The bed is against the wall as always, right below the windows that are slightly opened. Nothing slipped in either, because the screens are still on each window.

When my heart slows down a little, I go and check my phone for any messages. I see that it's almost three in the morning.

Maybe I'll buy a camera and videotape myself à la *Paranormal Activity* style. Then I'll be able to watch myself sleepwalking and getting up to make pancakes and then standing over Midnight dangling a piece of bacon.

Get some sleep.

I shut off the light and try to fall asleep.

I think of Lily again and dream of her being here.

Not so I can live out some crazy teenaged fantasies with her. Just so I can have another person to hold close late at night when the creepies come calling.

67. Living in the Moment

One thing you can't avoid no matter what high school you go to, whether it's a huge suburban one or a smaller country one that happens to be haunted:

Cheerleaders.

I see a pack of them coming my way as I'm getting some books out of my locker. It reminds me that there's a big football game coming up on Friday night. I guess the cheerleaders are trying to get some good old Harrington High spirit.

A split-second glance does it.

I'm getting my books and look up and then see an image in my mind that doesn't compute.

I look again toward the pack of six or seven girls and I see her.

No, that can't be.

Kelsey is walking with the girls, dressed just like they are.

I'm staring probably with my mouth wide open in shock when Kelsey's smile beams my way.

"Hey, Chris," she says.

I say hi, then one of them says something in a hushed tone that only girls know and the pack laughs. I don't think it's mean, because I don't think Kelsey has suddenly turned into a mean girl, but who knows.

What have YOU turned into, huh?

I'm still looking their way when I see her head turn around. She sees me watching her and seems amused.

I don't think she ever told me she was a cheerleader. Did she? I met her in art class and she was a quiet little mouse with her glasses and her braces.

Somehow, the glasses and braces have been replaced by long legs and a sparkling smile.

You're girl crazy, Chris.

Maybe I am. I don't know.

I just know that something's changed with Kelsey since last year.

Maybe we've both changed now that we're seniors.

Maybe that's just what happens to people.

Today is a strange day. First Lily texted me that she wasn't coming to school. I asked if she was sick, and she texted back a simple YES. That's all. And the rest of my texts today have gone ignored.

Then I see Kelsey dressed up as a cheerleader. That's what I keep thinking—that she's dressed up as one, not that she *is* one. But as I'm leaving the cafeteria early, since Lily isn't around, the cheerleader comes up to me as if to prove the point.

"Hey, Chris."

"Hi."

She smiles in an awkward way, and it comes as a relief. There's the Kelsey I remember. So not everything has totally changed in a short span of time.

"Where are your pom-poms?" I joke.

She laughs. "It still feels weird wearing this."

"Probably would feel more weird if I was wearing it."

This gets an even better laugh.

"You didn't tell me you were a *cheerleader,*" I say, stressing the word. "I mean—if only I'd known."

I see her blushing and know I'm overdoing it.

"Then what?" she says in a way that seems to reflect this new Kelsey Page I'm seeing.

"Well, then, I would have had to go out for football."

"You ran track, so you're fast."

"Yeah, but I play soccer. Maybe I could have been their kicker."

Kelsey looks older. She really does. And not just because the glasses and braces are gone. It seems like summer vacation really agreed with her.

"Do you have a minute?" she asks, looking around as though she's nervous that people are watching us.

I nod. It's funny. I no longer notice the people watching me. It's not like it was when I first started. People seem to have gotten used to me. Which is great.

"I was wondering—well, it's a big favor. And I just thought maybe to, you know—to ask you."

"Wait a minute," I say. "You want me to be one of those guys on the bottom of the cheerleaders who throw you up in the air and then catch you?"

Her face is lit up, and I know that whatever was there at the end of last year—especially during that dance at prom—hasn't gone away.

But you've gone away, haven't you?

"You're going to laugh, but it's kinda like that."

"Have you seen my arms?" I ask. "I think I'd probably drop you."

"No—it's nothing like that. But for homecoming—you know they have a big game and a dance the following night?"

"I didn't. I don't think I had moved here yet last year."

I'm trying to think of someone being a homecoming king of Harrington High. Then I realize I knew him—the wonderful Ray Spencer.

"Well—they always do something big, and this year, during halftime, the cheerleaders—we're going to do a special routine."

I nod, but suddenly I have an idea where this is going.

"And it's—it's going to be fun. I'm still not quite sure about all of this, but Georgia wanted me to go out for it my senior year. I mean—I never thought I'd make it."

"Come on. You're a natural."

"That's not nice," she says.

"What?"

"Well, I just—I need a partner, and I don't know any of the football players. So I was thinking—would you want to do the routine? With me?"

This is beyond surprising. And normally—if it were anybody else—I'd be shaking my head and saying, "Yeah, right."

But I'm standing here—today of all days on my own—and Kelsey is giving me that sad puppy dog look that Midnight has mastered. And I'm feeling bad for ignoring her ever since that last dance we had.

It's the least you can do.

"Sure," I say with a casual shrug. "Why not?"

But this isn't just because of pity or mercy or me being nice.

No.

Standing there—it comes back.

Stop, Chris, come on.

It comes back in a weird, strange way.

"And look—I know—the new girl and you—this isn't a big deal. I just wasn't sure who else to ask, so you know ..."

"It's cool," I say.

"Are you sure? You don't have to. You can think about it."

"No, it's fine."

"There will be practices after school. Can you make them? Just—if not, it's okay."

I want to say *Kelsey, please, it's fine,* but I don't.

I just smile and nod.

"Okay, great. I'll let you know when the first practice is. Okay?"

"As long as I don't have to wear a skirt, I'll be fine."

She laughs and then gives an awkward "See you later" before leaving.

I see a group of football guys walking past and wonder what I'm doing. Then again, I haven't really been thinking of the choices I've been making lately. I've been sort of just living in the moment. And saying yes.

All while trying to forget.

68. Harder to Breathe

Sometimes I still wonder.

When it's just me and I'm not doing anything, I wonder.

Those questions and those memories and those pictures that I've tried to bury start to suddenly spring out of the well like that dead girl with the long hair in *The Ring*.

It usually starts with thinking of Jocelyn.

It's been over eight months since the New Year's nightmare that I saw. And as long as those months might seem, I also know how incredibly short and sharp they are. I don't want to picture Jocelyn, but I still can. Sometimes she seems forgotten about, but then sometimes, for some reason, I'll think of her.

All the warnings, all the whispers, all the omens, all the strange things.

All boiling down to what? That I'm related to some guy?

So what?

I mean really—so freaking what?

There is still more to this story, but I don't know what. I still want to know. I need to know. But I also desperately want to be able to be alone and not think about all this.

I'm at the cabin watching television on the evening of the same day Kelsey asked me to be her partner, when there is a pounding on the door.

The mountain man with his dog!

I look up and see Lily at the window.

She pounds at the door again, so I get up quickly and open it.

She almost literally falls into my arms, shaking uncontrollably and crying.

"What? What's going on—Lily, what?"

I try to move to see her face, but she doesn't let me. She hugs me with a fierce hold and I just stay there, arms wrapped around her, her sweet smell covering me, her soft skin against mine.

"I'm scared, Chris—I'm really scared."

When I finally see her face, she looks tired and different. The beautiful confident aura is gone. Her face resembles a concrete sidewalk that's starting to crack.

"Lily—what happened?"

"Are you alone?"

"I'm always alone," I say.

"Can I just stay here for a while? And just—just not talk? Is that okay?"

I want to ask more questions, but I force myself not to. Instead, I just nod. She grabs my hand and leads me to the couch. She sits down and curls up in a ball, then rests against my chest and arm after I sit next to her.

This is becoming a habit, a nice one that I could get used to.

I'm able to keep my mouth shut and my questions to myself. For the moment. Because right now, Lily is in my arms, for some reason, and all those doubts and questions that I had before she came are gone.

Before she leaves, once the sun has long since disappeared and the cabin has grown dark except for the one light on in the family room,

Lily asks me a question out of the blue. She still has refused to tell me what's going on and has asked me not to ask about it. So her question seems even more mysterious than usual.

"What if you don't do what they tell you to do?"

For a minute I'm not even sure who she's talking about. Who's telling who to do what? But she knows about Staunch and Marsh. It's just—am I really doing what they want me to?

"I don't get the question."

"What if—I don't know. You said everything was going to be fine. What did you mean by that?"

"My mom is going away soon. To some rehab or something. For at least a week or two."

"And *that's* why things are fine?"

I nod.

"And why's that?"

"Because ..." I don't want to tell her the obvious.

"Let's leave."

"I can't—I already told you."

"But do you know any more about all the stuff going on?"

I know a little, but not enough. Not enough to make sense of any of it. I shake my head.

"With your mom gone—we can just leave."

"But what about *your* family—your mother?"

"Chris—listen," Lily says.

She stares at me for a moment. We're standing by the doorway, and I'm waiting for an answer or a statement or something.

She moves and kisses me.

Suddenly I forget about the conversation and kiss her back.

We lean against the doorway and block whoever might try opening it.

When she breaks away minutes later, she leaves me literally gasping for air.

There are no more questions, no more answers, no more solutions.

She just makes sure I have her full gaze and then she tells me with a seductive look, "Dream about me."

I'm left on my own, still finding it quite hard to breathe.

69. Texts

The week passes slowly.

All I can think about is Mom leaving. I'm dying for her to go to rehab. Such a son, huh?

The only break comes in seeing Lily at school. And having conversations with her on the phone. Or texting her.

A text comes from her asking WHAT ARE YOU DOING?

NOTHING.

YOU LIVE AN EXCITING LIFE.

IT WAS A LOT LESS EXCITING BEFORE YOU MOVED HERE.

WANT TO COME OUT?

NOW?

SURE, WHY NOT?

There's a pause.

HELLO???

IT'S A WEDNESDAY NIGHT.

AND YOU'RE UP.

MY MOM MIGHT NOT APPROVE.

DO YOU ALWAYS OBEY THE RULES?

DO YOU?

UM—DO YOU KNOW ME?

KINDA.

YEAH, WELL, THEN YOU WOULDN'T ASK THAT.

WHAT DO YOU WANT TO DO? I ask.

EVERYTHING.

STOP IT.

I'M JUST SAYING.

THAT'S NOT FAIR TO TEASE LIKE THAT.

I DO—I MEAN IT.

YOU MEAN WHAT?

I MEAN I WANT TO DO EVERYTHING. I WANT TO SEE EVERYTHING. I WANT TO EXPERIENCE EVERYTHING I CAN.

One minute I hear nothing from her. Then she texts me that.

OH.

WHAT'S WITH THE LITTLE TINY "OH"?

NOTHING.

STOP.

WHAT?

STOP SULKING.

I'M NOT SULKING.

YES YOU ARE.

You can't even see me.

Oh, I can see you and I know that look of yours.

Can you see me now?

Yes.

And what am I doing?

Smiling.

Pause.

I'm right, huh?

Yes I answer.

I'm always right.

Yes, you are.

So are you going to come out tonight?

I guess.

Don't guess with me.

You keep me guessing.

As I should.

That's not fair.

You think life is fair?

No.

Good. Get on that bike and act like a man.

I sense sarcasm.

Prove I'm wrong.

Maybe I will.

Maybe I'll let you.

Pause.

You there?

Pause.

Good.

70. Lovesong

We're riding in the darkness, going nowhere in particular.

We're off the bike hanging off the edge of a mountain and laughing.

It's like I'm back home again in Libertyville, laughing and loving life and feeling whole again.

Doesn't matter what Lily and I are doing or not doing.

I feel young and fun again, and this whole train wreck of a life that's happened in Solitary suddenly goes away.

I'm lovesick and she knows it and laughs and leads me on.

"What do you want to do when you're older?" Lily asks me.

"Where do you want to live?"

"What do you dream about?"

"Who do you want to be?"

She's curious and interested, and I talk more than I've ever talked before. The thousand thoughts in my mind are suddenly free to be uttered out loud. It's magical. It's freeing.

I don't think about midnight being near or school being tomorrow.

I hold her hand and tell her what I think about her, what I *really* think. She smiles as if she already knows all of this. It doesn't bother her. She doesn't feel the need to say anything back or react. Or even thank me. She knows and it's okay.

"I'm serious," I say.

"I think about you all the time."

"I'm slightly kinda crazy about you."

"You just make me feel better."

Lily takes my hand and kisses me. A sweet, soft kiss, but one that still leaves me wondering. It's a short kiss, and I tell her this.

"I know," she says.

"You send me mixed vibes."

"I know."

"You doing that on purpose?"

"Maybe," she says, then is off talking about something else.

My head is soaring, and this is just another school night for a senior.

Yeah right.

The silence and solitude are suddenly my friends, suddenly helpful in keeping the rest of the world away from my Lily.

This night, unexpected just like the curly-haired blonde walking through the door of my summer school class, soon ends. And I tell her good night. Wanting more.

71. Dr. Everything'll Be All Right

"I don't like leaving you here by yourself."

Mom has a suitcase by the door and is moments away from leaving.

It's a bit surreal, to be honest. It's like she's going on some vacation, but instead of going to an all-inclusive resort, this place won't have any perks and won't be fun.

"I told you Dad is going to try and get here tomorrow or Friday."

It's late September, and I have no idea what Dad might be up to. But I do know he's not coming here tomorrow or Friday or anytime.

"Tell him to call me—I've left you the contact information. I don't know how available I'm going to be to talk."

She looks pale and tired. And really old.

I should probably be more supportive, maybe ride with her to the place or at least give her a nice pep talk before she goes, but I don't.

"Chris—the envelope in there—it's money for you. For these next few weeks. I know your father—well, I don't want to seem like I'm leaving you here with nothing."

Oh, but that's okay, Mom.

"Just be careful. Okay? Anything—if anything strange happens. If there's anything—*anything*—that happens, let me know. Do you understand?"

I nod, but think she might have said this to me when we first got here.

There's too much to tell her. It wouldn't fill a book. It would fill a series.

Yeah, just keep reading, Mom. Edward and Bella show up in chapter seventy-five.

"Chris, I love you," Mom says, giving me a hug.

And that's when I feel like a complete and utter failure as a son. I don't tell her I love her back. Nor do I let the hug linger long. Nor do I tell her the truth.

Nope.

She gives me a look that almost looks like it could be the final look she gives me.

"I'm gonna get better," she says. "I promise."

I nod. Smile. Pick up the suitcase and take it down to her car.

Then I watch her get in and drive away.

Soon the car disappears and I'm left on my own.

In less than a year, I've ended up watching both my parents exit my life. And in both cases, I've been kinda glad.

I go back inside the cabin, where I feel something all around me.

Not ghosts or voodoo or sadness.

No. I feel the wonderful sensation of freedom.

I feel like turning up the stereo and doing air guitar in my tighty-whities and shades. But I don't have tighty-whities (no thanks), and my shades fell off while I was riding the other day. And I have no idea what song a young Tom Cruise was dancing to in his empty house. Actually, even if I had that song and did everything the same, I'd run out of room in this tiny cabin.

Instead, I select one of Uncle Robert's records and blast the first track.

I've heard it before, but not like this, not deliberately. I've seen it in a movie or a video or somewhere. I don't even know much of Prince's music.

But I get goose bumps when the crunching guitar kicks in and the song picks up at a hundred miles an hour.

Yeah, I can't help but dance.

Yeah, I can't help being happy.

The music is loud and all I wanna do is go crazy and get nuts. Just like the song says.

I'm seventeen, so sue me.

I've had a particularly bad year.

With the music cranking, I think about all the things I can suddenly do.

The little dark face on my bed stares at me. Midnight is wondering what I'm doing.

I'm trying to have some fun, want to join me?

I begin to mimic some air guitar that sends Midnight behind a pillow.

"Take me away!"

And with that, the song ends.

But I am just starting.

The screaming is downstairs, just like always.

I get out of bed and rush down, knowing that Mom is having another nightmare.

It's only when I turn on the lights in her room that I remember that she's gone. She's gone and the house is empty except for Midnight and me (as much as I tried for it NOT to be by texting Lily) and the bedroom I'm looking at is bare.

Except …

The bedspread. It's different.

I remember Mom had made her bed, and it looked fine when I picked up the suitcase earlier.

Now there's an impression on the bed as if somebody had been lying on top of it.

The scream sounds again, and this time I jump.

Wake up wake up you're just dreaming.

But I feel that scared falling sensation and I know I'm not dreaming.

The scream is coming from outside—maybe on the deck?

Don't go out there don't look.

It comes again. Like someone out of her mind. Higher pitched than my mom's scream. But just as awful.

The tiny light outside the front door is on, but it doesn't really shed much light. I go find a flashlight, then check out the deck from the windows. Nothing.

"Help me, they're coming!"

The voice sounds like it's right there in front of me. I actually duck because I think someone is going to suddenly reach through the glass and grab me.

But instead of glass breaking, I heard the sound of footsteps going down the steps.

My heart is racing, and I wonder what's happening outside.

Another scream. Growing more faint.

I curse and open the door.

Idiot.

I shine the light down the steps on our driveway. I spot my bike where I parked it earlier. And then—moving around like some ghost—

What the—

The face turns, and I see her clearly. Even though her eyes are darker and she's got blood coming out of her nose and mouth, I know who it is.

It's Heidi Marsh.

On my driveway. Screaming.

Hey, you broke into her house once.

I'm stunned and freaked out not just by seeing her there and by her screaming, but also by what she's wearing.

Or not wearing.

It's like a loose slip or something. White, but all stained with blood. The blood is all over her back, as if she's been cut somehow, and going down her bare legs. She looks skinny and frightened like a picture of a concentration camp victim suddenly let loose.

A hand goes up in front of her face, then almost seems to claw at me. Her scream is even wilder.

Then she's gone. Down the driveway and onto the road and into the night.

I might be crazy. I might have gone searching for Jocelyn when I knew she was in trouble. Or I might have gone down in those tunnels looking for whatever was there. I might have even gone into the woods behind Staunch's house to see Grandpa dearest.

But this—

No way.

I'm not about to follow that.

I get back inside and lock the door and wait. Wait to hear something else or see something.

But I'm waiting for a long time and nothing happens.

I guess I really did what Prince wanted me to do.

Let's go crazy. So I did.

Heidi Marsh—well, something tells me she's been crazy for a very long time.

72. Shadowplay

Suddenly, out of nowhere or somewhere, things start to play tricks with my mind. And heart. And soul, if such a thing exists.

These visions or nightmares continue.

As if Mom left and something or someone filled her absence. But not with the person I thought. It's been five days, and Lily hasn't brought her suitcase and started shacking up with me.

Instead, there's something else.

And the fact that I know that and just say it like I'm talking about the dog food on the ground—*hey, look at the dog food, and hey, there's an evil spirit in the fridge*—that proves that either I'm totally bonkers or that it's happening.

It's really happening.

Doors opening.

Faucets turning on.

Things hitting the windows. Or the side of our house. Things that I discover the next morning are birds struck dead by the force of the hit.

Stuff like this—it's only the beginning.

One night I discover the doors below my mom's sink opened. Sure enough, the plywood is off and I can feel the cool air blowing out from the open passageway. It takes me about fifteen minutes to nail it back into place.

And sure enough, the next morning the plywood is off again.

It's stuff like this. A freaking laundry list of hauntings. And by freaking I *mean* freaking out.

But that's kid stuff compared to the stuff I start dreaming about. Things that I see not only at night, but sometimes when I'm riding to school or sitting in class or staring into my locker.

I seriously begin to not want to close my eyes.

I remember what Marsh said to me.

"Horrific visions. Stuff from nightmares. Nightmares blending into reality. Am I right?"

Uh, yeah, you're always right.

"It's all part of the process. Just—try not to freak out."

Easy for you to say.

I wonder what "process" this is.

What am I becoming?

Then something strange happens.

Something that freaks me out in another sort of way.

One night I find a bottle of rum that my mom must have not thrown away once she came back from the hospital. Or maybe it was JUST IN CASE the whole rehab thing didn't work a hundred percent. I don't know. I was looking for something to clean up Midnight's puke off the carpet (I gave her too many hot dog slices again), and I found the bottle of rum.

Unopened.

Just waiting for someone like me to toast to the insanity.

So that night, after I spend the day begging and pleading for Lily to come over, I decide to get acquainted with the rum. I open a two-liter of Diet Coke and begin to play bartender. The strange thing is I don't feel the first two drinks I make.

On my third, I begin to feel the room spinning.

But this isn't the strange thing that happens.

Sometime later that evening, I fall asleep on my couch watching television and eating Doritos.

I don't hear anything strange that night.

I don't experience any nightmarish visions.

I sleep like a baby.

When I wake up, I see the bottle of rum and the clock saying I'm an hour late to school and I really can't believe that I didn't dream anything last night.

I look at the bottle again, thinking of Mom.

73. Finally

"Why have you been ignoring me today?"

It's Friday and I'm tired. Somewhere in between Marsh and Lily is a thing called biology, which just makes my brain hurt. The teacher is a drill sergeant and has no idea all the stuff I'm going through. I'm supposed to do homework in an empty home that I keep inviting Lily to. In an empty cabin that's continuing to be visited by ghosts.

Do I believe in ghosts?

Yep.

So I'm just tired and cranky and irritated that Lily is just playing games.

"No reason," I initially tell her.

Lily curses and tells me to just be real and tell her what I'm thinking.

We're sitting outside on a stone wall during lunch break.

"You *know* what I'm thinking," I tell her.

I look at her and see her whole expression and body language suddenly appear …

What?

I don't know what.

Almost—guilty. Like she knows exactly what is going on and she feels bad, but …

But why?

"I just thought—I mean one minute you're saying something, and then next you're not even there," I tell her. "And I thought that once my mom left … you know?"

Yeah, Lily knows.

She's known the first time she saw me look at her.

It's pretty much all over my face. And all the times she's held my hand and kissed me and flirted and texted and told me things—what am I supposed to think?

Lily's catlike eyes study mine for a moment. And even now, I'm so weak. So silly and stupid and young. I'm like a song put on pause waiting for her to press play.

She's about to tell me sorry and end things. I know it. I can tell because she's suddenly so serious and almost sad-looking.

"Okay, fine," Lily says.

"Fine, what?"

The sad, serious look only lasts for a few more seconds. Then suddenly, another look splashes over her face. Like a motion picture screen changing from black-and-white to a rainbow of seductive colors.

"You *know* what. So tonight. Okay?"

"Look, Lily—I just didn't know why—"

She puts a finger over my lips and laughs. "I shouldn't be doing this, Chris. I really shouldn't."

"Shouldn't be doing what?"

She laughs and brushes back that hair and seems to look up at the sky as if thinking *This is crazy.*

I've been thinking that since the very first time I found myself riding behind her on the motorcycle.

"I shouldn't be falling for you like this." She stands and looks down at me. "Pick me up tonight around six. I'll let you drive my car. So we can go on a proper date."

Suddenly I'm feeling nervous.

"Where do you want to go?"

No—make that scared.

"You choose, Chris. Tonight, you choose everything."

No—make that terrified.

I'm staring out the window in the class after lunch. Staring and thinking. Staring and imagining.

Between classes, I'm walking through the crowds and I see her walking toward me. Tall and beautiful. Smiling my way. Stopping by me.

I'm dizzy now without the rum.

I remain that way all afternoon.

Nervous. Wondering. Waiting.

It seems I've been waiting a long time. Not for any reason. Just waiting.

Some part of me feels like things will be better if and when this thing happens with Lily. I know it won't change anything about my life and what's happened or what's about to happen, but I swear that deep down a part of me really kinda thinks that it will.

It's crazy how all of this has led to this afternoon.

And to tonight.

When I'll finally get what I want.

Not just Lily. Not just choosing everything.

What do you really want, Chris?

Relief.

74. Slave to Love

Lily exits the door of the bed-and-breakfast wearing a strapless dress that's white with an exotic black and blue pattern. The loose dress shows off her long legs and seems to move and shift with each step she takes.

She tells you she's going to drive and you can barely catch your breath to say okay.

You're not hungry but make it through dinner anyway.

Soon you find you're laughing.

A lot.

Like the silly, stupid teenage boy that you are.

Some things shouldn't be laughed at but you laugh anyway because you feel unlocked and unhinged. You feel unleashed like a tiger in the night.

You know you're a pup but she makes you feel like a raging animal.

She laughs because she seems to be able to read your thoughts.

You're a fool but that's okay because you can't help yourself.

She holds your hand and leads you through the rain.

The storms swell above and the thunder cracks and you take shelter under a small alcove and then you feel her cradle herself close to you and you forget the day or the time or your age.

All this.

Every little bit.

Where did that gloom go?

Where did that scary story drift off to?

Did the writer suddenly take happy pills?

Or did the skies open up and she came down like a beautiful flower? A flower named Lily.

Opening and freeing and beautiful and intoxicating.

A year older and a decade wiser.

That's you and that's how you feel.

And when the storms pass and streetlamps are on and the moments seem to inch by, she asks you what you want to do.

"I want to go home," you tell her.

She just looks at you, serious and searching eyes. "You sure about that?"

You nod, but of course deep down you're not sure. You're not sure about anything anymore except this feeling deep down that never seems to go away.

"Okay, let's go."

You hold her hand as she drives in the darkness. And you don't even notice the SUV in the driveway of the cabin until she mentions it.

And in one short gasp of breath, you realize that your night has changed.

That everything has changed.

That this risky business has suddenly been found out.

And that somewhere up in the cabin above you, with the lights already on inside, your father is waiting for you.

75. Long Gone

Dad is sitting on the couch when I open the door. He gives me that look that I grew to hate and have never forgotten as he turns off the television. It's a look that can't hide his anger, a look that says he's trying to contain it but it's spilling all over that face of his.

"Where've you been?" he asks me.

It's almost been a year since we left, and not one single word has come from this man, and *that's* what he asks me.

Lily is already heading home. I told her I didn't want her dealing with this drama.

I also told her that I wanted—that I *needed*—to make up for tonight. Somehow and in some way.

She only smiled and kissed me on the cheek in response.

"Chris?"

"What are you doing here?"

He stands up and looks me over with questioning eyes.

"I'm here because your mother called and told me what had happened. She wanted to make sure you had 'called' me."

"Yeah. I know. I lied."

"Why?"

I rub the back of my neck and don't look at him. A year and nothing. No "How are you?" or any of that. Just riding me like he always did.

He looks the same. Dark hair parted on the side, a square and rugged face with lines on the forehead. I can see stubble from not shaving, something that rarely happens.

Something about him looks different, however. Yet I refuse to look at him long enough to figure out what.

"I think it's obvious."

"Chris—your mother has been in trouble—for some time now. Why didn't you call me?"

"I could say the same thing."

"I've been talking to your mother on a regular basis. As much as she would let me. Sometimes every week. I've always—always asked how you were doing. Always wanted to talk to you."

I look at him and know he's not lying. Christians don't lie, do they? At least they're not supposed to.

"Did your mother tell you that?"

"No."

He sighs as I pass him and go to the refrigerator.

"Chris, we need to talk."

"We're talking."

"So, what—were you not going to tell me what was happening with Mom? With her drinking?"

"Nope."

I pour myself some orange juice.

"She almost killed herself."

"Yep."

"You should've called."

I want to tell him about the lack of having a phone, or a connection, or a life. But I don't.

I keep my mouth shut.

"You had to go to summer school?"

I nod.

For a while, my father looks at me. The eyes that aren't that wide to begin with seem to sharpen like a knife.

"You're grounded."

"What? You can't do that."

"I'm your father, and I can make any decision I want when it comes to you."

"Not anymore."

He tightens his jaw and lips, and I see it, the anger and the frustration on his face. Just like always.

You haven't changed a bit have you.

"You should have called me."

I stand there not far away from him in this suddenly very crowded and very stuffy cabin. There are a thousand things I want to tell him he should have done. But I've learned that silence is sometimes the worst thing for someone.

"A part of me says I should just take you back home to Illinois."

A couple months ago I would have said "Please!" But not anymore. Not since meeting Lily.

"Chris, listen," he finally says. "You can't just shut me out like this."

"We left almost a year ago."

"And your mother has been making sure I had very little contact with you."

"You're an adult. You could have figured out how to get hold of me."

This seems to be a total slap in the face. He just stands there, the anger suddenly disappearing. He seems speechless. Which is a wonderful thing.

"Your mother said that Uncle Robert hasn't been around either."

I laugh. "Uh, yeah."

"She's been lying to me this whole time."

"About what?"

"About him being here."

"Are you serious?"

"All this time, I thought he was here."

"So that made you feel better, knowing there was a man in the house with Mom?"

"Listen, don't you—"

Then Dad stops and holds the rest of his thought.

"I'm going upstairs."

"I didn't want this, Chris. Any of this."

"Yeah, well, it looks like it still happened."

"Your mother is stubborn."

I look at the man across from me, the one who used to be a lawyer and supposedly a very good one. Someone who did his job and made a great living making sure that he proved his point. And he *always* seemed to prove his point.

"Yeah, I know," Dad continues. "I'm stubborn too. And that was the thing—one of the things that was so hard. But I didn't want to lose your mother. Or you. I mean it, Chris."

I just nod, trying to show no emotion.

He looks at me, and I raise my eyebrows as if to ask *Are we done here?* Then he nods and I head upstairs.

He might have not wanted to lose Mom and me. But he did.

And we're both gone.

Long gone.

76. The Routine

"You look tired."

Kelsey catches me still zoning out while I appear to be watching the cheerleader coach (or whatever she calls herself) explaining our dance number. Everybody is now getting up with their partners to start going through the motions of the dance.

"Sorry, I'm kind of out of it."

"Long night?"

I nod, then figure it's harmless telling her. At least she'll know I'm not making it up and won't think she's the reason I'm being a drag.

"My dad showed up."

"Are you serious? When?"

"This past weekend."

"Why?"

"My mom—she has some issues. So I was alone for a while. Guess my dad didn't want me being on my own."

"So how are things?"

"Oh, great. Mom was never home. Now Dad is always home. But I talk with him about as much as I talked to Mom."

Kelsey looks unsure what to say, so I tell her let's get started.

"Did you get all that?" she asks me of the instruction for the dance.

"Yeah, sure," I say.

Five minutes into going through the motions, or trying to, I confess. "Okay—I didn't really hear anything she said."

"Really?" Kelsey asks with a smile.

"I'm sorry. I just think it's the song that's throwing me."

Kelsey laughs. It's some jittery eighties tune that seems like the music on a *Saturday Night Live* spoof.

"I mean—couldn't they get something from this decade?"

"Well—you saw Ms. Zollinger."

I raise my eyes, nodding. "I think she's 'Holding Out for a Hero.'"

Kelsey laughs. "Come on. Here."

She takes my hands and forces me to pay attention. She goes through the moves. They're ridiculous. This is really beyond corny.

"Be the part, guys," Ms. Zollinger yells out above the song blasting in the gym. "Be the role of the hero."

Ms. Zollinger was probably one of those girls who never dated because she looks so square. Not square as in nerdy, just *square.* Like a block of wood with broad shoulders and hips and all that. This team doesn't need to form a pyramid to raise up one of the cheerleaders. All they need to do is have Ms. Zollinger squat at the bottom.

"You have to look at me," Kelsey says.

It's funny to hear her say that. She's really managed to become a little more outspoken than the girl I met last year.

"I don't know. I get kinda nervous when I do that," I joke.

"Stop it," she says.

I'm not exactly sure how this "dance" is supposed to fire up the football team. Perhaps if all the guys on the team were also in a glee club or something, then yeah, sure, maybe they'd get into this. But I don't know. I have a feeling this is simply for the long lost love who took Ms. Zollinger to prom and then danced with someone else on their final song.

"You have to really twirl me around. Like they're doing."

I look and see one of the guys who I know is a football player spinning his partner around. I nod and grip Kelsey under both of her arms and start to spin.

Of course it goes wrong somehow. Probably because I have no dance moves or cheerleading moves or moves of any kind.

The very light weight and very long limbs of Kelsey end up crashing on top of me.

I'm laughing while she's adjusting her cheerleading skirt and trying to fight the red on her face.

"Did you do that on purpose?" she asks as I help her back on her feet.

"I'd never do such a thing."

"Chris?"

"Okay, well, I didn't this time."

"We only have six practices to get this right."

"Six? Really?"

She looks at me in surprise. "You can't do them."

"That's a lot of practicing. I feel like I'm going to be part of the team."

"You know—if you don't want to, you don't have to do this."

I can't help but chuckle. "You're cute when you blush."

She smiles for a moment, but then something is wrong. Her face grows cold and serious.

"What? What'd I say?"

"Oh, it's nothing. It's wonderful to be called cute. Especially when, well—"

She glances over to the stands, and I follow her gaze.

Lily is sitting there watching us. She waves, and I can't help but wave back.

"You can go, it's okay," Kelsey says.

I want to tell her that it's fine, but I realize that our practice time is almost up.

I don't even get to tell her good-bye or good night or see you at the next practice. Kelsey disappears into the school, and I head up to the bleachers to see how Lily is doing.

77. Trying to Kill Me

"I didn't see you any today."

Lily nods and then pats the bleacher right next to her, like I'm a puppy who needs to sit for a treat.

I keep sitting, but I never seem to get the treat that I want.

"That was really cute down there," Lily says.

"You didn't answer my question."

"Did you ask me something?"

She's smiling, toying with me as always. "Lighten up—I got an excuse. When you're a girl you can come up with so many excuses. Just say 'girl stuff' and they excuse you."

"That's good to know."

"So that's the girl we saw at the party."

"Kelsey," I say, not sure if she's deliberately forgetting her name or not.

"That's right. Kelsey. Who is just *crazy* for Chris Buckley."

"Funny."

"It's true. But you know that, don't you."

"If you were somebody else, I'd almost think you might be jealous," I say.

"But I'm not."

"Jealous?"

"Somebody else."

These fun little games could continue for hours. And they often do, late in the night when we're texting each other.

"Any chance you can go out for dinner?" Lily asks.

"I told you I'm grounded."

"Until when?"

"Probably until Dad leaves." I don't really know, because he hasn't put a date around it.

"But you could do cheerleading practice, huh?"

"He knows how little I really want to do it."

"Does he know about me?"

I shake my head. "And I want to keep it that way."

"Fine by me."

"Lily, look—about the other night—I just want you to know, and I'm serious—"

She tightens those lips of hers to shush me. "No need to go back in time."

"What do you mean?" I ask.

"It was what it was. And here and now—just let's stay here and now. Okay?"

But I don't really get why she doesn't want to talk about the other night. I want to tell her that I haven't forgotten what was about to happen. And I want to bring it up because I want it to happen sometime soon.

Maybe she knows this, Chris, Maybe there's a reason she's shushing you.

I don't say anything, and Lily nudges me to try and make me smile.

"I really liked the song they chose for the routine," Lily says.

I can't help but laugh. "Maybe you should join the cheerleaders."

She sighs and lets out a gagging sound. "I couldn't stand the cheerleaders at my high school. Nope—that wasn't for me."

"So then, Ms. Lily-New-Student. What *is* for you?"

"Hmm—that's a good question. I like slow dancing to soft music when you can see the candlelight flickering off the walls and feel the breeze off the ocean coming in through the open doorway. That's what I go for."

I just look at her, again feeling the dropping sensation.

"What?" she asks.

"You're trying to kill me, right?"

"No."

"Oh, okay." I just shake my head.

"What'd I say?"

"You know now what I'll be thinking about all night long."

"Stop," Lily says.

"It's true. And I think you do that on purpose."

"No. It's just—it's so easy to tell you things I'm thinking."

"Yeah, well, sometimes—I don't know. Sometimes I'm just tired of all of that."

"Of all of what?"

I look at her, feeling like a two-thousand-pound weight is holding me back, inches away from her.

"Sometimes I'm tired of all the talking. And texting. Sometimes I don't want to talk anymore."

Lily smiles, takes my hand and squeezes it. "I know. And if only you weren't grounded."

"I can come home whenever I want. I don't care. Let's go somewhere tonight. Anywhere."

"That just means you won't be able to see me again for a while. And we don't want that, do we?"

I sigh. I hate being a teen, a boy, a high schooler.

I want to be an adult and take Lily to that place she spoke about. The tiny hut on the beach with the breeze and the candlelight.

"Come on, Mr. Cheerleader. Walk me to my car."

As we walk outside hand in hand, talking and laughing about something, I spot a car just starting to leave.

The driver has blonde hair a lot like Kelsey's.

That night I get an email from Kelsey.

Hi, Chris. You know—after thinking about things, I think it's probably best that we don't do the routine. I can find someone else. But thanks. I appreciate you trying.

Kelsey

I want to respond but I don't.

But she knew I was seeing Lily. She knew about that.

I decide I'll talk to her tomorrow.

I don't especially want to do the routine with her. But then again, I think it might be fun.

Kelsey's cute and sweet. I'm sure that she'll make some ordinary, nice guy very happy one day.

But I'm not ordinary and I'm not really particularly nice, either. Not anymore.

78. The Conversation

I'm sitting at the table eating a grilled cheese sandwich when my father comes inside from working around the cabin. The September evening is still warm enough to cause him to be sweaty. He takes off his work gloves and wipes his forehead, then grabs a glass of water before sitting down across from me.

"There's a lot that needs to be done around this place," he says to me in a tone that makes it sound like *I* should be doing the work.

I just nod and continue eating my sandwich.

Dad just looks at me for a minute and shakes his head. "Chris—come on."

"What?"

"Give me a break."

"What?"

I'm sounding like a broken record.

"No—I mean it. Cut the routine. Enough."

Before I can say "What?" again he keeps going.

"It's been three days. And look—I have no idea when your mother is coming home, do you understand that? You don't have to like the fact that I'm here, but you can at least act decent around me."

"What do you want me to do?"

"Stop with the hate," Dad says, wiping his face again. "Your mother has turned you against me."

"Mom hasn't done anything."

"She's done enough," he says.

I look at the figure across from me. Kyle Buckley, fortysomething, his face permanently set to look serious, his eyes two piercing daggers of judgment.

"I didn't want to move down here."

"I didn't want you to." His voice startles me with how loud it is. He breathes in and tries to calm down.

"You think God wanted this to happen?" I ask.

"Don't."

"Don't what?"

"Don't be that way. Don't be a smart aleck."

"I asked a simple question."

Dad just glares at me. "It's not a simple question, and you know it."

"You don't know everything that's happened down here."

"Then tell me, Chris. I've been here a week, and you've said nothing and told me *nothing.* About you, about Mom, about anything."

"What do you want to know?"

"Why are you so angry? What's happened to you?"

I finish the last bite of my sandwich and suddenly don't want to continue this conversation.

"I know you don't believe me, but I still love your mother and you. And I haven't given up hope."

"Hope for what?"

"That we can still be a family."

I let out a laugh. A laugh that's been wedged deep inside something tight and hurting.

"That ended the day we left Libertyville."

"I did not want that."

"You chose God. Mom chose North Carolina."

Dad shakes his head, angry, searching for something else to say, knowing I'm right.

"I didn't choose God, Chris. Do you really think I wanted this to happen? I quit my job, and things have been in a tailspin ever since. And I keep asking God why. I keep asking Him what He wants from me."

"Maybe there's a reason you're not getting an answer."

"Don't," Dad says. "Don't dare be that way."

You have not seen what I've seen. Or been where I've been.

"Don't become bitter like your mother."

"Should I be like you?"

Dad laughs, shaking his head, rubbing his palms together. "No. No, I hope and pray that you turn out far better than I did. Because I realize this, Chris, and you might not hear what I'm saying or want to hear it, but I mean this when I say it. I wasn't there for fourteen years of your life. And when I finally tried to be, it was too late. I know that now. I pray that I haven't completely lost you, but I don't know. I just don't know. Your mother—well, I can hope for something, but that's more complicated. And in her condition—it's just—that's something else. But I still love you. And I want the best for you."

The best for me.

I wonder what that looks like.

So many people want the best for me. But what about what I want?

Haven't you spent the last few months figuring that out?

"The only thing I know is this," Dad says. "God really does love you. And I don't want you to think of Him as your 'Heavenly Father,' because you have a really awful version down here on earth to compare Him with. So don't. But He is there, and He does love you. And that love—there's nothing like it, Chris."

Oh, here we go again.

I don't know if I roll my eyes, but Dad can just feel it.

He looks at me for a long time, and that's when I see the tears in his eyes.

In all our conversations and arguments and times back in Illinois, I never once saw him cry.

I think that maybe I should say something, anything, but he's up and heading to the bedroom. Probably to take a shower.

I sit there in the silence, thinking of everything he just said.

Maybe he's changed as much as I have.

79. Destiny

I finally manage to talk to Kelsey at school. I've seen her in the halls, but she's either avoided me or I've been talking with Lily and didn't want to suddenly go chasing after another girl. I know this about girls—they're impossible to figure out. So if things are going fine with even one of them (à la Lily), then that's great.

"Are we still practicing today?"

Kelsey looks at me as if I'm speaking a foreign language.

"I got your email—I didn't reply because I wanted to talk in person."

"I got someone else."

"Seriously?"

She nods.

"But I thought—look, I don't mind being your partner."

Kelsey raises her eyebrows. "Oh, you don't mind? Well, gee, thanks."

"I didn't mean it like that."

"It's fine. It's all taken care of."

Her bold blue eyes look away, and for the first time I notice how utterly distant Kelsey appears to be.

Do all girls have this ability to just completely shut down?

"Kelsey?"

"Yes, *Chris*?"

And do all girls have this snarky tone down pat?

I shake my head. I'm trying. I'm really trying.

"I just—what do you want?"

She looks at me, her expression softening and her head shaking gently. Those pretty eyes lock back on mine. "Nothing. Nothing at all."

The cute little girl who always used to look away doesn't look away right now.

And I gotta admit—it's kinda hot.

I see her friend Georgia coming and am smart enough to say good-bye. As I leave, I see her brush her hair back as if she's just gotten rid of a mosquito that's been hovering around her.

I always said that I was no good for her, and I still feel that way. I guess this just makes things easier.

Yet as I walk away to my next class, I can't get the image of her feisty stare out of my mind.

I'm walking out the doors of the school talking with Harris, who is in my last class of the day. He's become a pretty good friend. Not someone that I can tell everything to … but still someone I can talk to and laugh with and share our mutual love for Lily.

Lily isn't waiting here like she usually does, and we talk for a while as we wait for her. When she doesn't show, and the buses all file out of the parking lot, Harris takes off. It's Friday afternoon, and Lily and I were going to "hang out." I wasn't sure what that meant, but it did mean we'd be together. Now she's nowhere to be found.

I call her but get her voice mail. Then I text her, but don't get a reply.

Just as I'm about to get on the motorcycle and head toward town to see if she's anywhere around, a car pulls up along the edge of the sidewalk. It's a black Audi, a high-end Audi that seems a bit out of place around here. The window is rolled down, and I hear my name.

I glance in to see Pastor Marsh. He's wearing sunglasses and looks like he's off to go pick up chicks or something in his casual, hip clothes.

"Have a minute, Chris?"

No, not really. Please come back in seventy years.

"Why don't you get in?"

"Mom told me never to take rides from strangers," I say in a weak attempt at a joke.

"And how often have you listened to your mother?"

Good point.

"My bike is here."

"Your bike?" he asks as if to prove a point.

What's that word for someone who knows all and sees all?

"Don't worry—nobody will touch it," Marsh says. "We need to talk."

"Why?"

"Because it's September 30, and the timetable has been changed."

The timetable? For what?

"I'll explain, Chris. That and other things. Please—just get in."

It would have been strange to picture this months ago when I was chasing after this guy in the woods with a knife. But everything about Solitary has been strange. And I've continued to find surprise.

Opening the door and sitting on the soft leather seat, I know that some of the surprises have included my own actions.

As we drive toward downtown Solitary, I feel like a prisoner even though he's not technically holding me against my will. He has no gun or knife that I know of. But I really don't want to be here.

"I see your father managed to make his way here."

I nod.

"You're not having any ideas about suddenly becoming best friends with him, are you?"

I shake my head.

I can't see behind his shades, but I know those eyes are looking right at me when he's talking.

"Chris—you have to be very careful around your father. Do you understand that?"

I nod.

Suddenly a hand jerks my wrist, and I look at him and say yes.

"We don't have any more time for you to play dumb, do you understand?"

I take my hand back. "Where are we going?"

We're heading out of Solitary, away from the downtown.

"I'm going to show you something. Prove something to you. Okay? And then, maybe—just maybe—you'll start listening to me and start preparing."

"Preparing. For what?"

"To take over the work your great-grandfather is doing."

I look Marsh's way. He takes off his sunglasses to make sure I can see his glare.

"I'm going to prove to you once and for all that you are different. It's just one example, but it'll do. I can't show you everything. You'll have to learn it as you go. With your father here, and with all the things that have been happening—a date has been set, Chris."

"A date for what?"

He doesn't answer, but instead just whips the car around the curves of the mountain road. Maybe he's taking me back to the burnt-down Crag's Inn.

I could only wish.

Instead, he slows down and finds one of those nondescript dirt roads heading into the woods. Unmarked and barely visible unless you're really trying to get there. He carefully drives around the potholes in the road.

We drive maybe five minutes before he reaches a large boulder sitting on the side of the road and parks right next to it.

"It's a little hike from here, but nothing you can't handle," Marsh says. "It's all downhill."

The woods are shadowy and strangely silent. The ground is flat and clear where he walks, like it used to be a path but is rarely used anymore.

"Come on—I'm not going to do anything to you."

But honestly, how in the world can I believe that?

So why are you here Chris?

But I know it's for answers I've continually tried to get.

I hear a sound and suddenly know where we're going. We pass over flat rocks and boulders sticking out of the ground. Then we come alongside a running creek that leads toward the noise.

"Have you seen Marsh Falls from this view?" he asks.

I don't like this. Coming to this place with him.

The creek winds around, and then I can see it through the tree and bushes. The crystal-like water falling into a pool below. Boulders of all shapes and sizes jut up around the bottom of these falls—the same place where Marsh fell.

"Come on," he tells me.

We're soon standing on a massive flat rock right next to the stream flowing from the pool underneath the falls. It's warm here. Really warm. I study the water and wonder how deep it is directly under the falls.

Maybe someone could survive if he fell just right and the waters were deep enough.

But yeah, that's if the person already survived a plunging knife to the gut.

It's insane. Really, truly insane.

What are you doing here, Chris, get out get away.

"This is why your original great-great whatever first decided to settle down here, Chris. Louis Solitaire. He chose this place, according to the history we've been told, because of these falls. Because they're special."

I look at him standing by my side. I could take him in a fist fight, I believe this. He's not that big. I stand my ground, looking at the water but keeping him in my peripheral view.

"When he got here, he had to coax the Cherokee Indians to let him settle. The reason he left his small town in the French Alps—well, that's a whole other story, one of myths even wilder than those around here. But he came here desperate, his entire family destroyed. He chose these mountains because they reminded him a little of back home. Then he met the Indians and almost ended up dying by their hands. Until he showed them what he could do."

"What?" I ask. "Magic?"

"To them, he was a magician. A demon. Yet he managed to trick them into believing in his power. They knew these were special waters. But it was what Louis showed them *about* these waters that made them—believe. That made them start following him."

"I stabbed you. With a knife. And I watched you fall."

Marsh nods, moves away from me a bit, leans over and touches the water. He brings his hand back up to his face and sucks on his fingers.

"It even tastes different."

For a second I stare at the falls and the dark pool hovering at our feet. Then I glance back at Marsh and see him coming at me, something in his hand, something short and bright—

I hold a hand in front of me but he grabs it with his own, with a strength that I didn't know he had. Then he plunges the blade deep into my wrist. He gives it three deep, quick cuts, like he's trying to make sure he slices something just right.

Oh God no no no.

I grab my hand back and hold my right wrist with my other hand. Blood is gushing like the waters in front of us. My head is suddenly feeling light and woozy. I want to throw up.

Marsh is next to me then, one arm around me so I don't fall and bash my head into these rocks.

"Stay with me. I hate having to prove a point, but you're as hard-headed as these rocks around us."

"Why—what—I'm—the knife—why—"

"It's okay, Chris. Really."

I try to get out from his touch, but he holds me secure.

"Come on, now, let's just wait another minute."

"No no no …"

More than pain, a cold sick fear takes over me. I know just how bad those cuts were. The blood is everywhere. I'm going to die here right at the feet of this wicked pastor for no reason, none at all.

A part of me wants to cry out for help, for God, but I told Him right above these waters where He could go and what He could do.

"Okay, that's good, that's long enough," Marsh says. "If you weren't *here,* Chris, you'd die. Just like any ordinary person with a severed vein. But you'll see. Go ahead."

He lets me go and scramble away from him.

"Dip your arm into the waters. Go ahead."

I shake my head, but I'm feeling weak and know I'm not about to run away from him.

"Do it, Chris, or I'll do it for you."

I get on my knees and crawl over to the water, dipping both hands in at first and then plunging them in further.

"There you go. Keep them in there."

I'm on my elbows with both my arms in the water and the sound of the falls above me streaming forth and my heart beating fast and the sounds of the crickets and katydids all make my eyelids heavy and I can't help but close them just for a moment.

When I open them, I'm sitting up, resting against a rock. It feels like two days later.

"Here, drink this."

At first as I reach for the bottle he's giving me I feel pain in my wrist, but then I realize that's my imagination. I look at the hand that was just cut, the same wrist that was bloody and oozing and spilling out my life.

It's fine.

I touch it and think I'm dreaming.

"It's fine, Chris. Just like that."

"No."

He nods, then gives me the bottled water. I drink it, finishing it up.

"Good. I took that directly from those waters. Who knows. Drinking that much might give you the ability to fly."

I stare at him to see if he's actually serious, but he just laughs and takes the empty plastic bottle back from me.

"Nah, no flying. Not that I know of."

"What just happened?"

Marsh refills the bottle and comes back to kneel in front of me. He takes a sip, then stares at the falls.

"Louis Solitaire had a gift, the ability to see the spirits surrounding him. This place was full of them. Maybe because of the Cherokees, who knows. There weren't any white people here yet. He was able to do some tricks and get their attention. But it was only when he healed one of their very sick that they made a deal with him. That they actually began to worship him."

"He healed someone? How?"

"The same way you healed me, Chris."

I just look at those eyes in the glasses, wanting to know if he's kidding again. But he's not.

"These waters have always had a power to them. The Indians told Louis that the waters helped wounds and extended life and all that. But somehow, when combined with the abilities that Solitaire had, the water took on new power."

"How did I heal you? I tried to kill you."

Marsh takes a sip of the water. "Yes. You did. I should be angry at you for doing that, too. But that was my whole intent. To lead you to that cabin in the woods. Show you something that would make you *want* to kill me. Then lead you all the way here. Or, I should say, up there." He nods at the cliff at the top of the falls.

"Why?"

"To prove a point. To see if—if it was really true. And good thing, too, because if I'd been wrong, well ..." He raises his eyebrows.

"Why didn't you die?"

"You are part of the Solitaire bloodline, Chris. Sounds a bit creepy, huh? But it's true. Same with your uncle. And mother. But for some reason it's different with the males."

"What's different?"

"Their abilities. I've seen it with your great-grandfather. He should be dead, Chris. But these waters have extended his life. Along with others. But it's only when you combine this water—this water here, not the water bottled up and shipped to who knows where—with your touch. Your physical touch. Something happens."

"What?"

Marsh shakes his head, his eyes bright. Then he laughs. "I don't know. But it's real. That I know."

"No."

"Chris—please. Please do not say you didn't just see what happened. Twice now I've shown you. I proved it to myself, but that was also for you. How do you think I survived that knife in my stomach? Or falling over into these waters. I think I landed right over there, by those big sharp rocks."

I shake my head, but I can't argue with what he's trying to prove.

"This is just part of it, Chris. Just a fraction of who you are. And what you can do."

He's talking as if I'm in a comic book movie and he's suddenly going to tell me my new name is Thor or Captain America or something.

"I grew up hearing rumors of abilities like this, and then I saw it. I never believed in spirits and demons until—well, until I was proven very, very wrong. I long to have what your great-grandfather has, and what *you* have. But I don't. But I do know that it's real."

I look at my wrist, and it looks fine.

"If I told you this the second day you came to town, what would you have done? Probably taken the first bus out of here, if of course Solitary had buses running from it. You'd be delirious with fear and wouldn't believe it. But now, after seeing everything you've seen, do you believe me?"

I shake my head, sigh, then look at him and ask the question I still need an answer for.

"But what do you want from me? Why are you telling me this now?"

"Because, Chris. In nine months—less than that now—your great-grandfather is going to die. And you need to fill his place."

"Fill what place? To do what?"

"To continue the great work he's done. That your family has done ever since Louis came here and discovered this place and decided to make it his home. This is your home too, Chris. And it's time for you to grow up and be a man and *accept* who you truly are."

I still don't get it. "So who am I? What does my family do?"

"They're able—*you're* able to see on the other side. And with time, you'll be able to control the forces that are over there, no matter how terrifying they might be."

80. Angry

I ignore the calls from Dad. It's dinnertime, and I'm supposed to be home. And I'm heading home, my head floating in clouds of doubt and denial. And maybe deliriousness.

I need to see Lily.

Maybe I'll tell her everything going on. Just get it all out so that someone can help me make sense of it all.

The gunshot wound.

Thinking of Lily makes me think of this. And I feel shivers, thinking about what Marsh said to me.

Did they bring me to the waterfall and baptize me that night to heal me?

Maybe she can't make sense of this any more than I can, but at least she can make sure I'm not losing my mind.

It's maybe around six or something when I get off my bike and head up to the bed-and-breakfast. I wonder how long Lily is going to be staying at this place. Maybe I can move in here in an extra bedroom that Lily can slip into at night when her mother is asleep.

I'm almost to the door when I see the figures.

Lily is standing under a huge umbrella of a tree in the garden area to the side. There's someone next to her—no, make that attached to her. She leans against the tree and some dark-haired guy leans against her.

They're kissing.

No, they're doing more than kissing.

That's no ordinary kiss.

That's the guy she called an old friend, someone who went "way back" with her.

I stand there and watch, feeling worse than I did after Marsh cut me. Now I feel naked and stupid and angry and confused.

Her hands are all over this guy, and I see the two of them almost slide down the tree.

It'd be funny if it weren't Lily.

I wait one more second to make sure I'm really seeing this, then I turn around and quickly take off.

My motorcycle engine is loud, and I can see a figure emerging from the lawn just as I turn around to head back home.

I know it's Lily watching me, just like I was watching her.

Watching her and whatever guy she was with.

My dad almost grounds me again, but I tell him I could care less. I have less than nine months until I graduate and have freedom. Now that whatever I had with Lily seems to be over

And what DID I have with Lily, come to think about it?

it doesn't really matter if I get grounded again. You have to have things to be grounded from. And I don't. Not anymore.

I don't talk much to Dad tonight. He asks if everything is okay, and I shrug and say yes. But all I am thinking about is Lily.

I don't get a call or a text or anything from her. I know she saw me. And I know she knows I saw her.

It takes me a long time to go to sleep. I'm thinking of what Marsh said and what Lily did.

And all of it just makes me really, really angry.

81. Deliverance

Dad has been here a couple weeks when he comes to my room one evening. Studying is hard enough when it's just you and a textbook while the rest of the world has to wait. But when you have all the crazy thoughts that are going on in my head—well, that makes reading about biology even more difficult.

Make that impossible.

"I just spoke with your mother," Dad tells me as he stands at the doorway. "It looks like she's going to have to spend a little more time in the inpatient program."

"You mean rehab?"

"Yes."

I hate when people don't use the term that makes more sense. Like saying someone's an addict when they really should just say he's a drunk. It seems to let them off the hook in some way. Or maybe it makes it better when you have to say it out loud.

"What happened?"

"She just had a few setbacks."

I look at him, waiting for more. But more doesn't come.

I'm not in the mood to hear whether Mom escaped and hit the road in a convertible heading west. Or if she got caught with a two-liter jug of Diet Coke mixed with something.

"So how long is she going to be?"

"They don't know."

Dad looks as annoyed as I am. The lines on his forehead seem extra long and deep in the dim light of my room.

"You okay?" he asks me.

I nod. No, I'm not okay, not really, but that's been going on a year. Dad and I are on speaking terms, and things are fine so I just want to leave things like that. Just fine.

He looks around my room, at the sloped ceiling and the small desk. Then he just shakes his head.

"Chris, you need to understand something about Mom. Something about Mom and you and all of us. Something I believed back home and something I'm thoroughly convinced of now that I'm here."

He sighs, walks into the room, and sits on the edge of my bed. Midnight is by my desk, close to my feet like she always is when I sit there.

"I think our family is under a great spiritual attack. I saw it happening all the way back in Libertyville with your mother. Some of the things she said—and even did ..."

"I know what's wrong with her," I say.

"What?"

"She likes to drink too much."

He looks at me, nods, then clasps his hand tight.

"There's a battle going on. For your mother and you. For your lives. For your souls."

I shift in my chair.

"Don't roll your eyes," Dad says. "I know you don't believe in any of this. And I know I was wrong to suddenly come into your life and try to force you to believe in something. But the world is a dark place, Chris. You'll come to understand that."

"I believe that now."

"We can't do it on our own. I tried. God knows I tried for close to forty years. I tried and I failed. And I finally gave in."

"And everything's better?"

"Don't. Just, please, Chris, don't. I'm not forcing anything here. I've laid off. You gotta give me that. Right? I've let you be. Tell me if I haven't."

I nod, knowing he's right.

"This darkness—I think it's trying to destroy our family, the little bits we have left. I've prayed for your mother and you every day, numerous times each day. Not that you come back to me. But that you find God. That you find deliverance from this darkness. I just didn't know—I didn't know how bad it was down here. And I'm sorry I didn't just ignore your mother and come down here to see for myself."

I think of Iris talking about the dark and the light and the spaces in between. Then I think of the verses in Daniel that I read.

"There's only one way to fight this darkness. It's accepting Jesus. Not just a God above who is there to believe in. Because everybody—most people anyway—claim they believe in a God. I claimed this for years. But it's God's Son, Chris. His name. His sacrifice. His ability to take all of the bad stuff and make it go away."

I still don't get it. I really don't. "So your life has worked out perfectly since you 'accepted' Jesus?"

"The bad stuff is my own sins. Doesn't mean I suddenly become perfect. But it means that I don't have to carry those mistakes and hurts to the grave. They've been paid for. That's how He delivers us from the darkness."

I don't say anything, and there's a long pause. One that soon becomes a bit awkward. I'm too tired to disagree. I don't feel moved because I've heard this before and I just can't accept it. Not in light of everything going on. I don't think suddenly believing that Jesus Christ really did all the things He was supposed to have done will suddenly make my days and Solitary a lot brighter.

"I'm not trying to preach at you, Chris. If I were more eloquent, or patient, or a lot of things, maybe, you'd hear me out. But that's—I needed to say that. To tell you those things."

I nod.

"I love you," Dad says as he stands and then grips my shoulder.

He's got a strong grip.

He closes the door and I close my biology book, staring at the wall in front of me.

I sit there trying not to think of the words my father just said. But it's impossible.

82. Midnight City

The October days leading up to Halloween all feel gloomy, clouded, damp, and messy. I'm a fallen leaf stuck under a rut in the mud that's been driven over one too many times. Perhaps my English teacher might like that line, but I don't because it's too true and too tiring.

Lily tries to talk to me, but I refuse. She tries three different times but then seems to say *Okay, fine, I'm done with trying.* Which is fine by me because I'm done wondering what is going on with Lily. Obviously she has other things going on in her life. Other people in her life. Other guys.

Make that one other guy.

I just wake up and get out of the house without too much drama, then go through the motions of school.

I do my best at trying to avoid everything and everyone.

Lunch periods I walk around listening to my iPod. I have lunch sometimes with Newt, as long as he's not trying to make me do something I don't want to do. I hang around with Harris and others. I avoid Lily. And I'm still being avoided by Kelsey.

An advisor comes out of nowhere to meet with me and ask what I want to do with my life.

"Get out of here," I say, which he laughs at until he sees my expression.

My English teacher makes us read *Moby Dick,* and I come to see the whale as a symbol of the hope I'm looking for in this town. The hope I can't seem to ever find because everybody just keeps lying to me.

The Halloween dance is coming up with a special spooky theme, but I know I'm not about to go to a stupid dance. I'm not going to any dumb party afterward. Or then again, maybe I will, and maybe

I'll get so drunk I'll climb up on the roof and try to use the so-called magical powers Marsh says I have to zap some idiot with lightning.

Dad tries to make a point of having dinner. He's stressed and worried and at one point he said it has to do with finances but that I shouldn't have to worry about it so I don't.

Once I see the big SUV driven by Staunch coming my way on the street while I'm riding my bike, and I just pass it by as it slows to a stop. Maybe he wants to talk to me, but I sure don't want to talk to him.

I know I can't keep this up forever, this whole avoiding and going through the motions thing. But for a few weeks it seems to work pretty good.

And then I get friend request from Kelsey.

I never go on Facebook and I never update anything, but still she wants to be friends.

For a while I debate doing it, but I'm curious. I thought she hated me, and besides, I've seen her hanging around with some dark-haired guy, so why now?

Eventually I click accept.

Such a simple, stupid thing to say I "accept her friendship."

I thought we were friends, right, after all that last year?

Then what about the summer you stupid moron?

The voices in my head are getting meaner. I wish they had a volume knob.

I go on Kelsey's page and then, suddenly, the past few weeks and the endless dreary days seem gone.

She doesn't have many friends, and her settings are set to private. But she's inviting me in to see her little life.

I find myself on the beach with her. Bright-eyed and happy and glowing Kelsey. I'm on a city sidewalk with her, toasting to something. I'm with a group of girls all laughing and posing. I'm standing at the edge of some cliff looking over.

I don't know what it is about looking at those pictures and seeing all the things that Kelsey "likes." But it makes me feel better. It makes me feel normal. It brings me back to a place when I didn't have all of *THIS!* shrieking in my ears all day long.

I'm sad, and I don't want to be sad anymore. I want that smile on Kelsey's face. I want a family that seems as secure as hers. I want a future that seems as optimistic as hers.

And then, after looking at her life on display for a long time—so long I lose track of time—I see a message pop up on my screen. Not an instant message—I've got my settings so I can't get those. This just shows up in the inbox.

I click to find a message from the very same girl I'm looking at.

It's eleven o'clock, and dark and stormy outside, yet it's kinda comforting to find her still awake.

Thanks for accepting my friend request. Chris—I hope we're still friends. You've seemed quite blue lately. Yeah, I've noticed. But then again, I've always noticed.

I don't reply. But that night, all through the night, I think of Kelsey's words.

It seems like nobody, and I mean nobody—from my mother and father to my missing uncle and crazy great-aunt to the teachers to the students to the hot girl I fell for this summer to the mean man up the street and the freaky pastor—can be trusted.

Yet I trust Kelsey.

I've always noticed.

This is the first time I'm actually glad someone is paying attention.

I'm thinking of her cute, sweet face when I finally close my eyes.

83. The Boxcar

A couple of days before Halloween, I decide to head to the barn Jocelyn showed me that used to house Midnight. I'm not sure why I go there. Maybe I'm looking for answers. Or for Jocelyn to show back up in my dreams.

But you sent her away, didn't you? And that's not the only one you sent away either. Right, smart guy?

I hate it when my own thoughts mock me.

I'm heading down the tracks and I see the old railroad signal. Then I see something else resting in the shadows of the trees. An old boxcar is just sitting there on the tracks, waiting for the rest of the train to pick it up. It looks old, with a brownish-gray weathered color and no writing on it. The doors are shut and the wheels seem stuck.

I've come here a few times, and never once did I notice this boxcar. It's impossible to miss, even in the fading light of day like now.

Instead of going to the barn, I head over toward the tracks.

As I get closer to the boxcar, I feel something strange. It's the air around me, the way my skin feels, how something seems unsettled in my stomach. I'm sure it's just nerves—ominous boxcars suddenly appearing out of nowhere are enough to give anyone the shivers.

But it's more than that.

My heart races as I approach the freight car. It suddenly seems very dark outside. And I feel very alone standing here. I slowly reach out and touch the side of the car, just to make sure I'm not making this up. But it's real. It's made of wood that's cracking and faded.

I walk alongside it and come to a thick, rusted-over lock. A very simple lock, something that looks as though it was designed a long time ago. Perhaps when they actually ran this train.

It makes me think of the notes I made when I was researching this town and the tracks and the Crag's Inn for Iris. I still have the laptop she gave me. I still have the notes I was compiling.

A part of me wants to open the door. Out of curiosity. Out of sheer wonder. But another part fears seeing what's inside.

Something seems to enclose around me. Nothing physical, just a feeling. Like something is smothering me with fear and cold and dread. Like something else is pulling and stretching and clawing at me to get inside and pull me apart. I rub my bare arms, knowing I should've worn more than the T-shirt I have on. My muscles ache, and I have no idea why.

I move away from the door and circle the boxcar. On the other side, I make out some kind of marking. It's the number 1313 in big, bold paint that's started to fade away. There's nothing else, just the number in a dark color that is blurring out like the rest of the color of the wood.

As I get to the middle of the car on the other side, I hear sounds.

Moaning.

Not just one voice, but many.

They seem to be coming out of the railroad car.

They grow louder. A sickly, deathly sound. Almost wet and totally warped.

I hear movement.

Maybe it's all the zombie movies I've seen in my life, but this is what it sounds like—a bunch of waking zombies who I know are suddenly awake inside of that boxcar.

Those things are fast, remember.

I don't just walk away.

I bolt back down the railroad tracks to the town of Solitary.

Soon I can't hear anything else except the sound of my own gasping for air. I slow down a bit and look back over my shoulder and don't see anything behind me. Since the tracks have headed left a bit, I can't see the boxcar anymore.

I stop for a minute and suck in air and look all around me. I'll go see the old barn another day. Right now I head back to the grill where normally Mom would be.

I can't help looking back to see whether the boxcar is going to come out of nowhere, this time doused in hellish flames, racing out of control toward me with a doorway opened like some demonic mouth waiting to swallow me whole …

84. A Song and a Dance

What am I doing here?

I thought that this Halloween dance would remind me of last year, being in the gym with Jocelyn, but it doesn't. Primarily because of the music. I guess the country music and heavy rock DJ got replaced with the hip-hop and teen-bop DJ.

I'm not sure which is worse.

It's really awful seeing a bunch of white kids trying to dance to a Jay Z song. Doesn't matter if it's in Libertyville or Solitary. They're kinda just swaying at some of the rap songs while going crazy over the Lady Gaga type songs.

Yeah, I should not be here.

But I came with Harris, and he's fine dancing with half the girls out there. We're going to a party after this, where maybe the ghost of Jocelyn will show up. Or maybe Poe will come out of nowhere.

A pounding dance track begins with a female singer saying, "Don't hold your breath."

I've been here for an hour at least when I see her.

The tall girl with the long legs in the black mini-skirt.

And no, I'm not talking about Lily, who I haven't spoken with for several weeks. I'm talking about my Facebook friend and former art partner and potential cheerleading partner, who seems to have gone on some makeover show and turned into … this.

Kelsey's hair is straight and long, and she's wearing a long-sleeved pleated shirt that fits her just right. She's with her senior friends on the dance floor while the rest of the room, especially the guys, are watching them.

Harris, of course, is right there with them, dancing and smiling.

I take a sneak peek maybe, possibly. I don't know.

I'm not even bothering to hide my glance. At this point, it doesn't matter.

Yeah, maybe I've blown all my opportunities with Kelsey, and maybe she'd be wise to learn from those times.

But at the end of the song, her glance finds mine.

She smiles. As usual.

This time I smile back, not trying to hide anything.

It's nice to share a smile in this place.

"Did you, uh, come here with the girls?"

Kelsey looks at me. "No—the college senior brought me."

She smiles, and I know she's kidding.

"You look—different."

Her eyes dart down, and the old Kelsey, the shy and timid one, seems to suddenly resurface.

"Different as in really great. I mean—well, okay, this is going downhill fast."

"Is that supposed to be a compliment?"

I nod. "Sorry, it's just. I mean, you know—"

"This belongs to Georgia. My Dad would kill me if he saw me."

I laugh. "You look nice."

She smiles, and something comes over her face.

"What?" I ask.

"Nothing."

A slow song comes on, and this time I don't want to wait or wonder or let another second go by not doing anything.

"Do you want to dance?" I ask.

She looks surprised, but the nod is quick and I know she wants to. Not because I'm some magnificent catch here in this gym. No, not at all. I'm like some trout fish caught in a pond. Or maybe a worse kind of fish. I'm not a fisherman, so I'm not sure how to even rank the fish, but trout just seems sorta bland. I'm not cod, that's Gus. And I'm not shark. That's someone like Ray.

And why in the world are you thinking about fish as you're heading out to the dance floor idiot?

Kelsey puts her arms around my shoulders as I put my hands against her sides. I do this slowly because I'm hesitant, not sure how she's going to react to being this close. I know we've danced before and all that, but—

She pulls me closer.

Kelsey—sweet little Kelsey—is pulling me closer to her.

Okay, then.

We dance to a slow but upbeat R & B song, something where the guy talks about being alone at night talking to the moon.

I feel Kelsey against me and she feels right.

I calm down.

Staunch and Marsh and Lily and Jocelyn and Newt and Gus and Jared and Wells all go away for a moment. I'm no longer in this town. No longer in this stinky gym. No longer a teen.

The song seems to end before it even begins. It goes into another slow song by Beyoncé.

Kelsey looks at me for a moment.

"Am I hogging you from the others?" I ask.

"It's okay. They can wait. They've had four years to ask me to dance."

"You don't want to dance with any of them," I whisper close to her ear so she can hear me above the pounding bass.

She smells like some kind of bright fruit, and if I close my eyes I imagine some tropical place. It's a nice thought. I see us dancing like this at dusk to some Caribbean music.

"Kelsey, I'm sorry," I say into her ear as the song swells, just like my emotions are doing.

"For what?"

For pressing pause on that last dance and pressing mute on everything this summer and for trying to erase the track before it finished playing.

"For being a guy."

She looks at me, and I see everything in that look.

Suddenly I discover that I'm not the only one who's escaped this dreadful place through a song and a dance.

Kelsey's escaped too, and she's right by my side.

The dance is over, but the crowd of students doesn't seem to want to leave. I see that look on Kelsey's face again, the one I saw right before I asked her to dance.

"What?"

She only smiles.

"Come on—tell me what you're thinking, 'cause I know you're thinking something."

"Georgia was right."

"Right about what?"

"She told me to wear this outfit tonight. She said I'd be noticed."

I nod. "Tell Georgia I owe her one."

Kelsey flips her hair over her shoulder and gives me a playful, teasing sort of look. A flirty look. "She would probably tell you that you owe her a lot more than one."

I smile, knowing Kelsey is right.

Before I can say anything else, she leaves me there, speechless, breathless, lost for a short while.

It's a very short while, but at least it's something.

85. Temptation

I'm not exactly sure who is having this party. Harris thinks it's a freshman, and I feel sorry for the kid when I get there, because his averaged-sized two-story house on the corner lot is being destroyed. Inside and out. This isn't like the nice little chaperoned get-togethers that Ray used to have. This is an out-of-control party just waiting for the cops to arrive.

Cops to arrive.

It's a funny thought.

Somehow I want to stick around to see it happen.

But as it turns out, something else happens.

Someone else arrives on the scene.

I should've known that a nice night out would have to be ruined. How in the world could I possibly be granted a good night's rest after a fun time out?

"Chris, we need to talk."

It's Lily, looking stressed and serious and very *un*-made-up for a night out. She's in jeans and a blouse with a jeans coat over it, her hair up in a ponytail. Of course she still looks striking, as always, but she's dressed like she just woke up and threw on the first things she could find.

At first I shake my head and try to walk around her. I know Harris told her I'd be here, of course. It's okay. I figured she'd be here tonight. I just expected her to be a little more like her flashy self.

I feel a tug on my shirt, and I stop and turn.

"Chris, I need to talk to you. Now."

I sigh. "Maybe you should talk to someone else. Like—I don't know—the guy you were hanging out with. But I guess he wasn't really the talkative type, huh?"

She curses at me and then grabs my shirt in the front and jerks me forward.

"Just shut up, okay, and stop with all this. You need to follow me outside right now."

She's talking up close to me, but in a manner that I haven't seen before.

I nod.

Yeah, I'm not messing around with her. Not with *that* look.

I follow her outside of the mayhem that's not going to last much longer. Several guys run by holding beers in both of their hands.

Others are outside on the lawn in costumes. Somewhere back in the house is Harris.

"Did you drive?" she asks.

"No."

"I parked down the street."

"What do you—"

"I mean it, Chris, just shut up and come with me."

We walk down the street past a few houses. I get into her car and she starts it, looking all around us as she does. Then she heads down the street.

We're in the car for a few minutes before she decides to talk.

"I'm going to drive somewhere—I don't know where—just far away, okay?"

I nod. I'm suddenly a little worried. I don't think that it's just a Chris-Lily thing, not anymore.

She gets on the highway heading toward Asheville. The stillness is like an itch I can't scratch. I see her turn off on an exit that says Blue Ridge Parkway, then we drive for another five or ten minutes before reaching a small parking lot. She turns off the car and then opens her door, quickly climbing out into the cool night.

I follow, wondering if this is going to be some kind of dramatic, romantic gesture in the dark. Or if she's a psycho killer who's finally had enough of me.

We reach a short stone wall about three feet tall. Below it is just darkness that descends. I'm sure on a bright and sunny day the view from here is spectacular.

She breathes in and out as we stand facing each other, the cool breeze blowing against us. I can see the moon shining bright and it makes me think of that song that I danced to with Kelsey.

Maybe I'm a lucky guy who's really unlucky with girls. I don't know.

"Chris—this—I just can't believe how sick I feel," Lily says. "I haven't been this nervous about something for a long time."

Nervous about what? Is she pregnant with our child? Which would be funny since we were never even together.

She sighs and rubs her hands together. My eyes have adjusted to the moonlit parking lot we're in. I can see her clearly, that face still so beautiful, those eyes still so striking.

"I'm not sure how to say this, but I'm just going to tell you everything, okay?"

"Okay," I say.

"Just hear me out before you start—saying whatever, okay? Before you start asking questions. Do you understand?"

"Sure."

She nods and then decides to sit on the stone wall, taking my hands in hers and then guiding me to sit down across from her. She releases my hands even though I don't want her to.

"Chris—back in May, I was—well, let me back up. Last New Year's Eve my boyfriend, the guy you saw me with—twice actually—broke up with me. He's nothing but garbage. Nothing but bad news to me. Everybody around me has told me that, and I know it's true. But—well, it's been hard. He left me. Just totally left me with nothing and nobody."

Already I have questions, but I keep my mouth shut.

"By this springtime, I was pretty desperate. There's a lot of stuff you don't need to know about—some of my bad habits that cost a lot of money. Well, come April and May, I was desperate. And I met someone who offered me a job."

I nod, trying not to think. It's better when I don't think.

"The guy's name was Staunch. *That* Staunch. Yeah. Your neighbor. The guy who owns half of this town."

"You're working for Staunch?"

Whatever I might have expected, it's not *that.*

"Just—listen. Okay? Yeah, I've been working for him. He hired me to come to summer school, to come to high school. He hired me, Chris, for you."

"For me? Why?"

"So you could fall for me."

Blank.

"And just—look, when he met me—it wasn't even him, it was someone who worked for him, someone looking for someone like me, I was desperate and didn't know where to turn. And I'm still in that boat, Chris. I didn't move here with my mom. I don't even know exactly where my mom is. I have ideas, but it doesn't matter. My father bailed a long time ago. It's a long, sad soap opera that you don't need to hear."

Still blank.

"They set up this meeting with Mr. Staunch. He comes in here with all this money and with the promise of a better life for me. And all I had to do was make you start liking me. Nothing too serious, that's what they said. Just something that will 'keep a teenager's mind occupied.' His exact words."

Raging fire replacing the blankness.

"So you're not ..." but I can't even complete what I'm saying.

"My name is Lillian, Chris. Lily, Lillian, whatever. I'm twenty-four years old. I look older because, you know what? I *am* older. They chose me because I can act young and fit in."

She looks older because she is older.

I'm an idiot. And I just—I don't want to be here anymore.

I want to be back on that dance floor with Kelsey.

No, I take that back. I want to be back in Libertyville, back at school as a junior, back when none of this happened. Back when I was normal.

"Chris—the part of this that makes me sick—the you and me part—that's real. Everything that's happened between us—I mean it when I say you're a great guy. A special guy. And I swear—I expected to find just another guy wanting what all men want. But you—you were different. Even after everything happened. Or *almost* happened."

I try to swallow, but my throat is so dry and raw. I feel like throwing up.

"They were going to pay me for a year. And with everything happening back in Atlanta—that seemed too good to be true."

I feel dizzy.

Dizzy with lies and deceit.

"Everything was going great until Kurt came back and I messed up, Chris. I messed up."

"Messed up?"

My words are slow, just like my brain and heart and soul. Slow to grasp.

"I should have never—I should have been more careful," Lily says. "But then my ex found me and told me he loved me and all that, and I gave in. Just like I always did. You weren't supposed to see that, Chris."

"Sorry I messed up your plans."

She shakes her head, looking at me. "Listen to me—you can—you deserve to hate my guts for lying to you and messing with your mind. But you have to understand—the stuff I've told you, about the rose tattoo and you getting that card. Nobody knows about that. Only Kurt. And he has nothing to do with them, with Staunch. After you got shot and then suddenly seemed fine, I knew that there was something strange and crazy going on here. And now I'm afraid they're going to do something else. Maybe try and hurt Kurt. Or maybe hurt me."

"No," I tell her.

"No what?"

"That's not going to happen."

I still have no idea how to wrap my thoughts around this—this lie. But she's not going to die because of this and because of me.

"Why did Staunch want us together?"

"They didn't tell me, and I didn't ask," Lily says. "They just said to show a teenager some fun. But like I said, keep leading you on. They didn't want things to get to the next level."

I laugh. "Of course not. I mean, sure, lie and hire some girl to be with me. But not *really* be with me, because of course that would be far too kind for them, wouldn't it?"

"Chris—"

"So you're just like some hooker they got off the street."

She looks at me as if I've just slapped her in the face. Her face grows grim and her lips tighten.

"I guess I deserve that," she says.

All I can think to do is curse. I shake my head and look around me. "Why'd you bring me out here to tell me this?"

"I don't want them knowing about this."

"This is crazy," I say, laughing, standing up and walking a few steps away from her.

Some of the pieces seem to fall into place.

I told myself I wouldn't trust someone after Jared and what happens? Huh?

"Chris," she says, standing and walking up toward me.

"Please don't touch me. Like, ever again. You got that?"

She nods and waits for me to say something.

"And that other guy? Who you said was your father? Who was that?"

"The guy who first found me, someone who works for Staunch."

This is beyond ridiculous. Beyond mean. Beyond anything I can think of.

"Why would you do something like this?" I ask.

"Because there are worse things I could do for money," Lily says. "And I'm not going there."

"Wow, you deserve a medal."

This time Lily curses at me.

"But—why?" I ask. That's all I want to know.

"Why what?"

"Why did they hire you?"

"I told you, they wanted me to—"

"I know that, but why? What's the point been?"

"They wouldn't say. They just wanted me to keep you preoccupied. To keep tabs on you. To have you enjoy things."

"And then what? Were they going to pay you to marry me? Then send you away before the honeymoon?"

"I don't know."

I curse and look up at the sky.

This place is just bonkers.

"Listen, if you want answers, I know how we can get them," Lily tells me.

I shake my head.

"Brick sometimes like to brag about things in front of me. He once told me he had major dirt on Staunch. I asked what it was and how he knew, but he wouldn't say. But I don't think he was lying just to impress me. Maybe—maybe he has some kind of info on Staunch that we could use."

"That 'we' could use?"

"That you could use," she says.

"Why, then? Why were you going to go ahead and, you know. After they said not to. Just to lead me on. Did you feel that sorry for me?"

She grabs one of my hands again and places it in her own. "Chris—Chris! Look at me. Please. I'm not the monster here. I—I think you're adorable. I really do."

"Gee, thanks. Where's my ticket to Disney World?"

"Stop it. I told you—I was in love—I'm still in love. And love doesn't go away. Sometimes your heart doesn't stop bleeding, either, once it's broken. Sometimes your heart just keeps swimming in that dark pool. Unable to see anything. Unable to breathe. But somehow in some way continuing to beat."

"So then you went and broke mine?"

Lily shakes her head. "No, I didn't break your heart. I hurt your pride. And ended a flirtatious thing. But love—it's more than that."

"And you think you know?"

"Love is allowing someone to come back after they break you. Love is giving everything to someone. Love is being unafraid. Love is not sex. That is part of the greater picture, but never all of it."

I stare at her.

"You're still a kid. I've never met a seventeen-year-old so sharp, but you still are a teen."

"You have no idea," I say.

"I don't. But I do know this."

"What?"

"You're sweet," Lily says.

"I don't want to be sweet."

"But you are. And you're special. Something big is going to happen sometime down the road. It involves Staunch and that icky pastor and it involves you. That's all I know."

I close my eyes while she's still standing there, holding onto my hands, squeezing them now.

"Chris, I'm sorry. I'm sorry for lying. It's been—it's grown far too easy for me. But no more lies, okay? I promise you. I'll tell you anything and do anything. I just—I'm afraid something bad might happen if they feel I'm no longer doing my job. I mean—you won't even talk to me since Kurt came around."

I sigh. I'm angry, but I'm also confused and tired.

Yet I know I'm not going to do anything that manages to get her hurt or killed. I just won't.

"What do you want me to do?" I ask her.

"Forgive me."

She hugs me, and I finally manage to put my arms around her. But everything about her and about this is different.

I've been so stupid for what—how many months? Since June, right?

What do you guys want with me? And why send someone in to simply get my mind off things?

I have this scary thought. This sick thought.

All of this—everything bad that's happened—has come after my run-in with Marsh and my dare to God to come and hunt me down.

Maybe God decided I wasn't worth it anymore and took His ball and went back home.

Leaving me in the dark with liars and thieves and murderers.

Leaving me in the dark.

86. Temptation Remix

At the place where the dirt road leading to our cabin starts, I tell Lily to drop me off. She tells me to be in touch. I just nod and get out of the car and then begin walking back home in the dark.

It's a short walk, but it feels like the longest walk of my life.

I'm still too shocked—bewildered—freaked out—to shed a tear. I don't want to shed a tear for Lily.

Yet my own thoughts and actions betray me as well.

Would you have "fallen" so hard if she had weighed two hundred pounds and had pimples?

I want to be angry, but I fell for a fantasy.

They wanted me to fall for another Jocelyn.

They *knew* I'd fall for another gorgeous girl.

You're an idiot to have thought it could happen twice.

Maybe I'll keep walking past my cabin and up to Staunch's place. I'll just wave my hands and tell him to take me, the joke's over, the game is done, he's won.

Take me and then what?

Is there some special, secret throne I need to sit on? Where the rats will come nibble on my legs and take turns gnawing on my face and then I'll slowly grow crazy like that possessed king in *The Two Towers*?

I start to wonder about everything else that's happened.

Can I trust Mom? And Dad?

What about people like Harris? Or Brick? Or that whole sham of a summer school?

All I can think of is one person who I feel I can trust.

The same person I danced with tonight, a dance that made me forget.

I look at the moon and wish and hope that Kelsey is thinking of me.

If only she knew what kind of jackass I am.

Maybe she already does. But maybe she's okay with that.

Lily said that if things continue to appear like it's over between us—and if Staunch decides she's not worth keeping around—then she's in trouble. I wonder if someone like Kelsey could be in trouble as well.

Lies, lies, and more lies.

That's all I've gotten since coming to this cursed place. This cursed and damned and demented place.

Now I have to play their game. I have to suddenly start lying myself. Maybe that will be the only way I'll find out what their grand plan is. And how I can escape it.

Dad is up when I get back home. He's got his reading glasses on, but the book in his lap is closed. He greets me with a tired "Hi, Chris."

I say hi and then go to the fridge to get something to drink. I'm sweaty even though it's not hot outside.

Suddenly I have an urge to ask Dad something, so I go and sit across from him.

"Can I ask you a question?" I say, just to make sure I have his attention.

"Yes."

"Have you ever lied to me? Like—ever? About anything?"

Dad looks confused but immediately shakes his head. "No."

"No, look—I'm serious. Like recently—with Mom and the whole faith thing and North Carolina and your job. Have you ever once lied to me? About anything?"

"No."

"Do you swear?"

"Chris, I promise you. I haven't lied. I don't know what I'd lie to you about. Where's this coming from?"

I nod and stand up. "It's nothing—just life. Just this dark creepy place we live in."

"Who lied to you?"

"Everyone. At least that's what it seems."

"You know you can trust me. At least I hope you know that."

I nod and say yeah.

I know that now.

87. Clean Slate

The next morning I notice something on my desk. Something I look at every day for some reason. That picture that I discovered in my locker, the one of me smiling and looking carefree, the one that I never remember being taken. I almost threw it away because it was so faded. It looked more like a snapshot of the clouds than of me. But on this morning, the first day of November, I see the picture and then pick it up.

I examine it closely.

Good thing reality is continuing to be as foggy as ever.

I see the outline of my head and shoulders in the picture. It's still blurry and faded, but it actually seems to have come back into focus. Just a bit.

I'm imagining that.

But I know I'm not.

This picture means something. I know it.

Everything that's a bit off and abnormal means something.

Maybe it has to do with the bigger picture of what I know. Maybe the more I know, the more in focus the picture will become.

That's a nice thought. But who knows?

All I know is that I'm still aching from the deep cut I got from Lily.

I wish I could say that last night was a dream. But what I realized instead was that Chris & Lily—that was the dream and the fantasy.

Too good to be true.

As always.

RU OK?

I don't want to answer the text, but I do anyway. YEAH, I'M FINE.

Lily wants to know if I'm okay. That's so sweet of her. I don't want to tell her the dreams I had last night, the ones that involved me finding her with other men. I don't want to tell her that I don't think I'll ever be "fine," nor will I ever fully trust another female in my life.

SO EVERYTHING'S COOL?

I think back to Jocelyn. How she eventually told me what was going to happen, and how I didn't believe it until it was too late.

I don't want to be too late. Even if what Lily did was wrong. Not just wrong, but wretched. For no explainable reason.

YEAH, EVERYTHING'S COOL.

Lily looks like a New York runway model when I see her. And why shouldn't she? She's twenty-four stinking years old. She's probably exactly the age for a runway model. And she looks it in her long boots and skirt and top. But everything about her has changed. Everything.

When she sees me she tries to give me a hug, but I move out of it. Nobody sees it. It's just I don't want her hugging me or even touching me.

"Chris—"

"It's fine."

"Come on—let's laugh about things, okay?"

I let out a mock laugh that's a bit too loud and a bit too mocking. She stares at me with an intense look.

"I told you I'd do this," I say in a whisper. "But the more I think about things, the worse they are."

"I'm not going to spend the rest of this year begging you for forgiveness."

I chuckle. "You don't have to. Because it ain't gonna come."

She stares at me, and then we hear the warning bell for first period.

"Can you just act like we finally made up, and put on a good show for everybody?" Lily asks.

"I'll try. But I'm not as good an actor as you are."

But I'm proven wrong.

As we walk down the hallway, with Lily unexpectedly grabbing my hand and holding it, we pass by Kelsey.

And once again, Chris Buckley has managed to crush her bright spirit and possibly break that blossoming heart.

I'm in trigonometry, and I find myself wishing Mr. Taggart was here. Make *him* take this test. Make *him* sit and try to understand this.

He wouldn't have the first clue. So if he doesn't, why should we be expected to know all of this?

For some reason, I find myself thinking of, well, everything. But especially what my father recently told me about Mom. I wonder how she is, and despite all my anger and my attitude toward her recently, I miss her. I feel guilty, thinking I didn't do enough, thinking I should have tried harder to be a good son. But no, I was busy chasing some girl—no, some woman—hired to lure me into her trap.

I feel so weak.

Your passion and your strength.

I hear Iris's voice saying that. Saying that about me.

So it's easy to believe in the darkness, but not in the light.

It's strange how I remember this, but I do.

It's strange how she's right, how I can so easily believe in the darkness but I can't believe in that hopeful light.

Take heart and be strong.

I stare at the test, knowing I'm not going to do well on it. I stare at the pencil and the students around me and the clock on the wall and the dark chalkboard. I focus on that chalkboard that's usually so full of numbers and equations and explanations but now is just empty.

A clean slate.

I like the sound of that.

A year later, is it possible to be like that chalkboard, ready for things to eventually be written down on it?

Is it really possible to accept that light as easily as I can accept the darkness?

Can I actually, finally be ready to know what my place is in Solitary? What I'm supposed to do and why so many are so interested?

I want to pick up the chalk and start writing.

Start writing and not stop.

Guess I'm not the only one wanting a clean slate.

The lady who gets out of the car surely wants one. I see her from my window, and I can feel my heart beating, and feel this wonderful misery inside of me. I don't want to see her and don't want to greet her, yet I've missed her more than words can say. Maybe one day I'll learn to write out all these thousand thoughts in my head because God knows I can't actually speak them aloud.

She looks pretty.

So many pretty women in my life.

I hurry down the stairs and open the front door. Then I head down the wooden steps.

Mom stands there with her suitcase, looking younger in one way and older in another. She has tears in her eyes, and she smiles at me.

Then she hugs me, or I hug her—I don't know because we both go to hug each other at the same time.

There's a lot I want to say and ask her, but for the moment, it's enough that Mom is back.

That's a good thing. Especially around a place where people don't always come back.

88. Exchanging Information

I pull up to the little house I was starting to doubt I'd find. For a while I thought Aunt Alice's one-story rundown shack had gone bye-bye just like the Crag's Inn. But it's still there, still creepy-looking and hopefully still occupied by the living.

I park my bike a little ways down the drive so I don't startle her by driving up to the door. As I walk toward the house, the stench of death is all around me. But this time I don't have to wonder why. I see the outline of hairy clumps on the driveway and as I get closer can tell that they're dead dogs. Three of them, maybe fifty feet away from her door.

Last time a headless groundhog in her driveway, now this.

I don't want to examine the dogs very thoroughly, but they're dead, all right. If one suddenly jumps up and bites me, my heart will stop. Just plain and simple.

I wonder where the dogs came from and why.

But that's why I'm here. To get answers to some of the whys.

Mom and Dad don't know I'm here, of course. It's after school, and I've come with specific questions. I've come to learn a few things about my family. About *our* family.

Before I can knock on the door, it opens for me. And there she stands, a hobbit-like figure leaning against a cane, wild curly strands of thinning hair sticking up.

"Bobby, that you?" her ancient voice says in its deep Southern drawl.

"It's Chris."

"Who?"

"Chris—Tara's son."

"That's Bobby's bike."

"I know."

Her eyes seem to sharpen, and she appears suspicious.

"What're you doing with it?'

"I'm, uh, borrowing it."

She scowls at me. Her pet crow seems to caw in response, welcoming me in the same way.

I feel a shiver go through me.

"What do you want?"

I have a feeling she'd beat me over the head with that cane without a second thought. Maybe that's what happened to the dogs on her driveway. They sniffed by her doorway and got a big whack in response.

"Can I talk with you for a few minutes?"

"Think that's what we're doin'."

I nod, smile politely, continue to keep the cane in my view. "Yes, but I was wondering if we could go inside."

"I'm not for entertaining today."

"No, you don't have to go to any trouble. I just want to ask you some questions. About Walter Robert Kinner."

Her eyes somehow tighten even more, as if she's making a wish after blowing out a birthday candle. Obviously the name registers.

"What does he want now?"

"Do you know him?"

"My own poppa?"

Question number one already answered.

"Please, can I come in?"

Now maybe she knows why I want to come inside. Someone might be watching, or listening. Like they always are.

Plus, I want to get away from those dead dogs.

The place is the same. The black crow in the corner. Some weird mannequins. Candles.

The same stuff as before. Until I spot something on the coffee table.

One of those cards. The creepy cards that I saw at Ray's party.

Sure enough, next to the card is a flat dish with ashes in it.

The card has a long blade on it.

Oh that's just awesome. Where is the blood to go with it?

"I don't have anything to eat," Aunt Alice says.

"It's fine, thanks."

She hobbles to a chair near the crow and then sits down, urging me to do the same. I sit on a hard couch.

At this point, I just can't resist.

"What happened to those dogs?"

"They died."

Her reply isn't meant to be witty or smug. She says it in a matter-of-fact way, as if this sort of thing happens all the time.

"But why are they in your driveway—lined up?"

"To keep away the spirits."

I nod. "Dead animals, uh, keep away the spirits?"

"You see 'em, don't you? I know you do. You're a boy, so of course you do. A Kinner boy. Oh, how my poppa wanted a boy. He got us girls. Didn't know what to do with my sister—your grandma—but sure knew what to do with me."

She rocks back and forth a bit in the chair. If I just saw her I'd think that she was surely senile. But the way she talks—she's all there.

"Doesn't always work, but it helps. Other things do too, but you're young and you haven't been here long."

"Other things?"

"Bobby used to tell me that he'd smoke that special stuff just to be able to get some sleep and not see them in the blackness of his dreams."

I think of Mom drinking herself to oblivion and about my own experience the night I did the same at the cabin. No nightmares that night.

"Have you seen Uncle Robert?"

"He found love. That's what did it. I could see the cloud around 'im. Every time he'd come around. This black cloud of death. Told him he was a fool. But he didn't listen to me. Kinner boys don't ever listen. They gotta do what they gotta do."

"What happened to him?"

"Don't know. Do you? You got his bike."

I shake my head.

She's answering these questions more than I thought she would.

"Does Mom know about Walter Kinner being alive?"

"Her grandpoppa? How would she?"

I shrug. "Well—you told me."

She smiles, and I see a yellow set of teeth that have got to be fake. "'Cause you know. You seen 'im, haven't you? They tried getting to Bobby, but Bobby wouldn't do it. Poor tortured soul of a boy. Thought he'd be all noble and save the girl. But there's no saving anybody anymore. There's just death. That's what you'll learn, if you haven't already."

"What'd they want Uncle Robert—Bobby—for?"

"The same reason they want you. The last male pups left in the litter. Can't let you get away, can they? Their women they discard like those dogs out there. But not the men. Oh no."

I breathe in and feel like we're being watched or listened to. Maybe that's okay. Maybe they're fine with me finally knowing.

"Why do they want me?" I ask.

I'm here to confirm and compare what I know and what I've heard.

It's the only way I can do what Lily wants me to do: get proof.

"You do what they've always done. You take what you need and you leave nothing in return."

Her words seem like an ominous warning.

"But I just—what about the males—why the males?"

"You're their last great hope. Bobby was a lost cause. There was another hope, but I put an end to that. No son of mine would ever grow up black as that bird."

Son of mine?

I'm about to ask her about that, but Aunt Alice continues.

"All they want is for you to continue the sick, twisted bloodline. And you'll get whatever you want, son. *Whatever.* All for exchanging a small and simple thing."

"What's that?"

"Your soul."

89. Dirt

I'm standing at my locker at the end of the day when Lily stops by.

"Are you avoiding me?" she asks.

"I'm going to be seeing you in a few minutes."

"I know, but still."

I close the locker door and face her. "I saw you at lunch."

"Look, Chris—"

"Look what? There's nothing else to say. Is there?"

"What do you want me to do?"

How about go back in time, say no to Staunch's ridiculous offer, and never come across my path?

"Nothing," I say.

"But you're going to be like this, huh? Was the truth *that* bad?"

She's asking me if her lies were *that* bad?

"Ycah, thc truth was pretty bad."

"What part? The fact that I lied to you or the part about my feelings for Kurt?"

"How 'bout the part about you having no heart or soul?"

For the first time since Lily has come into my life like a wrecking ball, I see a break in her confidence. A look of astonishment and surprise on her face.

I wait for a response. She seems to wait for an apology.

I guess this is what they call a checkmate. No, make that stalemate.

In the corner of my eye I see two girls walking by. They're already past when I realize it's Kelsey and Georgia.

"I'll see you at Brick's," I tell her as I head down the hall.

I don't ask how she's going to get there. But she's old enough to have her license and have a car. And I'm tired of worrying about her.

We agreed to meet up at Brick's house after he told Lily he'd be more than happy to divulge the "dirt" on Staunch.

For now, I have more important things on my mind.

I speed up to get to Kelsey just as she walks outside.

"Hey, do you have a minute?"

Georgia catches me and locks an arm around Kelsey. "I'm sorry, but she's busy."

"Kelsey, please?"

She nods to Georgia and then stands still as her friend leaves, shaking her head.

"Listen—I just want you to know something. You have to know this, okay?"

Kelsey doesn't say anything but stands there, wondering when I'm going to say what I have to say. She looks serious, and I wonder if she's given up on me completely.

"I'm not with Lily, okay? We're not dating or anything. Okay?"

"Okay," she says just like a girl.

A girl who's acting like she has no idea why I'm telling her this.

"And maybe—I don't know. I'd like to try and make up for being an idiot these last few months."

"Just these last few months?"

"Well, an even bigger idiot than normal. That's huge, you know."

I see a tiny smile coming on her lips.

"Do you want to go out?" I ask.

"What?"

"This Friday."

"There's a game."

"After the game. I'll go to the game."

"It's away."

"Even better. I can pick you up. Then we can do whatever you'd like."

Kelsey laughs, looks at Georgia who's waiting in the distance.

"Why all of a sudden?" she asks.

"Because I've realized a few things. Okay? Just—you know how slow some guys can be."

"But you're not one of those guys."

It's comments like those that make me wonder why in the world she thinks so highly of me.

"I'm just as clueless as anybody or even more. But at least I admit to it."

"How about Saturday night?"

"I don't care about going to the game."

"I don't want to be wearing a cheerleader's outfit all night."

"Really?" I ask. "You look pretty good in it."

"Saturday, okay. Want to come over to my house around five?"

I nod and say yes without thinking about it.

It's time I stopped wasting time. It's time I started choosing wisely the friends I make.

Especially one who might one day be more than just a friend.

I've passed by Brick's house a dozen times or more since I've moved to Solitary. He's up the hill from the main town, the house sitting like a poor man on a slab of concrete, just wasting away with all its junk surrounding it. There are half a dozen signs everywhere that say to keep out and beware of the dog. But as I walk toward the open garage where I can see Brick, I don't see any animal.

"Where's the dog?" I ask Brick as he gives me both a fist bump and a hug.

"I'm the dog they need to beware of," he says with a laugh. "What's up, Big Buck?"

"Is Lily here?"

"Yeah. She's looking real excited to be here."

I walk past an old refrigerator sitting on a patch of dirt that maybe once had grass covering it years ago. When I reach the garage, I see an old car with the hood opened. Lily is standing next to it, looking uncomfortable. I give her a brief and subdued hi.

Brick comes back into the garage and looks at us.

"So you two want to know about Staunch, huh?"

"You might want to tell the whole world," Lily says.

Brick laughs and gives her a nod, then walks over and pulls the garage door down. It slams to the concrete floor with a loud thump.

"That better, princess?"

"Much."

Brick wipes his hands that seem to be covered in oil. "So what do you guys need to know? Height, weight, preference in women?"

I think Brick is joking, but I don't know for sure. Lily looks at me to let me do the talking.

"You said you had 'dirt' on him. What kind of dirt?"

"Oh, the dirtiest dirt you've ever seen," Brick says with a laugh.

"We're being serious," Lily says.

"Yeah, yeah, I know. What's your beef with Staunch?"

"Why do you need to know?"

Lily seems extra snotty today, while Brick seems extra amused.

Good thing we're not going on a cross-country trip or anything like that.

"I've had a bit of trouble with him," I tell Brick.

"'Cause of Gus?"

"Yeah, somewhat."

"You know, Staunch isn't a guy you want to mess with. He's loaded. Anytime someone's loaded it means they can do whatever they want. 'Specially around a place like this."

Brick picks up some engine part sitting on a bench and then throws it into a metal garbage can.

"Look, whatever," he says. "No big deal what you want to do with it, as long as it doesn't get back to him that the info came from me."

"It won't," Lily states firmly.

"Okay," Brick says in a suddenly urgent tone, mocking Lily.

"How do you know about him anyway?" I ask.

"I worked on his property one summer with a landscaping crew. That's how much dough the guy has. 'Oh, yeah, I'm going to need you to come work for me all freaking summer long.' Crazy. But it was good money."

"I hope you're going to say you have more than just actual dirt you played around with for your job," Lily says.

Brick has to think about her statement for a second. "Oh, yeah, funny. Good one. No, there were two things I filed away in the good old memory that nobody thinks I have. You know—you smoke dope and people just think you're stupid. But I remember. And I remember finding a tunnel leading into his house."

"From where?"

"You ever been there?" Brick asks. "Okay, then you know the stream just beyond his lawn? Yeah? The one with the nice little waterfall? We helped build that, thank you very much. Do you need any work done?"

"I'm good," Lily says.

"So one day I find this hidden door that was connected to a tunnel. I mean, there are tunnels all around this place, so that's not new, but this one was connected to his house. The other thing is this." Brick pauses and looks out a window just to see if anybody's around. "I swear he's got someone down in his basement. We heard things when we were working. Like, weird sounds. The guys I was with, half of them didn't speak English, so I didn't know what they were saying. But we all heard it."

"What'd it sound like?" Lily asks.

"Like some kind of caged animal. Screams. But if I had to guess, I'd swear they were human."

We don't say anything. I don't need to say anything, because I know. I peek a glance at Lily and see her looking quite anxious.

"The other thing—maybe even worse than that—we were told where to work and to avoid going farther downstream. There's nothing much down there, just woods. One day I decide to take off for a smoke, so I start to follow the creek in the woods. I keep going for a while until I reach a place in the woods that looks cleared off. Like just a circle or something, trees missing and everything. I took a look and—no joke, I'm not lying—there was like a huge hole in the middle of the woods, a crater or something, with a tarp covering it. The place just reeked, and I knew, man, I knew."

Brick curses and keeps talking about how ridiculous this might sound but how true it is.

"I took off one of the stones holding the tarp down and checked it out. Sure enough, there was a body. And I'm telling you, man, that hole looked like it could hold *a lot* of bodies."

"This is crazy," Lily says. "You're making it up."

"No way. I swear. No joke."

"And you think it's still there?" I ask.

"Yeah, why wouldn't it be? I mean, I didn't say anything. I got out of there fast."

"Why didn't you tell someone?" Lily asks.

Brick just laughs. "Oh, yeah, sure."

"What?"

"The stoner guy sees a mound of bodies in the woods just down from the Staunch house. Oh, yeah, that's going to go over well. I'll be in the mound, that's what would happen."

Lily looks at me as if she wants to leave.

There's something bright in this dark, grisly tale that Brick has told us.

This could get Staunch and others arrested. This is proof. More proof than just saying I was there when Jocelyn died.

And who knows what's in his house, too.

What's in the basement?

"I've never told anybody this," Brick says.

"Maybe because it's all made up?" Lily asks as she starts moving toward the garage door.

"I might do a lot of things, but when I say something's a fact, it is."

I look at his square face and buzzed head. I want to thank him for this information. But I realize I can't. The info is just too awful to thank anybody for.

Lily opens a door to head out of the garage. I tell Brick bye and then head out to follow her.

I can't tell if this information is going to help or if it's made things worse.

90. Nothing to Dislike

I come home to see Mom and Dad making out on the couch telling me not to bother them so they can make me a little baby brother.

Okay, this doesn't happen, of course.

Instead, I find my father packed and ready to go home. But before he goes, we're all going to go out to dinner.

This doesn't surprise me. Nothing does, not anymore, especially not with Mom and Dad. But the good news is that Mom is different. And so is Dad.

What about you, Chris? Have you changed as well?

Maybe that's what growing up really is. Not getting taller or stronger or wider or smarter. But just getting different with how you deal with the world and those around you.

"Where would you like to go?" Dad asks. "Anywhere."

It's Friday night, and we're going out like a regular old family. I can't say like we used to, because Dad was always too busy to do even routine things like that.

"I don't care," I say, because I really don't. "Maybe just somewhere outside of Solitary."

We end up at a Mexican restaurant that my dad had spotted recently while driving to Asheville for some errands. It ends up being the best Mexican restaurant I've ever eaten at. Perhaps the salsa bar seals the deal for me.

It's strange to see Mom drinking iced tea. Even my father has a Diet Coke. I remember they always liked to have margaritas with Mexican food. But I guess since Mom is trying hard, Dad is respecting that.

Before the food comes, Dad manages to start the conversation that lets me know why we're here, besides to eat dinner.

"Mom and I spoke about the holidays, and we agreed to work things out. With all of us."

"I've kept you away from your father, Chris," Mom says to me. "It wasn't right. I—we've talked about it. We think it would be good for you to spend some time in Chicago with your father around Christmas."

"We're actually thinking that I could come down here and pick you up before New Year's. Have you stay until school starts."

I nod, wondering why he's going to pick me up versus flying. A part of me wonders if he's going to do that specifically to check in on Mom and see how she's doing.

"Okay," I say.

It doesn't sound so bad anymore, going back to Chicago and getting away from Solitary.

"Have you thought anymore about colleges?" Mom asks me.

Yes, between figuring out why the dogs are dead on Aunt Alice's driveway and learning how to conjure up the dead from dear great-grandpoppa.

"No."

"I got a call the other day from your advisor urging us to get serious with your choices. You're already behind, Chris."

I nod at Mom and don't bring up the obvious. Like maybe the *reason* I'm behind. They're not talking to me in their typical way, however. Mom isn't annoyed. Dad isn't impatient and irritated. They're talking to me like an adult. Not that I think I am one, but I'm a year from being eighteen and it's nice to simply be treated with some kind of respect.

We talk about college, but I honestly don't have much of a plan. I have to take the tests—the ACT and the SAT—which means I have to study for them. But beyond that—I don't know.

"There are some good possibilities around Chicago," Dad says. "If that's where you want to go."

I nod, glancing at Mom. She doesn't say anything. I have honestly not thought beyond high school graduation. Everything leading up to that seems gray and blurry and distorted. It sometimes seems like I'll get my diploma and then the clouds will open to reveal a clear, blue sky full of opportunity.

I wish.

"Maybe during your break we can check out some schools," Dad says. "You know—a junior college isn't the worst idea."

I don't want to tell them that all I care about is getting away from this place. I'll go north or south or east or west. I don't care. Just nothing within a hundred miles of Solitary.

Our dinner comes, and the burrito on my plate is seriously larger than a football. That's awesome, because that means I might get a couple more dinners out of this. I'm already full from the three bowls of chips and the nine different salsas I've tried.

"Chris, I want you to know something," Dad eventually tells me after we've slowed down on our meals.

He's got his serious voice and face going. It makes me nervous and brings back bad memories.

"I wanted to tell you this in front of your mother. I just want you to know how proud I am of how you've handled everything. Of how you've helped Mom. She's told me some things. I just—I didn't know. I certainly haven't given you credit in the past. I'm sorry for that."

I nod and look at Mom, who has tears in her eyes. She reaches over and takes my hand, then squeezes it.

"I'm proud of you too," she says. "And I'm sorry."

I nod, and while I've been waiting and wanting these apologies for a long time, I just want this all to be done. I nod and smile because all of a sudden, there's nothing to dislike about Mom and Dad. They're just—people, just like anybody else. Except they're my parents, and they love me, and I know they're trying.

I want to apologize too for hating them so much lately, but I can't. I'm ashamed.

"Chris—if there is anything you need, I want you to know you can call me anytime," Dad says. "I'll be here if you need me. Okay?"

I nod again. And I believe him.

This belief is something I haven't had in a very long time. The realization that someone has my back, that someone might be looking out for me.

It's a nice feeling.

Especially knowing what I'm about to do.

91. Definitely Not Brotherly

At first when I email Kelsey about picking her up for our—well, yeah, it's called a date, so for our date, I say that I can see about borrowing my mom's car. She doesn't bring up the license issue, which is good. But she tells me to ride my motorcycle.

You think I can't ride on the back of a motorcycle? she asks in an email.

Of course not.

I'm not the wallflower you think I am.

I actually Google "wallflower" to see what she's meaning.

I never said you were I reply.

Good. See you tonight.

But Kelsey was right: she *can't* ride on the back of the motorcycle. Mr. Page greets me when I get to their house and then ends up asking me about riding with a helmet. Something I don't do.

"I think you need to drive, Kelsey," he says in a nice, friendly manner.

But the nice, friendly tone still doesn't mean she has a choice.

In her parents' other car, a four-door Honda, Kelsey apologizes for telling me to bring the bike.

"It's fine," I say. "I really need to get a helmet anyway. Or two."

"So where are we going?"

She looks cute in her jeans and boots and jean jacket. It's as if she dressed to go riding on a bike, looking a little tougher and more rugged than usual.

But she could never really quite look rugged.

"I was going to head to Solitary. Just park and walk around the downtown area a few dozen times."

"Stop."

She knows me well enough to know my sarcasm.

"I don't know. I was thinking—well, wondering what you like to eat."

"I haven't had Mexican for a while."

"Really? I know a great place in Asheville."

"You mind going that far away?"

"Do you?" I ask.

She shakes her head.

"When do you have to be home?"

Kelsey shrugs. "I don't have a curfew. It never really comes up. Even though the guys just keep coming around asking me out for dates."

"Maybe they're just intimidated by that shy persona of yours."

"Oh, yes, of course," Kelsey says with a laugh.

"I don't think you'd want many of the guys at Harrington asking you out. Would you?"

"I think they know I'm not particularly interested," she says, adding, "And that I've had my eyes on someone for a while."

The statement surprises me. I want to say something in response, a joke or a witty remark, but I don't want to make fun of what she just said.

She did something I rarely do—put herself out there for better or worse.

"It's about time he noticed," I finally say.

Kelsey looks at me with a whimsical sort of look. "Yeah, I'd say so."

For a while I'm seventeen again.

I'm not with a dark-haired beauty chosen to be a town's sacrifice for a reason I still don't understand, a girl tortured and facing the future by herself.

I'm not with the Goth girl who has always acted one way because of hiding another way she felt, only to be revealed too late.

And I'm not with the older girl posing as a high school girl to lead me down a troubled path.

Instead I'm with a cute girl who looks her age and talks her age but also seems to be more than just another seventeen-year-old girl.

There's something about her, something that continues to surprise me.

I don't exactly know what it is.

After dinner, while we're waiting on a tiny dessert I urged Kelsey to get and promised I'd help her eat, she brings up college. I guess this is the place to go to talk about the future.

"I've decided where I'm going to college," she tells me in a way that seems like she's been waiting all night to tell me.

"Where?"

"Guess."

I guess a few schools in North Carolina, like UNC and Duke. She's smart, and I know she has the grades to get in.

"Wrong state," she says.

I keep guessing until I eventually give up.

"Covenant College," Kelsey says.

I don't say anything, and she asks if I know where that is.

"Yeah, sure. Downtown Chicago."

"Surprised?"

I nod, because I am. "That's a long ways from here."

"It's a great school."

"I couldn't get in there even if I had a million dollars and my dad was the school president."

"Maybe I'll meet some nice Midwestern boys like you."

"Ha. Hopefully you'll meet some nice Midwestern boys who *aren't* like me."

"What are you going to do about college?"

"I'm thinking I'll just move to a big city. Start painting. Because, you know, I'm such a great artist."

This makes her laugh. We get the chocolate thing, and Kelsey takes a couple of bites as I tell her what my father said.

"Who knows," I tell her. "Maybe I'll follow you to Chicago."

She gives me a glance that doesn't go away. "Uh-oh," is all she says.

I know that Kelsey is suddenly acting all girly and strange when she pulls the car into the driveway and gets out. It should be me driving and walking her back to her home. But, oh well, nothing I can do about it. I know why she's being distant and quiet.

The date involving a great dinner and a cheesy romantic comedy movie is about to end.

What happens at her doorstep?

Do I get invited in?

Am I supposed to give her a passionate kiss good night?

Maybe the past year leading up to this gives me the confidence I need to let things be. For a while.

I still believe that I'm no good for Kelsey. But she'll go off to college, find a real man who can be her rock, and that will be it.

"Thanks," she says in that little chirp of a voice I got to know in art class.

"Thank you—for driving. And for hanging out."

"It was fun."

We're standing at her door, the light on, the crickets droning away. She's watching, waiting, surely wondering.

"You're a pretty awesome girl, Kelsey."

I move over and kiss her gently on her cheek. Not in a brotherly sort of way. But in an attempt—at least it's my attempt—to be a gentleman.

I look at her and smile at her in a way no brother is *ever* going to smile at his sister.

"See you on Monday."

She nods, telling me good night.

I see her open the door and slip inside, then hear the door shut and lock.

I go back to my bike and sit on it for a moment.

What's your plan now?

But I don't have a plan. Not with Kelsey. No plan, no intention, no goal. Just a guy hanging out with an awesome girl in the midst of a mad, mad world.

That's all. We'll go from there.

92. The Pit

It always seems that I'm heading down this creek when it's freezing cold outside. At least I have a pair of boots this time. Waterproof boots I bought not long ago. Maybe in the back of my mind, I knew I'd be hiking back downstream to the Staunch mansion at dusk.

I reach the small waterfall that I now know Brick helped build. It reminds me of Wade.

Now dead.

I remember coming here a year ago and seeing the figure on the deck. I now know that was Kinner, my great-grandfather.

Somehow, he seemed to know I was coming.

Can you feel me now?

I remember coming down here when I was just trying to figure out what was going on with Jocelyn.

Also dead.

It's dark and cold, and I'm heading to the place that Brick talked about, a big hole in the ground where the dead are buried. Or no, make that just thrown away. With a tarp covering them.

The farther I walk down the creek, the heavier I seem to feel. The faces and voices of the dead follow me. I feel like I'm carrying them, and I'm not doing a very good job of it.

I don't use a flashlight until I need to. But I've walked about ten minutes past the waterfall and the Staunch house when I turn it on. I'm walking beside the creek now, trying to see where the trees open.

Soon I find myself stumbling in the darkness, having second thoughts.

Maybe Brick made this up.

I go another ten minutes and then wonder if I somehow missed it and need to backtrack.

What am I doing here anyway?

I ignore the voice because I know why I'm here. For proof. For tangible proof that there's a monster living nearby and he's killing people. I've seen enough cop shows and *CSI* episodes to know what they can discover these days. Disposing of a body isn't as easy as it might have been when Count Dracula—I mean Solitaire—moved here years ago.

For a second I pause, feeling the slight wind chill my bones. That's when I hear the sound. A rustling in the woods, something coming toward me, moving and shifting the leaves and dead branches.

I scan the bare skeletons of trees looking for what's making the noise.

The sound is louder.

It's the dead and they've risen to greet you with decomposing arms . . .

Then I spot it.

It comes out of the trees and then stands, facing the beam of light with no fear. The first thing I notice are its pointy ears that are straight up.

The wolf.

It's the same one I saw when I came down here a year ago.

Does this thing guard the Staunch mansion? Does it turn into a demon dog that blows up into smoke?

Then suddenly it looks upward and howls.

I feel like someone just punched me in the stomach. Or I just landed on my back.

The air in my lungs suddenly disappears and I'm there trying to breathe but can't because I'm terrified at this high-pitched, awful scream.

I want to move but can't.

I want to bail but I can't do squat.

It howls for a minute, and I'm wondering if that's a call. If it's summoning up other wolves who will come and eat me. Or if this is a message for Staunch or Kinner or the werewolf in the *Twilight* books who never seems to have a shirt on.

The wolf then stops howling and races toward me.

I shut my eyes and hold my arms up toward my face.

Then I hear it rush past me and up the small bank I'm walking near.

I open my eyes and aim the beam to where the wolf is standing. He's on top of the hill, standing sideways, his head looking toward me.

He missed me.

But no. No way that tall and lean wolf missed me.

I see the white around its mouth as it howls again.

Then it does the weirdest thing. It starts to walk away, slowly, then it turns around and stares down at me.

Then it gives that freaky howl again.

It's like Midnight when she wants to play. She looks at you to throw the ball.

But this isn't a little Shih Tzu. It's a wild wolf in the woods.

It does the same thing again, disappearing and then coming back and looking at me.

It wants you to follow it.

I would laugh if I weren't so spooked. I stand there for a minute.

I'm freezing and know I need to do something.

So I take a few steps up the bank toward where the wolf is standing. He bolts off, this time with speed. I make it up the hill and then scan the dark woods to see where the wolf is now.

That's when I see the opening toward the gray sky above.

The wolf is leading me to it, to the place Brick told me about.

But that's as crazy as …

The bluebird by Iris's old place? That freaky thing in the woods by the wall to Staunch's residence?

I keep walking toward the wolf. He hasn't howled again, which I'm taking as a good sign.

Then I see it, a clearing in these woods where the ground starts to go down. But as I scan it, there's no tarp or covering on the oval-shaped dip in front of me.

Rather, the ground is barren and black. I walk down into it and kick some of the rock and dirt around. It's like a fire pit.

They torched the bodies.

I'm seeing the remains of a massive fire and ashes that were washed away from rain and snow and who knows what else.

I stand there just staring at the ground.

I can feel the evil here. It seems to cover me in an icy grip. I feel dizzy and sore.

I shouldn't be here.

I'm about to start back upward toward the Staunch house when I hear that awful howling again. I scan the edge of the woods with the bright beam of my flashlight.

The wolf buries his nose in the ground near a fallen tree. He does this several times.

Do you have a name? It would be easier just calling you by name.

I walk toward the wolf and watch him slowly move over from where he was standing. He's light brown and beautiful, so lean and muscular.

I get to the corner of the log and check out the ground. Sticking out of a clump of leaves and mud is something light-colored that doesn't look like it belongs. My boot taps it and then pries it free.

It takes me about a second to realize I'm looking at the remains of an arm. The skeletal remains, that's pretty much it.

I suddenly feel more than just woozy. I feel kind of sick.

This particular arm didn't make the roasting.

I fight off nausea and I head out, away from this awful place. I don't hear the wolf or see it anymore.

It showed me proof. The arm is proof.

I head back down to the creek. Otherwise I'll end up walking around these woods and be like those guys in *The Blair Witch Project.* Lost and freaked out and eventually

Bye bye.

I get to the stream and quickly head back up it.

Walking and trying not to think. Rushing and trying to make sure I don't fall.

Not thinking. Just walking.

And it's fine and I'm almost out of here when I make the mistake of looking up at the Staunch house.

I see a light on near the deck.

I see a figure on the deck, standing as it did a year ago, watching and waiting.

He's there. My great-grandfather.

Then I see an arm and a hand waving.

No, not waving.

It's gesturing me to come toward him. It's summoning me.

I feel my shaky breath as I try and think of what to do.

"Chrisssssss."

Maybe I'm imagining the voice in my mind, but I don't think so.

There are some things in this life you can put off. Getting a license, asking a girl to prom, deciding on a college, picking out what you want to do in life.

But this …

This isn't one of those things.

I swallow and start walking toward the Staunch house.

93. FEAR

The front door to the house is partially open. I knock on it just to be polite

even though that's kind of insane when you think of it

and then wait for several minutes.

Nothing.

"Hello?"

I don't see the figure who was waving toward me. I don't hear anything either.

If someone's in there, I'll see him soon enough.

I slowly open the door. Surprisingly, it doesn't creak. Doors always creak in the movies when they shouldn't. Right?

It's a small relief.

The house doesn't look completely empty since there are lights on. I wonder where Gus is and if he's going to wander out of the family room eating a fudge stick and picking his nose. I call out for anyone again but don't hear anything.

I am standing in the room full of dead animal heads hanging on the walls.

I hate this room.

The bulging shapes on the walls around me feel like an animal intervention. I definitely want to get out of this room.

I take a few steps and hear the wood floor creak. But that's all I hear.

"Christopher."

I jerk around. If my head weren't attached to my body it would be rolling around like a bowling ball. The voice is low, whispered but somehow loud.

It's that same voice. The one I heard when I crashed below the cabin right after moving here. The one I heard in the tunnel below my house.

The voice with the quasi-lisp.

"Chrisssss."

It's coming from upstairs.

Leave now get out of here right now.

I grip a fist and hold the flashlight.

No.

It's just in my mind. Like the nightmares I've been having and the visions.

"Move it," I tell myself, trying to sound like Coach Brinks.

The voice isn't the only thing that seems and feels … off. It's everything. Not just the fact that I'm in this huge house by myself. Trespassing.

No.

It's this feeling—the same feeling I've gotten ever since coming here. That something's right there in front of me, something I can touch or even taste, something right in front of my face, yet I'm alone.

What's that?

I hear something in the hallway behind me. In a room next to me. Footsteps. Voices. Shuffled, muffled, distorted.

I turn around and know someone's going to be there.

But nothing.

I feel cold as I begin to walk up the steps. Something brushes by me.

No that's impossible

But it *feels* like something—no, someone—brushes by me going up the stairs.

Again. Something touches my neck. Then my arm. Then wipes my leg.

I'm by the wide stairs and I sprint up them, the noise downstairs getting louder. Now I feel like I'm being touched all over, but I don't see anything.

I get to the top of the stairs and wipe myself all over like I've just run out of a cave and I'm covered with cobwebs. But my hand can't wipe off anything.

The voice comes again.

"Chrisssss."

I shiver, the wave going all the way to my feet.

Get out of here Chris now.

These little games began when I checked out that cabin behind my house. But this isn't an abandoned shack, and that voice isn't in my head.

I feel like I'm being watched, like there are ghosts and spirits all around me. It's hard to take in my surroundings as I head down the hallway to the first room on the left.

The door is open, a faint light spilling out of it.

I feel something dripping down my back. Again I try to wipe it away, but my hand comes back empty.

My arms and legs feel weak and loose.

Then I walk inside and see the figure sitting in the chair behind the big desk. He smiles but doesn't look evil or demented.

It's the man I saw that day on the deck of the house. The man who surely just got me to come inside.

He's bald, except for white hair on the sides. He's got a round face and smiles a friendly smile.

This can't be my great-grandfather, because this guy looks like he's only fifty or sixty.

But he's not Mr. Staunch so who is he?

"You've come to the right place, Christopher."

The voice is the same.

"Please, come in," he says.

I feel my heart beating. The room is spinning.

What am I doing here?

"You've come for answers, dear boy. And you've waited long enough. It's time, don't you think?"

I nod and look around, down the hallway and back down the stairs.

"We're alone, just you and me. Please, come in."

I take a few steps into the room but then stay put, close to the entrance and the stairs and the exit. The man leans back in the chair, tightening his narrow lips, gazing at me with eyes that don't seem to blink.

"I started right around your age too," he says in a voice, strong and Southern and in no rush to speak. "The visions, the dreams. Seeing things that weren't there. Feeling them too. It's okay. You will learn to control these in time."

"Who are you?"

"I think you know, even if your mind and heart doubt it. My name is Walter Kinner. They used to call me Wally as a child, but

I ended that soon enough. There is no dignity in Wally, don't you agree?"

"You don't look—"

"Old? Old enough?" He laughs. "Can't see the resemblance? I can see it, Chris. You've got the Kinner genes in you. Do you ever. Like your uncle. Except, well, I would say even more of a Kinner than Robert."

"Where is my uncle?"

He just shakes his head. The man who I still don't truly believe is my great-grandfather is wearing dress pants and a button-down shirt, as if he might be leaving for the office any minute. He wears a big ring on one hand—not a wedding ring, but something that looks as if it were made a long time ago.

"That is a good question, Chris. I was hoping you'd help find him. But he's no use to us, not anymore."

I look around the room. On one wall is a massive bookshelf with tons of books. There's a shelf unit with various things on it, like mementos or something.

"You won't find anything noteworthy in this room. The man of the house—he's too smart for that."

"How'd you know—can you read my mind?"

"It's not quite like that, Christopher. Tell me something. Do you have thoughts running through your head all day long? Like a tornado that just keeps going? Even when you're exhausted, the thoughts and voices keep going?"

I've begun to think that it's ADD, but then again that's what everybody thinks.

"Or tell me this," he says, his dark eyes never leaving mine for even one second. "Do you ever get the idea that you can hear what someone else is thinking? Of course, you just assume it's your own thoughts running wild. But how often does this thought occur to you? Right?"

"Are you really my relative?"

"Yes. This place is special. I know that the fine young pastor already introduced you to the miracles of the falls, correct? Amazing what the water can do to keep you looking younger."

He smiles, and I feel a wave of ice prickle throughout me.

"There is something that our family—the men in our family—have been able to do since our forefather escaped from France and came to this place. This place that's easily overlooked. This 'ability,' I'll call it, was something that has been transferred down. Sometimes, well, not always so successfully. Sometimes it drives men to madness, or to brutality. There's a reason the family line is devoid of males. But you, Christopher—moving away was perhaps the best thing that could have happened. It was always planned like that. And some plans work."

"What was planned?" I ask.

I'm feeling a little better now, now that I don't feel anything or hear anything other than his voice.

Go ahead, call him Walter, but don't call him Wally.

"The interesting thing," Walter says, ignoring my question as he shifts his chair back to stand, "is your issue of faith. Or rather, your lack of it."

I swallow. He doesn't come closer, but stands right by the desk. He's surprisingly tall.

"Do you know the greatest thing about the world today? It's

what people think of God and Satan and all the angels and demons. It's not that they openly disbelieve, Chris. It takes strength to do that, a strength like you have. But no. Most people are indifferent. Most people are *busy.*"

He says that word as if it sounds like "bussssssy." Or maybe that's just my imagination.

"They view God as some all-powerful buffoon. They view the Devil as a silly magician with horns and a pitchfork who raises his voice but in the end really doesn't do anything. Time and time again, God and Satan are put into tiny little boxes that people watch at the end of the day. But when it comes right down to it, they're no longer afraid, are they? They're more afraid of a hurricane or the stock market or a villain in a Batman movie than they are of these beings they've made into caricatures."

Walter moves toward me, and I buckle back. He stops and waves a hand, telling me it's okay.

"Chris—you have the power to see behind the mask. To go behind the curtains. To see what others cannot and will not see."

I wait. I wait because I want more. Because this is making no sense and all the sense in the world and eventually, down the road one day maybe, I'll connect the two.

"In Old Testament times, it was different. Men knew what an angel crossing their path looked like. They would fall down on their face in terror. Didn't matter whether that angel was fallen or not. But nowadays, nobody notices anything anymore. Nowadays, the supernatural and the spiritual blend in with the superficial and the simple-minded. Everything is a joke. Nothing is real. Nothing means anything."

He pauses, looking at me with hardening eyes and intense lips. "And *that* is where we get our power. *That* is exactly why the work we do is worthy. Why it continues to be necessary."

"What work? What do you do?"

"Do you believe what I'm saying?"

I shake my head. "I don't know."

"You've been saying that for a year. But all the things you've witnessed—after all of that, how can you not believe?"

"Believe in what? In God?"

"No, my boy." He laughs and shakes his head, going over to the bookshelf to pick up a book. He waves it at me. "This is a Bible, son. But this only tells half the story."

"Half?"

"Of course God is real. Even those who choose to say He does not exist know deep down that they're fooling themselves. It's not about believing in God. It's about believing in yourself. This whole mind-set of forgiveness and peace and love—those are the things that make people disbelieve, that make them angry. As they should, because that is where the fallacy comes in."

Again, I'm lost. I don't know what he's talking about or preaching for.

"The most powerful thing in this world, Christopher. The pastor told you what it was. It's not love. It's not for God so loving the world. It's fear. *That* is what drives this world, and that is what makes people like you and me so powerful. Because—once you learn to control those fears and have others fear you—then life ..."

He smiles.

I feel dizzy. Trapped. Cold. And confused.

"You wanted answers, my young man," he says, tapping the desk. "They don't reside in here. Nor do they reside with the owner of this house. What you will learn is that they reside in your heart. The answers you've been wrestling with time and time again."

"What if I—everything you say—"

"Come on, spit it out."

"What if you're just crazy like the rest of the people around here?"

Walter puts the Bible on the desk, then stands in front of it.

Then he does something utterly bizarre.

He stands there, about ten feet away from me, extending his arms and opening up his hands as if he's trying to catch falling raindrops or snowflakes.

"Crazy is not the word I would use, Christopher."

His eyes and lips turn into a mocking smile.

Then something happens.

Those hands of his suddenly begin to change.

They begin to turn

no

frail and bony. Then spotted. Then sickly.

This happens with his face too.

All of a sudden, he begins hunching over. His hair disappearing, his round face shriveling, the eyes

no no no make it stop get out of here Chris

suddenly no longer there. The eyes now just empty sockets.

Just like his teeth.

Just like his stare.

His mouth curls up showing rotting gums and a dark tongue that sticks out as it laughs.

"Welcome home, Chrissssss."

He then extends his arms as if to hug me.

And that's when I stumble backward out of the office and stagger down the stairs, grabbing the front door so hard I'm surprised it doesn't rip off. I open the door and as I plunge into the cold dark outside, I know I'm going to feel the bony, icy grip of the monster behind me grab me and pull me back in.

I sprint down the driveway.

I don't care anymore who sees me.

I want Staunch to find me.

I run and get to the road and keep running.

If I could run without stopping, I'd keep jogging far away from this place and this town and this state.

A state of wretched, ungodly fear.

94. So ...

You wanted answers, huh? There're your answers.

95. No Reply at All

The next day at school, Lily is nowhere to be found. She knew what I was going to do last night. Ever since I texted her with a short message saying I made it back safely, I haven't heard from her.

"So what's happening?" Newt asks by my locker.

You don't have enough time in your day.

"Later, okay?"

"Is everything okay?"

"Yeah, sure—just dealing with—everything."

I haven't quite figured it all out myself, so I'm not sure how to even begin explaining it to him.

Uh, yeah, well, the guy who first discovered Solitary came from Europe and was into some strange weird stuff that got passed down through the generations. Oh, and he can somehow see spirits, like ghosts and angels and demons. Some people inherit the gene of baldness. I inherit being able to see ghosts.

Even if—well, there's no way I'm denying this anymore—but even if every single thing that man who I still can't call my great-grandfather, not to mention Marsh and Stanch, said is true, I still don't know where it leaves me.

I'm supposed to continue what? What am I supposed to do?

This whole dark world needs hope. Hold on to it.

I hear the words Jocelyn wrote to me in her last letter.

She still feels so close sometimes.

I don't want her death to be in vain.

So what am I supposed to do? Take over *what?*

"You can tell me," Newt says.

But I only laugh, because how am I supposed to tell him this? That I've not only figured out who the bad people are, but that somehow I'm one of them?

Being related to one and being one are two different things.

I try to get hold of Lily, but she still doesn't reply. It makes me worry that something happened to her. Something to do with Staunch.

I go by the B and B after school, but the lady who answers the door tells me that "Lillian moved out a week ago."

Lillian.

"Do you know where she went?"

The elderly lady only shakes her head. I thank her and then send another text to Lily before leaving to head home.

Hey, Lillian. Just stopped by the B and B and hear you checked out a week ago. Are you gone for good?

I wait a few minutes for a reply, but nothing.

Later on at home, I keep my phone with me through dinner. No reply.

None that night and none the next day.

The weekend is coming and Lily is nowhere to be found or heard from and I suddenly start getting worried.

I'm worried that she's going to be another Poe/Rachel.

Or worse, another Jocelyn.

She lied to you so why should you care?

I still don't know everything—all the reasons and all the lies and the entire picture on Lily, but …

Nobody deserves what happened to Jocelyn.

Friday afternoon I send another text. Friday afternoon classes are the absolute worst. We're supposed to be reading in English class, but nobody is in the mood to read. It's raining outside. November rain. Too warm for snow, but still way too chilly to avoid jackets. I send a simple text.

WHERE ARE YOU???

And then, a reply.

I'LL SEE YOU LATER.

I start to reply again when another message pops up.

DITCH YOUR PHONE AS FAST AS YOU CAN.

For a while, I try to make sense of what she's saying.

And then …

I'm an idiot.

How could I forget? I didn't forget actually. I just sort of buried it along with everything else.

Seems like I've suddenly gotten pretty good at burying things. Jocelyn, Poe, revenge, answers, hope …

And the iPhone that Marsh gave me.

They didn't even have to try to monitor me. I've had a built-in surveillance on me for the last few months.

Maybe Lily discovered that the other day during her meeting with Staunch.

Or maybe that's not even Lily who answered you. Just like those emails from Jocelyn that Poe got after Jocelyn died.

Before the end of school, I have an idea.

Seeing Newt out of the blue reminds me that of all the people around here, he's one I can trust. So I go up to him.

"Newt, can you do me a favor?"

I explain to him what it's for.

"I don't want them knowing I'm involved," Newt says.

"Yeah, that's what you always say. Look—listen—you keep telling me I need to do this and that, but I need help, okay?"

"What if someone calls?"

"Don't answer it. It's just—if they can keep track of me, I want them thinking I'm with you."

"They'll know."

I force the phone in his hand. "Listen, I bet anything they already know, okay?"

"But then—"

"Just do this, okay?"

Newt leaves with my phone in his backpack. I watch him go and wonder if he is indeed safe.

Nobody around you is safe, Chrisssssssss.

I can hear my great-grandfather's sickening hiss in my thoughts.

I sigh and head out the doors of Harrington. Something in me expects Lily to be waiting there. But nope.

I arrive home. Mom is back to working, taking a few shifts just to get back in the swing of things. But no late nights. That's her promise. No mornings reeking of booze. That's her pledge.

I've been home for an hour when there is a knock on the door.

I pause for a moment, hoping.

Wondering what's going to be my next big surprise.

96. The Darkness Is Easier

Maybe I'm just a dumb guy, and this is what guys do. They open the door and look at the pretty girl and suddenly forget everything and everyone. I can't speak for other guys, but I can say that I'm glad Lily is standing there. One glance at Lily, and I know I'd still probably run away with her if she asked me.

Turns out, that's exactly what she wants me to do.

"We need to leave right now."

"And go where?"

"Far away. You still have your phone?"

I shake my head.

"Good. Come on."

"Like *right* now?"

"Yes, Chris, I mean *right* now. You spend any more time in this cabin or this place and you'll start having second thoughts."

"But—how do I know—"

"If I'm lying? You don't. This is now or never."

"Now or never—what do you mean?"

"You either come now or you'll never see me again. I almost left this place for good but I couldn't. Just—now, Chris."

I shake my head. It's not that I think I'm going away for good. But I don't want her leaving like this. I grab my wallet and keys and then follow her outside. Rain drizzles over us as we walk down to her car.

The black two-seater seems smaller than usual as I climb in and wonder what her plans are. She backs up and then speeds down the road.

"Are you okay?" I ask.

"I'm fantastic," she says in a mocking voice.

The wipers swish away the droplets as she winds around curves like some kind of race car driver. I glance at her, the jeans and thin leather coat, her hair curly and wild, her eyes more intense than usual.

"Where are we going?"

"Far away." She suddenly jams down on the gas. I hold the door handle and then put on my seat belt.

"What's gone on since Wednesday? What happened with Staunch?"

"He threatened me. Not just me, but my ex. And I just—I can't anymore. Do this. Deal with all of this insanity. These people are crazy. It's all crazy."

"Where is he?"

Lily gives me a look that says *are you kidding me?* "Where's who? Kurt?"

"I'm just asking."

She curses. "Don't even—Chris, please. This is serious. Don't give me that attitude."

"What attitude?"

"You know what kind of attitude. That one—the one that's all over your puppy dog face."

That stings. "It's just how I'm feeling."

"And how *are* you feeling? Huh? Sad that you didn't find love or sad you didn't get any?"

The car is in the middle of the road when another car comes around the curve. She quickly steers to the right without overreacting.

"You lied to me," I say.

"Oh, really? Open your eyes, Chris. Open them up." She curses again, and I'm not sure if it's directed at me or the situation.

The rain seems to start falling harder. The daylight is pretty much gone. I'm not sure where she's going and I don't know if she does either.

"My eyes are open."

"You're blind. There's something way bigger than you and me going on here. That's why this has got to stop."

"They'll find us."

She seems to spit out a laugh. "No, they won't."

"You don't understand."

"This place is the backside of nowhere. This stuff is going on because nobody pays any attention to anybody or anything around here."

"And you understand what's going on?"

She shakes her head, staring out through the rainstorm and the quickly-moving wipers. "I understand that we need help. That *you* need help. I could've left. I almost left, Chris. I did. But I couldn't. Because—it's just—I don't want—I'm afraid for you. Afraid they're going to get through to you."

"Through to me?"

"Stop repeating what I'm saying. Through to you. Getting you to turn."

You don't know me and never will.

"They're not going to get me to do anything."

She laughs. "They're smart enough to find others. I wasn't the only one. What about that guy who claimed he was your cousin?"

"What was I supposed to believe?"

"You're a good guy, and I don't want that to change."

"No, I'm not," I say.

"No, listen. I know. I know that there's something different about you. Something special. And I don't want that to change."

"I'm not some little kid, even if you think I am."

Lily rolls her eyes. "You can't see the obvious right in front of you in broad daylight."

She doesn't know I've been trying to see the obvious in front of me ever since I got to this wretched place. It was only after I met her that I stopped looking around for answers and uncovered mysteries and simply focused on one thing: her.

And that's exactly why they chose her, you idiot.

She curses again. "Listen, I know. I know that the darkness is easier. The night changes everything, Chris. It's there that you don't have to be afraid, that you don't have to see your reflection in all its ugly glory."

"You're not ugly," I say.

"Not in the night, not in the shadows. You know—if heaven is real, I don't want to go."

"What—why?"

"Because it's probably bright and sunny, and I won't belong there. They'll be able to see everything—everything—and I don't want anybody to see the things I've done."

The person behind the wheel is a lot like that other girl who once drove me around with all this baggage following her.

"People can change," I say, a bit weakly and a bit soft for the pounding rain.

"You remember when that Teacher-of-the-Year came to our summer school with that assignment? Remember what I read?"

That feels like a lifetime ago.

"You don't start over," Lily continues. "There are no do-overs and no second chances. There's just reality. The brutal facts of life."

"But—you don't have to be stuck—you can do whatever you want."

Lily only chuckles. "This isn't a cry for help, Chris. I don't need someone picking up my pieces. I'm fine. My choice in boyfriends—that's the part that hurts. And if only I could—"

She interrupts herself with a curse as she glances in the rearview mirror. I can see lights reflecting off it.

"Listen to me—" she says, then keeps cursing as she starts to drive even faster.

The road is heading downhill and swerving like a snake. I keep hold of the handle of the door, watching her, then staring back at the bright headlights behind us.

Following us.

"If anything happens—you listen to me. Don't mess with Staunch. He's the guy—just don't mess with him. And don't let them change you. You got that?"

She jerks the wheel as the street veers left, then jams it over as the car slides a bit as we turn right.

The vehicle is right behind us.

"It's going to be next May, whatever it—"

A loud cracking sound interrupts her as the car behind us slams into our tail and jerks us.

I feel us turning. Circling. Spinning, yet still racing ahead.

No

Lily screams. I reach out toward her with my hand grasping at her arm.

God no no no help

She's still screaming.

We're suddenly not on the road anymore. We're spinning, flying.

"Lily," my voice yells before the crunching breaking sound of glass and the thudding, pounding sensation.

97. Dream or Reality

"My dear boy."

I feel something wet placed against my forehead. I open my eyes and see a woman, a wrinkled but pretty face, calm and comforting.

"Iris."

She smiles at me.

"I thought you were dead," I say.

"And I thought you were alive."

I feel immobile, out of breath, weightless.

I'm dying or almost dead and this is my out-of-body experience.

"Where am I?"

"In good hands," she says.

"Your hands."

"No. But good hands."

"Where—am I?"

"On the edge of a mountain upside down crying out in pain and terror."

But I'm not doing that now. Or am I unconscious?

"I guess you wanted to do it your way, didn't you?" Iris tells me. "I wish I'd had more time. But the evil ones surprise us all, don't they."

"Am I dead?"

"No, Chris."

"Lily?"

I don't get an answer. I can't really see where I'm at—if this is a dream, I can't tell what I'm supposed to be looking at. I see a big flower—a sunflower. A window behind it. Trees. Lots and lots of trees.

"Chris, listen. There is a place, one of the places I told you about—it's tucked away behind an old church in the middle of everything. But if you go looking—if *you* go looking—you'll find it."

The room is growing dim.

"And then what?"

"Then you'll find me," Iris says.

I go to say something, but I can't. The lights go out, and I suddenly find myself in that place she was talking about, screaming in terror.

Then whatever dream or reality I'm in turns black. Again.

98. A Lost Battle

We all know what happens after this. The whole guy waking up in the hospital after a car crash scene. I've seen it a hundred times on TV, and I'm only seventeen. We've all seen it, so there's no need for another scene like that again starring me.

The thing nobody seems to know is how I got to the hospital. I should know because all I had was a concussion and some cuts and bumps and bruises. There is the fractured rib, but they say that will heal on its own. They ask if I play football, which is funny because I almost make a joke about being a cheerleader. But my head can't think fast enough to make a joke like that.

There's also that really deep gash on my thigh. The one where I lost enough blood to knock me out and get me close to death.

I want to ask if a thin, elderly lady carried me in on her back, but I don't.

Mom doesn't have an answer, and the doctors and nurses don't know.

Some cops—not Solitary cops, but actual regular-looking policemen—come in to ask me about the accident. Another person—a woman—does the same. I mention that Lily's car was hit from behind. I don't get into specifics. Of course not. I don't know who was driving the truck that hit us, but I have an idea.

Yeah, I'm pretty sure I know who did it, or at least who ordered it.

Mom is pretty shaken up. She doesn't leave my side except to use the restroom, and she makes that quick. I tell her not to tell anybody, not to call Dad. I tell her that I'm fine.

Except, of course, that I'm not.

When I close my eyes, I can still see Lily's body. Not next to me in the car. No. I can see her body mangled by a tree a dozen yards away from the crash.

I was wearing my seat belt. Lily wasn't.

I remember more about those moments sitting trapped in a sideways car with a tree branch jutting through the window and against my thigh. Feeling warm and cold at the same time. Looking over to see Lily. This once beautiful, breathing figure full of life. Now discarded like someone's trash.

In the hospital, then back home, the images of Lily remain.

There should be some kind of better ending. A more climactic ending. A more hopeful ending.

At least Jocelyn found hope.

But Lily …

I hear a thousand different statements from everybody. But the one that stands out the most is one from Dad.

There's a battle going on. Over your mother and you. For your lives. For your souls.

I think back to that new gold dream that I thought had accidentally walked into my life and swept me off my feet. I think back to the entire summer and the beginning of the school year.

Think I lost this battle, Dad.

But as the saying goes, maybe there's a war to win.

I just have to figure out how to get on the battlefield.

99. Elegia II

I sink back into school and homework and the crowd for the rest of November. I shut down again. I'm getting pretty good at that. Even Kelsey tries to comfort me, but I shrug it off as no big deal.

Both of us know better.

She seems to understand and gives me space. Guys who are emotional turtles do the same. Harris. Brick. Others.

And speaking of turtles, Newt goes back into his shell. The accident has freaked him out again. Too close and too real and too final.

As each day passes, I find that I miss Dad. That I wish he were here.

Those fairy tales he used to talk about sure sound good right about now.

I can't even understand this gigantic sky full of sadness and anger. It covers everything.

I just want a little blue to shine through.

I want a little light streaming down on me.

I want some truth to believe in.

When everything seems so hollow and empty, how in the world can I ever hope to feel full? Growing up sure doesn't seem like the solution, 'cause I have parents and uncles and great aunts and countless others who show me time and time again that age doesn't equal happiness.

Listen to you.

I know. I hate wallowing around, but there's nobody else to talk to.

Sighing just isn't enough anymore. And the answers that I desperately wanted and finally got ... well, they sure aren't enough either.

I need something more.

I need something real.

I need something whole to fill this empty hole.

More than music that drowns out, or silence that ignores, or pain that bleeds.

I find myself wishing Dad hadn't left, wishing he could be around to share a little more with me.

100. Whatever You Need

For a second, I look at the table full of every kind of Thanksgiving dish I could ever imagine, then I glance at Mom sitting across from me. This is surreal.

I remember my last Thanksgiving, eating turkey sandwiches in our cabin with Jocelyn. This is pretty much as opposite as you can get, and not just because of the food. I mean, there's turkey *and* ham. But no, that's not the reason.

It's because of the people at the table.

Kelsey sits next to me, then her brother sits next to her. Keith has brought his girlfriend to the dinner as well, a pretty and talkative girl named Diane. Kelsey's parents, Jack and Ruth, are on the other side of the table.

Ah, such a family affair.

I neglect to tell them that my quasi-girlfriend-that-turned-out-to-be-an-actress-for-hire just died a few weeks ago.

Maybe Jack and Ruth don't need to know stuff like that.

It took a lot for me to accept Kelsey's invitation, and it took Mom even more. But Mom does fine answering questions about life back in Illinois, about her work at Brennan's, all while trying to steer the conversation back onto the Pages and, unfortunately, onto me.

Maybe it's because I'm nervous, or because I haven't had a real, true appetite for weeks, but I end up having three platefuls of food. Turkey and ham and gravy and mashed potatoes and sweet potatoes and macaroni pie and stuffing and cranberry sauce and green bean casserole and corn bread.

"Save some room for our pecan pie," Mrs. Page tells me.

I nod, my mouth full.

My mouth has been full the entire meal.

Maybe it's because I don't want to talk. I just want to stuff my face.

The same reason people like Mom end up drowning their sorrows. I guess you can eat them away too. Then twenty years later wind up on a reality television show where some angry drill sergeant of a woman whips you back into shape.

"Get enough?" Kelsey jokes when I finally finish my third plate.

"I won't lick the plate, I promise."

"What'd you think of this good ole Southern cooking, Chris?" Mr. Page asks me.

"I like it."

"You'll have to come over more than once a semester," Mrs. Page tells me.

I smile and nod. "Yes, definitely."

Kelsey gives me that look of hers, the one that says everything. The big bold blue eyes that can't help sharing her thoughts.

I privately nudge her.

Then something deep inside nudges me.

Remember, Chris.

There's no way of not remembering.

I'm reminded of the reason I haven't been eating over here every weekend.

This is a good family. And Kelsey's a good girl.

And all along, I've thought the same thing. A good girl like her shouldn't be involved with someone like me.

Will she be next?

I try to turn off the voices. But I did that earlier in the summer. And that didn't work out so well for me.

"I didn't tell them," Kelsey says to me as we walk Midnight. She insisted that I bring her with us.

"Didn't tell who?"

"My parents. About Lily."

"Oh. Thanks."

It's a good thing, since I never told my mom either. There are plenty of others around school who found out what happened, but Mom has been living in her own little bubble since coming back from rehab. I figure it's best not to add any more heaviness to her world.

"I figured you didn't want it brought up."

I nod.

"But there I went and brought it up. Sorry."

"It's okay."

Kelsey stops by the side of the road as Midnight sniffs something. It's cold out, and we're wearing light jackets. The leaves have long since turned colors and are now mostly off the trees. The coming season is sort of how I feel deep inside.

"Did she have any family?"

I shake my head. I've asked a few times about family members and about a funeral or something like that. Sheriff Wells didn't have any answers. Whoever was contacted in Georgia about Lily's death didn't want anything to do with me.

So I guess the other familiar scene—the one where the grieving boyfriend wears a black suit and stands by a graveside—won't be in the film either.

"It's so sad," Kelsey says.

I nod.

"You know what I'm tired of?" I say without hesitation.

"What?"

"Being sad. It's like—ever since the stuff with my parents happened, it's all changed. Everything. And I'm just so tired of this—this sad stuff."

We walk for a while. "Can I share something if you don't tease me?"

"I'm not in a teasing mood," I say.

"You always tease me."

"Okay, I promise I won't."

"Our pastor shared this Sunday. He talked about being thankful in times when there's a lot *not* to be thankful for. People without jobs. People dealing with hurricanes or floods or something awful like that. He read a verse where Jesus says for anybody who's tired and heavyhearted to come to Him. That He'll give you rest."

"And how's He going to do that?"

"I told you—no teasing."

"No, I'm serious," I tell her, not in a defensive tone like I might have a year ago to my father. "How exactly does it work? Is it a Zen-like thing?"

Kelsey only smiles, shaking her head. "I don't think it's a Zen thing."

"But how? Because I know that people who believe that still have bad stuff happen to them."

"I don't know. I just know—when I pray for something, when I turn over my worries and doubts to God, I can feel a strength inside of me."

"But is it just because you believe the prayers are going to help out? So it's like something you did?"

"No, it's not anything I did. I just—I just believe that it's God giving me the strength."

For a while I don't say anything.

"Sorry for bringing it up," Kelsey says.

"Don't be. I'm just thinking. "

"About what?"

"I don't know." I sigh. "I wonder if God would let me take Him out for a test drive. Does it work that way?"

Kelsey gives me a humored look.

"Yeah, maybe not," I say.

"Have you ever tried praying?"

I nod. I think back to my last prayer. It was more of a cry for help as I lay dying in the car.

Who saved me then? Did God really hear my prayers?

I was saved, but Lily wasn't. So not all my prayers were answered.

"Pray for God to show you," Kelsey says.

"For God to show me what?"

She shrugs. "Whatever you need to be shown."

I like talking to Kelsey. And really, if I think about it, I always have. She's like visiting a favorite place alongside a river. No matter when you get there, you always find the experience enjoyable.

"Thanks for inviting Mom and me today."

"Thanks for coming."

I want to tell her more, like thanks for being patient with me, especially through the crazy past few months, but I don't.

I think Kelsey knows I'm thankful that she's here.

And I hope she knows that I need her around.

The only question—the question that always remains—is for how long.

101. Real

Maybe I'm like Doubting Thomas.

Oh, come on, I know the story. I know enough stories, at least. Like Noah and the big old ark that saves him from the end of the world. And Jonah and the big old whale. And how about Joseph and his big old coat of many colors. Okay, maybe it's not big and old. But I know some of the stories.

Maybe I need just a little more proof.

On this bleak December Saturday, I decide to get some.

Borrowing a short and heavy sledgehammer from Brick is going to help. I figure I might need it, and Brick was the person to ask.

I head to downtown Solitary. It seems abandoned, with only a couple of cars on the main street. There's nobody in sight. The town feels sad. It shouldn't feel this way in December. It should feel many things—commercial, busy, Santa Claus-ized—but not sad.

Maybe it's in the eye of the beholder.

I don't know. I'm not here to evaluate the town.

I'm here to check out that abandoned boxcar. Or to see if it's still there.

It takes me a while to get to it. But sure enough, it's right there in the middle of the tracks, just like it was when I first saw it.

It's gray everywhere. As I approach the railroad car, the sledgehammer in one hand, I can see the hazy fog around it. It's like some film director came in and used smog machines for added effect.

As I approach, I recall Newt's voice in my head recounting the myth he'd heard.

"Back in the old days, they used to run trains into town," he told me over lunch a few days ago.

I'd asked because I wasn't sure if I'd really seen the boxcar or it was just another of these great visions I was having. The gift in my wonderful bloodline.

"The story goes that the very last car on the train would be a 'special' car, one that nobody would open. They would simply unhook it from the rest of the train and leave it on the tracks. The townspeople wouldn't dare look in."

I stand next to the wooden boxcar, kicking the rusted metal of a wheel to make sure it's there. Just like last time, I feel it.

"People in Solitary started going missing around this time," Newt continued in a hushed whisper as he ate his bologna sandwich. "People thought it had something to do with a railroad car left in town. They wondered if it had people living in it. What if they were creatures of some sort. So a group of young guys—maybe our age—decided to open the doors."

I've reached the door of the car. I touch the bolt and feel the grime of it on my fingers. I try pulling it, but it doesn't budge.

Obviously. That's why I brought this stubby sledgehammer I borrowed from Brick's garage.

"The guys opened up the door in the middle of the night. Of course it was a dare. But what they found wasn't anything to laugh about."

I start pounding the bolt back. It doesn't move at first, but then begins to grind against the old wood and send bits of rust to the ground.

"They looked inside and found a bunch of bodies. Dead bodies of people who had lived in and around Solitary. People who appeared white as ghosts and drained of their blood."

The bolt eventually goes back, and I manage to swing open the door.

As I do, I hear the deep mumbling of something.

Or someone.

I can't see in the darkness of the boxcar, but I can smell what's inside. Decay and death.

I can make out shadows on the floor. Piles of something.

Then I hear the wailing. And moaning. And crying.

"Someone had been killing people in Solitary and sticking them in this boxcar. To get rid of them. Like some dead animals or something."

"Help us," a grainy voice says.

I hear shifting and twitching.

Something in the pile seems to get up. Slowly, as if it's on two knees.

"Hear us, let us go," cries another voice, this one a woman's.

I hold the sledgehammer in my hand, but know that it probably won't do much to the voices I'm hearing.

"Set us freeeeeeeee."

Then I feel the bony grip of something reaching out from the darkness, skeleton fingers squeezing around my neck.

A mutilated face suddenly appears in front of me. As it does, I hear what seem to be a thousand screams all go off from inside the car.

I fall back and brush away whatever's on top of me. The heavy hammer falls beside me.

Gasping and kicking and clawing, my eyes closed, I get whatever it was off of me.

Then everything becomes silent again.

I breathe in and open my eyes and sure enough, the boxcar is gone.

The sledgehammer is still there. The stench in the air is still there. And the pressure from the squeezing hand around my neck is still there.

I bet so are the marks.

For a while, I just lie back on the rocks next to the railroad tracks. I steady my breathing and think of what I just saw.

It was there. I saw it and felt it and yes, even smelled it.

What more do you want?

I don't need any more.

I believe in what people have told me.

I believe in what Marsh and Staunch and my great-grandfather said.

The thing about being able to see stuff that's not there.

This is why they want me and need me alive.

What they want me to do with this … I don't know.

But I know it's real.

And I know the creatures or monsters or demons that I heard and saw—those are real too.

102. What's in a Name?

Some of the puzzle pieces start to fit.

If the males in the Frenchman's line—the guy with the last name Solitaire—all had the ability to see things like I can, that means Uncle Robert must have been able to as well.

Maybe he couldn't handle it. Or maybe they wanted him to use his "powers" for something and he refused.

But this isn't a comic book movie, and I'm not a comic book hero. I wouldn't call the ability to see weird things a power, exactly.

And as for Mom and even Aunt Alice, maybe they have a little of it too. But it's different for some reason. And that's why Mom needed the booze. And why Aunt Alice is bonkers.

As for Iris … I'm still not sure about Iris. Was she like the good version of Staunch? Was she an angel or good spirit? And what about those dreams of seeing Jocelyn? Were those part of being able to "see"?

I remember Jocelyn telling me in one of those dreams that "there is a place that is somewhere between every day and every dream, a place like this."

Was that the place Iris referred to as a space in between?

Like the airport I saw Jocelyn in—a grown-up Jocelyn who wanted to talk.

Like the plane where I told her I was fed up with all these visions and conversations and where I told her to let me be.

How could I have sent her away like that? Especially if those were real conversations?

The deaths of the kids in the town—the sacrifices, I should call them—still don't add up. I don't understand why. Was it just part of this evil group or cult?

Are they wanting me to join them?

And if I do will I get some kind of membership card?

I see that even in the height of this hysteria, my brain tries to keep it mildly hilarious. I want to start laughing out like one of those *muaahhhhaahaha* laughs we all joke about. But then I realize everything happening and I begin to get scared.

If I'm really the last one in the family line, what will they do if something happens to me? Or if I refuse?

With answers come questions. And more questions only lead to more worry.

Thankfully I haven't seen or heard from Staunch or Marsh since breaking into the Staunch residence and then riding out of Solitary with Lily.

I've been waiting on them to come. I know it's only a matter of time.

A couple of weeks before Christmas, that time comes.

It's pitch black in the house when the knock comes on my door. It's locked. I always double check to make sure. I think it's Mom, but it's only eight and she's not due home for another hour or so.

Midnight lets out a few measly barks.

Why couldn't I have inherited a big scary dog?

I get up off the bed where I was reading, or trying to read, *The Old Man and the Sea* for English.

For a second I wonder if I should even bother answering.

The knock comes again, so I head downstairs, turning on the stairway lights and then turning on a lamp in the main room.

I see a head peering in the window.

It's Marsh.

I open the door and feel the cold outside.

"Almost started to think nobody was home," Marsh says.

"You knew where I was," I say.

"That's true. Can I come in? It's cold."

Once inside, Marsh takes off his black overcoat. "It's freezing in here. Why don't you have a fire going?"

"I wasn't cold."

"Gotta look after yourself."

For a second I just stare at him. His perfectly spiked hair, the perfectly styled glasses, the perfectly clear complexion. I hate him and everything about him.

"Chris, Chris, Chris—you're at it again," he says, openly mocking me. "Isolating yourself and planning things and keeping secrets. Have you not learned?"

I don't even hesitate.

I reach over and grab him around the neck with both of my hands, squeezing just like that monster from the boxcar. We both end up falling backward, and his head narrowly misses the stone edge of the fireplace. I'm on him and I know I weigh just as much as he does and my anger more than makes up for his age. I'm pressing down and gritting my teeth and squeezing and hearing him cough and choke and I swear with everything in me I want to kill him right here and now.

He chokes out a "Chris" and then a "help you" and I continue to drive my palms into his neck muscles and throat. His face is red and pink and purple. A vein is sticking out on his forehead looking like a pimple ready to pop.

"Can—help—Mom—you."

It's only the mention of "Mom" that makes me stop.

Suddenly I'm afraid.

He pushes me off him and coughs for a few minutes, spitting out and trying to breathe. Then he curses at me.

"What are you doing?" he asks.

"Pastors aren't supposed to use words like that."

"And teens aren't supposed to choke their pastors."

"You're not my pastor and never will be."

Marsh takes a moment to stop coughing and regain control. Then he looks at me while adjusting his glasses.

"I'm not the bad guy, Chris. How many times do I have to tell you that?"

"None, since I'll never believe you."

"Do you have any water?" he asks as he stands. "Man, you're strong."

"What do you want?"

You would think he'd at least want to try and knock my lights out for that move, but he simply walks over to the refrigerator and looks inside. He doesn't find anything, so he goes to the sink and drinks some water from the tap. He walks back over to me, wiping his mouth and shaking his head.

"Listen to me and listen good, okay?" he says. "Staunch doesn't know I'm here. But he's growing impatient."

"Don't you guys have this place wired or tapped or whatever you call it?"

"Staunch doesn't have to stoop to that level. But others do."

"You killed her."

"*I* didn't kill anybody, Chris. I keep telling you that."

"You helped."

"I had nothing to do with that. But I'll tell you this. You have only a couple more weeks. That's it. Come January first, the games end."

"You came here to threaten me?"

"I came here to tell you that. To warn you."

"Or what?"

Marsh rubs his neck. "Man, that really hurt."

"Good."

"You keep falling into the same old habits. I mean, I know you're only seventeen, but haven't you learned?"

"What habits?"

"These girls."

I think he's talking about Lily for a second, then realize he's talking about Kelsey.

I don't say anything.

"They will take whatever is important in your life away from you."

"Just like Jocelyn? And Lily?"

"Jocelyn—Chris, that was unexpected. I've already told you that."

"But why?"

"We do what we're told. Staunch, he's the one who gets the direct orders."

"From?"

"I believe you recently met him."

"Walter Kinner? Creepy great-grandpapa?"

He doesn't quite laugh at my slam.

"You want to change things, then do it yourself."

"What do you guys want from me?"

"I want you to see what's going to happen. You need to stop all this."

"All this what?"

"Avoidance."

"What am I supposed to start doing then? Is Yoda going to come out of the woods and start teaching me Jedi tricks?"

"You really are a smart aleck."

"Nobody said what I'm supposed to do."

"Running away with the girl isn't quite the answer."

"You don't understand."

"No?" Marsh asks. "I knew love once. But you will get older and learn. There's nothing wrong with desire, Chris. Desire is good. Love is bad. Love only makes you weak. And you—you can't be weak. You have too much going for you."

"She's dead because of all of you. You used her and then you killed her."

"That girl you're talking about drugged you the very first time you hung out with her at a party. Huh? Yeah, shake your head, but it's true. You just thought the beer hit you hard, didn't you? But *that* hard? So tell me—what kind of person would do that? Even if she was being paid."

"You don't know her."

Marsh shakes his head, staring at me for a second. "And you did? What did you think you were going to find? Did you think it was true love or something?"

"Until I learned the truth," I say.

"Oh, the truth. I see. Tell me something—what difference does it make who she was? You know exactly what you wanted, so what's the difference?"

"Everything."

"You're so naive. So young and stupid and naive. Love is a facade, Chris. Love is a fantasy, and this world paints it as something attainable, but you can never have it. Never. Look at your parents. They're just like the rest of the world. I tried and woke up and realized I'd never, *ever* have what I really wanted."

"No."

"Yes, Chris, yes. Love and happily-ever-afters are crutches. But, boy—you don't need crutches. The girl—she was yours. What was the big deal? What did you tell me? What? What did you want? You said 'relief.' And what did you get?"

"Lies."

"You got what you wanted, Chris. *Exactly* what you wanted."

"I thought she liked me."

"Of course she liked you. But what—did you want to go steady? Did you want her to fall in love? Chris—I fell in love once. And she managed to break every single inch of my heart until there was nothing left. Save yourself. Don't give your heart out to anybody."

"I'm not like you."

"No—I keep telling you that. You're not like anybody. You're special. Someone like Lily—there are a hundred Lilys out there

Chris. A thousand. You'll realize that when you get older. But you—people can't do what you do."

I curse at him, but he just laughs.

"You have the ability to see between the cracks. To see what's on the other side. You know that now, don't you? I don't have to tell you. Think about it. You always have been able to, even just a little, right? But once you manage to tap into that, everything changes."

"I don't want to tap into anything."

"That restlessness—those empty feelings—the questions and the pain—they will all go away. All of them. You just need to do something simple. And it will all begin."

"Do what?"

"It's a formality, really. Consider it a code word to enter the club. Just deny that Jesus is God. I mean—that's not very difficult for you to do, is it? Since you don't buy into the whole church thing."

"I'm not doing anything you want me to do."

"*I'm* not the one asking. I'm just trying to help you. Staunch is the one you have to be worried about. If you don't do what he asks, he takes. And takes. And keeps taking. I've seen this with my own two eyes. Lily—that was Staunch. He just had to say so, and it was done. Like that. He manipulates everything. He's been manipulating you from the very beginning."

"You don't know," I say.

"Did you ever think it was weird how Ray just popped into your life after you first got here? Staunch arranged that. Then he realized that social levels didn't appeal to you. He realized you needed to be watched and studied. Hence, there comes Jared. Your 'cousin.' You know how that ended. And then, Chris—he discovered it was so easy. Just put a pretty little hot thing in front of you, and you'll go following her with your little tail wagging. And that's where Lily came into play."

I curse, and just get a mocking laugh in reply.

"I'm telling you all of this so you know to be afraid of Staunch," Marsh says.

"I don't care—"

Marsh moves over to me quickly, more quickly than I'd ever give him credit for. Not to attack or hurt, but to simply grab my arm and get my attention.

"You'd better start caring," he says. "Or it will just keep happening. Your mother. Or father. Or the cute little blonde girl you've been seen with."

I don't say anything as I jerk my wrist away from him.

"It's two weeks away from New Year's Eve," he says like a warning.

"What are you guys going to do?"

"*He* will do whatever it takes for you to finally understand what's at stake."

Suddenly I feel scared.

Suddenly I feel like a teenager again.

Suddenly I remember Chris Buckley.

"Your great-grandfather just wants to hear it with your own voice. Nothing formal or anything like that. But he wants to hear you say it."

"Say what?" I ask.

"To reject Jesus Christ."

Marsh waits for me to say something, but I don't.

"Chris—take that anger and that fear and that hatred—the kind that I just saw wrapped around my neck—take it and do something with it. What's in a name you don't believe in? What's it to you anyway? You want to see power and control? Do this in front of the old guy. That's all he wants. Get it over with. And soon."

He stands there, and then says it again. "Soon. I mean it."

With that, he's gone.

103. Where This Will Lead

I know it's going to take a lot of persuasion and hard work to get Kelsey to agree with me. After all, I'm the guy who kept ditching her last year for Poe. And the guy who basically ignored her all summer. And yes, I'm the guy who showed up senior year arm in arm with Lily.

Thanksgiving dinner is one thing, but this …

It's probably not going to work, but I have to try. So I do it after lunch one day while we're standing in the hallway by ourselves.

"Okay, so I wanted to talk with you—alone—'cause I want to ask you something."

Kelsey looks curious and almost concerned. "Okay."

"I know it's a lot to ask. And it's kinda coming out of nowhere. But I told you this when we first met—there's stuff going on in my life—that's one reason I've avoided getting to know you, if you really want me to be honest. Because of just—this stuff. That maybe one day I can tell you about. I know it's the holidays, and I'm sure you have plans. But just—I'd like you—I'm wondering if you'd want to come to Chicago with me after Christmas. Right before the new year. And before you say anything, just listen. I know you're going to school there and I'm sure you've visited, but this could be another chance for you to go see the campus since I'm heading back up there with my father on New Year's Eve—"

"Okay."

"And it will only be for a few days and I can ask your parents myself if you want me to. I don't know if they'll think it's weird or anything—"

"Okay. Chris? I said okay."

"Like okay, you'll think about it?"

Kelsey laughs and looks at me with a surprised glance. "Why are you being like this?"

"Like what?"

"Like all nervous or something?"

I realize that I'm a jittery, talkative mess. She's right.

If you only knew, Kelsey. If you only knew.

"I'm sorry. Yeah. I just—it's probably weird me asking."

"Not really," she says.

"You'll go?"

For some reason I had it in my mind that she was going to say no. Perhaps because of the other girls in my life who have proved to be difficult when I needed them to be easygoing.

"Sure. That sounds like it'd be a lot of fun. My dad and I were just talking about me needing to check out the school again. They have something this spring, but still—this would be ideal."

I wait for a catch, but it's not coming.

I almost want to hug her.

She doesn't understand why I'm asking her. Why I'm desperate.

Nothing's going to happen to you, Kelsey. You're going to be by my side on New Year's Eve and you're going to be far away from this hellhole and nothing will happen.

"You think your parents will let you go with me? My dad is going to be there, of course. We'd stay at his apartment in Chicago. I haven't even been there yet."

"Of course. They really like you."

"Really?"

"But you already know that."

In some ways, yes, I guess I do. But I haven't paid much attention.

"Well, just—you want to ask and make sure?"

She gives me an excited and shy nod. And once again, those eyes tell me everything.

Do you know what you're doing?

Of course I don't. I don't know what this will mean for Kelsey and me. If this is leading her on or if I want to lead her on or if anything will happen and if I even want something to happen. I haven't thought through all of that and don't have time to.

"I'll let you know tonight," she says, then adds, "if you want me to."

"Yeah. Just text me. Or call. Whatever."

"Okay."

I head back to my locker wondering how that could have been so easy.

Things are never that easy.

I just hope there's no catch.

104. The Gift

It's just Mom and I on this cold Christmas morning. In some ways, it's kind of nice. The fire is going, and we're both in pajamas and sweatshirts with no worries of needing to get ready or shovel the deck or even bother to go outside. The tree doesn't have many gifts under it, but neither of us minds.

It's been a tough year for both of us.

Mom actually surprises me with a phone when I tell her that the one I had was busted. It probably is, since I chucked the old one into a Dumpster in Asheville. The new iPhone is just like the kind I had. Except I have a feeling this one hasn't been tampered with.

The phone isn't the last gift she gives me. She saves a small box for last, making me curious about it.

"Keys to a new car?"

She likes my joke. "Or maybe it's a wallet, for when you get your *license.*"

That's an even better joke. My negligence in getting a driver's license has become our joke now. She'll ask me about it and I tell her I'm working on it.

I open up the small box. It's a lighter. An old lighter by the look and feel of it. There's a logo of wings on it.

"Is this for all the cigarettes I smoke?" I joke.

"That's a Zippo lighter. An original. From World War II days. It belonged to your great-grandfather when he served in the army."

The mention of my great-grandfather makes me stop breathing. I look up at her to see if she's going to say anything else. To surprise me.

"What?"

"Nothing," I say.

"You just turned pale."

"Really?"

"Are you okay, Chris?"

"Yeah. This is great, Mom."

"His name was Walter Kinner. He died while fighting over in Europe, and this was brought back by one of his fellow soldiers and given to his wife."

Uh, no, Mom, he didn't die, because I just saw him, and while he looks a bit, well, unhealthy, I still saw him.

"I wanted to give it to you as part of our history. There's a lot about my family that I've tried to forget. Because of my mom and dad passing away. But family is family."

Right, Chrisssssss?

"Chris?"

"Yeah, that's great—thanks."

"What's wrong?"

"Nothing."

"Does it have to do with your father? Or Christmas?"

"Maybe both," I lie.

I lie because I have no idea what to tell her.

So my great-grandfather served in the army during World War II. Did he die over there, like Mom is saying?

Reports would have that, right?

Reports far away from this place.

I guess in some ways, it doesn't matter. The man I met the other day has enough issues. Whether or not he's lying …

Or whether or not he's dead …

"I want your trip to Chicago to be a nice break for you," Mom says.

"Thanks."

"I hope it's also a good chance for you and your father to start over—to actually be on good terms."

"Yeah."

I hold the lighter in my hand. "Have you tried to work it?"

Mom shakes her head, and I open it up and try it.

"Maybe if you took it somewhere, they could put some lighter fluid in it," she says.

"You trying to turn me into a pyromaniac or something?"

"If you do get it working, be careful. I'd prefer you keep it more as a memento."

"I'm not going to lose it, Mom."

Then again, maybe I should.

Maybe it will start lighting itself in the middle of the night.

I'm really curious about Walter Kinner now. Even more than I was before.

105. Chicago

The night changes everything.

So she told me.

Final words to her little boy.

In the passenger seat of the SUV, I look out and see the city. It glows and breathes and welcomes me. I hear the words and believe them.

I never knew Chicago could look so beautiful.

It's late and I feel like we've been driving forever. My ears are sore from the earbuds attached to my iPod. My butt is sore from sitting in place for so long. The last time we stopped was around Lexington. I'm ready to get out and stretch my legs and step back onto flat Illinois land.

Solitary is over a dozen hours away.

Not far enough, if you ask me, but it'll have to do.

It's quiet in the car. I look out the front window at the skyline in the distance. That's where we're headed, toward the city and not the suburbs.

The city means more people. More people means more help in case—well, in case of anything.

"You awake?"

I glance over at my father. "Never fell asleep."

"You closed your eyes."

Sometimes it's better that way.

I yawn and wipe my eyes.

"You're going to enjoy it here," Dad tells me.

"Yeah."

I don't really believe this. I want to. I really want to. But I just need to be away from that cursed town for a while. Maybe I can slowly begin to forget. Maybe I can slowly start to live again.

But that's what you tried doing in the summertime, and look where it got you.

I don't want to think about the last few months. The only thing that will bring is hurt, and I've got enough of that as it is.

"I think you'll like the apartment," Dad says.

"I think I'll like anything that doesn't have winding dirt roads around it."

Or secret hidden tunnels below it.

Dad doesn't know quite what to say. I don't blame him. He probably still aches for Mom. Maybe he's angry at himself for not being able to do anything more.

That's how I feel. Angry with myself with nothing left to say.

When someone dies all you can sometimes do is stay quiet and keep moving.

I thought that losing Jocelyn hurt. But this … this is different. This is worse.

The first time you did too little. But this time you did too much.

"Hungry?" Dad asks.

I was until I turned off the music and started hearing the voices. "No."

The city with its lights and life invites us in. I'm glad to see civilization again. I no longer feel so remote and so alone.

Yet there's a part of me that says I should have stayed.

There was no reason to stay.

There's so much to think about that my head hurts. I can't sort out the details. I think of the motorcycle, of the cards, of Marsh and Staunch, of Oli, of *him*. I can feel the Zippo lighter in my pocket.

Then I picture her face and feel the hurt again.

"I know Mom is proud of you."

I let out a chuckle and then keep my voice down. "Proud of me for what?"

"Proud of you for being strong for her."

It's been quite some time since I've felt proud or strong. The irony is that it's my father telling me this.

Seven months ago, there'd have been no chance ever that I'd be riding here with *him*.

But life sure has a way of crashing and burning around you.

The interstate eventually merges into Lake Shore Drive. Even though I can't see it, I know Lake Michigan is out there in the darkness. I can feel it watching and waiting in silence. Eventually we take an exit and drive for a few minutes down block after block.

"This place will be busy tomorrow night around this time," Dad says.

Everybody will celebrating and toasting and laughing and living.

Wanna know what I was doing last year on New Year's Eve, Dad? I was discovering that this girl I'd fallen crazy in love with had her throat slashed by a bunch of freaks in robes.

Even though Dad knows a few things, he doesn't know that much. He can't know much. I still don't know everything, but

I know enough now. I know a lot of answers to questions that circled inside my head a year ago.

Answers might fit the puzzle pieces together, but they still don't block out the gaping hole in the picture. The hole that's my heart.

I turn around and look in the backseat. A tiny ball of black is bundled up on the blanket. It's Midnight, the Shih Tzu that once belonged to Jocelyn and that I've been taking care of for a year.

For an incredibly crazy year.

Next to Midnight is Kelsey. I see the long blonde hair falling in her face, her head slightly turned.

"Is she still asleep?"

I nod at Dad. For a while I just look at Kelsey.

A determined voice reminds me again.

They're not going to take someone else. They've taken enough.

Dad pulls in front of a four-story brick building and stops, telling me that's the place. He says we need to find parking. But I'm in no rush.

I feel like a prisoner who's escaped his cell.

And any minute—any second now—someone will come and grab me and take me away.

Either take me away, or punish me for leaving in the first place.

106. Yesterday, Today, and Tomorrow

I'll probably always remember that day in Chicago, the last day of the year and what might be the first day to the start of a new life.

I don't know.

Maybe Kelsey and I will drift apart next semester, or she'll go off to school and I'll never see her again. I don't know.

I just know that at this moment she's safe with my father and me in Chicago. We spend the day sightseeing and laughing and eating and laughing more and crossing sidewalks and looking at more sights.

But that's a tale for another story, right?

I almost feel guilty, because I can't help remembering last year. Yet I can't tell Kelsey or Dad.

I imagine what it would be like to be able to tell this bright-eyed girl everything. And I mean everything.

It's a nice thought.

I'm trying not to look too far ahead with her.

All I can do is keep her by my side this day and this night.

The rest … well, whatever happens, happens.

So I let it happen later that night with the rest of the crowd sitting and standing in Grant Park near the edge of Lake Michigan watching the fireworks while Chicago's skyline surrounds us. It's too loud to say anything that can be heard unless you shout it. I don't want to say anything. I just smile.

Tomorrow will be a new year, and a new story will start to unfold.

But I don't want to worry about that right now.

Nor do I want to look back and regret all the awful things that have occurred.

There's a piece of me that is filled just being around Kelsey. I can't explain it, but it's always been there when she's been near.

I reach out and hold her hand. And as the countdown commences, we call out the numbers until we reach one, and everybody shouts and celebrates and wishes each other well.

Standing there under an unfamiliar sky, the fireworks going off, I lean down and kiss lips that seem to fit mine perfectly. The kiss Kelsey gives me isn't timid or weak, but fierce and somewhat mind-blowing.

I never thought kissing Kelsey would be like *that.*

When I move back and look down at her, I just know.

I finally realize this thing that on some level I've always known about Kelsey.

Not the cute smile or the crystal blue eyes or the long legs but something else. Something deeper and more important.

Something that a teenage boy doesn't always pick up.

She's never given up on me. She's been relentless in trying to win me over.

I can't speak for tomorrow. But for now, she's done her job well.

She's won.

And I'm lost.

And strangely, I feel better.

107. The Stranger

And so Chris Buckley lives life happily ever after …

I wish.

But I guess that life and all its surprises aren't finished with me just yet.

I realize this the morning of January 1 when I receive a message through Facebook. From someone named Jeremiah Johnson. The name gets my attention simply because of Jeremiah Marsh. Is this a code name he's using?

The message is short and to the point.

Take the Blue Line train and get off on Division. Go west about three blocks to a place called Bangers and Lace. Meet me there at midnight. Your mother's life depends on it. Don't tell your father or the girl.

My heart sinks.

Bangers and Lace. What kind of place is that?

It's nine in the morning on January 1, and the madness and the mysteries start again.

I go to the guy's Facebook page, and it shows a young Robert Redford. I guess Jeremiah Johnson is a character from one of his movies. I don't friend the guy because—hey, social networks can be terrifying. Not in a Solitary way, of course, but …

Shut up, Chris.

I do as I'm told.

Meanwhile, I try to get hold of Mom. I try several times. Then

I keep trying, all day long. She's not at home, can't be contacted on her cell, isn't at work …

Naturally I'm thinking the worst, because the worst usually happens.

All I can do is do as I'm told.

I'm supposed to meet Jeremiah Johnson tonight?

It's gotta be code for the pastor. Maybe it is him.

They have Mom and what?

Then what?

When I finally slip out of my father's apartment, it's a little after eleven. Kelsey is in the guest room while I'm sleeping in the living room, so it's easy to go out. I go down the back stairway and out through a narrow alley. I leave the door to the apartment unlocked, as well as the gate.

As I walk down the sidewalk, I try not to think of the past day spent with Kelsey. We had a perfectly enjoyable day together, having lunch at a little Mexican restaurant and then taking a train to Covenant College, which is right in the heart of the downtown area. It was New Year's Day, so she didn't have any scheduled meetings or appointments or plans. She just wanted to soak in the campus and see if it felt right.

At one point she asked me what was wrong. I did my best to shrug it off and act like I was there. And I was there, as much as possible. But all along I knew that I had to meet with some stranger to discuss my mother.

I get off the L-train early and have some time to kill. I head down Division Street the wrong way, then realize that and backtrack.

I arrive at the bar/restaurant called Bangers and Lace fifteen minutes before midnight.

As I approach, I see an open door and a crowd of people inside.

Then I spot a huge black dog sitting at attention. He's on a leash and near the doorway of the pub.

It only takes me two seconds to recognize the dog.

It's a black German shepherd.

The mountain man's dog. The big guy with the trench coat and grubby hair who seems to come and go as he pleases.

I walk around the dog and quickly dart into the entryway, hoping to avoid being mauled to death. That would really stink, to die now after making it out of Solitary alive.

I stop and study the crowd talking and laughing and drinking.

"Chris."

This isn't the voice I imagined the mountain man would have.

"Over here."

I guess I'm looking for someone big, because there right at the first table inside sitting on a barstool is an average-looking guy about my mom's age who looks a lot like Uncle Robert.

"He's big, but he won't bite. Not unless I tell him to."

I move closer to get a better view, and I see that it is indeed Uncle Robert.

Is he borrowing the dog? Or is this the dog's twin brother? Or maybe he killed the mountain man and ended up inheriting the dog.

"Go on, have a seat," he says as I walk up to the table.

Uncle Robert doesn't give me a hug, and to be honest, I'm not sure if I'd accept it.

He's got a nearly empty tall glass that I assume is a beer. His eyes are glassy, and he looks back to see if he can find a server. I sit down across from him.

Robert looks the same, just older. He's got dark stubble on his face and his hair seems a bit thinner. Just like the rest of him. He doesn't look like he's taken a shower for a day or two, and his clothes are wrinkled and worn. He looks at me and just nods.

"I was fully intending to stay out of your business forever," he says. "Just want to make that clear."

"Do you know where my mom is?"

"No," he says, looking into his empty glass. "Someone got to her."

I have so many questions that I can't even ask one of them.

"Yes, that's my dog, and yes, that big redheaded guy you've seen several times was me."

Say what?

"I just want to know," he says, letting out a loud and humorous curse and shaking his head. "How many times do I have to save your butt?"

"What?"

"At one point I even wondered if you knew it was me, to be honest. When you went off chasing after Marsh with that knife, for a while I thought you might use it on yourself. In the woods. Remember?"

"The knife disappeared afterward."

"Well, yeah. I thought you'd killed him."

"You've been watching me this entire time?"

"As much as I could."

A server comes and in a bubbly voice asks if we need something.

Yeah, I want to know about Mom, and Marsh, and Staunch, and Jocelyn, and the notes in my locker, and the gravesite in the woods, and the mysterious Marsh Falls, and Iris …

"Bring me another one of those—whatever I just had."

The woman says a beer that sounds French.

What is it with French things in my life?

"Yeah, sure, sounds great."

"Can I get you anything?" she asks me.

"Diet Coke?"

I want a beer like Uncle Robert.

"I'd give you a beer if I knew I wouldn't get in trouble, but they'd card you." Uncle Robert is serious.

"So all this time—you've been—wearing a costume?"

He shrugs. "You didn't have a clue, did you? Staunch doesn't know. That's the biggest thing. I'm telling you, Chris—you have no idea how bad things are for you."

"I think I know."

"No, you don't." His attitude is less good-to-see-you-again-nephew and more you're-in-deep-doodoo-Chris.

"I have an idea."

"Yeah, maybe, but just an idea."

"Where's Iris?" I blurt out.

"I don't know. Look—I'm not going to sit here and answer your questions 'cause that could go on all night. I came to tell you that you have to go back to Solitary and you have to go back tomorrow. Okay?"

"Mom was going to take us back."

"Not anymore."

"How do you know?"

"I know because she's gone. She disappeared. And there's only one person who could be responsible."

"What are you talking about?"

Uncle Robert just looks at me.

"What? What happened to Mom?"

Others around us look my way but I don't care.

Not Mom they can't do that to her too.

Our drinks come, and Uncle Robert downs half of his before he decides to answer me.

"Is she hurt? Is she—"

I don't even want to imagine, but of course I can and I do.

"I don't know" is all he'll say.

I want to burst out crying. Or wrap my hands around this guy's throat.

The reality burns my stomach.

"Why have you been hiding all this time?" I ask.

"That's my business."

"So why show up and tell me this now?"

"Don't get all annoyed with me. I've tried keeping you and your mother out of trouble."

"Oh, thanks." I'm angry now, now that I've been able to soak in the fact that Uncle Robert is alive and has known the hell we've been going through this last year.

"You don't have a clue what I've been through," he says.

"Looks like Mom and you have a lot in common."

He curses at me and finishes his beer.

"So I'm supposed to go back and do what?"

"Do what they tell you to do."

"For how long?" I ask. "The rest of my life?"

"Until I tell you what to do."

"Oh, okay. Will it be my uncle telling me or the spooky mountain man with the dog? Or maybe Jeremiah Johnson."

He tells me exactly what he's thinking. Which isn't exactly pleasant.

"Mom and I have been doing fine on our own."

"Not anymore. Something big is about to happen. I don't know what, but something big. Involving you. Involving him."

"Who?"

"The old man."

"You mean Walter Kinner? Your grandfather?"

"The old man," Robert says, teeth clenched as if he can't get himself to admit the guy is a relative.

"Why did you go into hiding?"

"What are you doing here in Chicago? Huh? Same thing. But you don't have an option. You have to go back. I don't think they've hurt your mom. Not yet."

"Why didn't you help us when we needed help?"

I see watery, cold eyes look at me. "You guys never should've come back. I told your mother that. But you did. It was out of my hands. You're not my problem."

"So then why are you here?"

He closes his eyes. When he opens them again, I see tears in them. He wipes them and shakes his head.

"You're not the only one who lost someone," Robert tells me. "Okay?"

He looks out the window next to him onto a dimly lit and empty side street.

"I'm not like them, Chris. I'm not like Marsh and Staunch." Uncle Robert reaches over and grabs my wrist. "But I'm not like you either. You've got—you've got something I don't have and never will have."

"What do I have?"

"The courage to stand up and fight."

He lets go of my wrist and then looks for the server again.

I sit there not feeling very courageous.

"Now go on, get out of here," he says. "Go back to Solitary, and go to Marsh and Staunch and the old guy and do what they want you to do. And—just shut up and listen—and you'll hear from me eventually. I just—I need time to figure out what to do. Okay?"

I want to say more. So much more. But I just nod.

"And be careful. They'll kill you if they decide you're no use to them. And just hope and pray that they haven't already killed your mother."

108. Remorse

The L-train shakes and hums and I don't want to get off. I want to stay on here all night. I want to stay inside here the rest of my life.

I feel a deep ache inside of me. Something worse than how I felt over Jocelyn or Lily. Because this ache is because—and for—me.

I'm tired. No, I'm beyond tired. I'm exhausted.

I just want some peace.

But Mom is missing and I know that peace is a long ways away. I'm scared for her and scared to find out the truth. I know I have to go back and know this is the nice little message they're sending to me.

I'm alone in this seat, and there's nobody watching. Nobody prying. Nobody bothering. It's just me. Just me and my Maker.

I know now that God is above, watching. But in many ways, I've always believed He was there. I had doubts and I could laugh it off or shove it away, but I sorta always still kind of believed. When Dad finally announced that he had made a big change, it felt all wrong. Of all the people in my life, it was *Dad?* The man who I didn't know, who had been out of our lives, the man now saying he had found faith.

That made me decide.

But deciding is one thing.

This ache—gnawing, twisting, hurting—won't go away.

I'm seventeen and oh am I stupid.

I'm seventeen and oh am I so silly.

I feel the weight of my problems and mistakes and sins spiraling inside of me.

A teen is supposed to have problems and make mistakes. But sins? Really?

But I know.

This isn't for show and isn't out of guilt. I'm not a kid anymore. A kid moved down to Solitary, but that kid grew up.

Now, inside of this empty car, the boy who became a young man sits there. Without any doubt, but unsure of how to move on. Unsure what to do next.

"I tried," I say out loud.

And yes, I did try. I tried to do it my way.

I even dared God to come hunt me down if He was up there.

Well, Chris?

I feel a shudder go through my body.

Well?

I feel warm and cold at the same time. The world circling around me without the help of a drop of alcohol or caffeine.

"What do You want from me?" I ask Him. "What do You want me to do?"

I feel tears blur my eyes and I let them stay.

I feel so heavy, so hard, so stuck.

"I'm sorry. Okay. Is that what You want to hear?"

I think of the words my father said:

But He is there, and He does love you. And that love—there's nothing like it, Chris.

I think of the words Kelsey said:

Jesus says for anybody who's tired and heavyhearted to come to Him.

And then I think of Jocelyn. This girl who knew she was on a one-way track like I am toward one single destination. And yet she still could find the way to say that she believed in the place she was going. That there was only good in that place, that she didn't have to fear anymore. Or have regret. Or apologize.

What do you want? Pastor Marsh asked me.

I look at my hands.

Everything feels so heavy.

All I want …

"I want the hurt to go away," I say in a loud voice.

I just want it all to go away.

I want to bottle it up and throw it out into the ocean.

I want to set a fire to it and watch it drift out into the night sky.

I want something to soak it up and then leave me dry.

I want someone to take this heavy hurt inside away.

He'll give you rest.

I tried running, but I guess He hunted me down after all.

I shiver.

"If You can, Jesus, take this—take all of it—take every little drop of it and take it away. Please."

This whole dark world needs hope.

That's what Jocelyn said. It was a year ago when she died. And when some important part of me died with her.

Or so I thought.

I hold the seat in front of me and stare down at the floor. Then I close my eyes.

"Take this hurt and replace it with that same hope that beautiful girl had, God. I'm sorry. I'm so sorry for trying not to believe. I'm so sorry for being so stupid."

I open my eyes and then look ahead. I wipe them and see the night outside.

I know that there is unfinished business back in Solitary, and I know I need to go back.

For my mom's sake. And for my own.

I just know that if I do go back—no, *when* I go back, that I need help on my side.

Help and hope.

And maybe, just maybe, God above will be kind enough to take some of the hurt away.

... a little more ...

When a delightful concert comes to an end,

the orchestra might offer an encore.

When a fine meal comes to an end,

it's always nice to savor a bit of dessert.

When a great story comes to an end,

we think you may want to linger.

And so, we offer ...

AfterWords—just a little something more after you

have finished a David C Cook novel.

We invite you to stay awhile in the story.

Thanks for reading!

Turn the page for ...

- **Three Recommended Playlists**
- **Behind the Book: Sixteen Candles**
- **A Snapshot**

Three Recommended Playlists

TEMPTATION PLAYLIST

#1 For the Walkman

1. "Elegia" by New Order
2. "New Gold Dream (81-82-83-84)" by Simple Minds
3. "Stop Me If You Think You've Heard This One Before" by The Smiths
4. "A Night Like This" by The Cure
5. "Behind the Wheel" by Depeche Mode
6. "Tonight Is Forever" by Pet Shop Boys
7. "Don't You (Forget About Me)" by Simple Minds
8. "Pretty in Pink" by The Psychedelic Furs
9. "Broken" by Tears for Fears
10. "Summertime Rolls" by Jane's Addiction
11. "Those Eyes, That Mouth" by Cocteau Twins
12. "Under the Milky Way" by The Church
13. "Lovesong" by The Cure
14. "Let's Go Crazy" by Prince
15. "Shadowplay" by Joy Division
16. "Slave to Love" by Bryan Ferry & Roxy Music
17. "Wrapped Around Your Finger" by The Police

18. "Doctor! Doctor!" by Thompson Twins
19. "My Foolish Friend" by Talk Talk
20. "The Chauffeur" by Duran Duran
21. "Listen" by Tears for Fears
22. "Temptation" by New Order

TEMPTATION PLAYLIST

#2 For the iPod

1. "Made For You" by OneRepublic
2. "Miracle Cure (Onetwo Remix)" by Blank & Jones
3. "Young Blood" by The Naked and Famous
4. "You Got to Go" by Above & Beyond
5. "Hellbent" by New Order
6. "Rolling in the Deep" by Adele
7. "From the Outside" by Editors
8. "City Lights" by Cause and Effect
9. "Forever Young (Hamel Album Mix)" by Alphaville
10. "Harder to Breathe" by Maroon 5
11. "These Changes" by Bad Lieutenant
12. "Wonderful Life" by Hurts
13. "Midnight City" by M83
14. "Alone" by Editors
15. "Talking to the Moon" by Bruno Mars
16. "Mirrorage" by Glasser
17. "Lilian" by Depeche Mode

18. "Set Fire to the Rain" by Adele
19. "Only a Few Things" by Above & Beyond
20. "Jigsaw Falling into Place" by Radiohead
21. "Temptation" by Moby

TEMPTATION PLAYLIST

#3 For the Movie

1. "Filmic" by Above & Beyond
2. "The Dream Is Always the Same" by Tangerine Dream (from *Risky Business* soundtrack)
3. "The Broken Places" by Moby
4. "Capricorn Rising" by Mike Simonetti
5. "Early Phone Call" by Thomas Newman (from unreleased *Less Than Zero* score)
6. "Startmusic (Mix)" by Johan Söderqvist (from *Earth Made of Glass* soundtrack)
7. "Sun in Your Eyes" by Above & Beyond
8. "Demons in the Dark" by David Julyan (from *Heartless* soundtrack)
9. "Breathturn" by Hammock
10. "Guido the Killer Pimp" by Tangerine Dream (from *Risky Business* soundtrack)
11. "In a Closet" by Thomas Newman (from *Welcome Home, Roxy Carmichael* soundtrack)
12. "Formula of Fear (Armchair Instrumental)" by Hybrid
13. "Lana" by Tangerine Dream (from *Risky Business* soundtrack)

14. "Julian on the Stairs" by Thomas Newman (from unreleased *Less Than Zero* score)

15. "The Photos (Mix)" by Johan Söderqvist (from *Earth Made of Glass* soundtrack)

16. "Murder" by New Order

17. "It's Ten O'Clock" by David Julyan (from *Heartless* soundtrack)

18. "Refrigerator Shrine" by Thomas Newman (from *Welcome Home, Roxy Carmichael* soundtrack)

19. "Sevastopol" by Moby

20. "In Odense …" by Ulrich Schnauss & Jonas Munk

21. "Turn Together, Burn Together" by Robin Guthrie

22. "Julian's Dead" by Thomas Newman (from unreleased *Less Than Zero* score)

23. "Love on a Real Train (Risky Business)" by Tangerine Dream (from *Risky Business* soundtrack)

Behind the Book: *Sixteen Candles*

Music matters. And teens know this.

Sometimes a song can speak for you. It says things you'd never dream of saying. It sums up how you feel. It sums up you.

Someone else can sing your sadness.

Someone else can come up with symphonies.

You don't know what's out there but you think you have ideas.

The songs spell it out with their suffering and their swelling hearts and their majestic lyrics.

You feel the despair of The Smiths.

You feel the fear of The Cure.

You feel the joy of New Order.

You feel the passion of Depeche Mode.

You feel things you've never felt before because you're growing up and your body is changing and your life is changing and you are absolutely terrified but trying to play it cool just like the music.

You are living in a decade called the eighties, and you have no idea how much things will change after that.

To you, sixteen is eternal.

To you, sixteen is epic.

A teen opens his eyes wide and takes it all in. It's only after enough years and enough broken dreams that he starts to shut them and drown out the songs.

The songs remind him of all the failed ambitions. Of all the lost loves. Of all those naive things that a teen can only think and dream and believe.

So many grow up and get busy and sometimes the music fades away.

You blink and find yourself forty years old.

But you are still a teen at heart.

The songs still matter.

And you still wake up and go to bed with your eyes wide open. Still dreaming in the good and refusing the bad.

You still find your heart swelling with these songs, these symphonies, these sweet melodies.

They will always—always—be a part of you.

They will always be remembered.

This eleventh grader wanted—no, he *needed*—a change of scenery. A big change. And boy did he get it. In the middle of his school year, he ended up moving. Not just to another city, but to another culture. The Windy City was calling his name, and he tried to never look back. But sometimes looking back allows the imagination to roam free.

For more information on Travis Thrasher,
visit www.TravisThrasher.com.